A SEAL'S SALVATION

BY
TAWNY WEBER

Published in Great Britain 2014
by Mills & Boon, an imprint of Harlequin (UK) Limited,
Eton House, 18-24 Paradise Road, Richmond, Surrey, TW9 1SR

© 2014 Tawny Weber

ISBN: 978 0 263 91227 2

14-0214

Harlequin (UK) Limited's policy is to use papers that are natural, renewable and recyclable products and made from wood grown in sustainable forests. The logging and manufacturing processes conform to the legal environmental regulations of the country of origin.

Printed and bound in Spain
by Blackprint CPI, Barcelona

To Birgit.
Here's to many fabulous books.
I think we're going to have a lot of fun together!

1

Ten Years Before

"GENNA, YOU'RE CRAZY. You don't have to do this."

"Of course I do. You dared me." Genna Reilly gave her best friend a wide-eyed look. The one she used whenever she wanted to appear extra sweet and innocent.

The sweet part was usually an act. The innocent part was pure truth, though. But fingers crossed, tonight was going to change that.

"I didn't dare you. Dina did. You could just take the truth instead. C'mon, I'll even ask a different question," Macy said, her desperate tone matching the intense worry in her eyes. She grabbed both of Genna's hands, hanging on tight as if her body weight could anchor her to this spot. Since Genna was a lean, mean five-ten and Macy topped out at five-two, as anchors went, the girl wasn't very effective.

"That's not how the game is played," Genna said, carefully extricating her hands, not wanting to hurt Macy but desperately wanting to be gone already.

She'd had no idea tonight's slumber party would turn wild. Oh, sure, the potential was there. That's why they always had sleepovers at Dina's, because her mom fell asleep by ten and didn't do spot breathalyzer inspections like Genna's dad. It was easy to sneak out and do fun things. Like play truth or dare.

She'd figured on a fun weekend with three of her best friends, one of the last leading up to graduation. But she'd had no idea it would be this fun.

She needed to do this. Now, while the anticipation was still zinging through her system, making her feel brave enough to take on the world. Or, in this case, to take down the sexiest bad boy of Bedford, California.

She wanted Brody Lane.

But he had practically made a career of ignoring her existence.

Time to end that.

Class vice president, squad cheer captain and the daughter of one of the most influential men in town, at seventeen Genna was no stranger to attention. Her exotic looks, long silky black hair and sky-blue eyes ensured that she got plenty of male attention, and not only in her high school classes. Nope, even though they were three years her senior, her brother's friends were always staring and flirting with her, too.

But she wasn't interested in any of them.

Not the boys in school.

Not the guys her brother ran with.

Not until he'd started hanging out with Brody last winter.

For the first time in her charmed life, Genna was smitten. Hooked. Hot....

Over a guy who was deemed off-limits. Not only by her parents, who were ridiculously overprotective. But by the town itself, all of whom considered the Lanes just this side of the devil's minions, and Brody as a hell-raiser with an overdue ticket to prison. Heck, even her brother, Joe, had told her not to be stupid when he'd caught her checking out Brody's butt.

And Brody? He looked right through her as if she were made of cellophane. It wasn't as though she expected everyone in the world to adore her. But the guy could drool a little when he saw her in shorts, couldn't he? Or at least stare when he showed up to give Joe a ride and found Genna in a bikini, strategically washing her car.

But did he?

Noooo.

The guy acted as though she wasn't even there.

Genna wasn't the contrary sort. She'd never had to be. But no matter who told her or how many times, she couldn't get Brody Lane out of her head.

So tonight, thanks to Dina's dare, she was going to do something about it.

"Genna," Macy pleaded, as if she were peeking into her best friend's thoughts. "Don't do this."

"And be known as the girl who doesn't meet her dares?" She'd rather be known as an ax-murdering floozy who wore designer knockoffs and ugly shoes.

"Maybe Macy's right," Sylvie said quietly, always ready to jump in as the voice of reason. "This isn't like daring you to stand up in Mrs. Bellevue's class and sing 'The Star-Spangled Banner' while shaking your tail feathers. If your dad finds out, he'll kill you."

"He'll kill *us*," Macy intoned wisely, knowing full well that Sheriff Reilly was just as likely to punish any possible accomplices as he was the actual perpetrator.

"My dad's not going to find out," Genna said dismissively, the negligent wave of her hand stirring a tiny breeze in the sultry night air. Her father was too busy keeping the peace and freaking out over Joe's latest escapade to pay any attention to what his little angel did.

"I hear he's wild. He likes kinky stuff."

She assumed Dina was talking about Brody now and not her dad.

"What kind of kinky stuff?" Twisting her carefully streaked blond hair around one finger, Sylvie sounded somewhere between fascinated and terrified.

Genna wasn't between anything. She was smack-dab solid in determination. And feeling hot, of course.

"I dunno. But I'll bet Genna can tell us tomorrow." When Dina's loud giggle earned her three glares, she slapped both hands over her mouth. But she didn't stop laughing.

It was just nerves over being on the rougher side of town combined with a little too much hard lemonade. Or maybe she really thought it was funny that Genna was going to put all her virginal skills to use and seduce one of the baddest of the town's bad boys.

"I don't kiss and tell," Genna decided. That sounded mysterious, didn't it? And kinda sexy. Besides, she figured any kissing she did deserved to be savored. Which meant kept to herself, where the gossips and tattletales couldn't whisper it around.

"You mean you don't kiss or do anything else," Dina corrected, rolling her big blue eyes.

"Dina," Macy moaned, wringing her hands in a way that proved Genna's assertion that her friend took far too many drama classes. "Don't encourage her. She'll do something crazy."

"Oh, c'mon. It's not like she's really going to jump the guy," Dina retorted. As usual, she'd picked the scariest dare she could think of when they were playing. She'd had no idea it was also her friend's secret dream. "This is Genna. She's gonna go in there, because it's a dare and she can't resist those. She'll try to flirt, Luscious Lane will do his brick wall impersonation and it'll all be over."

"The dare was to kiss Brody Lane," Sylvie pointed out

quietly, casting a nervous glance toward the golden glow emanating from the garage light twenty feet away. "Genna's not going in there unless she's gonna follow through. You know that."

Genna stood a little straighter, her chin a smidge higher at that character evaluation. She liked being known as a girl who followed through.

She looked toward the garage, the silhouette of a man working on a motorcycle. Since Brody's dad, Brian, was working behind the counter and probably three-quarters to drunk at the bar next door, that meant it could only be his son in there.

Time to put up or shut up.

"If I'm not back in ten minutes, head home," she instructed, fluffing her hair and slicking a coat of Racy Red on her lips, then tucking the tube into the back pocket of her jeans. "I'll call you in the morning."

Before they could launch into warnings, cautions or any more stupid arguments, Genna hurried off. Her sandals made slapping sounds all the way to the garage like some kind of early-warning seduction device. She shot a quick glance back at her nervously huddled friends, then figuring that warning Brody wouldn't serve her plans, she slipped off her shoes.

Barefoot, she tiptoed up the last few feet of sidewalk and carefully peeked around the open doorway.

And there he was. Brody Lane, in all his bare-chested glory. Black hair, as stick-straight as her own, fell across his eyes as he bent over the Harley. Facing away from her, she had the perfect view of his denim-clad butt. And oh, what a butt it was. She wanted to touch it. She wanted to run her hands down the hard planes of his back, glowing gold in the poor garage lighting. Then she wanted to curl her fingers over those biceps. Rock-hard arms were so sexy in a guy, she decided then and there.

Genna fanned herself. Because, oh, baby, he was sizzling.

She took a deep breath, hoping it did intriguing things to her form. When a girl wasn't blessed with a whole lot on top, she learned these little tricks.

Then she stepped through the doorway.

She knew it was impossible given the distance, but she swore she heard a chorus of gasps from her friends. Not looking back, she stepped over the threshold, leaning her shoulder against the door frame; she rested one hand on her hip in a seductive pose she'd seen in a magazine.

And waited.

Nothing.

Genna rolled her eyes. Even when he didn't know she was there, he ignored her. This definitely had to change.

"Hey, Brody," she called out, relieved when her voice only shook a little. "How're you doing?"

His body went still; his head turned. His eyes, golden-brown like a cat's, narrowed.

Slowly, like a dream, he straightened away from the bike, the light glinting off that sleek golden skin. So, so much skin. Her gaze traveled from the broad stretch of his shoulders down his tapered waist to his jeans, slung low and loose on his hips.

Her mouth went dry. Oh, wow.

"Genna?" He cast a glance behind her, then back with an arched brow. "Joe isn't here."

She knew that. After the third screaming match with their father that week, her brother had torn off on his motorcycle before dinner, heading for the highway. To see one of his girls, Genna figured. Leaving the way clear for *her* to pay a visit to his best friend.

"I'm not here to see Joe."

Not the answer he'd been expecting, if his frown was anything to go by.

"Then what's up?" he asked, grabbing a rag and sliding the wrench through it before placing the tool in its spot in the big red toolbox. The area around him was as an oasis of tidy organization compared with the chaos of the rest of the garage. His space versus his dad's, Genna figured.

At her continued silence, he took a step closer, then stopped. She almost pouted. It was as if he'd heard a signal warning that she was there for something naughty.

"You have a problem with your BMW?" Frowning now, he gave her a quick once-over. Not in a sexy way, more as though he was worried she was hurt.

Genna's heart sighed. Wasn't he sweet?

"Nothing's wrong," she said, having to clear her throat after pushing the words through a mouth as dry as the Mojave. "So how're you doing? Is something wrong with your bike?"

It was all she could do not to wince at her own inanity. *Seriously, Genna? That's the best you can come up with?* She gave herself a mental slap upside the head as if it'd knock her back to normal. Normal Genna had no problem talking. And she'd spent the last three months practicing her flirting skills for an opportunity like this.

One where it was just her and Brody. Alone. Together.

Time to put all that practice to good use.

"You came to ask about my bike?"

"I came to visit with you," she corrected, taking another one of those deep breaths. His gaze didn't drop to her chest, though, so she let it out. No point hyperventilating. It wasn't going to make her breasts any bigger.

"Why?"

"Why not? You're a friend of my brother's. You're over at our place all the time." An exaggeration, since he'd been over maybe three times in the last year. Sheriff Reilly didn't care for troublemakers on his property. But that was beside the point. "You never visit with me, though. I figure it's because Joe's such an attention hog. My mom says he takes the title 'son' in the wrong way, figuring the whole universe revolves around him."

She grinned, waiting for him to join her. When he just stared, those gold eyes intent and cautious, she dimmed the smile a little. Obviously friendliness wasn't something he was overly familiar with. No point scaring him.

"And tonight I was out and about, and saw a light on." She gestured to the bulb swinging overhead with its halo of moths. "Since Joe's not around, I figured why not stop by and say hi."

"If Joe were here, you wouldn't have bothered?" He looked around, then spying the portable phone, grabbed it. To call her brother?

Genna's lips twitched. Wasn't he the gentleman? That's what was so fascinating about him, though. He didn't play the games boys her age did. From what she could tell, he didn't play games at all.

"Do you ever smile?" She wanted to see those lips turn upward and his gaze light up almost as much as she wanted to feel his mouth on hers and his eyes filled with desire.

He didn't respond. Just tucked his phone into his back pocket, crossed his arms over that sexy chest and stared.

"You gonna tell me why you're here? You lose a bet or something?"

Won a dare. But he didn't need to know that.

"I'll tell you as soon as you smile," she teased, stepping farther into the garage. She was hit with the scent of hot concrete, metal and oil she associated with car repair, and something else. Something earthy and appealing.

Soap. And man. Her belly quivered and her thighs trembled.

"Genna."

The sound of her name on his lips sent shivers through her, eliminating every niggling doubt or cautionary concern.

Leaving only excitement and desire.

"Actually, I'm here to seduce you," she blurted out. As if her words were gasoline on a fire, the already sultry air flared even hotter.

Good.

She was ready to get hot and wild.

SHIT.

Brody Lane had been in trouble plenty of times in his life. So many, it'd be easier to count the times he hadn't been in trouble.

But he'd never been as screwed as he was right now.

He was smart enough to know that.

What he wasn't was smart enough to know how to get himself out of it.

Genna Reilly.

Sugar-sweet and wickedly exotic.

The popular, preppy princess who got good grades, cheered at games and helped old ladies across the street.

About as opposite Brody's type as an eighty-year-old nun.

And the star of four out of five of his sexual fantasies.

A problem considering that at the tender age of seventeen, she was pure jailbait.

And so off-limits, she should be wrapped in barbed wire and sporting an alarm button.

Nobody messed with Sheriff Reilly's little girl.

Nobody.

And nobody'd have to be a total dumbass to not only cross that line, but to mess with Joe Reilly's little sister. The sheriff was a mean son of a bitch, but Joe was meaner. He didn't believe in letting a silly thing like the law get in his way.

Joe's mean side rarely bothered Brody.

Unless he was facing the possibility of having all that mean aimed his way.

Smart thinking said shoo Genna right back out of his garage and out to the very edges of his life again. The edge where she only showed up on the opposite side of the street from time to time. And in his hot, sweaty dreams every night.

"Are you gonna offer me a beer?" she asked, tilting her head toward the six-pack minus one he'd left in the cooler.

"You're underage."

Eyes rounded in amusement, she gestured to the one he'd cracked open an hour ago, then forgot about after one swig.

"Pot, meet kettle?"

Brody's lips twitched. Damn, she had a smart mouth.

A very sexy, pouty-lipped smart mouth.

One he spent way too much time fantasizing over.

One he'd worked damned hard to ignore.

"I'm not aiding and abetting underage drinking," he said with a shrug. He didn't mind the hypocrite label. He'd sported worse. And he didn't think Genna, with any fewer inhibitions than she had already, was good for his peace of mind.

"So why are you here again?" he asked with his darkest glower. "Because we both know you're not the seducing kind."

He wanted to shove her out the door. Except that'd require touching her. So maybe he could mean her out instead. It always worked for his old man. The guy opened his nasty mouth and cleared a room in less than a minute.

"Why am I here?" she repeated, clearly buying time as she wet her lips and took a nervous breath. The move sent the ruffles of her halter fluttering in a way Brody had no business noticing. "I'm here because of a dare."

Figured. Brody crossed his arms over his chest.

"You're here to use me?"

Her lower lip dropped, then jutted out in a pout. He didn't figure she had the experience to realize just how freaking sexy that move was.

He did, though.

His rapidly hardening dick echoed its agreement.

"I wouldn't use you."

"No? So you came in here to talk to the bad boy of Bedford because you were craving my scintillating conversation?"

She started to giggle, then pressed her lips together, her face so amused she looked as if she were going to burst at any second.

"What?" he prodded with a growl.

"You said scintillating."

"Yeah? So? I know how to read, too." Damn, he hated this town. Everyone—even the sexy wannabe seductress in front of him—thought they had him so figured out. Labeled and dismissed, they never looked past his last name.

Hell, Genna's own brother, Joe, was way worse than Brody when it came to trouble. But people looked at his Harley, a brand-new, off-the-showroom-floor graduation gift, and smiled. They looked at Brody's, bought after years of scrubbing dishes in the back of the bar, pumping gas and wrenching at Lou's Garage, and saw trouble.

"I didn't mean to suggest you were stupid," Genna said with honest bluntness, her expression somewhere between indignant and horrified. "I just think it's a funny word."

"Right."

"I do. Like grandiose." Brody grinned at the way she seemed to relish the word, drawing it out in a tone worthy of a royal princess.

"You like things really big?" he mused before he could stop himself.

Her eyes lit, the worry leaving her face and her smile

returning like a ray of sunlight. It made him want to smile back. Almost.

"Participle?" She offered the word like a hostess offering a drink. As if inviting him to indulge.

"Does it dangle?"

Her laugh gurgled out, about the lightest, happiest sound to ever ring through this murky garage.

Brody couldn't help himself. He grinned. He just had to.

"You're cute," she decided, still smiling.

"Yeah?" He'd never been called cute before. Any number of other four-letter words, but not that one.

"Yeah," she said, stepping closer. Too close. Her scent wrapped around him, light and tasty, like the daiquiris he mixed in the bar on nights his old man passed out before closing.

Brody's smile disappeared.

Shit. She thought they were having a conversation.

He should have stuck to grumpy and silent.

"You need to leave."

Please.

"I don't think so," she murmured, her words so quiet they were a whisper on the heavy night air.

He could actually feel his brains start to slip away. Bad news, since he needed them. They were there to remind him to stay away from her. To caution him to keep his hands to himself. To warn him about those male relatives of hers. The ones he was supposed to watch out for. Whatever the hell their names were.

But she was close enough now for him to see the band of midnight encircling her pupils, all the more vivid against the pale blue of her irises.

"You really need to go." Desperate, he reached out to move her aside. Because if she wasn't leaving, he was.

But the minute he touched her, all thought of either one of them leaving fled. His fingers curled over the smooth, deliciously soft skin of her upper arms. She was so slender, but he could feel the muscles there. She was so warm, he felt like a tiny piece of him, forever frozen, was melting in his chest.

It was terrifying.

Those fascinating eyes huge and locked on his, she reached out to trail her fingers over his chest. Her touch was so soft and tentative, as if she were petting a wild animal. Or a rabid dog.

Brody wondered if he bared his teeth and growled, would she run?

He should try it.

But those fingers had shorted out his ability to think.

It was as if she'd reached in and flipped the last switch.

Brain, off.

Dick, on.

When she leaned closer, he realized she was the perfect height.

She fit perfectly against his body, her slender curves hitting all his favorite spots.

Her mouth was right there. Waiting.

He dropped his gaze, noting the slight quiver in the full, red cushion of her lower lip. He met her eyes again. No nerves there. Just heat. Pure, hot, intense.

Insistent.

"Kiss me."

"It's a bad idea."

"Sure it is," she agreed, her gaze not leaving his as she leaned in, closing those last few infinitesimal inches between them. Her breath warmed his mouth just before she brushed the slightest whisper of a kiss against his lips.

"So be bad."

2

GENNA'S ENTIRE BODY was quivering. Nerves. Excitement. Desire. She couldn't tell which was which. Just knew they were all there.

She stared up at Brody, her entire being engulfed by his presence. Everything was brighter. Stronger. Bigger.

The overhead light glinted blue in the vivid black of his hair as it fell over his forehead, stick-straight strands hanging in his golden-brown eyes.

Her heart beat so hard against her chest she was surprised it didn't jump right out and glom on to him. She wanted him so much. Breathing deeply, she filled her lungs with his scent. Clean like soap, but earthy. All male. All man.

Her lips trembled so much, she wanted to bite down to keep them still. But she was afraid that might discourage him from taking her *be bad* suggestion.

She really wanted him to be bad.

She needed him to take over. Because that kiss, that tiny little brush of her lips, that was about the extent of her experience.

"Please," she whispered.

Ah, there it was. The magic word. Brody closed his

eyes as if in prayer. When he opened them, the caution was gone. Instead, he was looking at her as though he was starving. As though he was the big bad wolf, and she was a delicious treat.

His gaze locked on hers, demanding that she watch him kiss her.

His lips were so soft. Tension she hadn't allowed herself to acknowledge seeped away as they rubbed over hers. Angling this way, shaping her mouth that way. So wonderful.

Then his tongue slid over the seam of her lips. Wet heat.

Oops, there came that tension again. And it'd brought a whole slew of wickedly enticing feelings with it. They whipped through her body, making her knees weak. Her heart race. And her panties damp.

His lips were just a whisper against hers. Still soft as he seemed to be memorizing the shape of her mouth with his tongue. He was touching only her shoulders, his hands so light she could barely feel them.

But the look in his eyes was so intense, so demanding, that she shivered. It was as if he were promising that she'd have to strip naked and share her every naughty secret. That she do all sorts of things she'd only heard in whispers, read in her favorite romance novels and sneaked peeks at on the internet.

She'd never realized that fear had a sexy edge. That the aching physical lure of it could beckon, even as her mind cautioned her that this kiss, this man, and whatever was coming next, were way, way out of her league.

Then, as if he couldn't stand the teasing any longer, his tongue swept into her mouth and, thankfully, his eyes closed. Releasing her.

He tasted so good. His tongue was pure power as it slid along hers, teaching her how he wanted her to respond.

Genna moaned, her stomach feeling as if she'd just taken a dive on a roller coaster.

Relieved, she closed her own eyes, concentrating instead on the clamoring of sensations spinning through her body. It was easier this way. It felt safer. As though she could just let go and not worry about what might happen next.

Her hands trailed, whisper-soft, over his chest. He was so hard, muscled but not bulky. Her fingers found a scar, long and rigid. As she wrapped her arms low around his back, she discovered a few more. She wanted to kiss them, every single one. To wish away the hurts she knew he'd suffered. She wanted to make him happy. To make him feel so good, he'd forget about all the bad he'd ever felt.

As if hearing her wish, her fingers—and she swore it was of their own volition—skimmed the waistband of his jeans. The fabric was soft. Worn. And so easy to slip her hand beneath.

His breath caught, the action pressing his hard chest against her aching nipples. He groaned, a low rumble against her mouth, before pulling away.

She wasn't sure, since her blood was pounding too hard for her to hear, but she thought she whimpered.

"No."

"Yes," she whispered back. She wanted to smile, to marshal together a clever argument that'd convince him that this was a good idea. But deep inside, beneath the crush that was driving her past reason, she knew it really wasn't. Just as she knew he wasn't going to listen to a thing she said.

Which left only one option for getting her way.

And that was physical.

More nervous than before her driving test, her SATs and opening her letter from Stanford combined, Genna took a deep breath to calm the dragons dancing in her stomach and leaned back a little. Not enough to put any real distance between her and Brody. Definitely not enough to give him the silly idea that they might be done here. But enough for her to reach up, sliding her hands under the heavy curtain of her hair. Her fingers quickly picked apart the bow tying her halter behind her neck.

His eyes wide and worried, Brody shook his head as if he could deny what she was about to do. But he didn't stop her. Instead, his gaze dropped, watching first her hands, and then the fabric of her blouse, drop to her waist.

Genna bit her lip to stop their trembling.

And waited.

His eyes weren't worried now. They were hot. Hot and intense and greedy.

His lids lowered, but didn't hide the sensual gleam. She could see the pulse beating, fast and furious, in his throat. He looked as if he could eat her up in one big, juicy bite.

So why didn't he?

She'd heard that sexual frustration was a bad thing, but she didn't think it was supposed to come with a big fat dose of anger.

Wasn't he supposed to do *something?* Be so overcome by lust that he grabbed her and took all the choices and moves and decisions out of her hands? That's how it happened in all the books. Clearly, he needed to read more.

"If you don't do something, I'm gonna kick you," she told him through gritted teeth.

"Baby, this is wrong."

Genna melted. The way he said baby, sort of low and growly, was so sexy and sweet.

"Then show me how to do it right."

He gave a laughing sort of groan. It was the first time she'd seen him laugh, she realized. The first time she'd been close enough to watch how it made his eyes light, his face look younger. Softer.

Sweeter.

"Don't you want to touch me?" Taking his hand in hers,

she lifted it to her bare breast. His palm was like fire on her skin. Her nipple tightened to an aching point, shooting a swirling shaft of desire straight down to settle between her thighs.

His pupils were so big, they made his eyes look pitch-black. His face was sharp in the shadows. She swallowed hard, wanting to ask if it felt as good to him as it did to her, but afraid to say a word.

Then he stepped closer. His body, hot and damp in the sultry night air, heated hers. A bead of sweat trickled down Genna's spine.

Eyes huge, nervous, she watched and waited.

As if he was moving in slow motion, Brody leaned forward, his hair sweeping down to curtain his face in black silk. It was so soft as it slid against her skin. Then he took her nipple into his mouth.

Hot and wet.

His lips brushed, his tongue swirled. Then he scraped the edge of his teeth over the aching bud.

Genna cried out, her fingers clutching his shoulders.

Brody sucked harder, his long, sure fingers pressed against the seam of her jeans. Need unlike anything she'd ever felt, more than anything she'd ever imagined, gripped her. Not sure what she was doing, how to quench the tightening demand of her body, Genna swiveled her hips in slow circles against his hand. Her fingers dug into the waistband of his jeans. Then, desperate to feel him, even as she hoped he'd take it as a hint to do the same, she unsnapped his jeans.

Lightning fast, Brody's hand grabbed hers and his head shot up.

It was like being speared by gold light, his eyes were so fierce. Nerves joined desire to swirl in an uncomfortable dance in her belly.

Genna bit her lip, waiting.

Was he going to stop?

Did she want him to?

Before she could decide, before she could even identify all the feelings bombarding her, he swept her into his arms.

Oh, God. Genna melted, body, heart and all, as he carried her three steps to an old bench-style car seat leaning against the wall.

It was so romantic.

They fell together onto the ratty black surface, with her on Brody's lap. He immediately rolled so she was underneath him. His mouth took hers again. This time it was harder. More demanding. He wouldn't let her play passive. He wanted everything she had to offer.

As soon as her tongue ventured out, sliding into his mouth, he rewarded her by cupping his hand over her bare breast again.

She flew higher. His fingers plucked at her nipple. She swirled, stars crowding the edges of her vision. She mewed in protest when his hand left her breast, then purred as it cruised down to her jeans. Her heart stopped, waiting for him to unsnap the denim.

He slipped right past the zipper though, again, pressing tight against her aching core through her pants. The heel of his hand rotated and his nails scraped.

Breath ragged, Genna tried to figure out what was happening to her body. It kept getting tighter and tighter, curling around and around, spinning out of control.

His mouth, so hot and wet on her nipple, moved away. She gasped when he blew on the wet flesh. Then he bit down.

And she exploded.

Lights flashed behind her eyes. Her pants were whimpers now. Her body on fire. She arched against his hand, wanting more. Needing more. Her thighs pulsated, the flesh between them throbbing.

"More," she murmured as she floated back to earth.

She slid her fingers into his hair, scooping it back off his face. He looked like one of those fallen angels. Too gorgeous to be real, too tempting to resist.

"I want more," she said again. "I want everything."

Brody looked as if he was at war with himself.

Before she could find out which side won, though, there was a loud racket by the door.

"Lane? Brody Lane? You here?"

Genna jumped so high, she was pretty sure she bruised her ass when she landed.

Passion fled so fast, it was as if it'd never existed. Panic gripped her belly in a greasy, vicious twist, making her want to whimper. She didn't have to look toward the door to know who was yelling. She'd heard that voice every day of her life.

Ohmygod. She was so dead.

They were off in the corner, out of view of the door. Were they hidden enough? Maybe if they didn't move, he'd go away.

Her eyes, wide and blurred by a haze of terror, met Brody's. His face, so soft and sweet and passionate only moments before, was like granite now. His lips pressed tight, his eyes chips of gold. He looked scary. As though he was taking that threat seriously and about to go to battle for his life.

Genna wanted to reassure him, to say it'd all be okay. That this wasn't going to be as bad as whatever he was imagining. But she was a lousy liar.

And that hadn't been an idle threat.

And she was pretty sure whatever he was imagining had nothing on the reality.

'Cause they were seriously dead.

When the knots in her stomach did a sickening lurch from side to side, she closed her eyes and breathed through clenched teeth and prayed she wouldn't puke all over Brody. Not that he was ever going to want to talk to her again after this. But still, that's hardly the last impression a girl wanted to make on the guy who'd given her her first orgasm just before her father killed him.

Maybe if they stayed here, didn't move, it'd all go away. Like the bad dreams she still had every once in a while. She just lay there, eyes closed, and waited.

The silence was broken by the sound of a shotgun chambering a round.

Genna gulped.

Waiting was probably out of the question.

Clearly in agreement with her brilliant assessment, Brody shifted. He didn't wait for her to pull up her top, instead yanking the halter so high she was afraid it'd end up tied around her mouth.

Taking her cue, she reached behind her and tried, three times, to tie it. Finally she managed some sort of knot that included a lot of her hair and a broken fingernail.

As soon as her fingers cleared the knot, he stood. If she'd had a voice, she'd protest his hurry. Didn't the guy know it was always better to put off ugly confrontations?

Genna stared at the hand he held out. The long fingers that, only minutes ago, had been teaching her what pleasure really was. At his impatient look, she grimaced and took his hand. He pulled so hard, she almost flew to her feet.

Midflight, she got a look at her father standing in the doorway.

Holy hell.

She tried to swallow, but couldn't get any spit past the knot of terror in her throat.

Her entire body started shaking, but this time she knew it was pure fear. Knowing it was insane to touch Brody, but needing the support all the same because her knees had just turned to water, she gripped the back of his jeans, the fabric still slack thanks to her quick work with his zipper.

"Hi, Daddy," she said, not at all sure he wouldn't pull the trigger.

FOR JUST A BRIEF, blissful few minutes, Brody had come as close to happy as he'd ever been in his life. Heaven couldn't feel as good as Genna Reilly did in his arms. And heaven, like Genna, was obviously not available to guys like him.

He should have known better. Hell, he had known better. Brody had to wonder when he'd finally learn. Anytime something looked too good to be true, it was. And a girl like Genna, she was not only too good to be true, she was so far off-limits that he was only surprised her cop father hadn't shown up earlier. The guy had to have a warning alarm planted on her somewhere. Brody just wasn't sure what'd triggered it. His hands on her body, or his lips on her mouth.

And it totally pissed him off that he considered both worth whatever price he was about to pay.

Teeth clenched, he eyed the shotgun. It was gonna be one helluva price, too.

"I'm gonna kick your ass," Sheriff Reilly growled, fury radiating off the guy in waves.

Brody braced, feet planted firm and fists loose at his side. His body was wired tight, ready to dive to either side. He'd spent most of his life facing one attack or another. He figured at least he'd earned this one.

He didn't wait long. The sheriff was on him in a flash. The guy was a lot faster, and in better shape, than Brody's old man. They flew backward, trapping Brody against the wall right next to where Genna had stripped down and blown his mind.

"Daddy!" Genna jumped forward, grabbing on to her father's arm and tugging. She was a tall girl, but as slight as a wish and no match for her muscular father when he shook her off. She fell backward, stumbling over Brody's bike and sending the Harley crashing to the floor. It barely slowed her down, though. She was back and grabbing on her father, tugging and demanding that he let Brody go.

Apparently unable to effectively threaten and deal with his daughter at the same time, the sheriff spun with a roar, grabbed his daughter by the shoulder, swept the shotgun off the floor where he'd thrown it before his dive. He shoved Genna toward the door.

"Get the hell in the car, Genna Yvonne. Now. I'll deal with you later."

"You're not going to hurt Brody. You can't. He didn't do anything." Tears soaked her cheeks, but Genna didn't budge from her position between her father and Brody.

"Don't you dare tell me what I'm going to do," her father growled, his face contorted in fury.

The cop raised his fist in the same move he'd pulled on Brody. Would he follow through? Rumor was that Genna was a pampered princess. Joe would have gladly outed his old man if the guy hit her.

Still…

"Don't."

That's all Brody said. He wasn't getting in the middle of family drama. He'd spent enough time in his own to know that bystanders were safer on the sidelines, and participants never appreciated interference. But he'd be damned if the guy was gonna get violent with Genna. Not in front of Brody, not later in private, not ever.

"Shut your mouth and sit down, Lane," the sheriff barked, confirming Brody's take on bystander interference. "I'll deal with you in a minute."

"There's nothing to deal with. I didn't break any laws, you have no reasonable cause to be here and this is private property," Brody pointed out quietly.

"You were in here with my daughter."

"When did a kiss become illegal?"

"When she's my daughter," Reilly growled, lunging again. Brody grimaced, knowing this time the guy was going for more than intimidation.

"Daddy! Stop or I'll call 911."

Genna's horrified cry was like a bucket of water over the man's head. It only took a blink for the rage to clear from his eyes and the cop-face to fall back into place. Brody didn't take a lot of comfort from that. He'd been kicked around plenty by cops wearing that same neutral look. But he wasn't worried about getting shot any longer.

"You touched my daughter."

Expressionless, Brody returned the dead-eyed stare, but didn't say anything. Why bother? The sheriff had walked in on them together. Lying was pointless and admitting it was probably admissible in the ass-kicking court the guy was convening.

The tension in the room seemed to ratchet up to the point that even Brody was shifting uncomfortably. He hated inaction. Kick his ass or get the hell out already. He managed—barely—to keep that suggestion to himself, though.

Finally, Reilly gave a grunt. He shouldered the shotgun, took his cuffs from his belt and gestured with his chin for Brody to turn around.

"You arresting me?"

Reilly's gaze shifted from Brody to Genna, then to the bottle of beer on the workbench.

"We'll discuss it." He lifted his hands, the cuffs dangling from one finger. "Turn around."

More intimidation. He had nothing. The beer was warm enough by now that it could have been Brian's, left there before the old man had gone to work his shift in the bar. Getting hot and heavy with Genna was stupid, but not a criminal offense. Fine. Brody sighed, then turned around. Let the guy cuff him and play hard-ass.

"Dad—"

"You say another word and it'll be on his tab," Reilly warned Genna, his icy glare making it clear the bill was already more than Brody could afford.

Whatever.

"Let it go," Brody murmured. Not that he expected her to take his advice. Hell, they didn't even know each other. But there was no point in her making it worse for either of them. Let it go and move on, was Brody's motto.

"I'll be right back," the man promised, giving the cuffs a smack that ricocheted painfully through Brody's arms.

"I'll be here."

Shifting his shoulders, trying to find an angle that didn't hurt like a son of a bitch since the guy had hooked the cuffs around the steel grip on a huge toolbox. To, what? Keep him from running away? Brody silently cussed up a storm and watched Reilly drag his daughter out of the garage.

The last sight Brody had of Genna was the tear-filled apology in those big blue eyes.

Damn, she was pretty.

He should regret it.

She wasn't his type, and she came with an insanely high price tag.

But the sweet taste of Genna was still on his lips. His fingers still tingled with the memory of her silky skin, the soft weight of her hair. Yeah. She was a mistake. But, even as he shifted again trying to ease the pressure on his shoulders, he couldn't regret making it.

"Took your time," he snapped when Sheriff Reilly sauntered back into the garage. Thankfully without the shotgun this time. He didn't look any happier, though.

"You in a hurry?"

"I have things to do." More importantly, he'd like to get

this over before the old man was off shift. Nothing pissed him off more than hearing Brody had been in yet another scrape with the law.

"You're gonna have to reschedule."

"Why? You're seriously hauling me in?" Brody wanted to laugh. Another black mark on his record wasn't going hurt, but it was gonna irritate. Worse, it was going to disappoint his gramma. And he'd been trying hard the last few years to stop doing that. Irene Lane had this crazy belief that Brody could build a good life. Could be the kind of guy she could tell her friends about, could brag on and be proud of.

"I figure there's only one answer to this little problem you've presented me with tonight."

His expression bored, Brody arched one brow in question.

"You'll have to leave Bedford."

Hell, yeah. It was like the guy had poked into Brody's brain and picked out his secret dream. Still...

"You can't kick me out of town."

"Boy, I can do whatever I damned well please."

Brody considered a testament to his control that he didn't roll his eyes. Because they both knew the guy was claiming powers he didn't have.

"Let's see. I've got you on underage drinking. Driving on a suspended. That fight last week with the Kinski boys, I'll bet they'd file charges if pressed. I can call that aggravated assault. Your bike has modified pipes, violating the sound laws." He went on reciting his list of minor offenses, boring the hell out of Brody. Was that the best he had?

Clearly reading his disdain, the sheriff shifted gears.

"You're a bad influence on Joe, and I know you're both involved in gang activity. I can make your life hell figuring out which gang, and what you're doing. Or I can put the word out that you're playing nice with me and let the gangs take care of you."

That caused a twinge, but Brody shrugged it off. He was clean and gang-free, but his friend wasn't. Still, Joe was a big boy. He knew what he was getting into.

"So that's all you got?" Brody asked, his laugh just this side of a sneer. "A handful of petty offenses and a few threats?"

Reilly stared. Just stared. For so long, Brody's neck itched and he wanted to squirm.

"Son, you're getting the hell out of here one way or another.

Hell yeah, he was. He'd spent the last four years saving up, cleaning up and getting his act together so he could see the end of Bedford.

Three more months.

That's all he needed to have enough cash to pay back the last of what his gramma had spent bailing him out of juvie, paying a lawyer to seal his records and covering his hospital bills. She'd mortgaged her house for him, and when he'd promised to pay it off himself, she'd doubled down with guilt, demanding he stay in town until it was paid. Her way, he knew, of watching over him as long as she could. She'd tried to get him to move in with her, but they both knew that was a bad idea. The few times he'd lived with her, Brian inevitably showed up, remembered he had a mother who might have some money and happily pounded on both of them. So Brody made a point to do as little as possible to remind the old man of Irene's existence.

But he hadn't been able to ignore her plea that he stay in town. The minute his slate was clean, he was outta there.

And never coming back.

"I'll be gone soon enough," Brody said. Then, pissed that he sounded weak, as if he were giving in to cop intimidation, he pulled out his best sneer. "You don't have to worry about your pretty little girl. I promise I'll keep my hands off her between now and then. No guarantees that she'll reciprocate, though."

Brody instantly regretted his words. He had no issue taunting the cop. But waving Genna around like that was cheap. Wrong.

And clearly the equivalent of a red flag in front of a charging bull.

Sheriff Reilly went from calm cop to furious father in an instant. His eyes, the same blue as Genna's, Brody realized with an audible gulp, narrowed into slits. His fists clenched, then as if making sure he hadn't broken any of his own bones, he slowly flexed his fingers before wrapping one hand over the butt of his gun. The sound of the release tab loosening was like fingernails on a chalkboard. Loud, painful and threatening.

Brody had spent the first half of his life a punching bag, the convenient focal point for every frustration, irritation or random violent thought his old man had entertained. He'd spent two idiotic years on the streets, honing his fighting skills and learning just how viciously painful a knife in the gut was.

But he'd never been scared for his life the way he was now.

"You won't hurt me," he said with his usual cocky assurance, even though he was nothing but. "You're not gonna risk your badge, or your self-respect, breaking those laws you love so much."

At least, Brody hoped he wasn't. Because Sheriff Reilly looked furious enough to kick his ass inside out, then rip the pieces to shreds.

And then the guy pulled it all in. Brody had to admire that, the way he could control all that fury, channel his emotions. It was seriously impressive. And not because it meant Brody wasn't gonna get beat up.

"As I see it, I have a couple choices," the sheriff mused in a cool tone. "I can do just what you said, and accept the results of those risks. Or I can make sure you get outta here."

"And I have no choice in leaving?"

"Actually, you do have a choice. You can choose army or navy. But that's about as much say as you're gonna get in this."

Brody laughed. There wasn't a damned thing funny in the sheriff's expression, but that had to be a joke. The guy could toss him in jail; he could probably get away with kicking his ass. But he couldn't force him to join the military.

"I'm not soldier material."

The sheriff smiled his agreement. "You're gonna be."

"Or?"

Reilly nodded, clearly pleased that Brody saw the reality. This was definitely an either-or situation.

"Or I haul your ass in on statutory rape charges. Genna's seventeen."

"We didn't—" Brody bit the words off, not about to share details of just what they had and hadn't done. "I didn't rape your daughter."

"Legal semantics," Reilly mused. "Statutory rape might not denote force, but that word, it's a lightning rod. And a case like this, the town bad boy and a straight-A student, a vulnerable girl whose life is now ruined? That'll make the news. Throw in your record, your rumored gang affiliation? I'll bet this goes national. Won't that be interesting? All that attention here on Bedford. Bet your gramma will be bursting with pride. She got anything left to sell off to pay legal fees?"

Brody swore a blue streak, yanking out every cussword and vile epithet he knew. The cop didn't blink.

By most accounts, Sheriff Reilly was a fair cop. He

cozied up tight to the letter of the law and prided himself on his position in town. But Joe had said more than once that his old man was a prick who cared more about appearances, about that precious rep of his, than he did his family. That he'd do anything to keep their reputation as shiny bright as he did his badge.

But Brody couldn't believe that included punishing his daughter with public humiliation.

Or maybe he just didn't want to believe it.

But shock didn't blunt his anger. He'd done a lot of shit in his life that probably deserved punishment. But not tonight. Not like this.

His gramma didn't hold out a lot of hope that her family would meet any decent standards. But having her grandson branded a rapist would pretty much kill her.

Genna would be publicly humiliated, dragged through the drama of a court hearing. She'd have to face reporters and gossips and nastiness in the form of support. Brody had seen plenty of that over the years, the gleeful joy others took in their hypocritical sympathy.

Numb, as if the fury had pounded itself out against his temples, he met Reilly's eyes. Brody wasn't a poker player, but he was the product of violence. He knew absolute determination when it stared back at him.

If he didn't fall in line, he'd pay.

And he was fine with that.

But Genna and Gramma Irene would pay, too.

Trapped, Brody quit struggling against the cuffs. His shoulders sank low and for the first time in his life, he felt defeated.

He vowed then and there that this was the last time he would ever let his dick get him in trouble.

3

The Present

"YOU BLOW MY MIND, DUDE. We've been on this aircraft carrier for what? All of a day and you're already making trouble?"

"Trouble? Dude, that wasn't trouble. Believe me, I know the difference." Petty Officer First Class Brody Lane, call sign Bad Ass, dropped to his rack with a grin, folding his hands behind his head and crossing his booted ankles.

"Farm Boy said some wet-behind-the-ears recruit threatened to kick your ass." Masters gestured to their teammate who'd returned from the poker game a few minutes before Brody.

Their SEAL team had hitched a ride on a navy aircraft carrier on their way back from a training mission. And while they weren't treated as dignitaries as they crossed the Atlantic, they were given a ten-man berthing area to use instead of having to bunk with the rest of the sailors.

"What'd you do, tell everyone between mess deck and our berth?"

Carter just smiled. Gossiping like an old lady clearly didn't faze him. With that fresh face of his, it was hard to believe he was a SEAL. Hell, it was hard to believe he was even old enough to serve, let alone two years older than Brody's twenty-nine.

"It was getting interesting, with the recruit mouthing off. And Bad Ass just sitting there counting his winnings. I thought the kid was gonna dive across the table. Then Bad Ass stood up and the wuss realized he was in serious danger of getting his ass handed to him."

"He was a NUB, Farm Boy. He didn't know any better." Brody had been a NUB, or new useless body, once. Fresh out of boot camp and on his first tour, thinking he was ready to take on anything. Anyone.

That kind of thinking had been forcefully adjusted pretty fast.

"Why are you playing with recruits?" Masters asked.

"I'd already cleaned out the officers," Brody admitted with a grin.

"Trouble," Masters muttered again, but he was laughing as he said it.

"We don't reach port till morning. What was I supposed to do? Sit in here like a good boy reading a book?" And the crew was providing Brody with a fat wad of poker winnings.

Masters snickered, then angled the book to one side. "I wasn't reading a book. I'm writing home."

Brody gave a jerk of his shoulder to show it was all the same to him. Truth be told, in his ten years of service he'd read a lot more books than he'd written letters home.

"You settle it or are we gonna be getting company?"

"It's done. He just didn't like losing." Too bad, since Brody liked winning. Not enough to cheat, though. He didn't need to. He was damned good. Something he made a point of being, with anything he cared about. Thankfully, that list was pretty short, so he wasn't spreading himself too thin.

"Mail call."

"You get demoted to mailman?" Brody grinned at Lieutenant Blake Landon. As officers went, the guy was all G.I. As friends went, Blake was aces.

"Nah, I came to make sure you weren't hiding a body."

"Did you have to tell everybody?" Brody gave Carter an exasperated look.

"I heard one of the seamen talking about a hosing some booter got in a poker game and how he was schooled by some visiting badass."

"And used mail delivery as an excuse to come by to make sure I didn't do more than pull rank?" Brody guessed.

"Maybe I just wanted to see your pretty face," Blake shot back, dumping a handful of letters on Brody's cot. "Or find out if you'd lost a bet and had to find yourself some pen pals. You're not known for your communication skills, pal."

"Snipers don't have to do a whole lot of socializing."

"Good thing. 'Cause you suck at it."

True. Probably another reason that Brody almost never got mail. He didn't do relationships. Oh, the occasional weekend fling or a few dates, but no woman had been able to hold his interest longer than a leave lasted. Definitely not long enough to reach the letter-sending stage. Sure, his gramma sent a letter and cookies every month, something that still made him squirm a little. But nobody else wrote. Hell, everyone else he knew was navy. His team here on the ship, or his platoon back in Coronado.

He snatched up the letters, all four of them, and glanced at the package. Yep, cookies from Irene. He tossed her letter on top of the box to read later and thumbed through the others. His brow creased. They all had Bedford return addresses. Two he recognized.

"Letters from home?"

Brody lifted the two while frowning at the third. "Guys I used to run with. I didn't know they could write."

"And that one?" Blake asked, poking his finger toward the last, the one with the flowing feminine writing. "Girlfriend?"

"From Bedford?" Brody's laugh held no humor. "Hardly."

No need to say more than that. Once, on a drunken bender, Brody had shared the details of his first hitch in the navy with Blake. Since the lieutenant had about the same love for his hometown and the people there, he'd gotten it.

Blake, ever the Boy Scout, didn't push the uncomfortable subject. Instead, he thumped his knuckles on the box he'd delivered.

"You bringing the cookies to Friday's poker game?" he asked, referring to their monthly game whenever they were on base in Coronado.

"Without a doubt," Brody confirmed. Irene's snickerdoodles were worth a buck apiece; her macadamia white chocolate anted up for five. And her fudge brownies? Those babies were pure gold.

Blake handed the other guys their much bigger bundles of mail and, after warning Brody to stay out of trouble, left them to enjoy their letters from home.

And Brody to stare at his.

The only woman who'd ever written him was his grandmother.

Not because he avoided women. But letter writing was nowhere on the list of things he did with them. Nope, they were a sweeter treat than the box full of cookies sitting on Brody's pillow. And they lasted about as long, too.

While Masters and Carter ripped through their mail, Brody looked at the envelope again.

Curiosity fought intuition. He wanted to know what woman'd be writing to him. But he had a strong feeling that opening that letter was gonna end up on his already-too-long list of things he regretted.

So he tossed it on his pillow, tearing open the one from Skeet Magee instead. It didn't take long to skim the page. There were only a handful of sentences.

Shit.

He blew out a heavy breath, hoping it'd relieve some of the pressure suddenly pushing on his chest.

He hated death.

Brody stared at the wall, seeing nothing but a gray blur.

He'd served on dozens of missions in his five years as a SEAL. He'd killed, and he'd watched death. He'd lost buddies and he'd mourned. That was the name of the game. A simple fact every soldier, sailor and military personnel faced.

So why was this hitting him so hard?

Knowing who the third letter was from now, filled with even more reluctance than before, he lifted the slender envelope off his pillow. The soft scent of something flowery filled his senses. Whether it was the paper itself or just a memory, he didn't know.

Sorta as though he was in a dream, Brody slid his nail under the flap, careful not to tear the writing. Wetting his lips, he took a breath and pulled out the letter.

Dear Brody,

I know it's been a long time, and I'm sure I'm the last person you want to hear from. But I felt it was important that I write, that I let you know that we've lost Joe. He never quite made it out of that self-destructive cycle, and after you left town, he sank deeper into ugly gang activity. He was in San Quentin on robbery charges and got killed last month in a fight.

*I know the two of you stayed in touch. I found
your letters, a couple of photos, in Joe's things.
Please, write me back.*

It was like being sucked, unwillingly, into a pit of memories. None good, except the ones that involved tasting
Genna. Brody didn't deny his life before the navy. He
wasn't proud of it, but neither was he ashamed.

But Genna was more than just a specter from his past.

He didn't think about her every day. He didn't dream
about her every night. He wasn't that big of a sap. But he
wasn't a liar either.

He thought of her.

A lot.

Too much.

In the navy, he'd found his calling. He'd found his pride.
He'd found himself.

And in a weird way, he had Genna Reilly to thank for it.

But he couldn't.

It was easier to keep the door to the past closed. To try
not to think about her, or everything that'd led up to his
ignominious entry into the navy. Too much.

And now Joe was dead.

And Genna wanted him to write her back.

Why?

What the hell was there to say?

Why'd they have to kick that door open?

All of a sudden, fury like he hadn't felt in years pounded
through him.

"Genius, got something I can write with?"

Masters spun a pad of paper across the room, Frisbee-
style. Brody caught the pen that followed, glaring at them
both for a second before taking a breath.

He sketched out a short sentence. Then, still riding on
a wave of anger he couldn't explain, he shoved the paper

into an envelope, used Genna's as a reference to address it and licked it closed.

Then, ignoring his cookie ante and the other letters, he headed for the gym to beat the hell out of something. Anything. Sweat, hard work and pushing his physical limits had saved him before. Maybe it would again.

GENNA REILLY HATED DATING. Seriously hated it. She'd almost be willing to marry the next guy who asked just to never have to date again. Almost.

It wasn't the interaction that bothered her—she loved people. And it wasn't that she was anti-relationships. She'd had a few, she'd given them her all. But inevitably they'd left her wondering what was the point. Now, she was just holding out for a great relationship. Her dream relationship. Which didn't include this "good-night at the door" awkwardness that made her want to scream.

"This was great. I'm glad we finally got to go out," Stewart said in a hearty tone, one foot forward already prepared to follow her into the house. For what? Coffee? They'd had it with dessert. A second round of dessert on her couch? Ha. Genna didn't think so.

"Thanks so much for the lovely evening." Before he could lean in for a kiss, Genna offered her brightest smile and slipped through the screen door, keeping her expression cheerful and giving a little finger wave. After a long second and a flash of irritation, he nodded and turned to go. She waited only until he cleared the bottom step before shutting the door.

Leaning against it, she held her breath and listened for the sound of his car. Too many of the guys she dated seemed to choose this point in the evening to suddenly forget their cell phones and need to make a call, or have a bathroom emergency, or worse, think she needed convincing that the night was so awesome it couldn't be over yet.

"Fun time?"

Genna pried her lids open to give her temporary room-mate a dead-eyed stare.

"Fun? The guy collects troll dolls, Macy."

The pretty brunette snickered once before plastering a proper look of conciliatory concern on her face. It was hard to hold it with all that newly engaged, soon-to-be-a-bride smugness she was wallowing in, though.

"Troll dolls? Those ugly little things with all the hair? He was probably just joking. C'mon, he's an attorney with great prospects. I don't think you're giving him a chance."

Genna wrinkled her nose. How much of a chance did a girl have to give? Either the guy made her heart go pitty-pat or he didn't. And Stewart definitely didn't. Genna wanted a guy who made her feel special with just a glance. A guy she could count on to be her own true hero. She shouldn't have to work at it.

"I went out with him, didn't I?" She dropped onto the couch next to Macy, who was multitasking her way through addressing her wedding invitations, eating a dis-gusting-looking diet bar and watching reruns of *Friends*. "I'd have had a better time staying here with you. Lousy food choices and all."

"Quite a statement, considering how much you love your food." Macy winked before taking a bite of the dry-looking carob-coated cardboard she claimed was going to slim her down a dress size in three months. "But one date isn't enough. You need to give guys more of a chance. When's the last time you went out with someone a sec-ond time?"

Genna sighed. First dates were testing grounds. Nobody got hurt if she said no after a first date. But second dates built expectations. Made guys think there was a chance.

"If I know on the first date that I'm not interested, why

would I go on a second date? That just leads to hurt feelings."

"That's silly," Macy said dismissively.

"Oh, yeah? I dated Kyle for a year, and when we broke up, he moved away he was so upset. I dated that dentist for two weeks, and when I didn't accept his invitation to a cruise to Greece, my mother cried for a week. My father pouted all through Christmas when I didn't go out with his new deputy after a few dates." Genna threw her hands in the air, as if to say *so there*.

"But that's the point. Those were all perfectly nice guys. I don't understand why you wouldn't go out with them longer."

"Because I didn't feel anything for them," Genna said, the words tight with frustration. Why didn't anyone accept that she didn't want to settle for just any guy? She wanted a special guy.

"But you're in a rough place right now. Maybe the date wasn't that bad, you just didn't want to be there?"

Although delivered in a gentle tone, the words had the blunt force intensity that only two decades of friendship could offer.

"I'm not in a rough place," Genna denied. "I just wasn't interested."

"And your brother was murdered two months ago," Macy reminded her quietly.

Genna wanted to ask what that had to do with her lousy date. But they both knew it had everything to do with it.

Stewart Davis had moved to town a year ago. Being a lawyer, he'd gotten to know her father fairly well—and had quickly become the answer to Sheriff and Mrs. Reilly's prayers. The perfect potential son-in-law.

But Genna had repeatedly turned down his invitations, not interested despite everyone's claims that they'd be perfect for each other. Until two months ago, after Joe's funeral. He'd asked her out in front of her father, and the way her dad's eyes had lit up, she hadn't been able to refuse.

So in addition to disowning his family, causing no end of stress for their parents, stealing her car and putting her in the unwanted position of the favored perfect child, she was laying blame for this date on Joe, too.

Damn him.

She sniffed, wiping a tear off her chin and looking at her fingers blankly. None of those were things to mourn. Why was she crying?

"It'll get better," Macy promised with a sympathetic pat on Genna's knee. "And your next date will be better, too. Maybe give it a week or so. Give yourself time to heal."

"I don't want to go out with Stewart again."

"You should, though." Macy shrugged off Genna's glare. "What? It's only fair. And your dad wants you to, your mom is over the moon at the idea of you dating a lawyer and you need to do whatever you can right now to help them out, to make them happy."

She paused and took another bite of her carob-coated cardboard, then offered a questioning look, as if daring Genna to deny it.

She wished she could. She felt like all she did was try to make her parents happy. The worse Joe behaved, the harder it hit their parents. The more miserable they were, the better she behaved to try to make up for it. It'd been a vicious circle.

Joe's first arrest and time in jail had put their mother in the hospital, making Genna give up her plans for Stanford to stay close to home. Joe's first stint in rehab had been followed by Genna's quitting her job in San Diego because the hour-and-a-half commute worried her father. By the time Joe had hit prison, she was working the most boringly safe job imaginable to go with her boringly safe life. It wasn't as if she wanted to jump out of airplanes or hitchhike across the country. But, man, she wished she had a little excitement in her life.

Instead, she'd been *this close* to being fitted for wings and a halo when Joe had been killed.

Now she didn't know where she stood. If he was done behaving horribly, didn't that mean she could ease up on trying to be perfect? Guilt poured through her, sticky and sour, turning her stomach.

"I'm getting something to eat," Genna said quickly, pushing off the couch as if she could run from her thoughts.

"You have mail on the counter."

Genna muttered her thanks as she headed straight for the freezer. She pulled out a pint of double-fudge ice cream, then got the milk from the fridge. She grabbed the jar of caramel sauce she'd made the previous week for good measure. Hopefully, it'd be hard to be sad while slurping down a chocolate milk shake with extra caramel.

Waiting for the blender to work its magic, she flipped through her mail with about as much interest as she'd felt in that date. Which was just about zip.

Then she came to a letter with an APO postal cancellation. There was no name, nor an address, so there was no way to know who it was from.

But she did.

Hands shaking, Genna didn't even notice dropping the rest of the mail on the counter as she held up the letter in both hands. Heart racing, she wet her lips, wanting to open it. Terrified to see what he'd said.

Ten years ago, Brody Lane had shown her an all-too-brief glimpse of awesome. In return, she'd landed him in the navy. She hadn't known where he'd gone at first. Partly because she'd spent a month on in-house restriction, partly because nobody—not her parents, not anyone in town, nobody—was saying a word. It wasn't until Joe had gotten out of the county lockup that he'd told her what Brody had done, had sacrificed. Because of her.

She stared at the letter, a little ragged and worn-looking against the soft pink of her manicure. She was the one who'd made this reconnection by writing him. She'd always wanted to. Always wished she'd had the nerve to tell him she was sorry for her part in landing him in the navy. But she'd been afraid. Afraid he'd hated her for it.

He was like the bridge between the two sides of her life. That side, fabulous and fun, filled with possibilities and excitement and wild times. And this side, with its day-in-and-day-out practicality, focused on doing what was smart, what was right, being perfect.

And she was scared that opening the envelope would somehow suck her right back to the other side of the bridge.

And even more terrified at how much she wanted to go there.

Figuring it'd be confetti soon the way she was shaking, she grabbed her brass letter opener, and with a deep breath, slit the envelope open. She gently pulled the thin paper out and, without blinking, unfolded it.

And stared.

Frowned and blinked. Then stared harder.

"Is he kidding?" she asked the empty room in bafflement. Then she looked at the paper again.

What are you wearing?

What was she wearing?

That was it?

She'd risked family disapproval, her father's fury, and had sucked up every last bit of nerve she had to write to him. She'd sent horrible news, informing him of the downward spiral and death of a guy who'd once been his best friend.

And this was how he responded?

Grinding her teeth, Genna held the letter out at arm's length, peering at it again. But the words didn't change.

What was she freaking wearing?

Jaw set, more alive than she'd felt in forever, she stormed over to the small rolltop desk in the corner and grabbed her stationery box. She yanked out a sheet of paper, ripping it in the process. She snatched up another and let her pen fly across the page.

She'd show him.

A teeny, tiny nightie the same shade as your Harley. You remember the Harley, don't you? Midnight-blue, so pretty it glowed. I used to dream you'd take me for a ride on that bike. In my dreams, I always thanked you by taking you for a ride in return. I could do that, in this little nightie....

BRODY READ THE letter for the fifth time, still not believing what it said. She was trying to kill him. That had to be it. Somehow, he knew this time he was floating in a submarine in the middle of the Atlantic Ocean with a crew of men.

He looked at the letter again and nodded. Yeah. She was getting revenge for something. Maybe she was pissed that he'd made her scream with pleasure, then hadn't called the next morning. Girls were weird like that, even when the not-calling excuse was being shanghaied into the navy.

Brody realized he was grinning.

How far could he push her? How far was she willing to go?

He grabbed a piece of paper and pen.

Might as well find out.

"DID THE MAIL COME?" Genna asked as soon as she cleared the front door, her arms filled with grocery bags, her purse and the box of fliers the mayor wanted folded just so for distribution.

"It's on the table." Macy gave her a narrow-eyed look. "You've been awfully interested in the mail lately. Are you expecting something important?"

"Important? Nope, not at all." Genna wet her lips, trying to be subtle as she edged toward the kitchen. "I'm just waiting for the latest *Cosmo*. I heard there are some great book recommendations in there."

"Books. In *Cosmo?*" Macy shook her head and went back to sewing tiny roses on an array of tulle circles. "I can just imagine what kind of stories those are. Naughty, right?"

"Very naughty. Red-hot, in fact, I read one last month called *Fearless*. Very hot," Genna said, spying the APO return and dropping her armload of stuff to grab it up. "And speaking of, I'm going to hop in the shower. Long day."

She might have babbled a couple more things as she hurried for the bathroom, her only guaranteed privacy. She loved having Macy here, but it'd sure be nice when her friend was married and Genna had her house to herself again.

The door locked, she twisted the shower on with one hand while ripping the letter open with the other.

> *You'd look good in a nightie while I bent you over my Harley. But you'd look even better in nothing.*
> *What'd you taste like? I wonder.*
> *What do you think I taste like?*
> *What would it feel like to find out?*

Whew.

Genna caught her reflection in the mirror as she puffed out a breath. Her face was red. Not from embarrassment. Nope, that was the color of sexual need. Hot, vivid, intense.

Seeing no other option, she stripped naked, turned off the hot water and slid under the icy spray.

And imagined Brody as she searched for relief.

I'm craving ice cream. Something cold, rich, delicious. I'll share it with you. But you have to eat it off my body. You can choose where to start. But to help you along, I'll pour a little drizzle of caramel sauce here, just below my belly button. Want to lick it up?

BRODY GROANED—actually groaned aloud—reading those words.

He'd always been more of a chocolate than caramel kind of guy, but now he wanted it like nobody's business.

He wanted Genna even more.

Grateful to be back in Coronado, in the relative privacy of the barracks instead of on a ship with a bunch of guys, he closed his eyes and visualized Genna as she'd been the last time he'd seen her. Then he imagined himself pouring caramel sauce over her body. Top down? Bottom up?

Aching hard, his body demanded the only solution possible. One he'd have to provide for himself, since no woman other than Genna would do.

He'd start in the middle.

I'd prefer a Popsicle to ice cream. Something long and hard I could watch you eat. You should run it over your lips first, so they are nice and wet and sweet when I kiss you. Then you can trace it around your nipples. The cold will make them rock-hard, like they're begging me to warm them. I'll do that while you move the Popsicle down to your thighs, leaving a sticky sweet trail for my lips to follow.

I think you're going to need another Popsicle. We melted that one.

GENNA LAY IN HER BED, the dim glow from her bedside light pooling over the blankets, shining on the paper. She imagined Brody, looking like he had ten years ago, writing those words. Pictured his eyes glowing with a wicked light as he watched her pleasure herself. As he brought her pleasure with just his words and the look on his face.

Her fingers slipped under the hem of her nightie, trailing over her skin in the same path he'd suggested she trail the icy treat. Reading the words again, she edged her panties aside and let her fingers go to work.

Nothing cold here.

> *I hope you like cherry. Because that's the only flavor Popsicles I like.*
>
> *I'm all sticky now. I need a shower. You can watch, but you can't join me yet. I've turned the water up so hot, the room is filling with steam. The shower nozzle is set to pulse. Fast, hard bursts against my skin, water droplets sliding down my aching flesh. I want you still. But you're not allowed in the shower. So while you watch, I'm going to pleasure myself and pretend it's you. I'll take the showerhead off its hook and slide it down my body. The water pools between my breasts, gurgling and bubbling before pouring down my body. I'm wet. And not just from the shower.*
>
> *What would you like to do about it?*

BRODY DIDN'T KNOW whether to damn Genna Reilly, or worship her. She'd got him into hot water when she was a teenager, now she had him living under a cold shower.

Brody ran a towel over his head, the rough terry soaking up the droplets and quickly drying his short hair.

Just the thought of a shower brought to mind Genna's last letter.

Of course, so did taking a shower. Seeing water. Hell, just breathing had the words flashing through his brain.

Scowling, Brody threw the towel on his bunk and grabbed his fatigues, shoving one foot in, then the other with enough force he was surprised the fabric didn't rip.

He wasn't writing her back.

This whole crazy game had to stop.

If he didn't respond, neither would Genna.

And they could both get back to living their lives.

He didn't fool himself into thinking he'd forget about the letters over time. If he closed his eyes, he could still remember the taste of her that night in the garage. He could still hear her soft cries of pleasure and see the rosy flush on her skin. Ten years hadn't dimmed that memory.

So, no. The images weren't going anywhere.

But the game was.

Brody finished dressing on autopilot, his brain ricocheting between the plan for the coming mission and every contingency. Their strategy was solid, they'd be solid.

"Lane. Heads up. The helo is ready to fly."

Brody nodded. All suited up now, so was he.

Time to rock and roll.

Habit had him glancing around before shutting the locker, making sure he'd left no traces of anything personal. Nothing was left out except the letter. Brody grabbed it, ready to tuck it away with his few personal effects. But it was like Genna's loopy handwriting was curled around his fingers, not letting go.

Damn. Brody felt like a fool.

He looked to the left, then to the right to make sure he was alone. He grimaced at his behavior, then pulled the letter from the envelope to read it one more time.

4

TIME TO ROCK AND ROLL. Brody, along with the rest of the team, loaded onto the Chinook helicopter. They didn't have to go over the mission. It was etched in their minds, every aspect of it not only committed to memory, but muscle memory. They were machines, ready to engage.

He eyed the extra guy in the bird, separate from the team. Watching. He didn't acknowledge them and as far as the team was concerned, he was just cargo.

Government cargo.

All SEAL missions were covert. Top secret was the name of the game, whether it was a direct action, recon or rescue.

Which usually meant no audience.

He puffed out a gust of air, then strapped himself in as the bird started liftoff. This wasn't his first rescue mission by far. But he figured it would be the first time he'd ever have the opportunity to meet the Cin C's right hand. He looked toward the passenger one more time, then dismissed him.

Tee minus five.

While the blades of the helo whirled their deafening hum, everybody went into prep mode.

The usual banter flew through the team as they did one last equipment check.

And then they went silent.

Brody had never worried about clearing his head before a mission. In the ten years he'd served in the navy, he'd learned a few things. Focus. Discipline. And confidence. Not the cocky bravado he'd perfected as a teen. But the absolute assurance that he was damned good at what he did and didn't have a thing to prove to anyone.

He was a finely honed weapon, trained with the necessary skills to carry out this rescue mission. He didn't have a single doubt that he'd do his job, and do it well. Because he had nothing, nobody, in the world that meant a damned thing to him except his team. His platoon. His duty.

He glanced around the belly of the plane. Cormack had his head tilted back, eyes closed as he muttered Buddhist chants. Masters looked fierce, as if he was going over the plan one more time in his head. But Brody knew he wasn't. The plan was imprinted; they didn't need to review it. Nope, the guy was mentally reciting *The Iliad*.

Brody usually thought about nothing at this point.

This time, just before he flipped the switch and became a military machine, the image of Genna Reilly filled his head. Her smile warming his belly, the wicked delight in her eyes reminding him of his past.

Was she still as bright as the sun, drawing people to her like a spotlight? Did her laugh gurgle the way it had when she was younger, deep and husky? And just how would she look in that little blue nightie she kept writing to him about? Or more to the point, how would she look out of it?

Was she still as sexy? Her hair a heavy curtain of long black silk, like in his fantasies? Did she make those same noises when she came? Or was sex just a way to pass time for her now? Like it was for him.

It was her smile that became his focal point as he let all

thoughts fall away. He shifted his shoulders, shrugging off everything but the mission.

"It's time," Landon said. His words were low and calm. His expression contained. He scanned the team, gave a nod. "Let's kick ass."

GENNA WAS GOING crazy with boredom.

It was like there was a switch in her head that enabled her to get through the same old boring job, blah life, day in-and-day-out monotonous yawn-fest of good behavior. And that switch had flipped off.

She knew she should find a way to flip it back on.

But she didn't want to.

If she did, she'd have to go back to making other people happy. Which still included Mr. Perfect, the troll collector, and all the pressures to go out with him on a second date.

The guy was boring.

Especially when compared with other people who needed to remain nameless, even in her own mind. People who wrote letters that made her melt before she'd even opened the envelope. People who were out living their lives, making a difference. People who, even though they didn't even sign their name to their letters, made her want so much.

Wish that things had turned out differently.

Lunchtime chatter faded into a buzz as Genna contemplated what her life might be like if she'd never taken that dare ten years ago. Or better yet, if her father hadn't ruined the best night of her life. If she'd rebelled instead of trying to soothe her miserable parents, and had done all the things she'd hoped to.

While her friends ordered dessert, she looked around with a sigh. She was like this café. Nice enough, but nothing exciting. Kinda like Millie, the café owner who kept the menu exactly the same month after month, year after year, so as not to upset her regulars by shaking things up.

"So that's an apple crisp with ice cream and a fruit bowl," the plump waitress ticked off, pointing her pencil at each woman as she recited their order. When her pencil aimed at Genna, she asked, "How about you? You want the last scoop of crisp? Or maybe some pie?"

With the nearest bakery in the next town, places like Millie's Café did their own baking. Genna eyed the display case. The toasted, almost-black meringue on the lemon pie was sliding to one side like a drunken mushroom cap.

"I'll pass." She softened her refusal with a smile. She'd stop by her house on the way back to the office and grab a couple of the turtle brownies she'd made yesterday instead. Maybe she'd take the rest of the tray back to the mayor's office. Last time she'd brought in treats for the city council meeting, everyone had raved. As they had when she'd baked for the school fundraiser, and her mom's ladies' tea. Sometimes Genna felt as if baking were the only area of her life where she was allowed to be free. Creative. To explore and experiment and indulge.

"Genna!"

"What?" Blinking a couple of times, Genna forced her attention back to her lunch companions. Macy was making notes in her wedding planner, but Dina was glaring.

"You aren't listening."

"Of course I am. You were saying you had juicy news."

"I do. And it's the juiciest. Better than anything you've got."

Dina figured her job at the hairdresser's should guarantee her the best gossip access, so it tended to drive her crazy that Genna often got better dirt first.

"Is it the news from this morning?" Genna asked.

"What news?"

"That Maury McCaskle ran the red light on Beeker

Street because he was yelling at his wife on the cell phone again?"

"Even bigger."

"That he was yelling at her because he found out about her affair with the pizza-delivery boy?"

"Bigger than that."

Genna's eyes rounded in faux shock. "Bigger? The pizza boy is only sixteen. How can you out-gossip that?"

This was what her life had come to, Genna realized with a morose sigh. Gossiping with her friends over a long lunch was the baddest she got to be. She thought of her little pen-pal project and her sigh turned dreamy. Now that was bad. So, so deliciously bad.

As bad as only a bad boy knew how to be.

Images filled her head, so vivid she swore she could reach out and touch them. Taste them. Feel them.

Thankfully, their waitress chose that moment to return with their order.

Whew, baby, it was much too hot in here for February. Even for sunny Southern California. Genna gratefully gulped down half the iced caffeine.

"This isn't gossip. It's more like news. Big, juicy exciting news," Dina said as she dug into her dessert.

Genna grimaced at the sight of the soft, cream-colored crisp. What'd they done? Scooped the leftover oatmeal from breakfast over canned apple pie filling and popped it in the toaster oven? At least they'd drizzled caramel over the vanilla ice cream.

"You just like to say it's news because gossip sounds so ugly," Macy said dismissively.

Easily ignoring them, Genna contemplated the many uses for caramel sauce. She'd offered up the sweet treat as a naughty suggestion in one of her letters to Brody. Especially her homemade caramel. Sticky sweet and buttery rich. She'd warm it up first, then drizzle it over her body and invite Brody to lick it up. She'd even let him choose. He could start at her toes and nibble his way up or start at her shoulders and taste his way down.

"When my information has to do with Brody Lane, I'd say it's news," Dina snapped.

Genna gave a start, almost spilling her tea. How had Dina peeked into her mind and pulled Brody's name out? What else had she seen while she was there?

"Brody?" she breathed. Excitement and fear hit her in equal doses, along with a big wave of lust.

"I was doing Irene Lane's hair this morning. She's Brody's gramma, you know." Dina waited for them all to nod, as if she'd just revealed some juicy tidbit. Since Genna spent every Saturday afternoon with Irene, she was pretty solid on who the woman was. "Do you remember when he ran away? What was he, thirteen? I heard he lived on the streets in L.A., a part of one of the uglier gangs and getting into all kinds of trouble. Four years he was running wild on his own until he was shot in the chest before his dad hauled him home."

He was fourteen, gone three years and knifed in the belly before his gramma had brought him home after he'd gotten out of the hospital. But Genna didn't correct Dina as she usually would. Talking about Brody made her nervous.

"I only have a half hour left of my lunch break," Macy interjected, her expression impatient. "Get to the point or get out of my way so I can refill my drink."

Dina sniffed, but didn't move out of the booth. Instead she leaned in toward the center of the table and with her most gleeful expression, whispered, "Brody Lane is coming back to town."

Genna choked on her tea.

"What? No way."

Brody, back here? Where she could see him? Touch

him? Hear his voice as he said all those words he'd put to paper?

Holy hell, she was in trouble.

"Brody Lane, back in town?" exclaimed their waitress, hurrying over as if proximity would get her more information.

"Yep, he's coming back in a couple of weeks. Irene said he was injured. Really bad. He was doing something military. He's army or a marine or something like that."

"He's navy," Genna corrected automatically. "He's a navy SEAL."

When three pairs of eyes locked on her, she gave an irritated shrug.

"What, he kept in touch with Joe. They were friends, remember. It's not like I'm in contact with the guy or anything," Genna lied. Not waiting for their response, she gave Dina a ferocious frown. "What happened? How was he injured? How bad is it?"

"And why is he coming here?" Macy added, sounding as though Dina had just announced the coming of Satan and his dancing minions.

"I don't know. All Irene would say was that she wanted her hair set extra tight so it'd hold during her flight to visit Brody in the hospital. She said he'd been hurt in a big mission. That they're calling him a hero now. After she left, I went on the internet. But I couldn't find a single bit of news. They are so weird about hiding all that military stuff. Like it's some big secret or something."

"Right. Military strategy and national security are such silly reasons to make it harder to share good gossip," Genna declared with an exaggerated eye roll. "I don't see why they don't post mission details and the names of all the Special Forces personnel on a website."

The brunette huffed, giving Genna an irritated look.

"Why are they calling Brody Lane a hero?" Genna

asked, figuring an opening to finish her story would pull her out of her snit. "Does that have something to do with how he got hurt and why he's hospitalized?"

"It does," Dina breathed, just as gleeful at sharing the gossip as she was with the attention. "I couldn't get much out of Irene. Just that Brody was on a rescue mission. It must have been someone really important, too. But something happened and Brody was hurt. Another guy even died. What do you think they were doing? I mean, Irene didn't even say where it'd happened."

Dina stopped to take a breath and preen a little because everybody in the room was hanging on her words. Even the waitresses had stopped pretending they weren't listening. Speculation flew, everything from the last big news story to involve the navy SEALs to people mulling names of navy personnel they might contact to get more inside dirt.

Genna didn't pay much attention, though. She was too busy trying to quell the miserable nausea churning in her belly at the realization that Brody could have died.

If it wasn't for her, he wouldn't be in the navy. Wouldn't be putting his life on the line for his country. His sweet, terrified-to-travel gramma wouldn't be getting her hair curled uncomfortably tight.

How badly was he hurt? Was he going to live? Would he be able to keep serving in the navy? Or was the injury so bad he'd be crippled? She imagined him lying in some sterile hospital bed, forever broken.

She pressed her lips together, breathing through her nose and trying to focus on something else. Anything else.

Brody healthy and whole. Strong and silent.

Or not so silent when it came to writing.

Letting the words he'd sent her fill her mind, she focused on them until her stomach settled.

Genna stared at the pastry crumble and soggy apples on Dina's plate as if they were about to sprout wings and fly. Brody Lane. Hot. Oh, yeah. Her blood heated and her mouth went dry. Brody, of the broad shoulders, tight ass and clever way with words. Who knew a guy who barely linked twelve words together at a time could turn her on with just the stroke of his, um, pen?

"If he's hurt, how's he coming back here?" Macy asked, interrupting Genna's hot little mental journey. "You said Irene is flying out there. Where is there?"

"He's in a military hospital in Virginia. She said she's gonna convince him to come back here as soon as they release him. How she thinks that's gonna happen is beyond me, though. Nobody has ever convinced Brody Lane to do anything he didn't want to."

"Here? Why here?" Macy said, her fingers pressed to her lips. "Shouldn't he recover in a hospital or tent or something?"

"You're so mean," Dina chided Macy. "Even the president of the United States thinks this guy is a hero, Macy. He might have been a little trouble when he was a teenager, but who wasn't? He's been serving his country for ten years. You'd think you could get over judging him by now."

It was all Genna could do not to roll her eyes. Every one of Dina's words had been playing to their audience, her way of looking righteous and caring.

Still, the recital had its intended effect. Macy blinked fast, her cheeks pink as everyone frowned. And from the looks on people's faces, Genna knew word that Brody Lane was a hero was going to be the gossip highlight of the week.

"What'd you mean about the president?" Genna asked quietly, glad that Brody would finally be talked about with respect. Even if it was only in gossipy whispers.

"Oh, did I forget to mention that?" Dina paused, pretending she wasn't aware that the entire room was holding their breath to hear the rest of her announcement. "The president of the U.S. of A. showed up at the hospital where Brody's at and pinned him with a Purple Heart. That's, like, rare according to Irene. She said he offered his personal thanks, and shook Brody's hand."

The room exploded as whispers turned to gasps, excited titters to loud exclamations. The president and Brody Lane? Fingers were flying over cell phones, and the few old-timers who didn't text were calling for their bill.

So much for the gossip being made in whispers.

Genna started to sigh at the ridiculousness of it all, then she caught her breath. Excitement sparked, still having everything to do with Brody, but this time having nothing to do with the image of him naked.

Maybe she could help fan the flames, bring this news to the attention of the right people. People who could make sure Brody got his due. People her father couldn't intimidate just because he was holding a grudge.

Finally, Bedford would see Brody as a hero. The same hero she'd always thought him to be.

She couldn't change the past. But maybe this would make up for it a little. And wouldn't it be fabulous if everyone thinking he was totally awesome helped her father see how great Brody was? That way, if anything did happen between her and Brody, he wouldn't have such a lousy reaction this time.

She almost laughed aloud at the perfection of her plan.

Not that she was thinking anything was going to happen between her and Brody. Not really. Although those letters could be taken as interest on his part. Or severe horniness, she warned herself, not wanting to get her hopes up too high. It wasn't like he'd even used her name. He could have been writing to anyone. But he'd sent the letters to her. That might mean something.

She propped her chin on her fist and gave a wistful sigh. Maybe.

"Do you guys remember that night we played truth or dare and Brody was the—"

"Did Irene say when she'll be back with Brody?" Genna interrupted Dina, looking up so fast she slapped herself in the eyes with her own hair. No, no, no. They were not revisiting truth-or-dare night. She'd never told them what'd happened between her and Brody. She'd played it off as if her father had busted them before anything had happened.

Nobody had ever connected that night and Brody's disappearance, either. Brian Lane had never said a word about his son's departure and if Irene knew Genna's part in her grandson's sudden desire to serve his country, she'd never let on.

Dina blinked a couple of times, clearly not happy to have her juicy gossip flow interrupted. Then, as if she'd just remembered that their little dare was a secret, and one that Genna had paid dearly for with a monthlong restriction, she made a show of dropping the subject.

"Subtle," Macy murmured, rolling her eyes.

Dina huffed. Then, realizing nobody else was paying them any attention, she shrugged and dug into her dessert.

"Irene said he's due to be released from the hospital next week. So depending on how long it takes to convince him, anytime between then and never."

Genna pressed her lips together and stared at the bland blob of dessert Dina was shoveling in, trying to keep her excitement to herself.

A week.

She might see Brody Lane again in a week.

It was going to be so awesome.

WELL, WASN'T THIS freaking awesome.

One minute his life was rolling along just fine.

The next it totally sucked.

He'd come full circle. Ten years ago he'd been a loser

badass with no prospects and a chip on his shoulder. He'd ridden to the top, an elite Special Forces SEAL living a life he loved. And now he was back in his hometown with no prospects, sporting that same chip. He figured it'd take about three days in Bedford before he could claim the loser title again.

His hands fisted around his crutches, Brody glared at the small house, its chipped paint and shutters sagging as if it was as enthusiastic to see him as he was it.

"Brody, sweetie, you sure you want to stay out here? I've got plenty of room in the front house. You can stay with me, where I can do a little fussing over you."

He wanted to be left alone. He wanted to be as far from fussing and people and, hell, life if he had his way.

But he couldn't yell that at his gramma.

Not because manners forbade it or that it was bad form. But because when he'd tried it in the hospital she'd smacked him upside the head, then burst into tears. He hadn't even felt the smack, but the tears had kicked his ass.

He'd given in to the guilt, and the nagging, and when the doctor ordered him to physical therapy at his home base in Coronado, he'd said he'd stay off-base with his family and come in for PT.

He hadn't wanted to return. He didn't want to face his team, to stay on base and pretend he belonged there. That he was still a SEAL.

His leg was jacked up bad. Shrapnel did a nasty number on flesh and muscle. But it'd heal. Unlike Carter.

Dead didn't heal.

The mission had been deemed a success by their superiors, as they'd achieved their target and rescued not only their target but three other hostages.

The mission has been a failure in the eyes of the team. Because they'd lost one of their own.

The mission had been the end as far as Brody was concerned. The warriors' creed demanded they leave no man behind. Dead or alive, they brought out their own.

He'd failed. It didn't matter that he'd taken a hit; he was trained to ignore injuries. It didn't matter that he'd had a little girl in his arms at the time of the explosion that'd knocked Carter on his ass. The only thing that mattered was he hadn't gone back. He hadn't gotten his teammate out in time.

Forcing aside the churning emotions battling it out in his gut, Brody turned to give his gramma a smile. Well, a shift of his lips. That was about as close as he was getting.

"I'll be fine here. I'm better on my own for a while."

For a while. Forever. Either worked for him.

"Now that you're out of the navy—"

"I'm not out," he snapped. Then, grinding his teeth to try to chew the rough edges off his tone, he continued, "I'm on convalescent leave."

Three freaking months of leave before a navy surgeon would reevaluate Brody's chances of full use of his leg. Twelve weeks to contemplate the end of the career he loved.

Once again, Bedford was akin to purgatory just before he dove into hell. He'd vowed when he left—or was kicked out, to be precise—never to set foot in this lousy town again. So why was he back?

He looked at his gramma and sighed. Why? Guilt. That's why. When an old woman who was terrified to fly crossed the country to pray at your bedside, you did whatever the hell she wanted.

Guilt, and the simple truth. He had nowhere else to go.

"Don't you think you'll convalesce better in the main house? There's a phone there, television. I can cook for you and make sure you're okay. These steps, they're not good for your leg. Or for my arthritis. Wouldn't you rather be close where I can keep an eye on you?"

Brody's ears sank into his shoulders.

How many times in his life had Gramma Irene tried to keep an eye on him? So many. Living with his father meant a filthy apartment over a bar, fending for himself from the time he was six onward. As Brian's drinking got worse, it'd included beatings that had escalated until Brody was old enough to hold his own. But it'd also meant freedom.

Gramma Irene's meant rules. Three meals, on time with clean hands. Curfew, attending school and talking. Oh God, the talking.

About his day. His dreams. His emotions.

Brody shuddered.

Nope. Guilt only got him to Bedford.

"The guest house is fine." He'd prefer a dark cave in the middle of nowhere. But he'd settle for no cable or phone in a doily-covered dollhouse with flowers on the walls.

"You're a good boy, Brody," she said, reaching up to pat his shoulder with a fragile hand before handing him the key to the guesthouse. "You might not like it. You might not agree with it. But you need this time. You'll heal here. And you'll be able to make some decisions."

He glanced down at the woman next to him, her silver-streaked black hair curled softly around a face lined by more worries than anyone should deal with in a lifetime. When he'd been a teen, Gramma Irene had barely come to his shoulder, she was so tiny. Now she seemed to hit just above his elbow. He'd filled out plenty in the last ten years. A daily regimen of kicking ass did that to a guy. But he hadn't gotten any taller, which meant she'd shrunk.

"There's nothing for me to decide," he told her as he unlocked the door and pushed it open. His face set, he gripped the crutches and navigated the concrete steps, numb to the pain in his leg. Numb to everything.

As far as he was concerned, his life was done. And he didn't give a single damn about what happened next.

5

Oh, man, this was it.

Genna stared at Irene's front door, the fresh white paint a glossy contrast against the peeling gray siding.

This was crazy. All she had to do was reach out and knock.

She visited here every week. Came calling with baked goods, cookies or cakes or whatever Irene was hungry for. At first, it'd just been to be nice to a lonely neighbor. But over the last few years, she and the older woman had grown close.

But she wasn't here to see Irene.

A plate of cookies in one hand, she pressed the other against her stomach, where it felt like butterflies were morphing into dragons.

After he'd heard that Brody was to be in town, the mayor wanted to hold a special parade and maybe a benefit luncheon. As community relations liaison it was Genna's job to arrange it. That's why she was here. Not because she was nosy. Or horny.

Well, she was both, but that wasn't why she was here.

She wet her lips, careful not to smudge her lipstick, then wiped her damp palm on her jeans before shifting the plate to it and drying the other. Maybe she should have worn a skirt. Something fancier. She was representing the city, after all.

Maybe she should go home and change. She glanced at her watch. It was close to dinnertime. Maybe she should come back another day. Yeah. Tomorrow. Or next week. That'd give Irene time to visit with her grandson. It was good manners to wait.

Her stomach stopped pitching and a little of the tension seeped from her shoulders at the decision. Which only proved it was the right choice.

With a relieved smile, she started mentally preparing her excuse to offer the mayor and turned toward the steps to leave.

"Genna?"

With a squeak worthy of a cartoon character, Genna jumped. She spun around so fast she damn near landed on her denim-covered butt, almost sending the plate in her hands flying across the tidy porch. Her heart pounded, blood rushing though her head so fast it sounded like a freight train passing by.

It took her three deep breaths before she could respond.

"Hi." She cleared her throat, then tried again. "Hi, Irene. How are you?"

"I'm good, dear. I've been so flustered this week. Flying in planes, it's not good for a body. Isn't today Tuesday? Or did we change our visit and I forgot? I was on my way to a book club meeting, but I can skip that. I'd much rather chat with you."

Looking as if those flights had definitely taken a toll, Irene pulled open the screen door. Genna hesitated. She was officially still on the clock, and supposed to be following her boss's orders. But Irene appeared tired. The lines in her face seemed deeper, dark circles etched under her usually calm eyes.

"I didn't mean to interrupt your plans. I wanted to drop off these cookies. They're a new recipe I made up, and was hoping for feedback," she prevaricated, holding up the plate as proof.

This would work out great. She'd get the inside scoop on Brody before she had to see him. Maybe she could even drop a few hints, mention the parade the mayor wanted to hold in Brody's honor, and get Irene behind the idea.

"Well, this is a treat." Irene stepped back, welcoming Genna into the house. The inside was as cozy and comfortable as the outside run-down, reminding Genna again to research how to scrape siding and look into exterior paint.

"Sit, sit. I'll put on coffee," Irene said, gesturing to the wingback chairs in front of the bay window. Knowing better than to offer to help, Genna sat. Acting as if all her attention was on meticulously pulling the plastic wrap from the lime-green plate, she surreptitiously looked around for signs of Brody.

Like luggage or a jacket.

Or his body.

Nothing.

"Flustered," Irene muttered five minutes later when she returned with the coffee. "I almost forgot your sugar. As if I don't know how you take your coffee. But a couple of days serving it black and I'm all mixed up."

Genna leaned forward to take the cup, murmuring her thanks. Anticipation rushed so fast through her system it was making her jittery. Figuring it was only polite, she waited for the older woman to get comfortable before grilling her about her grandson.

Before she could, though, Irene launched into the woes of traveling. She followed it up with the horrors of airplanes, with a few comments for the kindness of strangers, or the lack thereof.

Genna decided she should have been rude.

They were on their second cup of coffee and third double-fudge cookie and Irene was still talking about those lousy flights.

Yeah, yeah, traveling sucked. Recycled air was the work of the devil and the cost of a tiny drink was akin to highway robbery. She didn't care about the trip, though. She wanted to know about the treat Irene had brought home with her.

"How is Brody doing?" she finally asked, unable to continue politely waiting for the older woman to bring him up first.

Irene frowned. It only took Genna a second to realize it was worry, not annoyance over Genna's interruption.

"He's hurting," Irene finally said, staring into her cup and blinking a few times, as if shooing away tears. "Not just his body. He had horrible internal injuries, two surgeries and they're still not sure if his leg will ever be as strong as it was before. When I walked into that hospital room, I thought they'd lied to me. I thought I'd flown all the way across the country to claim his body, he was so bruised and cut-up and broken-looking."

Genna reached across the small table to curl her hand over Irene's fragile wrist, giving it a gentle rub.

"But he's okay, isn't he?" Oh, please, let him be okay. She'd had nothing to go on but gossip. Those in the know claimed that Brody had arrived with his gramma in a big blue car, and that while he was on crutches, he'd been sporting all his parts. "The surgeries were a success."

"He's alive." Irene pressed her lips together, her face closing up in a look Genna remembered seeing on her grandson's face. In all the years they'd visited, Irene never talked about family business. She might mention Brody in passing, but never did she complain or even brag. Whether it was an inherent dislike of gossip, or a defense against the years of fodder her family had provided, Genna didn't know.

But this time, Irene looked up with tears in those pale brown eyes, two shades darker than her grandson's.

"His body is healing, but more than that was hurt."

"What happened? Are you allowed to say?" Genna had only outright asked about Brody once, and that'd taken every bit of her nerve. Irene had said SEAL business was top secret and that she was doing her part to support her grandson by keeping her mouth shut. Given that Genna's question had been along the lines of *had she heard from him lately,* she'd taken the hint.

"He was on a mission. Something went wrong." Irene shrugged, the movement as helpless as her expression. "He doesn't say anything about it. But I can see the hurt in his eyes."

Her heart weighing heavy in her chest, worry pressing down so hard Genna wanted to cry, she could only shake her head.

"He's going to be okay. He's tough, Irene. He's a SEAL." From everything she'd read, which was everything she could find on SEALs—just out of curiosity—they were the elite, the best of the best.

"I hope so." Irene gave a shaky sigh, then her expression lightened a little and she peered at Genna. "You and Brody were friends when he lived here, weren't you? You're close to the same age, at least."

Her and Brody? Friends?

If she didn't wish that were true so much, Genna would have laughed. Brody as a teen had been gorgeous, sexy and fascinating. And that was from afar. Then she'd discovered his sense of humor and clever mind, to say nothing of his wickedly talented hands and delicious mouth.

And, of course, his writing skills.

But she was pretty sure none of that added up to them

being friends. She frowned. It hardly made them acquaintances.

"He and Joe were friends," Genna said, sidestepping the issue. She didn't talk about that night ten years ago, ever. To this day, she didn't know if Brody's decision to join the navy was his own, or if it'd been forced on him. Her father refused to discuss it, and by the time she was off restriction, Brody was long gone.

"Will you talk to him, Genna? Please, for me?" Irene pleaded, the worry in her eyes adding years to her creased face. "He's been here three days now and said maybe twice that many words."

"Irene—"

"I'm so worried."

Genna started to say she didn't think he wanted to talk to her, then stopped and sighed. For a million reasons, she wanted to talk to Brody. Heck, she was here specifically to do just that. And she wanted to do whatever she could to relieve the worry on her friend's face.

Why bother coming up with excuses she didn't mean?

"I'll talk to him. Is he going to be back soon? Or is he staying at the hotel?" She'd figured if he was, someone would have mentioned it. But he was a SEAL and had all that top secret mojo going for him.

"He's in the guesthouse. Just go on back."

On back? To the tiny building behind the house that faced her own backyard? Genna had thought that was a storage building.

"Now?" Genna was so nervous, the word took on three syllables and ended on a squeak.

"If you don't mind. You can take him some cookies. He does love your cookies," Irene said with a glint in her eyes.

Mind? Of course she didn't mind. Just as soon as she tamed the dragons suddenly doing somersaults in her belly. It was a toss-up what made her more nervous. That she was about to see Brody, for sure. Or that he was spending the next little while sleeping so close to her bedroom.

And Irene didn't give her time to figure it out.

The sweet old lady moved impressively fast, bundling the cookies and Genna out the back door, then standing there to make sure Genna didn't bolt across the alley.

Her fingers were damp again and her knees just a little wobbly. Genna was pretty sure they'd carry her home, though. She glanced over her shoulder and grimaced. Making an eighty-year-old woman run after her was rude, and the look on Irene's face left no room for doubt. Genna had been told to do something, she'd damned well better do it.

She took a deep breath that did nothing but spur the tummy-tumbling dragons to spin faster, and stepped up to the door. Holding the plate so tight her knuckles were white, she lifted the other hand to knock.

Okay, so maybe it was a tap, not a knock. But still…

This was it.

A chance she'd been dreaming about off and on for over ten years. A lot more on than off since she and Brody had started exchanging letters.

She didn't know what she felt.

Excitement, definitely. Brody Lane was her fantasy guy. He inspired feelings, reactions, emotions that she had no business thinking. At least, not while his gramma was watching.

She looked over her shoulder again to check.

Yep. Gramma was watching.

She tried to think nice thoughts instead. Good girl thoughts. Like dating. That was a possibility, right?

It wasn't as if he was off-limits anymore, either.

He was a hero.

The mayor wanted to throw him a parade.

Even her parents couldn't object to her dating a military hero, could they?

Not that she was counting on Brody's wanting to date her. Sexy letters aside, it wasn't as if they knew each other. Not really. And then there was the fact that their one and only kiss had gotten him corralled into the navy.

But who knew. Maybe all that postal flirting was going to turn into something else. There, Genna decided. Nice, delusional thoughts. Totally appropriate to entertain in front of his gramma.

Inspired, she knocked again. This time with enough force to actually make noise.

There was a loud thump inside, then the scraping sound of wood against wood.

Her stomach tumbled over itself.

She stood straighter, pulled back her shoulders and took a deep breath. The move had never done a thing to make her breasts look bigger, but a girl could hope.

The door opened.

Oh, please, let the whimpering sigh be in her head and not aloud.

Oh, my.

The years had been kind, indeed, to Brody Lane.

Even as his expression folded into a scowl when he realized she wasn't who he'd expected to see at his door, she couldn't stop staring.

It was as if Mother Nature had looked at the perfection that had been him at nineteen and decided to add a few layers of "oh, baby" gorgeousness to her work of art.

Arresting before with its sharp planes and brooding features, his face was more intense now. Even sharper, despite being unshaven and shadowed. His eyes were just as striking, like molten gold. They'd always been distant, except when he'd smiled. But now there was a chasm there, as though he was watching from miles away. Assessing. Her, the situation, their past, present and future, all without blinking.

It was kinda scary. Not sure what he was seeing, or more important, what he thought about what he was seeing, Genna bit her lip.

It was nerves as much as curiosity that made her peel her gaze from his to check out his body. And what a body it was.

Broad and muscular, his chest and shoulders looked as though they were sculpted from marble under his black tee. He still had that lean build, his waist tapering to slender hips.

Her eyes dropped lower and she gulped.

Oh, my, the blue cotton sweatpants did nothing to hide the muscle between his legs, either.

Little dots danced in front of her eyes. She realized she'd forgotten to breath.

A gulp of air cleared the dizziness, but the tingling didn't go away.

He was… Wow.

The things he could do with that body, she'd bet they were nothing short of amazing. And she wasn't just talking military things. Her mouth was dry and she was starting to feel a little dizzy again.

So she forced her gaze to climb back up to his face.

His unwelcoming scowl had turned into a ferocious frown.

She wrinkled her nose. She should have kept checking out the bod. He obviously wasn't thrilled to have company.

So what else was new?

"Hi, Brody. I brought you some cookies." As greetings went, it was lame. But she added her best smile. When that had no reaction, she held up the plate as proof. And, yes, as a bribe.

He didn't even look at the plate. Her lips threatened to drop into a pout.

"Um, it's me. Genna." She paused, brows arched. She

tried a friendly smile that was only a little shaky with nerves. When he didn't even blink, she swallowed hard, then added, "Joe's sister."

Your favorite pen pal, she wanted to say. But given his reaction so far, she was a little afraid to bring that up.

Genna waited. After five seconds, her smile dimmed. At thirty, she was straight-up frowning. Knowing a glare was imminent at sixty, she crossed her arms over her chest, the cookie plate hitting her in the shoulder, and lifted her chin.

"Well? Aren't you even going to say hello?"

Now her scowl matched his.

So much for dating. She couldn't even get the guy to talk to her.

BRODY KNEW THERE were many levels of hell. Why Genna Reilly had to keep showing up on his was surely a way of punishing him for any of his hundreds of infractions.

Did she have to look so damned good while she did it, though?

Why hadn't she aged in ten years?

She should have packed on some weight. Gotten bad skin. Hell, even a lousy haircut would be something.

But, no...

There she stood, long and leggy, her body still as slender as a dream. Her curves were more a whisper than a shout. Nature's way of keeping the attention on her gorgeous face, he figured. Her hair was shorter than she'd worn it as a teen, hitting her shoulders instead of flowing down her back. And those huge eyes, with their exotic tilt and lush lashes, were narrowed with irritation.

He didn't care.

He hadn't invited her here, so why should he play gracious host?

"Are you going to say anything?" she asked, sounding

exasperated. "Hello would be nice. Or even hi if you're only up for a single syllable. I'll settle for a grunt. Or if that's too much, you can simply step out of the doorway and gesture. You know, a silent invitation."

Brody's lips twitched.

Damn. He'd been so focused on remembering what it tasted like, how it'd felt, he'd forgotten all the other reasons he liked that mouth of hers.

All the more reason not to invite her in.

"Why are you here?"

"Oh, look. He speaks," she said in a cheery tone, lifting one hand to the empty yard as if inviting the worms and bugs to listen up.

Refusing to smile, Brody put on his most ferocious scowl. The one that made hard-ass recruits wish they were home hiding behind their momma.

Genna just smiled.

"I'm here for two reasons," she said in that irritatingly upbeat tone of hers. As if she really thought she could smile him out of his mood. "The first is an official welcome from Mayor Tucker, who would be honored if you'd join him one day this week for lunch."

Was she kidding?

Did he look like the kind of guy who did lunch?

Apparently asking herself that same question, Genna bit her lip and gave a frustrated sigh.

"I'm guessing from your excited expression that this invitation is the highlight of your week. But wait, I've got even more wonderful news."

She paused, giving him an expectant look. Brody just shifted, leaning his shoulder on the frame of the door so he could take his weight off the vicious throbbing in his leg.

"You know, I've been told I'm the best community outreach liaison this town has ever had. Now, granted, I'm the only one it's had, so there might be a little bias going on. But still, people are usually a little more impressed by my charm than you seem to be."

Oh, he was impressed by her charms, all right. He let his gaze wander again, enjoying the contrast of the vivid red sweater against her golden skin and the way her jeans molded her long legs.

Charming temptation. That was Genna.

"I'm not interested in company, cookies or invitations." He paused, then lied, "Of any kind."

Hurt flashed in her eyes for a second, assuring him that she'd gotten the message.

Good. He hated to waste his breath.

"I was hoping we could talk," she told him. She rounded her eyes and did a little head tilt thing, indicating the house behind her. "Your gramma asked me to."

He followed her gesture in time to see his grandmother's head disappear and the screen door shut. Nice. Gramma Irene was trying to save him with sugar—and he didn't mean the cookies.

"I thought you were the community outreach liaison here on the behest of the mayor."

"That, too."

Right.

"Not interested," he said again.

She huffed. Actually bunched one fist on her slender hip and gave a big huff. He wanted to grin but he figured it'd just give her crazy ideas.

He tilted his head toward the walkway instead, indicating she should go.

"C'mon, just five minutes. We'll ease your grandmother's worries and I'll be able to tell my boss I did my job." When his expression didn't change, she pouted.

He eyed the stubborn tilt of her chin. Another thing that apparently hadn't changed. It was as if the last ten years hadn't even happened.

It all crashed down on him.

Thanks to a bad leg, he was trapped in Bedford. Because of the mission that'd jacked his leg, his life sucked and he had no freaking hope for the future.

And here was Genna, the town princess. Shining bright and cheery. The sexiest thing he'd ever seen.

He gritted his teeth against the pain of it all.

She'd gotten him in trouble once before.

For his first year in the navy, he'd cursed her walking into that garage. But even as he cursed, he hadn't been able to regret it. Hell, he was already paying the price. What was the point of not enjoying the memory?

By his second year, he realized she'd inadvertently saved him. A girl like Genna was out of reach for a guy like him. An impossible dream that he wasn't stupid enough to think he'd had a chance at keeping. But because he'd touched that dream, he'd found a shot at a great life. At a life he was great at.

And now? Now it was all gone.

Despair poured over him like tar, black, sticky and impossible to ignore. Damn Genna for making him open the door, both to the guesthouse and to the past.

Done with the conversation, and all the emotions it stirred up, he turned away. Two excruciating steps, even though he tried not to put too much weight on his leg, and he let the door swing shut behind him.

With Genna on the other side where she belonged.

He closed his eyes, leaning his head back, and sighed when he heard the door *snick* back open.

He should have known.

"Brody, please, listen to me."

"I told you to go," he said, not turning around.

"Not until we talk."

God, was there no end to the woman's stubborn streak?

She still hadn't learned when to give it up. And why should she? She wasn't the one who'd paid for playing with fire.

He was.

Not because he'd been shanghaied into the navy. But because once there, he'd found himself. He'd found his path, his life. He'd made a difference, for himself, for his country. And now it was gone. Freaking blown to hell like his leg, and as dead as his friend.

And here she was, doing it again. Those big blue eyes gleaming with an invitation that spelled trouble. The delicious, mind-numbing, body-draining kind of trouble that made a man stupid.

Tempting him, stirring up longings and hopes that had no chance in hell of surviving.

Playing with a sweet thing like Genna could only end up with the same results as last time.

A glimpse of heaven, a little bit of delight and yeah, sure, probably a little happiness. But it wouldn't last. Nothing did.

And when it was done?

He'd be right back where he started, alone and empty.

With yet another memory of what he couldn't have.

Hadn't he paid enough already?

He had nothing left.

6

"CAN'T YOU TAKE A HINT?" he asked gruffly, turning around in time to see her set the cookies on a small table by the door. "Even when the hint is spelled out in short, simple words."

"I'll go in a minute. Right after I pass on the messages I'm supposed to." She put on that obstinate look he remembered so well, chin high and arms crossed over her chest. Fine. She wanted to see stubborn, he'd show her a thing or two.

He didn't say a word. Instead he crossed the room—what should be a quick task given that it was the size of his footlocker but was instead a study in pain. Genna's eyes got wider with every step closer he took.

Unfortunately, his body got harder with each step, too.

By the time he was standing next to her, his head was filled with her scent. Sweet spice, it wrapped around him like a warm hug that quickly turned hot.

He was trained to control his body. To ignore pain, to push through discomfort. He'd endured Hell Week. He'd trekked eight miles through a jungle in Bolivia once with a broken ankle. He'd won five hundred bucks once betting that he could sit through three hours of Farrelly brothers without cracking a smile.

But the scent of Genna's hair made him quiver. Sent his head into a tailspin and his body into overdrive.

He told himself to resist. Warned his body not to engage.

His body ignored the warning. It was as if she was jamming his radar and manipulating the signals.

He didn't like it.

"What do you really want, Genna?" he asked, furious at the frustration coursing through his system. Frustration that was all her fault, dammit. He'd been fine holed up here, ignoring the world and reliving every miserable detail of the end of his last mission. The explosion. The helplessness.

The memories gripped him with inky black fingers, trying to pull him down. But Genna's big eyes, sexy mouth and intoxicating scent held his attention, forcing him to stay in the here and now.

"I told you, the mayor asked me to stop by." She bit her lip, studying his face as if she were gauging just how much to share of the rest of the mayor's wants. "He wanted to extend his appreciation for your service."

Smart girl, she'd realized it was pointless to repeat the stupid luncheon idea. Brody narrowed his gaze when Genna looked away, her fingers twining together before she tucked them into the front pockets of her jeans. Clearly there was something else she hadn't mentioned. Whatever it was, he didn't care. The idea of him and the mayor having lunch was ridiculous. Ten years ago, Tucker had been just starting out as the county's assistant D.A., with a lot of ambition and an oft-shared goal of getting losers like Brody off the streets.

"I don't serve for appreciation," he said, his tone gruffer than he'd intended.

Genna opened her mouth, that full lower lip glistening with temptation. Then she snapped it shut and shrugged. He'd like to think that meant she was done and would leave, but he was starting to realize that she had a stubborn streak wider than his own.

"Your grandmother is worried about you. If you don't want to meet with the mayor and discuss getting a little of the recognition you deserve, fine. But at least talk to your gramma." She lifted both hands in the air, the gesture matching the exasperation on her face. "Why did you come home if you were only going to hide out?"

Good question.

Brody's scowl deepened when he couldn't come up with an answer.

"Time to go." He reached out, wrapping his hand around her arm to turn her in the direction of the door. But the move put pressure on his bad leg so he had to shift his weight to compensate. And ended up way too close to Genna.

Close enough to feel her body heat.

Close enough that her scent, teasing before, grabbed him in a choke hold, not letting go.

Close enough that he could see the darker rings of blue around her pupils, could see the individual lashes that made up the lush fringe around her eyes.

He yanked his hand away.

"If you wanted, maybe we could go to lunch instead." Her words were low and husky with curiosity, her eyes hinting at nerves and something more. Something that grabbed at Brody, made him want the impossible. "If you just needed someone to talk to, someone to help you deal with all the emotional stuff you're facing, I'm a good listener."

"You want to have lunch and talk?" he asked, sure he'd heard her wrong. "About my emotions?"

"If that's what you wanted."

Hell, no. He didn't talk missions, he didn't talk about the military. And he sure as hell didn't talk about emotions.

Brody pressed his fingers against his temple, trying to rub away the tangle she was making of his thoughts.

"You should talk to someone, Brody. Your gramma, me, anyone. You're hurt and you're back in Bedford for the first time since you left. That has to mean something." She paused, taking a deep breath that made him want to slide his lips along her collarbone, then she reached out. Her fingers came within millimeters of touching his arm, but didn't make contact. It was as if she was testing the electrical charge between them, seeing how potent it was.

The hairs on his arm stood up, his entire body reacting as if she'd slid those fingers over him. Touching, soft and gentle, everywhere.

"I don't talk," he said, irritated that the words were mellow, not abrupt.

"Not even about our night?" She gave a tiny wince, as if she knew she'd crossed a line. Then, typical of the Genna he remembered, now that she'd crossed it, she danced all over the other side. "I never forgot it."

"You need to leave." He'd said the words to her so many times, they were like a catchphrase now.

"Brody—"

No. He couldn't deal with this now. Not her, not the memories. Not the feelings she was stirring up.

"Don't make me do something you'll regret," he warned quietly.

For a second, Genna stilled.

Then, damn her, she gave a soft little laugh and pressed her hand against his chest. Not to push him away. Simply to touch.

Her fingers burned his flesh, fired his needs.

"You won't hurt me," she said quietly, the absolute confidence in her tone baffling. Did she really trust him that much? Did she have no clue the things he'd done, the things he'd seen?

"I won't have to hurt you."

There were so many other things he could do to her. With her. On her and under her.

Her letters, always there tucked away in a private corner of his mind, surfaced. The door he'd slammed shut flew open, giving him access he hadn't allowed himself since his last mission.

The memories of those letters were a reward, a treat. Special. Something he'd enjoyed as he reveled in how freaking awesome his life was. The words played through his mind. The images of caramel, pulsating water and blue silk all crashed together in his brain in a huge, horny wave of need.

He wasn't interested in need, though.

He just wanted to be left alone. Physically, and mentally.

As always, he used the tools at hand to win the battle. He didn't go for guilt himself, but that didn't mean he didn't know how to wield it with laser precision.

It was only fair that he give her one last warning before he moved in.

"We're done. You delivered your invites. I turned them down. Time to go." His tone was low, menacing. He shifted his weight just enough, pulling back his shoulders and angling his chin so he loomed over her.

Intimidating.

She swallowed loud enough for him to hear her teeth click. Her pulse raced. He could see it thrumming in her throat. But her expression didn't change. She just kept looking at him with that cheerful smile and calm eyes.

Damn, she was something.

And *something* was the last thing he needed in his life right now.

WELL, THIS WASN'T going very well. Genna didn't know what she'd thought would happen when she talked to Brody. She hadn't let herself imagine that far, figuring the reality was going to be so much better than anything she'd imagined.

Disappointment sat hard and tight in her belly.

She hadn't let herself imagine what it would be like. But she'd entertained a few worries about what she'd hoped it wouldn't. Like that he'd be holding a grudge for that night before he'd left for the navy. Or that he'd be involved with someone, possibly serious. Or maybe that he'd only see her as Joe's little sister and want to talk about her brother.

Turns out she hadn't worried nearly enough. She needed to work on that.

"You're not leaving." His statement was so matter-of-fact, it was as though he was simply accepting the inevitable.

Genna wanted to smile, to pretend they could move on to rebuilding—okay, building outside of her imagination—their relationship. But she wasn't stupid. Right beneath his calm words was a whole lot of anger and nothing that invited building anything except space between them.

She should leave. She knew she should, but she was so afraid if she walked out this door, that'd be it. Her last, her only chance to talk to Brody, to find out what'd happened after that night. To discover how he felt about her...

Her fingernails cut into the soft flesh of her palms as she debated. Run or stay. Smart or stupid.

Then Brody moved and took the choice away.

"You ever been warned not to play with fire? Not to poke a sleeping tiger? Not to take candy from strangers?"

Despite his serious tone, her lips twitched.

"I'm not playing, I'm talking. You're awake. And I brought you cookies, not the other way around. You're welcome to offer me candy, though. I like peanut butter M&M's best."

His eyes lit for a second, then he shifted closer. His expression was hard, making her doubt the flash of humor she'd seen. She tried to step back, but realized he had her back against the wall next to the door.

He was only inches away.

So close she could smell his soap, clean and fresh, and see every detail of the stubble covering his chin. A couple days' worth, she realized, her hand aching to rub it and see if it was soft or rough.

Her gaze shifted, meeting Brody's eyes. His stare was intense, as if he were looking into her soul and figuring out all of her secrets. What he planned to do with them was what worried her, though.

"You should listen to good advice. And warnings." He leaned in closer, not touching her yet, but making her feel as if his hands were sweeping every inch of her body. "You never know when ignoring them will get you into trouble."

Genna's heart raced so fast, she swore she could feel it vibrating under her skin. Her body went into meltdown, needy and wanting more. It'd been so long since he'd touched her. Since he'd kissed her. Was it as good as she remembered? Was he better now?

She didn't care how stupid it was. She wanted to find out.

So when he leaned closer, his expression pure intimidation, frown and all, she leaned, too.

Right into his lips.

Oh. Her head spun, slow and intoxicating. Her body almost melted, he felt so good. She'd have thought that frown would make his lips hard. But no. They were soft. Welcoming.

Yummy.

Afraid to move, afraid to close her eyes, Genna stared up at Brody. Waiting.

Her heart raced, anticipation pounding through her veins. Surely he wouldn't turn her away. Would he? As he stood, rock-still, disappointment started to edge out the anticipation. Genna sighed against his mouth, preparing to move away and begin her descent into humiliated horror.

Then he took over.

He grabbed her arms, just above the elbow, lifting her higher so her toes barely brushed the floor. His mouth shifted, angling. Taking. His tongue plunged, dark and demanding as it drove deep into her mouth.

Genna's head fell back, giving him control. Giving him anything.

Her breath came in pants, her mind swirling with sensations even as the intensity of their kiss worked its magic on the rest of her body.

He was voracious.

His mouth took hers as if he were starving and she a feast, there to feed his every need. She'd never been kissed like this. Never felt this edge between passion and fury.

That he was angry was clear.

At her? At himself? At the situation? That part was up for grabs.

It didn't matter. She was sure she could soothe the anger with a few kisses. That she could reach inside and fix whatever made him so sad.

She shifted closer. Not quite plastering her body against his—she wasn't sure where his injury was and didn't want to hurt him. But close enough to feel the heat radiating off his body. To brush his chest with the tips of her breasts, sensitive even through the nubby knit of her sweater.

When she moved, his kiss changed. He pulled back, his lips softer now. Distant. Afraid he was going to end their kiss, she called up all of her nerve, wrapped her hands around the back of his neck to hold him in place and plunged her tongue into his mouth.

It was like flipping a switch.

No more anger. No more distance.

Just passion. Pure and sweet.

His tongue slid along hers and his hands wrapped around her waist under her sweater. Flesh against flesh. She shivered at the feel of his fingers, rough and strong against her skin.

His palm closed over her breast, making her whimper. It felt so good. Her nipples ached with a delicious kind of pain, so hard she was surprised they didn't rip her silk bra.

"More," she breathed against his mouth.

"Is this what you want?" he asked, his hand pressing between her thighs, the seam of her jeans riding against the swollen flesh and driving her crazy. "Is this how you want it?"

She'd rather have it naked, but she was too far gone to speak. She wasn't positive she was even breathing. All she could do was feel the amazing sensations rocketing through her body.

His fingers scraped over the seam of her jeans again, making her whimper. The sensations intensified, her entire body feeling like it was electrified. Desire coiled, tighter and tighter between her thighs. His lips closed over hers, tongue plunging before he lured hers into his mouth and sucked.

She exploded with a tiny whimper. Tiny sparks of light blew to pieces behind her closed eyes and the room spun as the orgasm poured through her. He slowed the kiss, then as her pants became shuddering breaths, trailed his lips over her cheek to bury his face in the crook of her neck.

Genna sighed, feeling as though she'd run a marathon.

In her jeans.

Again.

The guy had given her the two best orgasms of her life, and she hadn't gotten her jeans off for either of them.

Time to change that.

But suddenly, she was nervous.

This wasn't Brody, her brother's friend.

He was different now.

He'd seen things, done things that were beyond her comprehension. He was a soldier. A SEAL. The best of the best at doing the impossible.

Since there was nothing impossible about what she wanted him to do to her, this should be a piece of cake.

As if he'd read her thoughts, he slowly pulled back. Genna ran her palm over his cheek, smiling and ready to make a joke.

But the distance on his face was a little off-putting.

She took a shaky breath, trying to calm her racing heart.

She'd never felt this way before. Her body was still humming and she was ready to strip naked and do all the things to his body that she'd dreamed of for years. Things she'd had zero interest in doing to other guys' bodies. Brody things.

"You need to go," he growled. "Now. Before this goes too far."

Go? Was he kidding? The climax was still working its magic on her body in delightful little shudders.

"I think it needs to go just a little bit further," she corrected softly, nibbling kisses along his jaw and down his throat. He gave a low moan when she got to that spot beneath his ear, emboldening her. One hand still gripping his biceps for balance, she grazed the other down his side and across his rock-hard abs, taking a second to give her own moan of appreciation. Then, still nibbling, she slipped her fingers beneath the elastic waistband of his sweatpants.

Before she could explore, or even touch anything interesting, his hand shot out and grabbed her wrist.

"Further," she whispered in his ear, dipping her tongue along the rim before adding, "Please."

"Genna—"

"C'mon," she cajoled. "Let's see how good we are together. This is it, finally we get to give us a chance before you have to go back to being a big, bad SEAL heroically saving the world. Let's do it now."

It was as though the hard, hot body in her arms had turned to ice. She pulled back to look at him, trying to figure out what was going on.

"I'm not a damned hero," he ground out.

Genna laughed. "Of course you are. Even the president says so."

"I'm no hero and there is no we," he said with a laugh so bitter it made her mouth hurt. When Genna shook her head, he shifted aside. As if moving away from her body would make the differences between them all the more obvious. Since he was hard and she was panting, it was a smart strategy.

Genna wanted to thump her hand against her chest to force some air past the knot in her throat.

He was so big, looming over her. His body was like a solid wall of muscles. Even through his T-shirt, she could see them bunch, hard and firm beneath the fabric.

"Brody—" she said slowly, then went silent. She had no idea what to say. This wasn't the Brody she'd held in her mind all these years. The one she remembered as her gallant hero, the one who wrote her incendiary letters. The one who made her melt with just a look. Okay, maybe he was that last one, but not the rest. And she wasn't sure what to think about it.

"Look, we should—"

"No," he interrupted. "There is no we. There's you, the pampered princess. And there's me."

He paused, giving her a once-over that made her go hot and cold both at the same time. "Not interested."

Despite her confusion and the sick feeling in her stomach, hot passion was still gripping her limbs and pooling between her thighs. Genna dropped her eyes to the very large, very visible proof pressing against his sweatpants.

"No? You look mighty interested to me," she taunted without thinking. As soon as the words were out, though, she wished she could pull them back.

"Sweetheart, you want to get naked and do me right? Fine, let's go. I'm willing to let you. But that's not interest. That's over the minute I roll off your body."

His words hit Genna like a kick in the gut. Swift, well aimed and brutally painful. Emotionally reeling, she tried to take a breath, but it hurt so much.

"But I thought—" She broke off, not about to admit what their letters had meant to her. Or what these kisses were a sign of. And definitely not a peep about the fantasies, the dreams and the hopes she'd built around him over the years.

"You thought what? That because we played the old-school version of sexting that there was something going on? That because I'm willing to do you against the wall, it's special?"

Ouch. Genna frowned, suddenly feeling very naive. Apparently they taught mind reading in SEAL school.

"I didn't think the letters were a secret code for *let's run away together*. But neither did I think they were your version of a girl in every port." Wishing she were anywhere but here, Genna tried to ignore the tight knot of misery in her stomach, where only moments ago had been white-hot desire. "Did you write me just to be mean? For some kind of revenge? Is that what this was all about?"

For a second Brody looked as if he was going to protest. Then his expression smoothed again, back to stoic military machine.

"A day where we learn something isn't a day wasted," he told her in a sanctimonious tone that made her want to kick him in the shin. And not the good one.

"Well, I guess today is fabulous," Genna said, tears burning her eyes. She lifted her chin, daring them to fall. "I learned that you weren't the man I thought you were. I found out that you make an excellent bully and that you have no problem playing games and deliberately hurting someone."

She waited for him to protest. To claim she was wrong.

She wanted, desperately, for him to be that guy she'd always thought he was. To be the one who fought the odds, faced down the bullies. The one who protected her. That Brody was her hero.

But this one? His expression didn't change. She struggled to accept that this was the real him. The boy she'd known was a distant loner with a rough reputation and a questionable attitude. But she'd always been sure that was just a defense mechanism, maybe because his father sucked and he'd had such a bad childhood. On their night together he'd joked, he'd smiled. He'd been so sweet.

"But then, you've never known me, have you?"

Again with the mind reading. Genna wasn't sure if she wanted to cry, or to throw cookies at him. It wasn't as though she'd spent the last decade waiting around for him. But still, their relationship had been a cherished memory, that one thing that'd always made her feel special. Made her feel as if whatever else was lousy in her life, the hottest guy she'd ever crushed on had cared enough about her, about her reputation, to give up his freedom.

But it looked as though she was the only person who gave a damn about that memory.

Humiliation washed over her, making her blink fast to clear the burning from her eyes.

"I guess I don't know you. Not any better than anyone else around here. You're either the badass troublemaker son of the town drunk. Or maybe you're the abused grandson of a sweet lady who thinks you need saving. Or, wait, I know," she snapped, "you're the big bad hero the mayor wants to honor for your incredible service to your country. But whatever you are, it's not what I thought."

"Well, then," he said slowly, his words like gravel. "I guess that says it all. Maybe now you'll go?"

It wasn't his words that broke her heart, though. It was the look in his eyes. For one brief second, so much pain and loss flashed in those gold depths that she didn't know how he could survive it.

Genna didn't remember leaving the guesthouse. She wasn't sure if she ran across the alley, went around the house or sprouted wings and flew into her bedroom window.

She'd thought he'd forgiven her.

She'd thought he was interested in her, that those letters had meant something. That maybe he wanted her. The real her, not the perfectly behaved, please-everyone princess he'd so accurately dubbed her.

She'd thought they had something special between them. That those letters, that one night, they were proof of the passion and connection they shared.

Genna pressed her lips together, trying to stop the tears that were trailing, fiery hot, down her cheeks.

Now she was afraid he was a stranger.

One who hated her.

7

THERE WERE TIMES, miserable times, that a girl needed work. When it was good to have a job to focus on, to serve as a distraction from heartbreak.

This was not one of those times.

Real life sucked when she didn't have her secret fantasy to fall back on. After her mind-blowing climax, a nasty descent into reality and the proceeding all-night crying binge, Genna had tasked herself with getting over Brody. It shouldn't be that hard to get over a hero who had never existed, should it?

Three days later and she still hadn't figured out how. But hey, she had the rest of her long, lonely, dull life to work on it. She'd get there eventually.

She arranged coffee cups on a tray, making sure to add sugar in the form of cubes, granulated and raw. Yet another pathetic example of how sad her life was when the highlight of her day was getting the exact same amount of sugar in each bowl. It was enough to make her scream. Or maybe that was because her boss was still talking about his new favorite subject. Hometown Hero, Brody Lane.

"This event will be fabulous. We need to be sure enough press is invited. Not just lifestyle. I want current events, politics. War Hero Welcomed Home by Loving Town With Parade. That'll make a great headline."

"It needs work," Marcus Reilly said from his spot at the opposite end of the table from the mayor. "You're putting up a lot of fuss over a guy who, what? Did his job?"

Glad her back was to them, Genna freely rolled her eyes. *Did his job?* Leave it to her father to be a little black rain cloud. The sheriff had never been what anyone could call effusive. But over the last few years, the worse Joe's behavior was, the more withdrawn their father became. Almost as if he'd been expecting Joe's death and had figured on getting in some mourning ahead of time.

"Fine. We'll let the papers come up with the headline. Either way, hometown hero appreciation is good PR. A parade is good commerce and after all, it is election season," Tucker pointed out, those words saying it all.

The cookies arranged just so and coffee balanced on the tray, Genna turned toward the men gathered around the long teak table. An informal monthly meeting among Bedford's movers and shakers included the mayor and sheriff, of course. A couple of high-profile businesspeople, the bank owner and, she sighed, one perfect lawyer rounded up this month's powwow.

Avoiding the lawyer, Perfect Stewart who was still angling for a second date, she moved to the other side of the room with her tray. She wasn't sure how her job as community liaison had come to include playing hostess. But given that her job was more a backroom agreement between her boss and her father, she figured the mayor was looking for whatever he could to justify her paycheck. She'd protested the job once, wanting to quit and find something that she'd love. But that night Joe had been hauled in by Highway Patrol on drug charges. Her father had left midprotest to deal with the fallout. By the time he'd bailed out her brother, smoothed over the furor and glossed away the damage to his sheriff's reputation, Genna had given up arguing.

"Coffee?" she asked the room at large as she set the tray in the center of the table. Then she stepped back, returning to the counter to prepare the backup plate of cookies she knew they'd want soon.

It was bad enough she had to hostess these things. She drew the line at being waitress. As appreciative sounds and compliments on the cookies started flowing around the table, she admitted she didn't mind playing caterer, though.

Besides, she'd been on a baking binge for the last four days, ever since her encounter with Brody. Every counter in her kitchen was covered in some treat or another. And that was after sharing with all of her neighbors, her friends and the senior center.

"Genna?" Mayor Tucker called around a mouthful of cookie. "Have you spoken to Lane again? Has he agreed to meet with me?"

Go back and see Brody? The man who made her insides melt, turned her body into a panting puddle of passion and then summarily rejected her?

No, no and hell, no. Genna tried to think of a polite way to reword that. Before she could, her father gave a garbled protest.

"What? You sent Genna to talk to him?" The sheriff straightened, his cookie crumbs blasting across the table. His face turned a worrying shade of red and his mouth worked as if he was chewing up words to keep from spitting them out.

Looks of shock and worry flew around the room.

"Of course," the mayor said slowly. "That's her job."

Genna's face heated. Unspoken, but heard loud and clear by everyone in the room, was that it was a job her father had actively solicited, then called on all his parental guilt pressure to get her to take.

"I don't want her near Lane. The guy is a loser."

It was too much. He decided her job. He tried to control her dating. And now he was railroading her boss as to what her duties were? Anger bubbled up, slow at first but rapidly heating.

Forgetting her desire to stay as far away from Brody as possible, Genna stepped forward to argue. Both against her father's high-handed mandate as he continued to try to run her life, and at the idea that Brody was a loser.

Thankfully before she got a word out, and caused a scene that would send her father into yet another meltdown and her mother to the hospital to have her heart checked, someone cleared their throat.

"Brody Lane?" Stewart asked, confusion clear on his face. "The guy we're planning a parade for? The navy SEAL recently recommended for a Silver Star?" He let the words hang in the room for a few seconds, then gave a baffled shake of his head. "That guy is a loser?"

"No, no," Tucker broke in, giving the sheriff a quick glare before plastering over it with a cheesy smile. "That's old history. Sheriff Reilly remembers when Brody Lane was a troubled teen, well before the U.S. Navy turned him around. It's quite a rags-to-riches story. Something to include in the article, don't you think?"

"Get him yourself, then. Genna's not going near the guy."

Holy crap, she was sick of men. Sick of them deciding what she could or should do. Sick of them treating her as if she couldn't make her own decisions, or if she did, of them proving to her just how stupid some of those decisions might be.

"I'm standing right here," she pointed out in her chilliest tone. "If you want me to do something, or would rather I didn't, why don't you tell me directly?"

"This doesn't concern you, Genna," her father said dismissively.

Genna's jaw dropped. It wasn't her reaction that goaded her father into recanting, though. It was the expressions on the rest of the faces in the room.

"What I mean is that protecting the citizens of Bedford is my job, and this is part of that," he said, giving Genna a paternal look. The kind a proud father gives a little kid, loving and indulgent and just a little patronizing.

It made Genna want to throw a tantrum just to justify it.

But the minute she snapped, the family drama would start. Guilt, games, hospital trips. Every freaking time.

Her throat closed up and black dots danced in front of her vision. Genna felt as if she was choking. It was all she could do to breathe, which was probably just as well given the words that were trying to trip off her tongue.

Finally, she sucked in a deep breath, lifted her chin and gave her father a chilly smile.

"I guess you don't need me, then, do you?"

Ignoring the uncomfortable looks ricocheting around the room, Genna packed up the rest of her cookies. They'd all gotten a big old dose of gossip fodder. They weren't feasting on her baking, too.

The last thing she heard as she swept through the door with all the majesty of the princess title Brody had pinned on her was her father's muttered words.

"I'm gonna kick Brody Lane's ass."

BRODY STOOD BY the small lake down the hill from the park, noting that the cattails were chest-high now and the surrounding trees had created a canopy overhead. He used to come down here with his buddies after dark to drink. Or, every once in a while, with a girl, since not much action could be had on the backseat of a Harley. Some enterprising kid had tied a rope to one branch, right above the no-swimming sign.

Bet the local law loved that.

He missed the ocean.

He missed activity.

Hell, he missed reveille, spot inspections and mess hall chow.

"So this is where you're hiding?"

Brody sighed.

What he didn't miss were people. Which was one of the reasons he'd chosen this side of the park. It was rarely populated.

"If I was hiding, you wouldn't be able to find me." He didn't turn around when he said it, just kept staring at the murky water.

"You don't look surprised to see me," Masters said as he reached Brody's side, mimicking his stance of both hands in his pockets staring over the lake.

"I heard you stomping down the path." And he'd been expecting him. Irene had passed on a half dozen phone messages, each one more demanding than the last. Brody had ignored them, of course. But nobody put Masters off for long. If the guy wasn't so brilliant, his call sign would be Bulldog instead of Genius.

"I came to haul you out of hiding."

"I'm not hiding. I'm recovering." Brody gestured to the uneven path. "Walking, working the kinks out, pushing my limits."

"Moseying through a cozy small-town park at dusk pushes your limits?"

Brody shrugged.

Leaving the house pretty much pushed his limits these days.

"The doctor's report said you're ready for PT. Actually, I'm paraphrasing a little. What it said is that you should have reported to base to start thrice-weekly physical therapy a week ago, as soon as you got back to California."

"I'm on leave."

"Convalescent leave. Which, according to the manual, means you're off duty but still obligated to fulfill your duties, such as they are laid out by your superior officer."

"You read too much."

"We've all got our faults." Masters shrugged, kicking around the rocks and gravel beneath their feet.

"I figured I'd take another few days. Start physical therapy next week," Brody said. Not really a lie. If he'd thought about it at all, he'd definitely have put it off.

"Why?"

Brody hunched his shoulders, glaring at the water and wishing he'd opted for a nice, anonymous hotel room in some remote city to recuperate. Masters still would have found him, but it'd have taken the guy a couple extra hours.

"I'm not ready."

His teammate was silent for a few seconds, still stirring the rocks with his foot as if searching for gold. He bent down, grabbed a flat rock and sent it skipping over the lake. Three bounces. Not bad.

"PTSD?"

"I jacked up my leg," Brody snapped. "Not my head."

"Dude, that mission went straight to hell. Landon is still chewing on asses over the intelligence breakdown. And you bore the brunt of it. Nobody'd think less of you if you were having trouble processing it. There's no shame in that."

Brody puffed out a breath. He wasn't dissing guys facing it. Post-traumatic stress disorder was real, and from what he'd seen, it was pure hell. He thought about pointing out that he'd gotten through debriefing just fine, but he knew Masters wouldn't buy that. Debriefing didn't mean jack. Guys came back from missions, left the military all the time with their heads inside out. A guy didn't do or see the kind of things SEALs did without it taking a toll.

"I'm not ashamed. I'm just saying that's not the issue."

"Then you'll report for physical therapy tomorrow."

He quickly marshaled a handful of arguments. His bike was on base, so he didn't have wheels. His right leg was damaged, not in any shape to operate a car. And he couldn't ask his sweet little gramma to drive him the two-hour commute back and forth to Coronado. He wasn't even sure she had a license anymore.

He didn't offer up any of them, though. SEALs didn't make excuses.

"You could consider it an order," Masters said in a contemplative tone, bending down to pick up another stone, then winging it across the lake.

Brody grimaced. Not that the guy scored five bounces. But that he'd resort to pulling rank.

"Deal with whatever's going on. You need someone to talk to, give me a yell. But don't take forever. The team is waiting for you to finish this little vacation and get your ass back to work." Masters waited a beat, then added, "Besides, we miss your cookies. Can you get your gramma to send a care package with you when you come in tomorrow?"

Brody snorted.

Then, straightening his shoulders, he faced reality as he had so many times in the past. Orders were orders, no matter how ugly they were or what degree of reluctance he felt about them. He'd do PT until reevaluation. What he did afterward, well, time would tell.

"You need a ride?"

"Waste of resources," Brody pointed out, thinking of the car that'd dropped him off from the airport.

"Dude, we're on leave. The team will take turns playing taxi until the doctor green-lights you on your bike. Or you could rent something safe. A Smart Car, maybe."

Brody laughed, turning to face Masters for the first time since his buddy had joined him. The guy looked good. Normal, except for the seven stitches holding his cheek together. They'd all taken a hit on that mission.

But Brody had been the last man out. Well, second to last. His smile dropped, Carter's face flashing in his mind just before the guy had gone flying through the air.

"You okay?"

Brody blinked, then shrugged.

"Other than being ordered to see some dumbass who's gonna play with my body? Yeah, I'm fine."

After a long, narrow-eyed inspection, Masters nodded and turned to go.

"Don't forget the cookies," he called over his shoulder.

Brody let his mind go blank. It was a lot easier than facing the questions Masters's visit had planted in his mind. Questions that'd been there already, nicely buried. Thanks to his buddy, they'd made their ugly way to the surface. Much harder to ignore.

But not impossible.

The sun was sliding low when he finally made his way up the hill. He wanted to blame the chilly weather for the stiffness in his leg and pain shooting from ankle to shoulder.

He'd just cleared the hill, beads of sweat coating his forehead with an icy chill. He hunched his shoulders and ignored the pain.

"Hold it right there," growled a familiar voice.

Brody's fists clenched in his pockets, his jaw tight to hold back the cusswords.

Was there a beacon that went off whenever he cleared the lake? How many times in his life had this guy busted him right here, in this very spot?

And what the hell was with today? Had he missed the note on the calendar calling it face-your-demons day? First Masters with the reminders of the mission. Now Reilly was here to throw off the careful barriers Brody had slammed around any thoughts of Genna. Or more particularly, of the piss-poor way he'd treated her.

His attitude slid downward, from rotten to pure crap. He forced himself to pull it back. It'd been ten years. He was too old to play rebel badass. Besides, he'd made his peace with the sheriff's actions years ago. No point in holding a grudge.

"Lane." Reilly gave him a once-over, his tone as cool as the look on his face. "You have a reason for being here?"

Looked like time didn't do a damned thing to blunt other people's grudges.

"Walking is against the law?"

"I see the service didn't do anything about that smart mouth of yours."

"Actually, it improved it. Nobody swears or smarts off with the same finesse as a sailor."

Reilly just stared. Cold, with layers of anger that said he'd be more than happy to take off his badge and kick Brody's smart ass.

Brody grinned, amused for the first time in weeks.

Did the guy actually think he was intimidating? Brody had been stared down, shot at and ordered about by hard-asses that made Sheriff Reilly look like a cute little pussy-cat.

"Stay away from my daughter."

What? Had Genna run to Daddy, complaining that the big mean guy had kissed her?

Brody's grin slid away.

He made a show of looking left, then right. Then, just to prod the guy a little further, he glanced behind him before offering the sheriff a shrug.

"I don't seem to be anywhere near your daughter."

"Clearly the navy didn't teach you respect," Reilly muttered, resting his hand on the butt of his pistol. What, like he thought that'd get him the quote-unquote respect he apparently wanted?

Since Brody could have that weapon out of the guy's possession and neutralized in twenty seconds—an extra ten because he was injured and hadn't trained in a couple of months—he was having trouble finding the will to be intimidated.

Nor was he finding any for this conversation.

Before, the highlight of his discussions with the good sheriff was to see how far he could push the guy. To find each particular button and give it a good jab.

Now, he just didn't care.

"You looked me up for a reason, Sheriff. Why don't you get to it so we can both be on our way?"

Reilly blinked, then frowned. His hand shifted to his belt as he gave Brody a searching look.

"I told you, stay away from Genna."

"I haven't gone looking for your daughter."

"But you've seen her."

No point denying the truth. But neither was Brody stupid enough to fill in any blanks, either. Instead he just waited.

"Genna's not smart enough to know when she's being taken for a ride," the sheriff said, for the first time looking like a concerned father instead of an uptight cop. "She's got some starry-eyed idea that you're a hero. Same way she thinks drunks are safe to talk to and that her brother was gonna rehabilitate."

Brody rocked back on his heels, his mind adjusting to the lineup he'd just joined. Drunks and a prison-shivved junkie. Talk about perspective. The kind that grated down his spine. But as much as it killed him to let it slide, he didn't take the bait.

"Sounds to me like the person you need to talk to is your daughter," he said instead.

"I'll be talking to her. But I'm warning you, too. She's vulnerable, and not good at seeing through bullshit. Naive and easily confused."

Were they talking about the same woman? Genna Reilly, leggy spitfire with a wicked mouth and an attitude that didn't quit? Did the guy know his daughter at all?

"She's spent a lot of years getting her life on the straight and narrow, and keeping it there. She doesn't need any bad influences dragging her off."

"When did Genna fall off the straight and narrow?" Like the man's earlier one, this image simply didn't compute. Genna might be pure temptation wrapped in bold sassiness, but she was still the epitome of the town sweetheart.

"The only reason she didn't go the same way as her brother is because her mother and I kept a tighter rein on her. Kept her away from influences like you, made sure she works the right job, lives in the right place."

In other words, they'd tucked her under their thumb and hadn't let go.

Damn.

Brody felt like an ass. It was bad enough that he'd been a total jerk to her. Now to find out he'd only been act 1 in the ass brigade marching through her life.

He'd been fine justifying his treatment of Genna when it was only the two of them. But knowing her father was giving her shit for something she hadn't done seriously pissed him off.

"You've been warned," Sheriff Reilly snapped, turning to leave.

Brody wanted to hate the guy.

Still…

"Sheriff?"

Reilly stopped and looked over his shoulder.

"I'm sorry about Joe."

Grief-laced anger flashed, raw and painful in the older man's eyes for a second, then he blinked it away. He gave Brody another one of those searching looks, offered a silent nod and kept on walking.

Jerk.

Brody was still fuming when he got back to his hidey-hole of a house, his leg screaming protest at the extra pressure his stomp home had put on it.

For the first time, he looked past the guesthouse to the house on the other side of the alley. Lights glowed, the windows glistening against the darkening sky.

Then he glanced at the door of his hidey-hole.

Brody debated for all of three seconds.

Time to have a chat with Sheriff Reilly's little girl.

8

WHAT THE HELL was wrong with men?

Were they good for anything besides the occasional orgasm and spider removal?

"Genna, your mom called. Again."

"I'm not here."

Macy huffed in the kitchen doorway, then made her way into the bowels of temptation as she called it. Genna called it therapy. She looked around the counters covered in pies, cookies, cakes and her latest experiment, cookie-pops.

"You're gonna have to take her call," Macy said, her tone distracted as she stood a good foot away from the counter but leaning so close she was almost bent in half as she sniffed the coconut cake. "Otherwise she's going to send the EMT over again."

Focusing all her attention on the ziplocked bag of graham crackers she was crushing with a rolling pin, Genna just shrugged.

Since there was no impact in sending the cops, given that Genna's dad headed up that game, Cara Reilly had taken to calling for an ambulance when her daughter ignored her. After all, the only reason Genna could ever not respond was that she'd fallen in the shower, or slipped down the staircase, or cut her head off while slicing to-matoes.

Genna beat the bag so hard the seams exploded, send-ing graham cracker crumbs all over the counter. It was un-thinkable that her daughter might not want to talk.

"If you talk to her, she'll quit calling," Macy said with an impatient look.

"If I talk to her, I might actually need an EMT." Genna swept the crumbs off the counter into her hand, her moves jerky with irritation.

"What'd she do that's so bad?"

Genna shrugged and grabbed a paper towel to clean up the mess instead of answering.

What was the point?

Macy didn't get it. She saw Genna's parents as poster-perfect, the epitome of what every parent should be. At-tentive, helpful and always there to offer advice on their daughter's life. What she didn't see, or chose to ignore since Genna had pointed it out a few million times, was that they were smothering her.

"I'm going to stay at Greg's for a little while," Macy finally said, sidling closer to a triple-layer coconut cream cake and swiping a fingerful of frosting.

"Because my mother keeps calling?" Wow, maybe her parents' nagging and interference had finally paid off. Not that she didn't love Macy, but she was seriously tired of justifying her mood, choices and entire freaking life.

"No. Because you keep baking. In the last three weeks, you've made enough food to stock a fancy bakery. I can't take it. I'd rather stay with Greg and risk a big fight be-fore the wedding than stay here and ensure I can't fit in my dress."

Genna winced. Shaking the cracker crumbs off her fin-gers, she finally turned to look at her friend.

Macy's face was creased with concern. Another reason

to leave, Genna supposed. No bride should have worry lines on her special day.

"I'm sorry," she murmured, glancing around the room and seeing what her friend probably saw. Holy cow. It did look like a bakery had relocated to her kitchen. "I have no idea what I'm going to do with all of this."

She'd been so focused on baking to avoid her thoughts, she hadn't considered what to do with the results.

Macy backed away as if the very question opened the door to the possibility of her eating it all. Then she stopped, sighed and scooped up another taste of coconut frosting.

"You won't burn yourself out before you need to make my wedding cake, will you?"

Genna laughed for the first time in three days. What was Macy going to obsess over after mid-May?

"Of course not. I love to bake. I can't imagine ever burning out on it." Of course, she hadn't been able to imagine her heart being stomped on and her dreams trampled while she was still quivering from a mind-blowing climax, either. So what did she know?

"Will you be okay here by yourself?"

"I'll be fine."

Better than fine, actually, since all she wanted right now was to be left alone. She didn't want to talk, she had no interest in sharing her heartbreak or hearing advice. And if Macy wasn't here, she could turn off the phone altogether. After putting in a call to the EMT center to let them know to ignore her mother, of course.

Nope, she'd rather be alone, baking and contemplating the useless dissatisfaction that was her life.

Fun, fun.

"Go, live with your fiancé," she said, shooing Macy out of the kitchen before she gave in to self-pity and changed her mind. "Have wild sex, play house, try togetherness on for size."

"Genna," Macy protested, blushing. "We don't have wild sex."

What was the point of getting married, then?

Not wanting to prolong the departure, Genna kept that question to herself. Instead, she wiped her hands and helped Macy carry a half dozen bags and boxes to the car. A quick wave, a few warnings and reminders to call her mom from Macy, and voilà.

Peace and quiet.

Exhausted but not willing to go to bed at—she glanced at the clock and winced—7:00 p.m.? Pissed off, miserable and frustrated made for an exhausting cocktail.

She stepped back into the kitchen and looked around.

It did look like she was stocking a bakery with goods.

Maybe she could set up a stand in the front yard. Three cookies for a dollar. A few hundred dozen and she might have enough money to afford a sheriff-approved storefront.

Playing with that dream, a nice distraction from her earlier thoughts, Genna returned to building her cheese-cake crust. Butter, graham crackers, ground almonds. All yummy goodness.

She was entertaining the mental debate over decorating her dream bakery in modern teal and brown, or going with a fun black-and-pink palette when there was a rap at her back door. Loud enough to make her jump and almost drop the cream cheese. Her heart pounding just as loud now, she shifted to the side of the kitchen to look out the window.

Brody?

She blinked, moved closer to the window in case the porch light was casting illusions, then looked again.

Tall, sexy and gorgeous. Yep, that was Brody all right.

She scowled. What did he want?

She debated for all of three seconds before checking to see that the lock was engaged, then jaw set, took the cream cheese back to the mixer. When the knock came again, she flipped the mixer on high to drown it out.

"It's usually better to hide in another room if you're pretending not to be there when someone knocks."

Genna jumped, but managed to contain her scream. She was so proud, she gave herself a couple seconds for her heart to slow again before turning off the mixer. Had he learned lock-picking in SEAL school? Or was that a leftover from his badass days? Pasting on her most distant expression, she tossed a cool expression over her shoulder.

"It's usually better to take the hint. When someone doesn't answer the door it means they don't want to see you."

"I've never been good with subtleties."

No question about that. Brody and subtle didn't even belong in the same sentence. Genna pulled her gaze back to the creamy mixture in her bowl, wishing he didn't look so good. A quick glance told her he'd lost some of that pallor, the crisp evening air and scent of the outdoors adding to the healthy impression.

Too bad.

She'd been imagining him wasting away with guilt, miserable over having rejected her and pining away to nothing.

"Saw your old man tonight," he said, letting the door slam shut behind him. "So what's the deal? You tell your daddy I'm being mean to you?"

"Wow, not subtle or polite," she said, pretending to measure the vanilla instead of just pouring it into the bowl to give her face time to cool off. Damn her father.

"Genna?"

Pressing her lips together, she finally turned to him. And immediately crossed her arms over her chest. Both to keep her hands to herself, and to hide the instant evidence of her body's reaction.

He was so damned sexy.

His leather jacket did nothing to disguise the breadth of his shoulders, and instead of sweats he was in jeans tonight. Jeans that molded nicely to his hard thighs. Whew, it was hot in here.

"Well?"

Well, what? Did he want her to say it out loud? That he was gorgeous or that she went into instant meltdown just being in the same room as him.

Then she replayed the conversation and grimaced.

"I didn't say anything to my father. He was at the meeting when the mayor asked if I'd contacted you again. I said no, my father said never, I walked out. End of story."

Brows furrowed, Brody stared long enough to make her want to squirm. Then he nodded and looked around the room. His eyes got wider as they passed from counter to tabletop to counter.

He gave a baffled shake of his head. "Do you run your own bakery? Or are you supplying treats for the Fifth Fleet?"

Starting to get a baking complex and wondering if she should look into a twelve-step program, Genna followed his gaze and sighed.

Then, not willing to relax her guard since the minute she did all those schoolgirl dreams would come floating right back, Genna gave him an arch look.

"Why are you here?"

All the way in the room now, he was peering from tray to plate, then chose a butter pecan cookie and popped it into his mouth.

"I told you," he said around the cookie. "Your father came to see me."

"And told you I said you were mean?"

"Actually he warned me to stay the hell away from you."

Genna closed her eyes against the humiliation. She was twenty-seven and her father warned away guys he didn't like. Her mother called her three times a day and sicced emergency personnel on her if she didn't respond. Could her life be any more pathetic?

Forcing herself to meet his gaze again, she offered a stiff smile and a shrug.

"Okay. So he warned you. That shouldn't be a big deal since according to you, you don't want to be anywhere near me anyhow." She waited, but his expression didn't change. "So I'll ask again. Why are you here?"

"I told. Because your father told me to stay away."

"Seriously? You're here to defy my father?"

"Sure." He shrugged. "Why not?"

Genna was pretty certain she wouldn't have been more shocked if he'd stripped naked and asked her to eat cookies off his body.

It was all Brody could do not to laugh.

The look on Genna's face was priceless. Baffled fury, coated in a pink wash of embarrassment.

She was adorable.

And he was pretty sure that was the first time in his life he'd ever used the word *adorable*.

The kitchen timer dinged. After a couple of blinks and a bewildered shake of her head, Genna grabbed a cloth and hurried to the oven. As soon as she opened it, a spicy rich scent filled the room. Giant cookies, the size of his hand and studded with chocolate, covered the tray. His mouth actually watered.

"Let me get this straight." She set the tray of cookies on the counter, opposite Brody and too far for him to sneak one. A frown between narrowed eyes, she gave him a long look. Strikingly similar to her father's look, actually. Brody's lips twitched. She probably wouldn't want to hear that.

"I write to give you bad news, and you hit on me by mail. I come to see you to pass on an invitation and a message—neither of which are from me—and you feel me up then kick me out. And today my father, clearly overstepping both his parental and legal bounds, warns you to stay away from me." She paused, as if waiting for him to dispute anything she'd said so far. Since she was pretty much on track, he just shrugged. "And now that I am, according to someone who has no say in it, off-limits, what? You want me?"

"I didn't say I wanted you," Brody corrected quickly. No point giving her the wrong idea. Or in this case, the right idea that he planned to ignore.

"Ah, my mistake." She tossed her hands in the air, the move sending the scent of fresh-baked cookies through the room. Brody's stomach growled. Risking her glare, and the spatula she was currently smacking against her palm, he snagged a cookie from the closest tray.

It melted in his mouth, rich molasses goodness coating his tongue and sliding down to create a celebration in his stomach.

Incredible.

He lifted the small piece left in his hand, peered at it, then looked closer at the trays around the room. He knew these cookies.

"I've had this before."

"I brought you a plate of them less than a week ago."

He shook his head. "I tossed those out."

"You threw out my cookies?" Outrage and shock rang out, her voice rising with each word. Eyes wide, mouth half-open, she kept trying to say something but the words seemed to be stuck somewhere. Instead she shook her head and gestured, tried again, then settled on a low growl.

Brody smothered a laugh.

Well, well.

He'd intimidated her.

He'd groped her.

He'd put on his meanest face and tried to scare her.

And she'd had a sassy comeback every single time.

But now he'd finally done it.

He'd rendered Genna Reilly speechless.

All it'd taken was to insult her cookies.

He couldn't help it. He laughed out loud.

Shock faded, leaving Genna's expression blank before it slowly shifted to fury. Red washed over her cheeks and her eyes sparked enough fire to turn the cookies to charcoal.

"I'm sorry?" he offered, trying to smother his laughter. It was hard, though. She was so damned cute with her outrage.

"For...?"

What? She wanted a detailed list? Oh, no. He might limit his experience with women to the length of a long weekend. But he wasn't stupid. The minute he started confessing, she'd start keeping score. Since she was ahead of the game anyway, he wasn't about to hand her that kind of ammo.

"You know," he said slowly, changing the subject. "Every month my gramma sent me a care package. Wherever I was, I'd get a box of cookies. Sugar cookies in Cairo, spice cookies in Dubai. In Korea I got a box of chocolate chunk that were so good, the entire SEAL team was licking crumbs out of the box."

"So?" Her expression didn't change. But the way her eyes lit with pleasure assured Brody he was right in his suspicions.

"So, for the last eight years, I've been getting cookies from my grandmother. Except they weren't from her."

"Did she say they were?" Genna asked, moving the cooled cookies to a rack before turning back to whatever other delicious concoction she was whipping up.

"Nope. Not once did she say, 'Brody, I made these cookies myself,'" he acknowledged. "But neither did she ever mention they were from someone else."

He waited a beat while Genna poured white batter into what looked like small pie tins.

"Any idea what's behind the covert cookie care package?" he asked as soon as she set the bowl down.

"Maybe you should ask her," Genna said, leaning forward so her hair swung down, hiding her face as she arranged the tins in a pan of shallow water.

"I'm asking you."

Genna slid the tray into the oven, then with a sigh deep enough to do interesting things to her apron ruffles, she faced him with a shrug. Her shoulders hunched and she dropped her chin to her chest.

"I made the cookies," she confessed with more guilt than most insurgents he'd watched be interrogated.

"No! Really?"

Some of the shame faded as her lips twitched. But the odd look didn't leave her eyes. Like she was hiding something still. Something ugly. What? Since he hadn't dropped dead, he knew she hadn't poisoned the cookies.

"Why?" he asked. When she pressed her lips together, he shook his head. "C'mon. Why would you send cookies all that time through my gramma? How'd you get her to go along with it? She's not known for keeping secrets, but she never hinted. Even when I thanked her to her face for the treats and told her how much the guys loved them."

"She told me that," Genna said softly. He assumed her affectionate smile was for his grandmother. Then, after giving him a long look and probably realizing he wasn't going to give it up, she lifted both hands in the air.

"Look, it's no big deal. I'd just moved in here and was going around meeting the neighbors. I took Irene cookies and when I realized how lonely she was, I started taking them by each week. She mentioned once that you'd loved cookies when you were a little boy. So I gave her extras. What she did with the extras was totally up to her."

There was more to it than that. But Genna had that stubborn tilt going with her chin, so he knew he wouldn't get the rest of the story. Yet.

Just as well.

The idea of her sending him cookies, of her thinking about him every single month for the last eight years. That did something to him. A warmth Brody had never felt spread through him, soft and gentle. Probably heartburn from eating so many sweets on an empty stomach, he told himself.

Still, better to drop the subject than risk feeding that feeling.

"So, seriously. What's with all the food? Is that what you do when you aren't playing messenger for the mayor? You have a bakery?"

"No. And I'm not the mayor's messenger. I'm the community liaison. I work with the various businesses and organizations on things like outreach, civic issues, beautification and events." She looked around the room and must have noticed there was three square inches of counter space available, so she pulled out a big bowl and started gathering ingredients.

"That's your real job? I thought it was something you did like volunteering. You know, being a good citizen and all." He grabbed a muffin, figuring if she was baking something else she could use the room.

"Why are you here again?" she asked, lifting her chin and giving him as cool look. "You just wanted to visit because my father put me on the off-limits list? Or did you get lonely there in that tiny house all by yourself with nobody to insult?"

Brody grinned. He loved her claws.

But she had a point.

And while he wasn't big on apologies, he did owe her something after the way he'd treated her before. He looked at the muffin in his hand and grimaced. He hated explaining himself. Especially when he didn't really understand why he was here. Just that he'd needed to see her.

"I didn't realize how hard things might be for you," he said slowly. When she frowned and shook her head in confusion, he clarified. "Here, after. I figured you'd skate through, you know? Pampered princess and all that."

She pulled a weird spoon thing made up of wires out of a drawer, running it through her hands as she considered his words.

"After? You mean when my father shanghaied you into the navy?"

Brody almost choked on his muffin laughing.

"Yeah. After that." Leave it to Genna to tell it like it was.

"I'm pretty sure you're the only person in the world who thinks I'm a pampered princess," she said, rolling her eyes and ignoring the rest of his words.

So. She didn't want to talk about what it'd been like.

Too bad. Brody did.

"What happened? I thought you were going to some fancy college. Didn't Joe say you'd gotten into Stanford?" Not that Joe bragged about his sister. If Brody remembered correctly, Joe'd been bitching that Genna's accomplishments were putting pressure on him. Apparently their parents were starting to nag that he get off his ass and do something with his life.

Genna pressed her lips together, all of her attention on the milky sugar mixture she was stirring with that weird spoon. After a few seconds, she shrugged.

"That didn't work out. I ended up staying here and did the community college thing instead."

Maybe it was because all he'd ever wanted to do was

get the hell out of Bedford, but Brody just wasn't buying that she'd given up so easily on leaving.

Or maybe it was the way she refused to look at him.

Deciding this was going to take a while and he might as well be comfortable, he pulled out one of the ladder-back chairs, turned it backward and straddled it.

"Comfy?" she asked, the sarcasm as thick as the cream she was stirring.

"I could use something to drink," Brody responded. "But otherwise, thanks, I'm pretty comfortable."

After a long look, she walked over to the sink, took a glass out of the cabinet and filled it with tap water. Since it gave Brody a great view of her butt, he couldn't complain. Except that he wasn't here to look at her butt, he reminded himself. He was here to find out what the hell had happened to her life after he'd left.

"You didn't get to go to Stanford because of what happened between us?" he guessed, watching her face closely. "Was that your punishment for getting too close to a bad influence?"

She sighed, looking defeated for the first time he'd ever seen. Her entire being, face, body and spirit, seemed to sag.

"Do you blame me for your impromptu commitment to the military?" she asked, sidestepping his question. Again.

"No." For a couple of years, he'd wanted to. But he'd never quite been able to justify it as fair.

"Then you shouldn't have any trouble understanding that I don't blame you for my parents going off the deep end with the overprotective control issues."

"What happened?" Brody was as surprised at his words as Genna seemed to be. He never asked questions like that. He always figured people overshared anyway, so why encourage more? But all of a sudden, with Genna, he wanted to know everything.

Maybe he was suffering delayed reactions from his injuries. Or was in desperate need of a distraction from the upcoming therapy and return to base. But he couldn't let it go. He had to know what had happened.

The buzzer chimed just then and she slid a thick mitten on her hand to pull out the little cake things she'd put in earlier. She touched the tops, added more water to the pan, then slid it all back in the oven and reset the timer. That should have given Brody plenty of time to talk himself out of the idiotic idea brewing in his head.

He didn't quite manage it, though.

"Maybe we could try something new," Brody said quietly.

Spooning the fluffy white cream she'd been stirring into a triangular shaped plastic bag, Genna glanced over. Heat flared in her eyes, making it clear she'd be interested in trying quite a few things. She wet her lips so they glistened, tempting him to ignore his conscience and give in to the need to taste her again. But instead of making any suggestions that could open the door to tasting, touching or anything else that'd feel great and show incredibly bad judgment, she arched one brow in inquiry.

"What'd you want to try?"

Brody tried the words out in his head, but they sounded too stupid to say aloud. Holy crap, he felt like a dorky schoolboy. Any second now he'd be shuffling his feet and, God forbid, blushing.

"Brody?"

He sighed, then faced the words the way he faced Hell Week, that sky full of empty air when he was jumping from a plane, and enemy fire. With a deep sigh, a straight spine and an unbreakable resolve.

"I thought we could try being friends."

9

FRIENDS.

She and Brody Lane were friends.

Or at least, they were trying to be.

She wasn't sure how she felt about it, though. She'd agreed because, well, she wanted to know the real Brody Lane. To find out if he was different from the guy she'd spent years fantasizing about.

Over the last couple weeks, she'd discovered three things.

He was completely different from the guy she'd thought he was. He was controlled and strong-willed, and didn't hesitate to voice his beliefs.

He was exactly the same as the guy she'd thought he was. Quiet, almost to the point of being taciturn, clever and fun when he did have something to say, and so sexy that she got turned on just watching him breathe.

And, over the last few days, she'd come to realize that they actually could be friends. That they had enough in common, similar interests and values. That they'd found a rhythm and flow that felt good. And as great as that was, she would absolutely, positively, unquestionably go crazy if all Brody would ever be was her friend.

Genna peered into the mirror, trying to see if there was crazy shining in her eyes yet. Nope. A few hints of stress and a whole lot of sexual frustration, but no signs of crazy.

Just her normal blue gaze stared back at her, albeit wearing a little more makeup than usual. Her eyes were smudged in kohl, with a dusky gray shadow giving her a smoky, do-me-all-night look she'd practiced for hours. Pale pink lips with a hint of shimmer on her cheekbones and she was as close to sophisticated sexy as she figured she'd ever get.

She leaned back from the mirror, lifting her hair this way and that. Up or down? Down said casual, just two friends going to dinner. If anyone saw her and Brody together, she could play it off as just a friendly meet-up with a distant acquaintance. Up said fancy, maybe a date. There was no way to pass off fancy hair as a casual get-together. Fancy hair said she'd put in time, effort. That she was looking to score.

Which she was.

But she didn't want anyone else knowing that.

Including Brody, who seemed completely determined to keep their relationship—or friendship, as he always corrected her—on his terms. Which included his stopping by at random times over the last week, eating cookies, testing her new recipes and nagging her to do something with her baking instead of giving it away. He didn't talk much, but listened just fine as long as the conversation wasn't about him. Which meant Genna did all the talking. She hadn't realized how much she had to say, things she couldn't say to the other people in her life. Frustrations and worries, dreams and fears.

But nothing about them. Nothing personal. The minute she'd bring up that night ten years ago, Brody would shut it down. If she mentioned their first meeting two weeks ago, he changed the subject.

And the few times she'd tried flirting?

He'd walked out.

Genna dropped her hair and pressed her fingers to her temples.

Clearly, it was going to be a hair-down kind of evening.

But she wanted it up.

She sighed. Yeah. She was going crazy.

"Hey."

Genna jumped.

She'd been so focused on her image, she hadn't heard Macy come in.

Her stomach tightened with nerves that had nothing to do with Brody, but everything to do with her relationship with him.

"What're you doing here?" she asked, glancing from Macy to the clock. Brody wasn't due for twenty minutes. Hopefully she could shoo her friend out before he got here.

"I came by to borrow your printer. The caterer emailed me the final contract," Macy said, her tone distracted as she gave Genna a suspicious twice-over. Clearly the first glance had tipped her off. Genna brushed her fingers over her hair, hanging loose and casual, and bit her lip.

"What're you doing?" Macy asked, stepping farther into the room. Her gaze swept from Genna's dress to the three others tossed on the bed, then landed on the tangled pile of shoes next to the closet. Her arched brows demanded information.

Genna didn't want to give it to her, though.

Macy would judge. And since Brody had been stubbornly reluctant to take his hero dues, especially in public, the gossip had shifted. Now the lunchtime buzz wasn't as much about Brody Lane, the military hero. It was more speculation with a whole lot of rehashing his past.

Macy, like Genna's parents, would buy into the speculation, rather than trusting the hero buzz.

"I'm just trying on outfits. You know, playing girl for a change." Just because she lived most of her life in jeans didn't mean she didn't have a great wardrobe of things she never got to wear anywhere. Especially the shoes. A girl who stood five-ten barefoot and only seemed to date insecure men never got to wear heels. Since Brody was secure as hell and six-two, she'd figured this was a great time to scuff those soles.

But she didn't want to tell Macy that, either.

"You're going out?"

"Maybe."

"With Stewart?" Macy said, looking at the four-inch, pointed-toe stiletto pumps on Genna's feet.

"Eww. No. He collects troll dolls. Remember?"

"Then who are you going out with?"

Crap. Genna gave the clock a wincing glance and realized she wasn't going to get out of this. She took a deep breath and put on her most confident face.

"With a friend for a friendly dinner. Sort of repayment for a few dozen cookies, a cake and a couple of pies. You know how everyone pays me for my baked goods in favors or in exchange?"

"I don't remember you getting all dressed up when Mr. Jenson bought you lunch last month for making his granddaughter birthday cupcakes."

"That's because Mr. Jenson bought me a hoagie and a side of fruitcake off the lunch truck and he didn't even invite me to the party." And, of course, there was the fact that the sixty-year-old pharmacist looked nothing like her hot and hunky SEAL.

"So. Who's been eating your cookies?" Macy asked suspiciously.

Sadly, no one. Since Macy wouldn't understand or appreciate that joke, Genna just shrugged.

"Genna…"

"Brody Lane," she blurted out, throwing her hands in the air. "There. Now you know. I'm going to dinner—a casual, just-between-friends dinner—with Brody Lane."

From the horror in her eyes and the drop of Macy's chin, maybe it'd have been better if she'd said she was going to dinner with an ax murderer.

"Like I said, it's just a thank-you meal. No big deal."

Macy's mouth worked, but nothing came out. Good. Genna knew she wasn't going to like hearing it when her friend recovered.

Pretending her spine wasn't so tight it'd take a chiropractor and a sledgehammer to crack it, she moved to the full-length mirror to check her dress. Was it too fancy for a simple dinner between friends?

Red and fitted with a sweetheart neckline that made the most of the very little she had, the bodice hugged her body to the waist before flaring into full pleats to just above her knees.

She sneaked a glance at Macy's expression in the mirror. The other woman looked like she figured a straitjacket would be a better fit.

"Okay. What? Go ahead and say whatever you have to say. But do it fast, because Brody's going to be here in ten minutes and I'm leaving."

"You're crazy. Don't you remember what happened last time you chased after this guy? How furious your parents were? In case you forgot, your mom ended up in the hospital and your brother in jail."

Praying for patience, Genna reminded herself that this was her oldest, dearest friend. And that she was too heavy to throw out the window.

"Joe stole a car. That had nothing to do with me, my actions or Brody. He would have gone to jail even if I was sitting at home eating popcorn and watching reruns of *Friends*." Something she'd told herself, and her parents, a million times over. Dammit, she wasn't to blame for her brother's choices. "And Mom went to the hospital because she had an asthma attack. Again, in no way related to my actions that night."

"Her asthma attack could have been brought on by stress," Macy said, parroting Cara so perfectly that it was all Genna could do to not look around the room for her mother.

Or cry.

"That doesn't mean I caused the stress. Joe gets the lion's share of the credit for that. Or it could have been brought on by the heat." Genna frowned, wondering why the hell she was always to blame for everything when she was the least of the contributors. When did she get to stop paying for her brother's choices? And when the hell would someone trust her to run her own life?

Trying for patience, she smiled through gritted teeth. "Macy, my mom is a hypochondriac. Even the doctor says so. My brother was on a collision course with himself."

And Genna had paid, and paid and paid and paid, for that night. As horrible as she felt about Joe's choices, about what'd finally happened to him, she was tired of paying.

"It's no big deal. Seriously, don't get all weirded out." Genna wanted to check her lipstick, but figured primping would negate her entire pitch. "Brody is staying at his gramma's while he recovers, so he's living across the alley and we've run into each other a few times. Partially because the mayor wants to do an event for him. Hero's welcome and all that."

Something Brody had no interest in. Still, Genna had started putting together tentative ideas, in case she changed his mind. After all, he was a hero and maybe if he saw how much the town appreciated his service, he'd have a different opinion of Bedford. And of the idea of visiting here more often after he'd gone back on duty.

And maybe after seeing Brody praised and paraded, everyone would see what a great guy he was. A much better guy than someone like, oh, say Stewart.

"It's really no big deal," she said again. This time as much to convince herself as Macy.

"You're going on a date. For Valentine's Day."

"We're going to dinner. On a Tuesday," Genna corrected, checking her purse for necessities. "Valentine's isn't until Friday."

Lipstick, keys, license and credit card, condom, twenty-dollar bill, cell phone.

Looked as if she was all set.

"Hey, there's nothing between us. We're friends. That's it. That's all he wants." She met Macy's eyes and straight up lied. "And that's all I want."

"Fine." Macy huffed, then handed Genna the black leather gloves and wool jacket from the chair, as if covering her as much as possible before she went downstairs was going to keep her virtue intact. "When's he leaving?"

Leaving? The thought was like a jagged knife ripping through her gut. She hated thinking about life without Brody.

"He's going to Coronado four times a week for physical therapy now, so I'd imagine he'll be back to full use of his leg before the end of the month." She gave Macy a big smile all the brighter for being fake. "So he should be back on duty in two weeks."

A smart girl would start steeling her heart against the end. A smarter girl would cut things off now, before her emotions got tangled any tighter.

Genna was smart.

Damned smart.

Smart enough to know that she was already in too deep. She had been for years. She was smart enough to know that nothing was going to make the heartbreak of Brody leaving any easier to take. So she was going to get every second of pleasure, of fun and of anything else she could from these couple of weeks together.

And she didn't care if it took her thirteen of her fourteen days. At some point before he left to play hero again, she was getting him naked and naughty.

Right on cue, the doorbell rang.

"Don't you have something to print?" she asked, hurrying around her friend and heading for the stairs. "Go ahead, take your time. Lock up when you leave."

Never one to take a hint, Macy followed her right down the stairs and stood there like a grumpy rain cloud, waiting for Genna to open the door.

Trying to ignore her, Genna tossed her coat over the hall bench, took a deep breath, put on a big smile and opened the door.

And almost melted as the chilly evening air washed over her. Oh, he looked good. Black slacks and dress shirt suited his bad-boy image and fit to perfection. So used to seeing him in jeans or sweats and a tee, she had to swallow a couple of times to keep from drooling.

"Hi," she finally said.

"Hey. You look nice." His tone was light and friendly, but his eyes were hot as they swept over her body, leaving the kind of tingles that led to tight nipples, damp panties and, hopefully, multiple orgasms.

Yes. Genna wanted to do a happy dance right there in the doorway. Finally, he was looking at her as something other than a friendly cookie machine.

Maybe they could skip dinner and get right to dessert.

The loud cough behind her burst the sexual bubble as effectively as an icy cold blast from the hose.

Brody looked over her shoulder. She followed his gaze and sighed.

"Brody, this is my friend Macy. She was just leaving," Genna said pointedly.

"Hi," Brody offered with a polite nod.

Looking distant, as if she were holding her breath in case he was carrying a bad case of cooties, Macy gave a jerky nod.

Brody glanced at Genna, who just rolled her eyes and gestured him inside.

"You look great," she said as the door closed behind him. Her fingers itched to straighten his collar, to feel the fabric of his shirt and see if it was as soft as it looked. "I didn't realize you had fancy clothes with you."

"I stopped by barracks after physical therapy today."

Brody shifted from foot to foot, almost as if he'd rather be in front of a firing squad. Whether that preference was over what he was wearing, his visit to his barracks or this evening's plans was up in the air.

"You sure you want to go into San Diego? We can eat someplace here in town instead. That way you don't have to drive," he said, referring to the fact that while he'd come back on his Harley after his last physical therapy session, he didn't have a car.

Nope. Dinner in San Diego was more romantic. A drive would give them time to talk. And if they stayed here, people would see. Then they'd talk. Her father would hear and things would get ugly. Worse, her mother would hear and head straight for the hospital.

"Good question. You should eat in town. I hear Ziapatta's is serving lasagna tonight," Macy broke in. Stepping forward, she started reciting the menu as if her life—or Genna's virtue—depended on convincing Brody to eat there.

Genna scowled. The woman couldn't say hello, but she saw a chance to ruin the night and she turned into a chatterbox.

"We have reservations," Genna interrupted smoothly. "And I don't want Italian food."

She wanted her date, dammit.

"Good night, Macy," she said emphatically.

As huffs went, Macy was a champion. Muttering warnings the whole way, she skirted around them to yank open the front door, then stormed down the walk.

Genna grimaced at the scowl her friend threw over her shoulder before climbing into her car.

"I'll bet she's on the phone by the end of the street," she predicted, letting the door slam shut with a satisfying bang.

"Gossip?" Brody guessed.

"Tattling."

He glanced out the window at the departing car, then arched a brow her way.

"To whom about what?"

"To my parents about us," Genna said, heading over to grab her purse and coat off the bench.

She didn't make it far.

Two steps and she was stopped by Brody's hand on her arm.

"Hold up a sec. So let me get this straight. Your friend is going to run to your mommy and daddy and stir up trouble when she tells them that you're hanging out with me?"

Genna frowned for a second at his use of hanging out instead of dating. He was working hard to keep that wall between them. Or maybe it wasn't hard work on his part and he really did only think of her as someone to hang out with while he was stuck in town.

Then, taking a deep breath to shake that off because she was sure she'd change his mind eventually, she focused on his question. And the irritation on his face.

"Totally obnoxious, right? I know she's my best friend, and she really is a sweetie. But she's always doing stuff like this. She thinks she knows best, and just has to interfere."

Genna started to move toward the bench and her coat again, but Brody didn't let go of her arm.

"What?" she asked.

His irritation had settled into a scowl.

"Tell me something. Other than your friend, does anyone know you're hanging out with me?"

Again with the hanging out? Genna huffed, then shrugged. He let go this time, but shifted so his arms were crossed and his legs wide. She had the feeling that even if she did get her coat, she wasn't getting past him to open the front door.

"I don't know," she said, throwing both her hands in the air. "I suppose your gramma knows. And people have seen us together, right?"

At her corner grocery store. The little café on the edge of town. The movie theater matinee. Nobody who knew and might report back to her parents. But that was beside the point. They were still people.

"You ashamed?"

He said it so matter-of-factly, with no inflection at all, that it took a few seconds for the implication of his words to sink in.

"Of course I'm not ashamed to be *hanging out* with you," she protested, ignoring the guilty little tickle in the back of her throat at the words.

He didn't look convinced. In fact, if Genna didn't know better, she'd think he was a little hurt. But Brody didn't care about things like approval. And, despite the fact that they were playing this *let's be friends* game of his, she doubted her opinion registered in his world.

"Yeah? But you're worried about your friend ratting you out. Worried enough about word getting around that you only wanna be seen with me if we're out of town." Brody pulled a contemplative face and rocked back on his heels, then gave a decisive nod. "Yep. You're ashamed."

Genna's jaw dropped in a shocked gasp. She took a step backward, but figured pressing one hand to her heart might be overkill. He wasn't buying it anyway. Brody was still giving her that pitying look, as if she'd just admitted to sleeping with his photo cut from a high school year-book under her pillow. Which she hadn't done for at least nine years.

"Oh, and you're one to talk," she tossed back. "If it hadn't been for my father warning you to stay away from me, you'd never have come over."

He just stared, no expression in those gold eyes. Damn that SEAL training of his. So Genna pushed harder.

"What's the difference? Isn't you being with me your own form of rebellion? A way to give the finger to the guy who shipped you off ten years ago?"

Well, that changed his expression. Right from casual suspicion to icy distance.

Oops. Maybe she'd pushed a little too far.

"I'm your rebellion?"

Genna winced. Leave it to him to home in on that one particular statement. Couldn't he focus on the insult instead? It'd be a lot easier to smooth that over.

"Aren't we going to dinner?" she asked in her brightest, let's-change-the-subject tone. "We're going to be late if we don't get on the road, and I'm starving already."

His expression didn't shift.

"I don't think you're doing it right," he mused, his slow contemplative tone at odds with the cold look in his eyes. "If you want to rebel, you throw your actions in people's faces. You don't hide your bad side away hoping nobody will notice."

You did if you were afraid of their reaction. Genna pressed her lips together to keep that confession to herself.

"Then, by your own definition, I'm not rebelling," she pointed out with a teasing smile, hoping to charm him out of pursuing this conversation. "And we've already established that I'm not ashamed of being seen with you. So why are we wasting time talking about this? Especially since chitchat is right up there with wearing pink on your list of manly things to do."

"Because I don't like being played."

This was getting ridiculous. Genna took a couple of deep breaths, trying to push away the edges of panic that were pressing down on her. She was so close to her dream. So close to having something—maybe not a relationship, but something—with Brody. And now it was shattering so fast she couldn't even see where the pieces were flying.

"I'm not playing you. I'm not ashamed of you." She shifted, lifting her chin and giving him a direct look filled with all the sincerity she had. "And I'm not using you to rebel."

"Right."

There was so much sarcasm in that single word that Genna was tempted to look at the floor to see if it was dripping on her feet. What was his problem?

"Don't you think you're blowing this out of proportion? I just said that Macy was a tattletale."

"Exactly. C'mon, Genna," he said, shaking his head. "You're all grown up and still living under your parents' thumbs. What better way to wiggle out than to piss them off by dating the guy they blame for introducing their princess to the dark side?"

"Why are you doing this?" she asked quietly. "Are you trying to pick a fight? If you didn't want to go to dinner, all you had to do was say so. Friends don't hurt friends, Brody."

DIRECT HIT.

Brody grimaced at the baffled pain in Genna's eyes.

Why was he doing this?

He shoved his hands into the pockets of his slacks to keep his fists from finding a wall to pound on. He had so much anger broiling inside him, but it wasn't aimed at her.

He didn't give a damn if she was rebelling. Hell, she deserved to. Her parents were manipulative assbites who were ruining her life with their fears.

It made no difference to him if she hid their relationship, either. She was the one who was going to have to live with the talk after he was gone, not him.

As she said. Friends didn't hurt friends.

But Brody was a lousy friend. Just ask Carter.

"I should go," he decided.

"No," she said quickly. "What is going on? I thought we were going to dinner. I thought we were friends. So either feed me or talk to me, but you aren't leaving until you do one or the other."

She was so damned cute when she got feisty. Brody couldn't help but smile a little. Actually, she was so damned cute all the time, feisty or not. And sexy. Fascinating, entertaining, fun.

His smile fell away.

Maybe that was part of the problem.

He'd thought they could be friends. He hadn't been able to resist spending time with her, and had thought he could control the intense attraction he felt for her. That he could channel it into making up for some of the lousy deal she'd gotten after he'd left.

But he felt as if he'd signed up for a torture project. Days spent talking and joking. Watching her bake, listening to her dreams. Nights spent hard and horny, diving into dreams so hot he thought the bed was on fire. He was a man used to pushing through the pain, well trained to overcome his body's weaknesses. Except, apparently, the ones Genna inspired.

"Look," he said, taking a deep breath and hoping for

some semblance of tact and diplomacy. "This friendship thing, it was a mistake."

Her eyes widened, surprise and hurt flashing. Then, with a sweep of her lashes, her expression changed. Intensified. It sent an itch down Brody's spine.

"We're not going to be friends anymore?" she asked in a calm, friendly tone. If it wasn't for the fact that she was saying the right words, he'd have figured she hadn't understood him.

As soon as he nodded, she gave him a brilliant smile and tossed off her coat. It hit the floor with a swoosh just as she reached behind her back. The move was quickly accompanied by the sound of a zipper. And Brody's hiss.

"What, exactly, do you think you're doing?" he asked, hoping like hell it wasn't what he thought she was doing.

"Seducing you."

Damn.

That's what he'd been afraid of.

Brody's breath was a little labored, but he tried to reel in his reaction. This wasn't happening, he warned his dick. No point getting ready for a party they weren't gonna attend.

His dick, always ready to party, ignored him and hardened rock-solid anyway.

"Genna—" he started to say.

But she interrupted before he could figure out the rest of his protest.

"I figure this is part one of a two-part solution to our problem," she said. "You were trying to pretend we're just friends. Except we aren't. We might be building a friendship. But what we are is crazy attracted to each other. So part one is to act on that attraction once and for all. The total act, with you naked. I'm willing to be on top if you're still holding on to that friendship myth of yours. That way you can tell yourself I took advantage."

Brody couldn't help but laugh. Sure, the sound was strangled and a little painful. But it was the best he could do with the blood streaming south so fast his head was spinning.

She tugged at one sleeve, the red fabric tight from wrist to shoulder. Then she tugged at the other to loosen it, too.

"And then there's the issue of you thinking I'm ashamed of you. I figure after we've had our way with each other's bodies a few times, we're going to be hungry. We can go to the nearby café and get something to eat. Since I figure you're really good at sex, even if I am on top, what we'll have been doing will be obvious. That should take care of that issue."

He made some sort of choking sound, sure if he had any blood left in his brain it would have been words of protest.

Then she let her dress fall to the floor. Brody actually gulped trying not to swallow his tongue.

She was gorgeous.

Ivory limbs glowed like silk, the long sleek length of her interrupted by tiny pieces of black lace. He didn't know where to start. At the top, where the lace cupped the gentle slope of her breasts. Or at the bottom, where it was barely held in place by two tiny strings.

His gaze as hot as the blood rushing through his body, he decided to settle for the middle. At the cherry-red jewel decorating her belly button.

Screw friendship. And screw good sense.

He was gonna let Genna Reilly seduce him.

10

GENNA HADN'T HAD many opportunities to be ballsy and brave in her life. So she figured she'd been saving up, and this was the perfect time to put every bold instinct she possessed to work.

She didn't want Brody's thinking she was ashamed of him standing in the way of whatever they were building together. If it took being outed to her parents to prove that, then fine.

She wanted Brody Lane.

And, dammit, after ten years, she was finally going to have him.

Except he was standing there, fully clothed and still wearing his coat, one hand flexed as if reaching for the doorknob.

And she was standing here, almost naked except her undies and high heels. It wasn't that she minded the almost-naked part. It was the clothing inequality that bothered her. And the fact that he wasn't making any moves to change it.

Her bravado waned a smidge. What had she been thinking? That he'd take one look at her underwear, lose his mind and do her against the wall? Clearly her thinking needed an adjustment. Since her state of nakedness did, too, her fingers itched to grab her dress.

Then she saw the look in his eyes. It was as if the golden depths had turned molten, his gaze was so hot. She saw his jaw clench, and the pulse at the base of his throat was pounding hard.

Relief surging through her, washing away the nerves and making way for desire, Genna almost did a happy dance right there in the entryway.

He wanted her. Maybe not enough to grab her and do her against the wall, but that look made her think that maybe she could change his mind.

Knowing that, she didn't feel naked anymore.

She felt powerful.

"C'mon, big boy," she said, her tone husky and suggestive. "Let's see what you've got."

Brody laughed, just as she'd hoped he would. Then, his eyes still hot and locked on her body, he shrugged off his jacket and stepped closer. Close enough to touch.

She didn't wait for him to make the first move.

She'd said she was seducing him, and she meant it.

So she grabbed hold of his shirt and pulled him closer, ignoring the ping as one of his buttons flew off and hit the wall. In heels, she was tall enough that all she had to do was tilt her head back to meet his mouth. So tilt she did, one hand wrapping around the back of his neck and holding tight.

As his mouth took hers, she was grateful she was holding on. Oh, my. Her mind spun in a slow, delicious circle.

It was like he was starving and she a feast.

His tongue swept in, plunging deep. Demanding a response that was hard to offer while her body was melting into a puddle of lust.

But Genna did her best. Her tongue danced with his, their lips sliding in hot need against each other. The moves rolled, one into another, and she could barely think as the passion pounded through her veins.

His hands swept along her arms so light and soft they were barely there, leaving tingles of needy heat. He reached her wrists and bracketed each loosely between his fingers.

Then, so fast she didn't even realize what was happening, he had her up against the wall.

Genna almost came right then and there. Her core throbbed, wet and hot. Her thighs trembled and her mind went completely blank. All she could do was feel. And she felt incredible.

Trapped between the cool plaster and his hard, hot body, she wrapped one leg around his thigh to pull him closer. He gripped her hands, both of them, and lifted them above her head, anchoring them there with one of his while he slid the other into her hair to lift her face closer.

His kiss was voracious.

His teeth scraped her lower lip, tugging it into his mouth, then sucking. Genna whimpered. His tongue swept over the tender flesh as if soothing it, then plunged into her mouth again.

His fingers skimmed along the back of her neck, tugging at her hair to hold her mouth in place, totally at his mercy. A part of her reveled in the power he had over her. That he demanded.

Another part, though, wanted to make demands of her own. She wanted to touch him. To run her hands over those muscles and feel how hard they could get. To measure the tantalizing width of his shoulders, the rigid length of his thighs. And all the other hard, wide and long things he might be willing to share.

She shifted to release her hands from his grip. But he wouldn't let go.

A thrill surged through her system, from the tips of her

fingers to the aching bud between her thighs. She tugged harder, but his grip didn't change. He was in control.

Or so he thought.

Unable to use her hands, Genna slid her foot down the back of his thigh to his calf, using the move to press her core tighter against his hip. Then she slid her foot back up, gripping him tight.

He growled, low and sexy in his throat.

She arched her back to press her breasts against his chest. The move made her nipples tighten to rigid buds, aching for attention.

As if he'd heard their plea, he skimmed his hand down the side of her throat and slid it between their bodies to cup her breast. She swelled, aching and needy, against the lace of her bra trying to get closer to the hard warmth of his palm.

Her breath came faster now. Her pulse raced and her heart pounded so hard, she was sure he could feel it.

"More," she breathed against his lips.

"How much more?" His fingers dipped between the edge of her bra and her skin, rubbing his knuckles back and forth along her nipple. She squirmed, pressing herself tighter against his thigh, desperate to ease the mounting pressure there.

"Everything you've got," she gasped.

He leaned back. She gave a shuddering sigh, her arms moving to reach for him. But although he lowered his hand so her arms were bent above her head, he didn't let go.

Instead, he used his free hand to pull the lace cup of her bra down so it lifted her breast. For a long, exhilarating moment he stared. His eyes were hot, intense. His breath short and the look on his face as needy as the desire contracting low in Genna's belly.

He brushed one finger, just the tip, over her nipple.

Genna whimpered.

He leaned forward, this time touching his tongue to her pebbled peak. He pulled back just a little and blew.

Genna's thighs quivered, her clitoris trembling. She pressed harder against his thigh, undulating, desperate to relieve the pressure.

His free hand skimmed over her stomach, fingers leaving a hot trail all the way to the slender elastic band of her thong. He traced the lace from front to back, then reached out to cup his large hand over her butt, squeezing her cheek and pulling her tight against him. Angling her perfectly.

Oh, God.

Her body started shaking.

He bent his head, taking her nipple into his mouth. Sucking hard. Swirling his tongue around, nipping, then swirling again. His hand slid beneath her thigh, his fingers touching the wet bud there. He gently pinched her clitoris, making her cry out.

So close.

Her body was so tight.

The orgasm right there, just out of reach.

Now.

She needed it now.

He didn't bother pushing her panties aside. Instead, with a quick snap of his fingers, he ripped the lace so the fabric fell to the floor between their feet.

Sucking hard on her nipple, it wasn't until he pinched the other one that she realized he'd let go of her arms.

Unable to remember what she'd wanted to do with her hands, unable to do anything else, she gripped his shoulders so tight her nails dug into his flesh.

He slid two fingers along the length of her swollen clit. Up, then down, then up again.

The climax coiled tighter.

Then he thrust one finger inside her, swirling while his thumb worked her bud.

The climax snapped.

Genna's head flew back against the wall, her eyes closed tight as stars exploded in time with the orgasm pounding through her.

He didn't stop sucking or thrusting.

She didn't stop coming.

Not until everything went black, the stars behind her eyes fading. The orgasm was still coming in tiny shudders now, her slick flesh still vibrating around his finger.

Her breath tore from a throat so dry, she had to try three times just to swallow.

He shifted, leaving a chill where his body had been.

"Where are you going?" she cried, not done with him yet.

"I want to taste you."

Ohhhh. The walls of her insides quivered again, a tiny orgasm exploding at his words.

But as much as she wanted to score as many climaxes as she could, she wanted something else more.

She wanted to touch him.

To see him.

For more than ten years, she'd dreamed of seeing him naked. Fantasized about what his body looked like. She wanted—no, needed—to see it. Now.

She grabbed his shirt, still loose around his shoulders.

"Not yet," she said, shaking her head.

His eyes met hers. The golden depths were molten with desire, narrowed in question.

"Strip first," she told him. "It's only fair."

His lips quirked to one side and he gave her body a considering look. Genna followed his gaze, realizing he'd pushed her bra beneath both of her breasts, the black lace vivid against her pale white flesh and berry-red nipples. Her panties were shredded, leaving the only other thing on her body a belly-button ring and a pair of black heels.

"I can strip later," he said, his words husky as he reached out one finger and slid it between her legs before lifting the wet proof of his handiwork to his lips. "I'm hungry now."

Genna's knees almost gave out. She had to take a couple of deep breaths to clear the haze from her eyes, then she forced herself to shake her head.

"Strip," she repeated, pushing the fabric of his shirt off his shoulders. And oh, baby, what shoulders they were. Pure muscle beneath silken flesh. Leaving him to deal with the buttons at his cuffs, she smoothed her hands over those shoulders. He was so warm, so hard.

She shifted forward, her lips brushing against that flesh.

She breathed in deeply, inhaling his scent, filling herself with his essence. Forgetting her orders, forgetting everything but exploring his chest with her mouth, she kissed her way over the delicious range of muscles, pausing to flick her tongue over one nipple before continuing her exploration.

She heard a thud, followed by another. But it was the weight of his slacks and belt hitting her toes that got her attention. Because that meant he'd gotten down to the good stuff. The stuff she wanted to play with most.

Unable to resist one last kiss, she then leaned back to check him out.

And almost came again, right then and there.

"Oh. My."

It was like she'd died and gone to heaven.

He was even bigger than she'd dreamed.

Her eyes locked on his penis as he stepped out of his pants, his toes pushing his socks off one foot, then the other. The move made that very, very large erection bounce.

Before she could look her fill, he dropped to his knees.

"What are you doing?" she objected.

"I stripped."

With no further explanation, his hands cupped her butt cheeks and pulled her closer. His tongue pressed between her damp curls, flicking and sucking.

Genna felt herself drowning again as desire washed over her.

"No," she gasped desperately. "Not yet."

His tongue paused. She moved fast, before he could overrule her. Or put that tongue back to work. One more lick and she was going to explode.

She fell to her knees, pressing him backward so fast he was too surprised to protest. As soon as he was on his back, she leaned down and took him into her mouth.

"Hey, now," he growled.

Still bent low, her hair trailing along his thighs, she shot him a mischievous smile.

"But I'm hungry, too."

He arched one brow, then shifted. Grabbing her by the hips, he lifted and turned her as if she weighed nothing. Now her knees straddled his chest and she was flashing him everything else. Before she could be embarrassed or self-conscious, actually before she could even blink, his tongue was back at work.

What's a girl to do, she thought, letting the sensations take over and bending low to slide her lips over the long, hard length of his arousal. Her head moved up and down, her mouth sucking and tongue swirling in time with his. His fingers gripped her thighs. Hers were braced flat on the floor. He pulled back just a little, blowing cool air over her wet flesh.

Genna's breath was coming in whimpering gasps now. She was so close, her body tight, the climax coiled low and intense. She lifted her head so her tongue danced around the velvet tip of his penis, then she sucked it into her mouth like a lollipop.

He growled.

His fingers gripped tighter and his mouth stilled for a moment, as if he were focusing on keeping control. Then, with a breath that gusted over her thighs, he sucked her clitoris into his mouth one more time, then thrust his tongue deep into her throbbing passage.

With a cry of shock, Genna exploded.

Her entire body shook with the power of her orgasm. She rode the waves, panting and oblivious to everything except the sensations, bigger, stronger than anything she'd ever felt in her life. More intense than anything she'd even fantasized about.

She didn't know how long it lasted. She didn't even realize that Brody had moved until she finally floated back to earth and realized she was lying on the floor now, wrapped in Brody's arms.

"Bed?"

"Here," she demanded, still panting from the power of her climax. She felt as if she'd climbed a very tall, very hard mountain. But she still had one more peak to scale. She slid her hand up and down the rock-hard velvet of his erection, then knowing how fast she could get distracted if she started touching him again, she quickly shifted away, grabbing her purse off the floor.

She didn't have a clue how he was going to top that incredible orgasm. Or even if he could.

But oh, baby, she was more than willing to let him try.

BRODY GROANED, NOT sure what he missed more. The warmth of her slender body against his. Or the feel of her talented fingers working their magic. He started to grab her back, then realized she was already on there, a condom held between two fingers like a trophy.

It was as if she'd read his mind. His grin was fast and just a little tight as need pounded through his system.

He reached for the foil wrapper. Quick as a cat, she

pulled it away. Wiggling her brows, she tore it open her-self, the move slow and deliberate. After a quick glance for placement, she locked her eyes on his, forcing him to meet her wicked gaze as she slid the latex over his throb-bing cock.

The effect of her eyes watching his reaction, and the way she slid her fingers around the base of his dick, made him groan.

"Now," he growled, reaching for her. It had to be now. He'd never wanted anyone, anything, as much as he wanted her right this second. He was terrified he might even need her. But since most of the blood in his body was currently partying down south, his brain couldn't muster enough energy to worry about that.

He'd have plenty of time to worry later.

Now, he had to have her.

Since relinquishing control wasn't something he did long or well, he jackknifed into a sitting position, taking her mouth. Her eyes widened with surprise, then blurred with passion. He grabbed her waist and shifted their po-sitions so she was beneath him. Her fingers clutching his shoulders, she wrapped her legs around his hips.

Mouths still locked together, he slid into her in a single smooth move that felt more natural than breathing. Buried deep, Brody had only a second to wonder at the sense of coming home before his body demanded more.

Eager to get past the strange emotions buffeting him, he slowly pulled away, sliding almost out. Then he plunged.

Pulling her mouth free of his, Genna gasped.

He plunged again. And again.

He arched his back, shifting higher on his knees so her hips were off the floor. Her feet anchored to the small of his back, she met his every thrust with a panting moan and a tiny undulating move of her own.

Those tiny moves were killing his control.

Brody's breath came faster.

His body tightened.

He thrust faster. Harder. Deeper.

More.

He had to have more of her.

He wanted all of her.

Genna's moans turned to whimpers, higher and higher. Her thighs locked tight around hips, her fingers trembling as she dug her nails into his biceps.

He slid back out, leaving just the tip of his dick in her warmth. Her eyes flew open and she gave him an urgent look.

Staring into those blue depths, Brody plunged again, burying himself as deep as he could get.

And watched her explode.

Her cry echoing in his head, her climax pulsating and clenching his cock, Brody followed her right over the edge. The orgasm was so seriously mind-blowing, he didn't know when he'd be able to think again. Instead, he collapsed against her, twisting just before they came together so they were on their sides.

And he held tight.

GENNA'S BODY FELT like it'd been used, and used well.

She throbbed in places she'd never been aware she had.

Her skin tingled.

Her lips were too swollen to talk.

Her muscles too lax to move.

Thankfully, Brody had still been sporting the manly mojo. Somewhere between minutes and hours after they'd guaranteed she'd get turned on every time she walked through her front door, he'd swept her into his arms and carried her up the stairs.

When they'd fallen into bed together, she'd thought they'd sleep. She'd been almost there when he'd started the whole amazing experience over again. He'd claimed he wanted to see how it compared on a mattress.

Snuggled close, her face buried in the crook of his shoulder and his arms tight around her, Genna had to say it had compared pretty darned well.

"I'm thinking you had a lot more fun this evening than if we'd gone to dinner," she said quietly, her tone teasing as she swirled her fingers through the light dusting of hair on his chest.

"I'm sorry about that," he murmured against her hair.

"I'm not," she said with a little laugh. "This was much, much better."

"I had to go by barracks today to get something to wear," he finally said, sounding as though he'd just confessed to wearing her undies. Maybe someone had given him a bad time about dressing up for a date?

Still floating on a cloud of sexual delight, Genna sighed at the memory of how hot he'd looked all dressed up. "And I tore your buttons off. I'll sew them back so you don't have to go get another shirt."

It was sweet, though, that he'd thought a dinner that was just two friends hanging out necessitated a trip home to get special clothes.

"I haven't been back since the accident. Since before we shipped off on that last mission." Brody's words were quiet, just a hint above a whisper. But Genna's heart clenched at the pain in them. Her smile fell away, her breath knotting in her throat. She wanted to shift up onto her elbow so she could see his face in the moonlight, to try to figure out why he was hurting so badly. But knowing he'd hate that, she kept her head on his shoulder instead. And waited.

"We lost a guy on that mission. Seeing his empty bunk was a reminder, you know?"

It was only a few words. But there was so much pain in them, Genna could barely control her sob. She swallowed hard, blinking to clear the burning from her eyes and trying to get control. She knew the only thing Brody would hate more than sharing his emotions was her dumping hers all over him.

"I wanted to let you know," he said, his words a whisper in the night. "You asked why I was such an ass when I got here. It wasn't you. It was that."

Her teeth clenched tight to keep the hot torrent of tears from falling, Genna had to take a couple of breaths through her nose before she could find enough control to respond.

"Hey, now," she finally said softly, proud that her laugh was only a little shaky. "I never called you an ass."

"I was acting like one."

"I'm not denying that," she said, finally in control enough of her expression to shift to her elbow and look at him. "I'm just saying that I didn't call you that."

His smile was more a twitch than a grin, but she'd take what she could get. The moonlight softened his features, casting a warm glow over the bed. It didn't blunt the impact of his vivid eyes, though. Genna was pretty sure nothing could.

"So that means you're not going to hold a grudge over dinner?" he teased.

"Well…"

"I knew it." This time his smile was real.

"You can make it up to me, though."

"Yeah?" he asked, his eyes blurring with desire and one hand cupping her breast. "Did you have something in mind?"

"Actually, I was hoping we could try it with me on top this time," she said, wriggling her brows suggestively. "Now that I've had my way with you, it's your turn. Show me what you've got, big boy."

That made him laugh. And thankfully, to lean down

to kiss her. Genna was grateful. She needed something to distract her from the tight ache in her heart.

The first two times, their lovemaking had been a wild ride, fast and furious with shades of desperation.

This time, Brody was calling the shots.

His moves were smooth, gentle. Pure confidence and delicious control. His lips never left hers as he shifted their positions so she was flat on her back. Fingers entwined, he trailed kisses over her cheek, along her jaw and down her throat.

Genna moaned when he reached that spot at the base of her neck, right where it met her collarbone. Desire coiled again, low in her belly. But this time it was mixed with a tenderness, a gentle sort of emotion she wasn't sure what to do with.

So she ignored it and focused on the rising passion.

His hand swept down her side, cupping her waist before sliding down to her thigh. Fingers gentle, he trailed his hand along her leg in a teasing move until he'd reached her aching core. Soft as a whisper, he worked her until she begged.

Then, finally, he shifted, looming large and hard over her before he slid, smooth as silk, into her welcoming warmth.

The minute he plunged, she exploded.

It was like floating on a sea of sensations. The orgasm just kept pounding, washing over her in wave after wave. His moves were slower, as if he wanted to prolong her delight.

By the time he gave over to his own body's demands, Genna had lost count of her orgasms. It wasn't until he slid out and moved away, then lay back down to pull her tight into his arms, that the sexual aftershocks started to abate.

Well. Nothing like incredible sex to clarify a few things.

Not that Genna had had incredible sex before tonight.

Mediocre, okay. Decent sex, yes. But tonight, Brody had shown her the difference between a nice orgasm and a mind-blowing, ongoing, multiclimaxing meltdown.

Her fingers tangled in the soft hair of his chest, she snuggled in closer and sighed. His scent wrapped around her as tightly as his arms, keeping her close, making her feel special.

Tonight had shown her what great sex was, yes. But it'd also made her realize that she'd been fooling herself that this thing she had for Brody was just a fun, easy thing to enjoy while he was home. Something she'd be able to look back on with a smile as a fond memory.

It'd been one thing to nurture a decade-old schoolgirl crush. To see him as a hero on a white horse who'd someday ride in to sweep her into his arms. As someone who'd magically transform her life from blah to amazing with just a kiss.

That'd been a little silly, a lot sentimental.

So she had plenty of experience with what a crush felt like.

But now?

She'd had incredible sex, yes.

But she'd seen the real Brody. The man beneath the hero. The one who had fought hard to overcome an ugly beginning. Who had a sense of honor, of loyalty that was beyond her understanding of the words. A man who had made himself a real hero in the truest meaning of the word, but didn't see himself that way.

A man who could withstand all manner of pain, except the pain of feeling like he'd failed.

Finally, she felt as if she knew the real Brody.

And she was sure, absolutely and without any doubt, that she was 100 percent, head over heels in love with him.

And that—unlike the crush—was going to end up breaking her heart.

Genna snuggled in closer, trying to get as close to him as she could. As sexually fueled exhaustion pulled her down, her last thought was that whatever heartache she experienced, Brody was worth it.

11

WHO KNEW THAT a steady diet of cookies and mind-blowing sex could change a girl's life?

Three days of lovemaking, of sharing secrets and cuddling up with Brody, and she was a new woman.

A sexy, powerful, confident woman who could turn her big, bad SEAL into a panting puddle of lust with just the brush of her lips. Depending on where she brushed her lips, of course.

A strong woman who could handle anything. Including gossip, teasing and no shortage of envious looks from the women around town when they saw her with Brody.

A confident woman who knew what she wanted. Who was getting all kinds of brave and making the changes she'd dreamed of for years.

"You're sure of this?" Mayor Tucker asked, gesturing with the resignation letter in his hand. Standing in front of her table—her position didn't merit an actual desk—Genna followed his glance and took a deep breath.

But there were no nerves to chase away.

She felt incredible.

"I am. I've enjoyed working here and I'm grateful for the contacts I've made." Especially as they'd be such a big help to her starting her own business. "But I think it's time to move on."

"I'll wish you all the best in your new venture, then. As someone who's enjoyed your baking over the years, I have no doubt you'll be successful." Refolding the letter into a tidy rectangle, Tucker gave her a considering look. Then, using the same direct diplomacy that'd gotten him elected twice, he asked, "Have you thought through all of the ramifications of leaving, though? While I wish you the best and am sure most people will as well, some might be a bit concerned."

Genna's stomach clenched as the image of her father's furious face flashed through her imagination. Concern? Talk about an understatement. When her parents found out, they were going to have their own version of an all-out kicking and screaming tantrum.

She wasn't looking forward to it.

But neither was she going to let that kind of thing run her life. Not anymore.

"I know I'll have a few issues to overcome, but I'm sure I can handle them," she said, pretty much lying since she wasn't sure at all. But she wanted to be. And that was good enough for now. Especially since her father wasn't due back for another couple of days. Plenty of time to shore up her nerve and strengthen her spine.

Looking as though he wanted to say more, Tucker sighed, then nodded. Then, with a grimace, he offered, "If you need anything, just let me know. Business advice, a recommendation, a mediator."

Genna laughed.

"I'm glad you understand," she said, truly grateful that he was making it so easy. Then again, maybe he was looking forward to having her—and her interfering father—out of his office.

"You've been great. Even though this position wasn't

my idea, you've been a wonderful asset to the city. It'll be hard to replace you."

"Thank you." Genna hesitated, then figuring she had nothing to lose, she asked, "Can I ask a favor in return? I'll need permits and licenses."

"You want me to waive them?" Tucker asked, a small frown creasing his brow.

"Oh, no. I'll get them all like I'm supposed to. Just, well, can you make sure they don't get blocked?" She didn't need to add who the potential blocker would be. They both knew as soon as word of this got back to her father, he was going to make things ugly. She might need Tucker's mediation skills after all.

"I'll take care of it," the mayor assured her, patting her shoulder as he passed by. Then he stopped and turned with a frown. "One thing before you pack your bags. We need to finalize the arrangements for the hero appreciation day. Did you have any luck convincing our erstwhile military man to participate?"

Pleased that the event for Brody would be her last job here in the mayor's office, Genna pulled a folder from the stack in her tote.

"I've organized all of the vender donations, as well as coordinated with the high school band and the ladies' groups," she said, handing it to him. "As soon as we finalize the date I'll contact the sheriff's office to arrange to close off the pertinent streets. Custodial is already giving an extra polish to the town hall so it'll be ready for the luncheon."

Tucker gave an impressed nod.

"And you've got Lane on board with it?"

"Well, not exactly on board." Genna bit her lip. "But I think I can convince him."

As soon as she got the nerve to ask him again.

She was sure he'd say yes. Okay, almost sure. Sort of.

Maybe it'd help if she asked while they were naked.

He seemed to be willing to do anything she wanted then.

Tucker didn't look very assured. Given that he didn't know Genna's secret weapon, she couldn't blame him.

"I'll get a commitment," she promised.

"By tomorrow," the mayor prodded. "The press needs lead time to build some buzz. We want to be above the fold and it's going to be hard to top his being decorated by the president. See if he can get a few other SEALs to attend. That'd make great press."

Genna kept her smile in place while the mayor continued his excited recital of plans on his way to his office. At his door, he gave her a finger wag. "Tomorrow. Get it done."

She waited for his door to close before dropping her head into her hands.

Convince Brody to play hero. Do it by tomorrow. Build buzz and drag in a few extra SEALs for a more colorful photo op.

Easy peasy.

Genna's head snapped up when the front door ricocheted off the wall.

Her father strode in, looking as though he wanted to shoot somebody.

Guess he was back in town. And he was clearly up to speed on the gossip about his daughter's love life. She wondered how long it'd take before the hospital called.

"Hi, Dad," she greeted him, getting to her feet. No point letting him look down on her any further than she had to.

He barely glanced her way.

"Tucker in?"

"He is." Genna was tempted to let it go at that. He could have his powwow with the mayor, she could sneak out and start her new life. But that was the weenie way. So she cleared her throat and said in a rush, "But I need to speak to you before you go in."

"What's up?" The sheriff gave her a questioning look. "Tucker giving you a rough time? Working you too hard? Want me to talk to him?"

He'd do it, too. Go in there and tell the mayor of Bedford to quit picking on his little girl, the mayor's paid employee. Genna had always thought it kind of sweet, knowing she'd always be looked out for. But now it was stifling, like the very thought was choking all the air out of her life.

"Tucker's fine. But it is about my job," she said.

Then she ran out of words.

She wanted to ease into it. Make sure he understood how important this was to her. How excited she was about opening a bakery, that it was her dream job. If she could get that across first, then he'd take the news about her job much better.

A half smile on his face, her father arched one brow.

"Yeah? What about your job?"

"Um, I just quit." Well, Genna wrinkled her nose. That was eloquent. Any chance he'd clued in to how excited she was by her shaking tone?

"You what?" Looking as if he was going to burst a vein, he didn't wait for her to repeat the obvious. Instead he stabbed one finger toward the mayor's door. "Then get in there and ask for it back."

"I don't want it back," she said quickly, pushing the words through her nerves, knowing she had to take a stand or give up her dream altogether. "I quit because I'm going to bake full time."

Her father sighed. He took off his Sheriff ball cap, ran one hand through his still-thick hair as if trying to comb away a headache, and tugged the cap back on.

"Genna, we've discussed this." His tone shifted from angry to reasonable. So reasonable that Genna was almost nodding before he'd said another word. "You'd be dealing with complete strangers day in and day out. You'd have no stable income, no insurance, no sick pay. You simply don't have the experience or the knowledge to run your own business."

And he had no respect for her, Genna wanted to yell. But that'd get her nowhere.

"This isn't some impulsive craze," she defended instead. "I have a BA in business, and this is exactly what I studied for and it's time to make it happen. I'm calling it Sugar and Spice. I've made arrangements with the café and three of the restaurants in town to carry my desserts. Even Mr. Jenson is going to sell my cookies from the pharmacy. I've got orders already, enough to carry me through the first month, possibly three. Then I can look at getting a storefront."

A cute one over on Beeker, maybe. Right between the dress shop and the library. It'd get great foot traffic, plus there was a good-size parking lot across the street.

Summer, she promised herself. She'd be decorating her own shop by summer.

"When did you do all of this?" her father asked slowly, his fingers tapping on his belt as he frowned at her. "I've only been gone five days."

A girl could get a lot done in five days when she was motivated. And Genna was. She wanted this job. And more, she wanted to prove to Brody that she could make things happen. That she wasn't a wimpy little daddy's girl who couldn't stand on her own two feet.

"It's something I've been dreaming about for a long time. I've been making notes, sketching out ideas, for years. Once I decided it was time, it was pretty easy to do," she said, reaching into her tote for the expandable file folder filled with ideas, plans and orders that she'd shared earlier with the mayor.

She bit her lip, excited to see how impressed her dad would be with her work.

Before she could show him, though, he was shaking his head and giving her that cop look of his. The one that made a person want to confess to crimes they'd only thought of just to get him to look away.

"Have you been seeing Brody Lane?"

Genna pressed her lips together. Seeing, doing. Neither was something she wanted to discuss with her father. Especially given the way he felt about Brody.

She tried to settle the nerves gnawing their way through her stomach. She'd known word would get out. If Macy hadn't told—and surprisingly, she hadn't—someone else would have since she and Brody had been out in a lot more public places the last week or so.

"This has something to do with that troublemaker," her father accused, reading her face much too well. His wasn't tough to decipher either. Fury came across loud and clear.

"No. Starting a career is my decision, something I came to all on my own. It has nothing to do with Brody," Genna said quickly, her fingers knotted together to keep her hands from shaking. Well, it did. But not how her father meant. "This is my dream. It's something I've wanted for years."

"And you just happened to decide it was time to make it happen this week? When I was out of town?"

That had definitely made it a lot easier.

But Genna shook her head. "I had a house filled with baked goods to find homes for. The more people I shared with, the more people talked about how they'd buy from me, the more I couldn't see any reason to wait."

"I can think of plenty of reasons. You go talk to Tucker and get your job back. Then we'll sit down and go over this reasonably. You, your mother and me. If it's the best thing for you to do, we'll support you."

No, they wouldn't. They'd do exactly what they'd done

every other time she'd gone to them to share her plans. They'd talk her out of it. Or they'd guilt her out of it. One or the other.

"No," she said quietly. She untwined her hands, flexing her fingers once to shake off a little tension, then took a deep breath. "I've already made my decision."

"This is that damned Lane's fault," her father growled. "He's trouble. The only reason he didn't end up in jail is because the military had him locked down and under control."

"If he was as bad as you seem to think, he wouldn't have made it in the military as long as he did. Nor would he be a part of the elite Special Forces, or a decorated SEAL," she pointed out, trying to sound reasonable. She didn't want to come across as a defensive lover. That wasn't going to score points with her father.

"He's just as bad as your brother was. It's his fault Joe went the direction he did. That he found so much trouble and couldn't climb out."

Genna had to look away to clear the tears from her eyes. Not over her brother's path of self-destruction. He'd made that choice and she'd cried plenty about it over the years. But that her father was so blind to his part in Joe's choices. That he would blame someone else, someone who'd never been as bad as Joe, who'd been gone for the worst of Joe's hell-bent-to-worthless years.

"Brody isn't Joe. He never was." She didn't need to say that Joe had been raised with every privilege, often more than he'd appreciated. While Brody had been raised with nothing. No fancy toys or fast cars, no designer clothes or cool trips. Not even three healthy meals a day or a safe home. Or love. "And neither was I. But you punished me for Joe's actions. The worse he became, the less freedom I had."

Maybe because Joe blithely ignored every punishment

their parents set. Whereas Brody had taken her father's punishment and used it to build a life to be proud of. And that, she figured, said it all.

"I'm seeing Brody Lane. And I'll keep seeing him as long as I choose to," she told him quietly. Her nerves wound so tight, she felt like her hair was going to fly off. Her stomach churned, sick with nausea. But she kept her chin high and her eyes steady. "You can't run him off this time. You can't put me on restriction and take away my privileges."

"You'd be surprised at what I can and can't do." Looking every inch the cop he was, her father seemed to tower over her. Like a threat. Or a jail sentence.

Like a light flashing in the dead of night, the truth washed over her. All of a sudden, her head started spinning. She had to stop and breathe through the dizziness.

"That's what you've been doing all along, isn't it? You didn't like my choices, so you and Mother systematically took them away from me. You, with your rules and guidance. All along, you've kept me on restriction."

"You're being melodramatic."

"Am I? First it was college. Then you used your influence around town to make sure I stayed between those narrow lines you drew. I lived where you wanted, worked where you chose."

Sure, she'd realized her dad was a pain in the butt when it came to being overprotective. But until now, she'd refused to admit how bad he was. How much he'd restricted her every single freaking choice.

And the ones he'd somehow lost control of? Her mother swooped in to play the health card for the win.

How many people saw what she'd been so reluctant to face? Brody did. All his comments, his questions suddenly came into brilliant focus. He'd seen it. Her friends had commented from time to time. Even Macy, although her comments usually supported Genna's parents.

Brody had accused her of using him to rebel. She hadn't lied when she'd denied it, because she hadn't been brave enough to take that kind of risk.

But he was right. She had used him. The truth was, she'd used him to find herself again. It was only through Brody that she'd been able to reconnect with her own wants, her own needs. With her own self.

That she'd had to was demoralizing.

"Everything we did was for your own good, Genna." Still using his father-knows-best tone, her dad stepped forward as if to take her hands.

Genna stepped back.

His scowl made her want to add a few extra steps to her retreat.

"You can't run my life, Dad. Not anymore."

"I can, and will, do whatever I think is best for my family," her father shot back.

"You're so busy forcing your family to follow your rules, to fit your preconceived ideas, that you're destroying it." Genna swallowed hard to get past the tears clogging her throat. Her dad might be bossy and overprotective, but he was still her dad. She hated hurting him. But she couldn't—wouldn't—let him continue to run her life. "If you can't accept my choices, then maybe it's better if you just stayed away."

Her eyes blurred, she hurried past him and out the door before he could respond.

BRODY STEPPED INTO the room that'd once fit him like a second skin. This bunk, a cot in a tent, a rack on a ship. It didn't matter. They'd been home. Barracks were all the same. Coronado, Little Creek, Pearl Harbor or Afghanistan. He'd fit. He'd belonged.

Now?

He looked around the bland room, his gaze avoiding the bunk next to his. Carter's bunk.

Now he wasn't sure.

"Dude, you're back?"

Brody turned in time to catch Masters's hand in a tight shake and gave a half shrug.

"Just finished physical therapy."

"Finished a session? Or finished completely?" Masters asked, his green eyes intense.

"Both."

"Yeah? You're cleared for duty?"

"Gotta see the doctor on Monday. But the physical therapist said I'm solid."

"Nice timing. We ship out in a month, start training next week."

A week. Brody was silent. Genna's face flashed through his mind. What would she say if she knew? After that first night, they'd never talked about his service. For the first time, he realized they'd both been avoiding it.

"So what's the deal?" Masters asked, reading the stress in Brody's tone. "You thinking about opting out?"

"I don't quit."

"No. But if you can't give it one hundred percent, you're not an asset."

A brutal statement by some standards. But not Masters's. And not Brody's. He knew it was the truth. Their commander ran the team with a strong hand, demanding the best from each man, pushing them all to their limits, then shoving them right past to find new limits. A SEAL carrying baggage was a detriment. To himself. To the mission. To the team.

"So what's the deal?" Masters asked, grabbing a wooden chair and spinning it around before straddling it. He waited until Brody had done the same, then he picked up the deck of cards on the table between them and started shuffling. "You've been cleared of PTSD, right? You say you didn't B.S. your way through testing. So it's gotta be something else."

Brody debated while Masters dealt.

He wasn't a sharesies kind of guy. He didn't believe confession was good for the soul. And whatever nasty crap he had in the closets of his mind was just fine hiding out there. He'd lived through plenty of ugly in his life and ignored it all just fine.

So why was this different?

He lifted his cards, tossed one down.

"You ever question your ability to do your job?" he asked quietly, taking the new card Masters flipped across the table.

His buddy stared at his hand for a couple heartbeats. Brody knew he was thinking. The guy didn't say boo without considering all the ramifications. Finally, Masters looked up and gave a jerk of his shoulder.

"No. That's probably not what you want to hear, but it's the truth. We're the best. We do what nobody else can do. And we're damned good at doing it."

Brody nodded. He used to believe that, too.

"You questioning the job you did?" Masters asked, his words quiet as he rearranged his cards.

"I failed." There. He'd said it. Some people might think confessing their deepest shame was cathartic. Brody had news for them. It sucked. His gut ached and his head throbbed as he heard his own words.

He'd left Bedford a loser with little or no prospects. Ten years later, he was back and not much had changed. He still had the hots for the town princess. She was sneaking around seeing him on the sly. And his prospects? Pretty freaking lousy.

He met his friend's eyes with a shake of his head.

"My failure cost us a brother."

Masters pursed his lips, that computer brain probably replaying the mission statement and everyone's assignment, the operation itself, and the postmission assessment.

Then he shook his head.

"You saved a little girl. A kid who wasn't supposed to be in that compound. Despite spotty intelligence, you listened to her old man, went back in and found her, and hauled her out with a bullet in your thigh just before the place exploded all to hell. That's your job. You did it. What's the problem?"

"I wasn't the last man out."

Masters's face stiffened for a second, his jaw tight. He gave a short nod.

"Carter went down. It happens, man. We all know that going in."

"He took a chunk of concrete to the back. He went down fast, but he was alive. I should have grabbed him then," Brody said, staring at the cards in his hand but not seeing them. Instead, images flashed of that mission. Of his friend's face, fire flaring all around them, the air filled with concrete as sharp as shrapnel.

"You had an injured kid in your arms and a damaged leg. You were ordered to get her out."

"I almost went back. I could have carried them both. She was hardly more than a handful. But she was terrified. Started screaming and crying when I turned back. I figured I'd drop her at the helo, go back and get Carter."

"That's SOP."

"The building blew before I could get back."

"It blew before any of us could get back." Masters's words were toneless, easy. But Brody heard the pain in them. Knew the guy was struggling with his own demons. They'd all had a job to do, had all been focused on getting it done. But they should have gotten Carter out.

"No man left behind." Brody's jaw clenched so tight he had to force the team slogan past gritted teeth. "I failed."

"If you'd gone back, you and the kid would have gone down, too. You got out of there with five seconds to spare."

"I should have grabbed him."

"Did you show the president the big fat *S* on your chest when he pinned you with that medal?" Masters asked, rolling his eyes and laying down a straight. "I thought your call sign was Bad Ass. Not Superman."

Despite the misery curled in his gut, Brody smirked.

"Talk it out, hit the gym, visit the range," Masters suggested, folding his arms over the back of the chair and meeting Brody's gaze. "But get over it."

"You been reading psych books again?"

Masters didn't smile. Instead, he slid his cards together, tapped them on the table a couple of times, then met Brody's eyes. His own gaze was steady, rock-solid.

"I'm damned choosy about who I serve with. About who I trust to cover my back. I'd serve with you without question," the guy said, his words too matter-of-fact to be taken as sappy or sentimental. "I have complete confidence, not only in your ability to do your job. But in the simple fact that if I go down, you'll do everything in your power to get me out. I can't offer up a higher trust than that."

They were SEALs. Bred for action. Words were rarely necessary, and other than to geeks like Masters who obsessed with books the way some guys drooled over porn, they didn't mean much.

But hearing his teammate's trust, knowing the guy wouldn't hesitate to take the field with him again, it went a long way to bridging that gaping hole inside Brody. The one he could no longer ignore.

"Thanks." Taking a deep breath, Brody faced the decision that'd been lurking for the last two months, waiting for him to man up. "But until I know it, too, I'm no good to the team."

Brody laid down his cards, stood and clapped his buddy on the shoulder, and strode out of the room.

Just before he hit the door, he heard Masters mutter, "Son of a bitch. Royal flush? Does he ever lose?"

12

So THIS WAS what life was like without daily PT, constant training and an ongoing need to challenge himself to push the limits. No missions, no range practice, no combat.

It was sort of mellow.

Settled on Genna's couch with her curled up at his feet working on her latest brainstorm, Brody watched familiar scenes flash on the television.

Mellow was an odd speed for him. He wasn't sure how he felt about it yet.

For ten years, he'd been going at full tilt.

The nineteen years before that had been spent on edge. Always ready to fight, always ready to run.

The last few months felt like turmoil.

But maybe, this week, he'd found peace. Or at least now that he'd pretty much decided his future, he wasn't battling his own brain. That was close enough to peace, wasn't it?

The irritating nag of a million doubts ran through his mind, mocking him. Okay, so he wasn't at peace. So what. It wasn't as if he'd ever been before.

He was happy, though.

His gaze shifted from the bomb-ravaged scene on the TV to the woman sitting at his feet.

Genna's hair gleamed like black silk in the lamplight. He could only see her profile, but had to smile at the way her lips were moving as she made silent comments about whatever she was writing. Her enthusiasm, her whole-hearted excitement over her new business, was pretty awesome. She didn't let the obstacles, the issues with her family or the various questions he'd heard tossed her way slow her down. This was her dream and by damn, she was going to make it happen.

She was his dream, he realized.

Not just the hot sweaty kind. Although she'd ratcheted those up a few notches over the last couple of weeks. He'd never been a man who shied away from great sex, but clearly he'd been clueless to just what great was.

But Genna was more.

Sweet and fun, she believed in him. She gave him a feeling of contentment, of happiness, he'd never had. Never even knew existed.

As if clueing in that he was thinking about her, she flashed him a smile.

"Mr. Jenson said you and he had a fun chat today," she said, looking up from where she was cozied between his thighs in front of the coffee table. She had a slew of papers spread over the surface, notes and sketches, at least three calendars and God knew what else. But it seemed to be making her happy. And that's what he wanted. Her, happy.

"I stopped in the pharmacy to pick up my gramma's prescription and he wanted to talk. I guess there aren't too many people to share his Korean War stories with."

"Well, there is the VFW and the American Legion. But everyone there has heard his stories. You're fresh blood. And you've got rock star status, being a SEAL and all," she teased.

Brody hoped she'd take his grimace as a smile.

Rock star.

Right.

That'd change in a heartbeat once word got out that he was leaving the navy. He'd be back to being a loser and deadbeat in everyone's eyes. Except Genna's. Which was all that he was going to let matter. He'd rather see the relief in her gaze than the worry he figured would be there if she had to see him leaving on mission after mission.

"How are the business plans shaping up?" he asked, wanting to change the subject.

"I'd thought it'd take a lot longer for word to get out that I'd started Sugar and Spice. I mean, I know this is mostly curiosity and test orders. It'll level out in a month or so. I just hope it doesn't level too much lower," she mused, looking at a list of potential restaurants that were interested in carrying her desserts. "Or that my father would intimidate people out of ordering from me so I'd have to climb back under his thumb. I'm setting up a website. You know, a lot of bakers are having big success with next-day orders. And that way, even if my dad scares away locals, I'm still in good shape."

Good plan. Then, his brows furrowed, he hit the pause button to freeze Jeremy Renner on the screen.

Would her old man really go that far?

"Have you talked to him at all?"

"My dad? Not since I told him I'd quit my job." Genna shrugged. "But I have heard from the mayor four times this week."

"He wants you to come back to work for him?"

"More like he wants me to talk you into changing your mind about being the guest of honor for his Honoring Our Heroes event," she said, making it sound like a joke.

Brody's jaw clenched and something ugly churned in his gut. Not happening.

But he'd already told her that a dozen times, so he didn't bother repeating himself.

As if sensing his irritation, Genna shifted onto his lap. Liking how she fit there, he wrapped his arms around her waist, but his frown didn't budge.

"You going to be okay with this?"

"With what? Sitting on your lap? Or playing messenger for the mayor?" she asked with a teasing smile.

He didn't give a damn about the mayor.

"With the crap from your parents. I don't like you taking heat for seeing me."

Her sigh was a work of art, complete with a roll of those pretty blue eyes and a tap of her fingernails against his shoulder. Damn, she was cute.

"My father isn't punishing me for seeing you," she finally said. "I told you, I'm the one who told him to stay away unless he could accept my career decision. Not the other way around."

"Are you thinking he'll try scare tactics when the freeze-out doesn't work?"

"Maybe," she said with a shrug. "But I told you, I've already figured out how to counter it if he does. I bartered a cake with a gal who does web design for her son's graduation. She's already working on an online store for me."

"Look, I don't want you to worry about the money stuff or let it slow down your progress. I know you're set for the next few months, but if you run into trouble, let me know. I can help out." He might not have a clue what he was doing with his life, any idea of where he fit in the world now or even where he'd be sleeping in six months.

But if he could help Genna make her dream come true, he figured he was set.

HE WANTED TO HELP HER?

"You're serious?" she breathed.

It wasn't a proposal, or a big emotional declaration. To Genna, it was even more. It was a promise that he'd be around. That they had a future, whatever that might look like.

Her heart melted in her chest, warm, soft and gooey. Unable to resist, she wrapped her arms around his shoulders and hugged him tight.

Her smile was wide enough to split her face when she pulled away to brush a quick kiss over his lips. Then, happier than she could remember, she shook her head.

"No, but thank you."

"What? Why not?" Brody scowled.

"That is the sweetest offer and I appreciate it." Probably more than he wanted. But that was just one more reason she was madly in love with him. And yet another reason to be careful to protect herself. It was enough that her heart counted on him. She couldn't risk her business, too. "But you stepped in to save me once. I don't want that to be the basis for our relationship, you know?"

"I thought the basis for our relationship was sex," he teased.

"Exactly," she said with a relieved laugh. "Why mess with a good thing?"

He nodded, but the serious look didn't leave his eyes. "Fine. You go it alone. But if you run into trouble, let me help you. I've got plenty saved up. I can afford to buy my way into a lifetime supply of cookies to keep you from losing your dream."

Her eyes soft, she reached out to cup his cheek in one hand and kiss him again.

"You are so sweet," she said when she lifted her lips from his.

"The hell I am."

He looked so embarrassed, she decided to give him a break and change the subject.

"Did you want to see the site design?" Shuffling papers,

she grabbed the sketch pad. "Maybe tell me what you think of the colors and logo we're doing?"

"You're kidding, right?" Brody gave her a pained expression. "You want a taste tester, I'm your guy. But you start talking colors and decorations and crap, I'm outta here."

"I've been horrible, haven't I?" she said with a laugh, tossing the sketch pad aside. "Not only do I keep asking you all these questions you have no interest in answering, but I've had you try every recipe I've made in the last week."

"Well, you've kept me pretty well compensated," he mused, that sexy glint in his eyes making Genna shiver. She loved how he looked at her. As if she were the key to his every sexual fantasy.

"Would you like a little compensation right now?" she asked in a teasing tone, shifting so she was straddling his body, her hands anchored on the couch behind his head.

"Sounds good," he murmured against her throat. His kisses sent shivers through her, but it was the hot rod pressing against his zipper that had her all kinds of excited.

"What'd you have in mind?" she said, sliding against his erection in a slow, undulating move that was making it hard to breathe.

"A cookie."

What? Genna pulled back to look at him. His smile was as huge as the hard length pressing against her aching core. Laughing, she leaned in to kiss him, reveling in the taste and texture of his mouth before shifting back just a little.

"You can have a cookie afterward," she promised.

Before she could get started, though, his cell phone rang. As much for the fun of wiggling in his lap as to be helpful, she reached around to grab it off the side table.

"I've already had my way with you once today," she

said, placing a teasing kiss on his chin. "Go ahead and take your call. I'll compensate you afterward."

"No."

Brody stared at the readout. The phone went silent, then black before he blinked, then tossed it onto the coffee table. It bounced twice before skidding into the popcorn bowl. Genna tensed, looking at the phone, then back at Brody's face. He didn't appear angry. Just distant.

"Is everything okay?" she asked quietly. She didn't want to pry. But she couldn't ignore how upset he seemed.

"Fine." He blinked, and it was as if she'd imagined the closed look on his face. In its place now was a cheerfully charming smile.

She frowned.

Brody didn't do cheerful.

Something was definitely wrong.

"That was Blake," he said, giving a first name to the "Lt. Landon" she'd seen on the screen. "He's got some irritating mother-hen tendencies."

"So he's calling to check on you?"

"Probably." Brody shrugged. "I don't feel like talking, though."

Shock. Brody Lane didn't want to talk?

Genna knew she should ignore her nagging sense of worry. But since she doubted his teammate was calling to discuss feelings, relationships or their rocky past, she couldn't. Not when he looked so unhappy. But whatever was bothering him, she knew he wouldn't share.

So maybe she should ask about what was bothering her. Nervous, but knowing she'd never get a better opportunity, she swallowed hard and forced herself to say, "So... You'll be going back soon."

He grunted. She took it as a yes.

"I know you don't get to say where you'll live or how long you're in any one place." And it wasn't as if she was asking to follow him around. Although she would if he asked. "Do you think, maybe once in a while between missions. If, you know, you're stationed at Coronado. If, maybe, you'd come back and visit?"

Genna mentally cringed. The only way she could sound more hesitant and unsure was if she'd thrown in a whining tone with all those maybes.

Brody didn't cringe, though. Nor did he get that distant look that told her she'd stepped into classified territory. Instead, he gave her a long stare, then smiled.

She wasn't sure why the smile made her want to cry.

"I've got some career options ahead. I've decided not to re-up in May. I'd be leaving the navy. So maybe instead of visiting, we can just see each other all the time."

Genna stared, her mind spinning.

She'd hoped, in that way-back secret corner of her mind, that the option of an online business would make it easier for her to keep her dream if she just so happened to be following Brody from base to base.

But now Brody was leaving the navy? He was moving back. And he wanted a relationship with her. Not just a "distance, naughty letters, and the occasional phone call or conjugal visit" kind of a relationship. But a day-in-and-day-out one.

She wasn't sure if she should giggle, jump up and down with happiness, or freak out.

"You cool with this?" he said after a solid minute of her mindless staring.

Genna yanked herself out of the reverie, starting to smile. Like a blooming flower, joy spread through her bright and shiny. The smile turned to a grin, then into a giggle.

For the second time that evening she threw her arms around his neck, hugging him close while the giddy laughter poured through her.

"Cool with it?" she asked, so excited she'd have bounced in his lap if she wasn't worried about damaging anything she was going to want to celebrate with soon. "I'm so happy and so excited. I love you so much."

She froze.

Her smile disappeared and the giggles fled.

No. She wanted to grab those words back. Her mind raced, trying to think of some way to play them off, or something to say that'd be shocking enough to make him forget she'd said that. But she couldn't come up with anything more outrageous than blurting out her love.

Cringing, she watched Brody's face.

Instead of looking distant, though, his eyes softened.

He ran one hand through her hair, his fingers tangling in the strands by her ear as he pulled her mouth to his. The kiss was so soft, so sweet, Genna swore they were floating on a cloud. Fear fled, worry faded. All that was left was the most intense sense of happiness.

Brody shifted, so she was on her back on the couch and he was poised over her. Their clothes disappeared between kisses, their breath mingled, quickening as their hands slid over each other. Except for the time it took to slip on a condom, Brody's mouth never left hers.

Fully embedded, he slowly pulled away to meet her gaze, his expression filled with the same emotions she felt churning through her.

Then he started moving. Slow and sweet.

And whispered, "I love you, too."

So this was what it felt like to have your dreams come true. Brody loved her. And he was happy that she loved him. Even in her favorite fantasies over the years, she'd always figured that if she ever accidentally let that slip, he'd run faster than a bullet left a gun.

But he hadn't. He'd smiled. He'd said he loved her back.

And then he'd made the sweetest love to her as if in testament to their words. It was the most amazing feeling. As if someone had reached inside her heart and lit the happiness light as bright as it could be.

She looked at the pages spread over the table, the tidy list of orders color-coded by type and arranged by date. She'd spent the morning on the phone with wholesale suppliers, thrilled to be able to rattle off her business information and place orders.

She should be ecstatic.

Sure, her father wasn't talking to her. They'd actually passed on the street the day before and he'd pointedly looked the other way. It was almost funny. In a *holy crap, are you kidding with the immaturity* kind of way.

And yes, her mother was calling daily to keep Genna in the health-crisis loop. The hospital trips, a migraine and a cold in the last week. Her last message had included a warning that if Genna didn't do something about her stress-inducing behavior, she'd be forced to take drastic measures. Since she hadn't included details on what those measures might include, Genna had ignored it.

Because her business rocked and her love life was a dream come true.

Well, to be precise, her business had the potential to rock, if it didn't fall apart. And while her sex life was amazing and her heart was happy, there was something nagging in the back of her head.

Brody was leaving the navy?

Why?

She'd asked, but all he'd say was that it was time.

That was good, right?

It'd be so much easier to have a relationship with someone who was actually around, instead of off fighting secret missions most of the time. He'd be safer here. Nobody would try to blow him up or shoot his leg full of holes. The only secrets he'd have to protect were her recipes.

That was good.

Wasn't it?

The doorbell chimed, loud and distracting.

Grateful for the interruption, Genna almost ran for the door, her stockinged feet sliding on the hardwood. Please, let it be someone with an elaborate baking order that would require a lot of focus and attention. Or anyone she wasn't related to who didn't want to talk about her family issues.

She pulled the door open to a blast of cold air and a total stranger. Frowning, she shifted her grip on the door so it'd be easy to slam if necessary.

The guy looked as if he could be plenty dangerous, but he didn't appear to be a threat. Supershort brown hair, blue eyes and a friendly smile, she mentally cataloged as her father'd taught her. About six foot wearing jeans, a black turtleneck and a leather bomber jacket.

Nope, he didn't look like a threat. But he didn't look like he was there to order a cake, either.

"Hi?"

"Hi." His gaze was laser sharp, the inspection quick and impersonal. Still, it left Genna feeling as if he'd just accessed all her secrets, her entire history and her driving record. "I'm Blake Landon. I'm looking for Brody. His grandmother said I might find him here."

Ahh. Genna's frown shifted to a smile. The SEAL friend who kept calling Brody.

"He's not here right now. But I expect him soon. Did you want to leave a message?" She relaxed her grip, letting the door swing open a little more.

Dark brows creased, the guy gave a quick glance over his shoulder at the BMW parked in front of Genna's house. She followed his gaze to see a woman in the passenger seat. Seeing their attention, the redhead gave a friendly wave.

"My wife and I were hoping to see him. Can you suggest a restaurant or bar in the area? We'll grab a bite to eat and come back in an hour or so."

It was three in the afternoon on a Thursday. Too late for lunch, too early for dinner at any place worth recommending. Genna debated for all of two seconds before waving back, then gesturing to her entryway.

"I'm really not sure how long Brody will be, and all I have to serve are desserts. But if you'd like, you're both welcome to wait here."

He gave her another one of those laser looks, this one a little more personal with a hint of curiosity. Then he nodded and turned, gesturing for his wife to join them.

"Alexia would like that. She's a fan of all things dessert. And of Brody's. So be warned, she's going to ask a million nosy questions."

A million?

Before Genna could reconsider, the redhead joined them. Gorgeous and leggy, she wore stunning knee-high black leather boots, jeans and a white wool coat.

"Hi. I'm Alexia. And you must be Genna." The woman's friendly smile negated all of Genna's worries. "I'm so happy to meet you. Brody is one of my favorite people, so I know you will be, too."

Suddenly at ease, Genna smiled at the friendly enthusiasm and invited them both inside. Within minutes, they were seated around the table. The coffee on, Genna brought plates and a tray of cookies and tarts over.

"Oh, these look wonderful." Humming a little, Alexia considered her choices. Then, her plate gratifyingly full, she gave Genna a brilliant smile.

"So, let's chat. You can tell us all the great backstory on Bad Ass, and we'll bring you up to speed on the last few years."

"Did you just call Brody a badass?" Genna asked, not sure if she should laugh or be horrified.

"It's his call sign," Blake told her quietly, getting up and helping himself to coffee. "It seemed to fit."

Didn't it just.

"What's yours?" she asked.

Pausing in the act of pouring for all three of them, Blake looked her way and grinned. "Boy Scout."

Genna looked at Alexia, who rolled her eyes again and gave a little shake of her head. So Blake might always be prepared, but if his wife was to be believed, he was anything but a goody-goody.

"You want to know what Brody was like growing up?" Genna asked, trying not to imagine just how ungoody-goody Alexia could coax Blake to be.

"No secrets," Blake insisted. "Don't invade Brody's privacy."

Alexia rolled her eyes, her mouth too full to talk. Blake looked uncomfortable, as if dishing dirt on his teammate and friend was something he'd only tolerate because he adored his wife.

Genna liked him all the more for that.

"Well…" she said, drawing out the word to its fullest impact while she chose a pecan tart with caramel swirls. Inspecting the golden-brown perfection of it for a second, she raised her eyes and gave Alexia her best gossip face.

"Growing up, everyone in town called Brody a badass."

Alexia looked blank for one second, then she burst into laughter. Blake, on the other hand, just looked satisfied as he finally took a cookie. As if Genna had passed some secret test.

"Fair enough," Alexia said, exchanging glances with her husband. Genna envied how they seemed to have an entire conversation between blinks. "So maybe we'll chat about the SEALs instead. Do you have any family in the military?"

Genna set her half-eaten tart back on her plate and shook her head. "No. My father's in law enforcement, though. I know it's not the same, but there is a similar sense of service and focus, I think."

"There is," Alexia agreed. "It's not just a job, it's who they are. Their identity, their purpose. In a way, it's their life."

Genna frowned at the ease of the other woman's words.

"Doesn't that bother you just a little? I mean, not that I don't appreciate what you do," she told Blake, who didn't seem at all offended. Then she looked back at Alexia. "But if your husband's entire world is the military, where do you fit in?"

Alexia's eyes sparkled as if Genna had just asked the perfect question. If she'd been a teacher, she'd have pulled out a gold star.

"No, no. I said the military was his purpose. I'm his world," she said with absolute confidence. "But I'm not his priority. Not while he's on duty, at least."

The smile the couple shared told Genna that Alexia had no problem demanding all of Blake's attention when he wasn't on duty, though.

"And you're okay with that?" Genna asked, wondering if she could be.

"I wasn't at first," Alexia said quietly, her fingers curling over her husband's. "I grew up a military brat and was carrying a lot of baggage about it. But even without that, it takes a special woman to be able to handle the secrets, the risks and the long separations. To be able to build a life that fulfills her, but is still dedicated to a long-distance marriage. Military men are strong, but their women are stronger."

"Really?" Genna's laugh was a little skeptical, but she couldn't help it.

"Really," Blake said, answering for his wife.

She glanced back and forth between the couple, realizing that there was more than one kind of strength. And wondering if she had the kind it took to wait for her man, knowing he was in danger, knowing his duty came first.

"And it's just that easy?" she wondered.

"Hell, no."

"Of course not," Alexia said at the same time. She and Blake exchanged smiles. "But no marriage is easy. Nothing worthwhile in life is, really. But it's special enough, and we're strong enough, to make it work."

Genna tried to absorb that. She and Brody weren't even close to talking marriage. And he was leaving the navy, so it didn't matter if she wasn't strong enough to be a military wife or not. Did it? Or was that why he was leaving? Was it significant that he told her he loved her and that he was leaving the navy at the same time?

"You're wondering why I'm telling you this," Alexia guessed.

"Well, yeah." And when they were done, maybe they could tell her what to do, too. An ironic hope, since she'd spent years trying to get people to *stop* telling her what to do.

Alexia leaned forward, her face intent as she searched Genna's. Then, apparently liking whatever she found there, she said, "We want you to help us figure out how to convince Brody not to quit the SEALs."

13

FUELED BY GUILT over talking about Brody behind his back, and a stomachache from too many tarts, Genna pulled into the dingy parking of Slims. She'd been searching for Brody for the last two hours, and while she couldn't imagine why he'd want to come here, it was the last place inside city limits she could think of to look.

Parking next to a patch of weeds as tall as the bumper of her car, she puffed out a breath. She hated going in there. Not just because it was three shades of sleazy with a whole lot of gross on the side. But because it seemed to be the epitome of Brody's late father. Ugly, mean and under many circumstances, plain dangerous.

But two o'clock on a Friday afternoon shouldn't be bad. She hoped.

Steeling herself, and making sure her Mace was in her pocket, she slid from the car and crossed the gravel lot. She was careful to avoid the multitude of oil leaks—apparently the clientele at Slims wasn't big on auto maintenance. Pushing the scarred wooden door open, she stopped short inside to let her eyes adjust to the dim light.

Chairs stacked on tables gave testament that someone had at least pretended to clean the floor. The neon signs behind the bar glowed blurrily through a sea of dust motes. Floodlights similar to those she had in her back garden were lit and aimed toward the stage, if that's what they called the three pallets pushed together in the corner in front of the mike.

But there weren't any bodies.

Genna considered, then bent low to squint under the tables.

Nope. No bodies.

Dammit. She bit her lip, not sure where to look next. His Harley was still at his gramma's. So he had to be in town somewhere. Didn't he? Maybe she should just go home and wait for him.

Except the conversation with Blake and Alexia kept playing through her head, urging her to find him as quickly as possible.

They thought Brody leaving the SEALs was a big mistake. That he was doing it for the wrong reasons, even though neither of them had been willing to tell her what they felt his reasons were.

She knew, though.

When he'd lost his friend on that last mission, he'd lost his faith in his ability to do the job he expected from himself.

What she didn't know was what to do about that. Trying to help him through the emotional issue was pointless. She knew from experience dealing with her father and brother over the years that since she wasn't a SEAL, wasn't military and wasn't a guy, she wasn't qualified to try to talk him out of whatever he was feeling.

Until her visitors today, she'd figured that all she could do was be here, support him and then when he was ready to finally talk, listen.

But now she knew she had to do more. She couldn't let

him walk away from something so important to him unless he was really sure.

Unless he had already thought it through and *was* sure.

And as much as she'd always dreamed of Brody being in her life, she didn't want it to be at the expense of his own dreams. But if it was something he wanted to do just because, well. that was different.

She shoved both hands through her hair and tried not to scream at the conflicting thoughts battling it out for top spot in her mind.

Then she heard a noise. Her heart skipped. The scraping sounded again off the room behind the bar. Balanced on the tips of her toes, she shifted to run out the door.

Then she heard voices.

Brody?

Panic fled, leaving a frown as she stepped cautiously toward the bar.

As if her movement triggered a signal, Brody and Leon, the bar owner, stepped out. Leon looked bored, as usual. Brody's face flashed with surprise, then something that seemed like irritation that went too fast for her to be sure before he gave her a questioning look.

"Genna? Why are you here?"

"I was looking for you," she said, figuring that should be obvious. Her boots sticking to the floor in places, more proof that the chairs on the tables were a fake-out, she made her way across the room.

With each step, tension drained away, both from discomfort of being alone in such a sleazy setting, and from her worry over where Brody had disappeared to. Leaving plenty of room to wonder about why he'd disappeared to here. She'd think it'd be the last place he'd want to see.

"I got stuff to run to the bank. You cover for me?" Leon

mumbled, tucking a grungy sack into the front of his pants, then buttoning his flannel over it.

At Brody's nod, the older man skirted the bar and left, not glancing once toward Genna.

Even though she was apparently invisible to him, she still waited until the door closed before reaching across the scarred bar to give Brody's hand a squeeze.

Before she could say anything, he asked again, "Why are you here?"

"I told you, I was looking for you."

"I've got a cell phone." His words were short, his expression stiff. "Just call. Don't come looking, especially at a place like this."

Since she didn't like seeing him in a place like this, she couldn't blame him for feeling the same. But still, why was he here? Given the history, that his father spent most of Brody's life here drinking himself to death, you'd think he'd want to stay clear of it, too. Her frown deepened and she glanced at the small room behind the bar, then at the hand-lettered bartender-wanted sign on the stool.

She'd turned her life upside down and quit her job. She'd faced off with her father and offered her mother a silver platter full of health woe excuses. Thanks to Brody, she'd found the nerve to finally move forward with her life.

Her stomach knotted and bile rose in her throat.

And what? Thanks to her, he'd moved back?

She gazed around the dingy bar, the sense of desolation and despair as real as the dust and dirt. Back to this?

She was pretty sure when Prince Charming had ridden in to save the princess, he hadn't give up the castle to end up in a hovel.

As much as she hated to mess with what had this morning been a pretty awesome outlook for her life, they had to talk. She had to know, for sure, that he was going to be happy with his decision.

Otherwise, she thought as her heart sank into the toes of her sticky-soled boots, there was no hope for them to be happy together.

"BRODY, SERIOUSLY. WHAT are you doing here?"

Brody scowled. How the hell had she found him? He suddenly felt dirty. As though every nasty memory he'd had of this place was crawling over him. He figured he'd better get used to it, though.

"Leon had been bugging me to stop by and clear out the old man's stuff."

Genna moved closer, standing on tiptoes and making a show of trying to see over the bar.

"His stuff is back there?"

"You heard Leon. He asked me to man the bar for a half hour."

Her face as distant as he'd ever seen it, Genna took a deep breath, crossed her arms over her chest and gave him a long look. He damn near shuffled his feet, her eyes were so intense. It was if she was looking inside him. As if she was checking out all his secrets.

He hoped she had plenty of time. He had a helluva lot of them.

"I heard Leon was looking for a new bartender."

"So?"

"So. Did you take the job?"

Shit.

Brody had spent most of his life answering to nobody. The last ten years answering to the navy. He'd sorta thought this round he'd answer only to himself.

He'd sorta thought wrong. At least, he had if he wanted Genna in his life.

And he did.

More than anything, more than everything, he wanted Genna. Even if it meant trying to justify his decisions.

Even the ones he couldn't quite come to terms with himself.

"I've gotta work," he said, irritated that he sounded so defensive. "Look, this is a good thing."

Her mouth dropped open and she blinked a couple of times, then shook her head as if clearing a buzz from her ears.

"A good thing? You, quitting the navy. Giving up being a SEAL. To what? Tend bar in the same sleazy dive you grew up over? Why? You missed all the happy memories?"

Damn. She had a smart mouth on her when she wanted. And a wicked way of kicking her point home right where it'd hurt most.

"Well, there's not a whole lot of jobs in Bedford requiring a sniper." He shrugged. "I'm trained to fight. To perform covert operations and carry out military strategies. Believe it or not, those skills aren't big moneymakers in the civilian world."

"But they are skills you love. Skills you're proud of." She lifted both hands in a classic WTF gesture. "So why are you throwing them away to pour drinks for drunks?"

Brody ground his teeth together to keep the cusswords from spewing out. Yeah. She was aces when it came to the well-aimed shot. This one didn't hit his ego, though. It went straight for the gut.

What a deal. Giving up a life of excitement, adrenaline and power to schlep booze for drunks. Traveling the world to hole up in the town he'd spent most of his life trying to escape. But that was his problem. And he was willing to do it if it meant a life with Genna.

Why was *she* pushing this? Most women, outside the frog hogs as the guys called the SEAL groupies, wanted a guy who was around. Who was around for Friday night dates, holidays and more days in the month than he was gone.

Maybe she just didn't get it.

"Look, this is a good thing. You should be happy," he said, despite the fact that she appeared about as far from that as he'd ever seen her. "This means I'm sticking around. You get that, right? That I'm here, that we can be together. No deployment, no long missions, no part of my life locked up and labeled classified."

Her eyes softened and some of the tension left her posture. For a second, he thought he had her. But Brody knew better than to relax.

"I want to be with you," she said, her words soft and sweet to match her smile. She stepped forward, taking his hands in hers and lifting one to her cheek.

Brody wasn't a mushy kind of guy. But that move, it slayed him. Especially when she was looking up at him as though he was her whole world and she was ready to love every second of it.

Then, with a quick brush of her lips over his knuckles, she released him and shook her head.

"You can't do it, though. You can't quit being who you are. You won't be happy."

"I'd be with you. That'd make me happy." Happy enough, he promised himself. The two of them building on what they had. That'd be enough. He'd make it enough.

Her eyes so bright they lit up even the dim dust of the bar, Genna smiled. But there was a line between her brows that got deeper as her smile faded. Slowly, she shook her head.

"I want to be with you. So much. I love you," she finally said. Her words sent a thrill through Brody. Not because they were some he'd rarely heard in his life. But because they came from her. And they meant everything.

"But you can't put that on me. I can't be the reason you leave the military. I can't fill the hole it's going to leave in your life."

"I'm not leaving because of you."

"But you're not leaving because you want to."

Brody scrubbed his hands over his face. God, this was stupid. Why the hell was she arguing with him? For a brief second, he missed the navy so much it hurt. For no other reason than in the navy, when someone issued an order or made a decision, everyone shut the hell up and accepted it.

"Look, I've made up my mind. I'm through. I can't be a SEAL anymore. And if I can't be a SEAL, I won't serve." He gestured to the bar. "This is a job. It's honest work and will pay the bills until I figure out what I want to do."

Honest work to pay the bills. It took Brody a moment to figure out why the words tasted so bitter. Then he remembered his father yelling them at his mother. Every argument they had over his drinking, his living at the bar, had ended with that statement.

Apparently they sounded just as good to Genna as they did to him.

"So this is it?" The wave of her hand was more a slap at the bar than an encompassing gesture. "Your future? Tending bar, holing up in that dingy apartment filled with ugly memories and despair?"

"Leon already rented out the dingy apartment. I figured I'd live with you." Clearly not in a joking mood, she just hissed. So he shrugged and amended that to, "Or in the guesthouse behind my grandmother's."

Her glare was just as threatening as an AK-47, making it clear she wasn't interested in smart-ass responses.

Okay, fine. She wanted the truth, she could find a way to deal with it.

"My future was being a navy SEAL. I worked my ass off for that, Genna. I trained for it, I lived it, I breathed it. I was it. And now I'm not." Brody glared right back, hating that she was forcing him to say the words aloud. "So excuse me if I make the best of the lousy hand I've been dealt."

She gave him a long look, then slowly nodded.

The vicious knots of tension gripping Brody's gut eased a little. Good. Maybe now she'd let it go.

"You don't have to take this deal. You have plenty of other options, including returning to duty."

Why? He wanted to drop his head into his hands and give it a good shake. Why did he ever believe she'd take the easy path? The one that tidily avoided all that emotional crap.

"What in the hell do you know about it?"

"Blake and Alexia came to see me earlier," she said. "I know your friend said the surgeon cleared you to go back to the navy. That the decision to leave the SEALs was yours."

If she'd hauled an Uzi from under her skirt and shot him, he couldn't have been more stunned.

Blake and Alexia had been in Bedford? Specifically to visit Genna, obviously. What the hell? Since when was it the lieutenant's job to play retention officer? Why did he care? Didn't he realize the team was better off this way? That any team was better off with a solid group of dependable men?

Brody didn't let any of that show on his face, though.

Any sign of weakness, of surprise, and she'd never let it go.

"Landon was right. It's my decision. And I decided to stay here."

"So… What? You're just going to spend the rest of your life here at Slims, pouring drinks and hiding from life? You really are taking Brian's place, aren't you?"

Her implication was like a slap to the face. He wasn't his old man. He wasn't a bitter, angry asshole who loved his booze more than anything else in his life.

He was just a bitter, angry asshole.

"I don't drink." Brody almost rolled his eyes at that

stupid statement. He was really hitting the bottom of the barrel on pathetic now.

"No? Why not?"

"My body is a military machine. A tool for Uncle Sam. You don't take care of your tools, they don't do the job they're supposed to. Alcohol dulls the senses, it slows re-action times. I'm not messing up hours of intense training for a cheap buzz."

His words trailed off as he realized he was speaking in the present tense. But his body wasn't finely tuned any-more. And his mind was jacked-up trash.

That realization crashed down on him along with the full impact of how hard he'd worked, how long he'd striven to be the best, to finally be someone people admired. Gone.

All fucking gone.

Brody didn't even realize he'd grabbed the whiskey bottle until the scent of Jim Beam hit him.

His eyes cut to Genna's.

Instead of the appreciation and understanding he'd grown used to seeing in those warm blue depths, this time there was contempt.

His gaze cut away, focusing on the whiskey hitting a dingy glass.

"Well," she said quietly. "I guess you have made your decision. You're going to turn your back on a career you apparently loved. One you're so good at, the president of the United States acknowledged you. One you've made such a difference in, the mayor of Bedford is throwing an event in your honor."

Was she still harping on that? The entire team was up for the Silver Star, not just him. For the good and the bad, it was always the team. He wasn't a hero. And he wasn't a part of the team anymore.

"I told you from the beginning, I'm not doing that

damned event. I'm not a windup toy sailor to be paraded back and forth for someone else's ego."

She threw both hands in the air, giving him an exasperated look.

"This isn't about ego, Brody. It's about you accepting your due. It's about you being treated with the respect you deserve from a town that sucked at giving it to you before."

Respect?

For what?

If they knew the truth, everyone in town would see that he was the same loser they'd always judged him to be. The only one under any illusions was Genna.

"I'm not a damned hero. I'm just a guy trying to make a life here so we can be together. You don't want people to know you're dating a badass, that's your issue. If you don't know who I am, if you can't accept me for what I am, fine. But quit trying to make me into something I'm not to soothe your own ego."

The look of shocked misery on her face made Brody want to throw himself on an IED. Crap. He shoved both hands through his hair, totally at a loss. He didn't want to hurt Genna. But neither did he want to defend his decision. Because, as everyone in this room clearly knew, it was a lousy one. But he wasn't changing his mind. He wasn't fit to be a SEAL. And if he couldn't be a SEAL, he wasn't going to serve.

With that same sass he'd always admired, Genna took a deep breath and shook her head.

"The man I know, the man I've had a crush on since I was seventeen, the man I fell in love with? He's a hero. He's a badass with a miserable history. A man who overcame adversity, an abusive home and a knife in the gut to make something of himself. Something to be proud of. If that's not a hero, I don't know what is."

She sniffed, took a shaky breath, then shook her head

again as if she were trying to figure out where he'd gone wrong. "And now look at you. You're what? Throwing it all away because you are having identity issues. It's not because of me, Brody. Don't you dare pin this on *me*."

"Identity issues?" he sneered, wondering just how long she'd spent with Alexia. That shrink talk was apparently contagious.

"That's what I'd call it," she shot back. "You're either the guy who turns his back on his past to be a big bad SEAL, a hero with no ties to anyone or anything. Or you're the badass bad boy from the wrong side of town, the son of the drunk who lets the past limit his potential and shape his every decision."

Holy crap. Brody shook his head, wondering if Alexia had dropped off a psych profile to go with her contagious talk.

"You've got it all figured out?" he mused, anger wrapped around him so tight he felt that he was suffocating. "And, what? If I'd returned to the SEALs, or even to the navy, you'd have stood by me? Like you'd give up your golden life here as the pampered princess or walked away from your happy new business to live on base. For me? Yeah. Right."

For just a second, her chin trembled. Then she lifted it high and gave him an arch look.

"I guess we'll never know, will we? But for the record, yes. I'd have stood by you, whatever your decision. If you talked to me, and were honest about what you wanted, I'd have done anything for you. Stay here, hand out fliers for this lousy bar. Or follow you all over the world, waiting while you defended our country. I'd even built my happy new business around the idea of being portable, of doing it from anywhere. So I could be with you."

A single tear slid down her cheek, glistening in the dim light like a diamond.

"But then, you never asked. You decided to destroy your life instead." With that and an ugly look at the glass in his hand, she turned on her heel and sashayed out.

Not stormed or stomped. Nope, not Genna. She knew exactly how to hit him where it hurt, so she took her time, hips swinging and head held high.

Wrapped in bitterness, he watched her go. She shoved the door open, letting a blinding beam of sunshine into the bar before it slammed closed with a bang that ricocheted through the room. Leaving him in the dark.

Brody stared at the door for a long second.

Then, damning his entire life to hell, he tossed back the whiskey in a single gulp.

YOU'D THINK IF A steady diet of cookies and sex was incredible, bingeing on just cookies to get over not having the sex would at least be okay.

Instead, it was rotten, sucky and miserable.

Genna stared at the pink polka-dotted fuzziness of her socks, one crossed over the other on the coffee table strewn with cookie crumbs, candy wrappers and an empty box of tissues.

What a cliché. Could she be any more pathetic? At least she hadn't given in to the urge to call friends to join her in the pity-fest.

Nope. This was not a side of herself she wanted to share. Or even admit.

As if on cue, her doorbell rang.

Genna sighed, shifting her feet off the coffee table and tucking them under her hip as she curled into a ball on the couch.

For three days, every time someone came to the door, she'd wiped her face, jumped up and run to see if it was Brody.

It never was.

Whoever it was this time, they'd go away.

"Genna? Can we talk?"

Unless they had their own key.

"I was worried about you."

Too tired to even get mad, she shifted her head but didn't lift it off the pillow.

"Not now, Dad."

"Your mom plans to come over this afternoon."

Genna sat up so fast her head spun. Blinking away the dizziness, she plastered on a cheerful look and brushed sugar off the knee of her sweatpants.

"I'm fine. Let Mom know you saw me and nothing is wrong. I was just taking a nap."

Standing in front of her now, her father scanned the littered table and gave a contemplative nod.

"Yeah. Those sugar crashes get ugly without a nap." Then, looking unsure for the first time Genna had ever seen, he offered a hesitant smile. "Or a hug from Dad?"

Her lips trembled and her eyes filled.

Before Genna could say yes or no, he was there. As he'd always been. With a hug and a strong shoulder. A solid wall she could depend on. Whether she wanted to or not.

He didn't say a word, though. No lecture. No *I told you so*'s. Just a hug.

Genna burst into tears.

He let her cry it out, grabbing napkins when he saw the tissue box was empty. He patted her back. He made sympathetic murmurs. She heard his teeth grinding at one point. But he didn't say a word.

Finally, whether because she was cried out or because she was worried keeping his opinion to himself was going to put her father into dentures, she pulled herself together.

"I yelled at Brody," she said quietly.

"Did he deserve to be yelled at?"

Genna frowned, peering through swollen eyes at the

man next to her. He looked like her father. He sounded like her father. He even smelled like him. But this was where her father would be offering up lectures and realigning her life to suit his vision.

Instead, he was watching her patiently. Waiting for her to respond.

Wow. Maybe they'd both grown up.

"I don't know if he deserved what I yelled," she confessed. "But I hated seeing him at Slims."

"What the hell were you doing at Slims? More to the point, what the hell is he doing there?" There he was, her normal father. His anger made her smile.

"Brody's working there."

"Why? He's got a job. He's a SEAL."

"He's quitting."

Genna waited.

But her father didn't explode. He didn't rant about losers and how he'd always been right. Instead he took a deep breath, which did nothing to clear away his frown, and nodded.

"That's why you yelled at him."

"Yep."

She waited for the interrogation. She saw a million questions in his eyes. But he said nothing. He just waited, letting her call the shots.

She wasn't sure she knew how. It was a little mind-boggling.

"You know, I've dreamed of him coming back for years," she said. "I never thought it'd really happen. It was one of those 'prince on a white steed sweeping in to save me from a life of blah' things."

"That's a lot to put on someone," her father said quietly. "As someone recently pointed out to me, we can't expect others to fill the empty places in our lives. That's something we have to figure out how to do on our own."

"I didn't have holes in my life," she said automatically. At her father's arch look, she sighed and shrugged. "Okay, so I wasn't happy. But it's not like I was sitting here stewing in misery, waiting for Brody to save me."

"Why did you wait until he was back to stand up for yourself and the things you really wanted then?"

Because it wasn't until she was with Brody again that she'd realized how much of herself she'd let go over the years. With him, she felt strong and clever and able to face any challenge. With him she felt safe. Like whatever happened, she could handle it.

Because he was her hero.

So instead of making him feel all those same things, she'd yelled at him, attacked his choices and all but called him a loser like his father. She'd tried to railroad him into doing what she thought was best, then had thrown a heavy dose of guilt on top of that just to make sure he got the message.

Her stomach churned. She swallowed hard to keep the cookies from making a reappearance.

Brody hadn't pushed her into her decisions. He hadn't nagged—granted, the idea of Brody Lane putting together enough words at one time to be considered nagging was strange. He'd just listened to her and let her figure it out for herself.

"I ruined everything," she said quietly, staring at her hands as if the reasons were written there somewhere. "I figured I knew what was best for him, and I tried to force him to do it, despite his own feelings."

"You had to get something from me besides your good looks," he said with a sympathetic expression.

Genna gave a shaky smile. Then she sighed.

"What do I do?"

For a second, her father's eyes lit with a controlling gleam. Then he banked it and shook his head.

"It wouldn't do me any good to tell you what to do, Genna. You need to figure it out yourself." He hesitated, then as if he couldn't resist, added, "Whatever it is, you need to make sure it's right for both of you. And that it's something you'll be comfortable living with for the rest of your life."

For the rest of her life?

Since she wanted to spend that with Brody, whatever it was, she'd better make it good.

14

"LANE."

Brody sighed, taking a second to rub at the pain knotted between his eyes before turning around. He set the case of beer he'd been carrying on the bar just in case he needed both hands.

"Sheriff."

"We need to talk."

"I'm still officially enlisted in the U.S. Navy on medical leave. If you're looking to drive me out of town, you're going to need a new game plan."

Reilly offered a chilly look, then gave a quick nod.

"Good to know."

"You might also want to know that I'm not playing this time," Brody said, figuring he might as well lay it all out from the get-go. "You have an issue, you deal with me direct and we hash it out. You're not calling the shots, but I'm willing to work with you to make Genna's life easier."

Reilly's stare grew contemplative.

"Actually it's Genna I'm here to talk about."

"I figured."

"My daughter isn't happy. I accept my share of the

blame and I'm working on that. I figure you need to step up, too, and deal with yours."

Sheriff Reilly wanted him to fix things with his little princess? Brody tensed. That, he hadn't figured.

"Isn't this why Genna stopped talking to you?"

"There's a difference between looking out for someone, in trying to help make their life a little smoother, and in trying to force them to live their lives the way you want."

"So wouldn't your being here fall under the forcing things category?" Brody asked. Even when he wasn't trying to run his daughter's life, the guy still had to poke his nose in?

"I don't see that I'm forcing anything. Just having a conversation."

"Nice." Brody rolled his eyes.

"Genna said you're leaving the navy. Why?"

"Why the hell do people keep asking me that?" Brody shoved his hand through his hair, even more irritated to feel how long it'd grown since he'd been on leave. Just another sign that he didn't fit, wasn't himself. "I'm getting out. End of discussion. I thought that'd make Genna happy. Don't women want guys who are around more than a few months a year?"

"I can't claim to be an expert on women, but I think they'd want a guy who's honest with them. One who lives his purpose, even if that purpose doesn't revolve around them. If you leave the service because you think it's what she wants or because you think that's the only way you can make a relationship work, then your odds of going the distance are pretty slim. She's either strong enough to handle your career, or she's not. Don't put the burden of her happiness on your shoulders."

"Quite a statement from a dad who spent the last ten years putting that burden on his daughter."

Cheap shot, but Brody was feeling mean.

The sheriff took it like a man, though. Instead of snapping back, he simply nodded. Leaving Brody to feel like an ass.

"I won't be getting any parenting awards. In retrospect, I'm pretty sure Cara and I made every mistake in the book. And our children paid for them." Reilly paused, clenching his jaw and his face tight with grief. "Genna and Joe paid for our mistakes. The same as you paid for Brian's."

"Not even close to the same thing." Shaking his head, Brody grimaced. "Whatever mistakes you made, and I'm not saying there weren't some head scratchers, you always loved your kids. You acted out of concern. They knew that. Both of them."

He didn't bother to add that Brian hadn't had an ounce of love to offer anyone, let alone his son. And his only concern had always been himself.

"I'll deny it if you ever repeat this," Brody said quietly, feeling like an idiot but scanning the empty room anyway to make sure he wasn't overheard. "But I used to be jealous of Joe having a guy like you for a dad. I always figured if I had kids, I'd do a lot of things the way you did. Not all of them, since I'm a fan of learning from other people's screwups. But some."

"Thank you," Reilly said quietly. His face wasn't any less tight, but he'd lost that miserable look in his eyes. "I guess it's only fair that I tell you that there weren't a few times after you shipped out that I didn't wish Joe were more like you."

Holy crap. Brody jerked his shoulders, trying to shake off the emotional impact of that. This was getting ridiculous. A few more exchanges like that and they'd be hugging and offering to do each other's fingernails.

Still, he knew what it must have cost the guy to say that, so he could only offer honesty in return.

"I'm not leaving the navy because of Genna."

The sheriff arched one brow and waited.

Brody ground his teeth. This definitely wasn't one of those "jealous for Reilly as a father" moments.

"I failed. You know how that goes, right? Despite any random thoughts you might have had to the contrary, you've called it plenty of times when you said I was a loser."

The sheriff rocked back on his heels, both hands in his front pockets as he considered that.

"You're talking about the guy who was killed on this mission?"

Brody went hot, then cold. Fury iced in his veins, freezing out his regret over how things had gone down with Genna. What the hell? She'd shared what he'd told her? Fists clenched, he wondered if the bar would withstand a few solid punches. As the fury coiled tighter, he realized he didn't care.

Before he could release his anger on the decrepit wood, the sheriff held up one hand.

"The mayor pulled strings, called in a few favors to get the basics for the hero event he put together. Nothing classified, all approved by your admiral."

Tension seeping away, Brody wondered how many different ways he could feel like an ass in one conversation.

"I figure that kind of thing, losing someone like that, it might give you second thoughts. Inspire a little worry. Maybe even fear."

"I'm not afraid," Brody said dismissively. Shaking his head at that crazy thought, he laughed and went back to stacking cases of beer. Time to call an end to this conversation.

"Not for yourself."

Brody froze. He took a deep breath, slowly lowering the box onto the bar. Okay then. The conversation wasn't quite over.

He gave the older man a questioning look.

"No? Then who am I afraid for?"

"Only you can answer that." The sheriff shrugged. "If it were me, though, I'd probably be worried about my teammates. Maybe a little concerned that I couldn't pull off the mission perfectly, so that means I was flawed. That I wasn't a solid SEAL."

Brody had taken plenty of hits in his day. Some he'd been braced for, others had come as a complete shock. But nothing had knocked him on his ass quite like the sheriff's words.

He had to take a few breaths to pull his thoughts together. A few more to shake off the creepy feeling that the other guy was peeking through his brain for information.

"Your teammates are SEALs," he finally said, matching Reilly's light, conversational tone. "They're trained to kick ass and if they thought you were afraid for them, they'd kick yours."

The sheriff's lips twitched.

"And the rest?"

Brody shrugged. The rest was right on target. But he wasn't a pansy-ass. He'd spent most of his life being called a loser, feeling like his situation flawed him in one way or another. He'd overcome it before, he could overcome it again.

"You know, I was a green rookie right out of the police academy when I married Genna's mother. I was so damned cocky, so sure I could handle anything." Reilly smiled, a reminiscing look on his face. "Then I got a domestic abuse call. Before I could knock on the door, the guy shot me."

Brody frowned. Obviously it hadn't been fatal. But still…

"My first thought as I hit the ground was Cara. That she was going to freak, want me to quit the force. My second thought was that it hurt like a son of a bitch, and that

I wasn't as invincible as I'd figured." The man paused, whether reliving the moment or for effect to let those words sink in, Brody wasn't sure. "But Cara didn't freak. She never asked me to quit, and if she worried, she never let on. And you know what? Not being invincible made me a better cop."

If he'd taken a huge stick and smacked Brody upside the head with it, the guy couldn't have hammered the message home any stronger.

It wasn't just his own fears Brody had been nursing like a dirty little secret. He'd generously assigned a whole slew of them to Genna, too. Fears she'd never once voiced, probably hadn't even considered.

But worrying about her fears, protecting her at his own expense? That'd been a hell of a lot easier than admitting his own.

Brody dropped his head back, staring at the ceiling and trying to figure out how he'd lost sight of the simple facts.

Genna was sweet, loving and sassy. She was clever, gorgeous and talented. And she was strong. Strong enough to tell him what she wanted. And what she didn't want.

But he hadn't given her a chance.

He'd done the same thing he'd cussed her father out for. He'd made the decisions for her, all in the name of protecting her.

Maybe he was more like the good sheriff than any of them realized. And that wasn't necessarily a good thing.

"Figure it out?" Reilly asked after giving Brody a few minutes to stew in his own stupidity.

"I blew it," Brody confessed. Then he shrugged and shook his head. "I'm surprised she didn't kick my ass before she walked out."

"You want to make it up to her?"

No. He'd rather find her, kiss her crazy until she forgot all the stupidity of the last week, then lose himself in her body for a few hours. But he didn't figure that was the answer. Nor anything her father needed to know.

So he shrugged instead.

"Tucker went ahead with that event. The hero thing? It's happening in about, oh—" he checked his watch "—ten minutes."

"Without me?"

"Our esteemed mayor doesn't like to waste a chance to show off for the press."

Damn.

The only thing Brody wanted less than facing the crappy thoughts tangled up in his head was to stand up in front of a bunch of people and be declared a freaking hero. He wasn't one.

But Genna saw him as one.

Which, he finally let himself admit, made him feel pretty damned good.

Besides, if he went it'd make her happy.

And he wanted that more than he wanted to hide.

"I'm not saying I changed my mind," he declared, grabbing the bar keys from under the counter, then snagging his jacket. "I'm doing this for Genna. So she knows I'm not a total ass."

And, maybe, so she'd forgive him.

Then he could get rid of this sick feeling in his gut. And maybe, just maybe, they could talk about the future and how she'd feel about sharing hers with a SEAL.

Maybe.

If he changed his mind.

Following Reilly to the cop car, Brody realized that while he'd ridden in a few over the years, this was his first visit to the front seat. Then the sheriff hit the road.

"Where are we going? Town hall is the other way."

"We gotta stop by your place. Your gramma made arrangements for your dress uniform to be here in case you decided to do her proud today."

Dress whites?

Shit.

A HALF HOUR LATER, Brody flexed his shoulders to try to get the heavy fabric of his uniform to lie comfortably. His hat tucked under his arm, he took a second to glare at the spit-shine polish on his black shoes and wonder if his gramma had done that. Then another moment to absorb how special it was that she had.

"C'mon," Reilly said quietly.

Since the cop had parked illegally in front of the town hall, all they had to do was mount the steps and push through the wide doors. All the way, Brody focused as if he was approaching a mission. No room for emotions. He was here to do a job. A job that he was trained for, one that his military résumé claimed he was qualified to do.

A deep breath, his emotions locked tight in some far corner he never saw when he was in the zone, he entered the battle—or as everyone else called it, the main hall.

And stopped short.

Damn, this was bigger than he'd expected. It looked as though the entire town had crowded into the huge room. Off to one side were a handful of strangers, cameras and recorders in hand. The press. On stage the mayor stood at a lectern, Genna seated to his right. To the left was a row of chairs, all but one filled.

His team. To a man, they were all here. Like him, they were all decked out in dress whites. He tensed, his eyes widening when he saw who was seated in the command position. Admiral Pierce? Wasn't it bad enough being declared a hero in front of a team of men just as heroic? But they'd brought in the brass, too?

Then he noticed the large framed photo propped before the podium.

Carter.

This wasn't about him, Brody realized.

This event was to honor Carter.

The real hero.

Reeling with emotions so strong they almost knocked him on his ass, Brody's gaze cut to Genna. She stared right back, her chin high and pride in her eyes. She'd arranged this. She'd understood what he hadn't.

His gut ached with the power of his feelings.

He looked at his team.

And knew they were all feeling the same thing.

Pride and loss.

Knowing, accepting, that he belonged up there next to them, Brody nodded to Reilly, then made his way to the front of the room. After his salute to the admiral, he took his seat.

"Ladies and gentlemen, thank you for joining us today," the mayor said, his tone holding jovial respect. "I'd like to offer a special thanks to our honored guests. Admiral Pierce, Bedford's own Brody Lane, as well as the United States Navy SEAL team he serves with."

Mayor Tucker dived into his speech with gusto, reveling in the attention but keeping a sober, respectful tone that made it clear that this was more than just a promo op for him.

After he wound up his words by expressing pride that the town could call one of their own a part of such an esteemed group, he handed the lectern over to the SEALs.

Brody joined his team as they honored their fallen comrade. Like the others, when his time came he stood and said a few words. Not about heroism, or about his own loss. He spoke of what it meant to be a SEAL. Of why they did what they did. It wasn't for glory, or even for acknowledgment. That's why their missions were classified. They did it because they were the best. Because they were the ones who could.

As he finished, he looked at his team. Landon, Masters, Castillo and the rest. Their faces echoed the pride he felt. By the time he stepped away from the lectern, he'd found peace.

His gaze found Genna's.

And there, he'd found love.

He figured it was a lucky man who could claim both. And an idiot who'd let either go.

GENNA WIPED THE tears from her cheeks, but they just kept coming. Thankfully, nobody was looking at her as she moved off the stage. All eyes were on the SEALs as the men stood to leave. She wouldn't have been surprised if the building didn't tilt to one side, everyone moved toward them so quickly.

"Genna."

After another quick swipe over her cheeks, she turned to offer the mayor a smile.

"That was fabulous. Wonderful," he gushed, almost bouncing in his Gucci loafers he was so excited. "I wasn't sure about the changes at first, but you were so right. Kudos. If you ever want a job with me again, it's yours."

After a quick pat on her shoulder, he made like a whirlwind toward the press. Leaving Genna to blink. Wow. The man had never been that effusive when he'd actually had to sign her paycheck.

"Nice offer."

Sighing, she turned to face her parents. "I'm not going back to work for the mayor."

"Of course you're not, darling," her mother said, elbowing her husband. "I've been playing hostess at the dessert table. Sweetheart, your offerings are amazing. And the money people are paying!"

Genna and her father exchanged smiles. Nothing turned Cara Reilly's opinion around faster than other people's opinions. Especially when those opinions were made in cash.

"I just wanted to sneak away for a moment to give you a kiss and tell you how proud I am," her mother continued. "Now I'm going back to the table. I want to make sure every sale includes a flier for your business. I'm keeping a list, too, of people who've expressed interest. I'll be happy to follow up and remind them to buy stuff later."

As excited as if she'd thought it up and pushed Genna into starting Sugar and Spice herself, Cara gave her daughter a quick kiss, then hurried off.

"Thank you," she said quietly to her father.

"I didn't change her mind," he said with a shrug. "And I'm still not completely sure this is a good idea. There are a lot of risks. But I do believe you can handle them."

"Then thank you twice," Genna said with a reluctant laugh. "For believing I can handle myself. And for bringing Brody."

Her dad nodded, his gaze cutting across the room. Maybe it was the white uniforms, or just the general air of command, but the SEALs stood out as if a spotlight were shining on them.

"He's a good man," her father told her. He offered a bittersweet smile. "The kind of man anyone would be proud to have for a son."

Oh. Genna had thought she was through with tears. Knowing how hard that was for her father to say, to even think given his guilt and anger over Joe, all she could do was offer a hug. And sniffle a little more.

"Go on," her dad said after giving her a quick squeeze. "You have things to do."

"No." She looked around the room, so glad she wasn't ever going to have to plan one of these things again. "My part is done."

"That's not what I meant."

Genna looked toward the podium, her eyes immediately finding Brody. She'd done this for him. To honor what she thought he believed heroism to be. To give everyone, including herself, a chance to show their gratitude for what he and others like him did. And, maybe, to give him a little closure.

She hadn't thought about after, though.

And now that it was here, she was nervous.

"Maybe later. This is his moment. I'll talk to him after the crowd disperses." Or at his gramma's. Or maybe she'd write a letter.

"Excuse me."

"Or you could try now." With an inclination of his head and a twitch of his lips, her father gave Genna an arch look and said, "Good luck." And left.

Just like that. Years of overprotective hovering and he chose this moment to let her sink or swim?

Her nerves jangling so hard in her system, she was surprised her entire body wasn't vibrating, Genna pressed her lips together, took a breath and turned around.

Oh. He was so gorgeous.

She'd never been one of those women who swooned over a guy in uniform before. But Brody in uniform? Delicious.

"Can we talk?" he asked quietly.

She wasn't sure she was ready to. She'd been so nasty to him before, then instead of trying to fix things, she'd arranged an event he'd specifically said he didn't want.

"Seriously? *You* want to talk?" she asked, trying to sound as if she was teasing instead of nervous. She gestured to the group of still-surrounded men. "It looks like the admiral is leaving—shouldn't you say goodbye? Why don't you spend this time with your friends? I'll be here if you want to talk later."

Here, home, somewhere.

But Brody didn't even look around. Instead, those golden eyes stared, intense and hypnotic. Genna wanted to squirm. Not from nerves this time, though. Nope, that was pure sexual heat in that gaze. The kind that made her want to strip him out of that delicious uniform and taste everything underneath.

"C'mon," he said, taking her hand. Fingers wrapped around hers, he led her to the door. "I can talk to them later. We need to talk now."

Later?

Unlike Brody, Genna looked back. She caught Blake's eye. The other man, admittedly dashing in his uniform, gave her a slow nod. For the success of the event? Or because he thought Brody might be returning to his team? Blake's expression didn't give anything away. Damn, these men were hard to read.

Still, she didn't ask. Not while Brody led her out of the building. Not when he looked around, then guided her over to the small gazebo across the street from the town hall. Not when he took off his hat, tossed it on the bench and took her hands.

She did melt a little then, though. It felt so good to touch him again. It wasn't until this second that she realized how afraid she'd been that she'd never be able to again.

"I'm sorry," she said quickly, before he could say a word.

"What for?"

"For yelling at you. For trying to push you into doing what I thought was best. For going ahead with this event, knowing your feelings about it."

"For thinking I was a hero?"

"Hardly." Genna gave him an *are you kidding* look. "If you don't want to see yourself that way, that's fine. I mean, who wants a guy who thinks he's so awesome he should be declared a hero?"

"Say what?" Looking confused, Brody shook his head as if trying to clear his ears. "I thought you thought…"

"That I thought you were a hero?" she finished when his words trailed away. At his sheepish nod, she pulled both hands out of his to frame his face. Staring into his eyes, she smiled. "I don't think you're a hero. I know you are. You're my hero. Whatever else you do, whether it's saving the world or pouring whiskey, you'll be my hero. Because you saved me. From myself, from my fears, from wasting my life."

He started to shake his head, so she hurried on before he could interrupt.

"You helped me realize that I have to stand up for myself. And that even if it isn't welcome, that sometimes we have to stand up for others."

She waited to see if he understood that she didn't blame him for trying to protect her. Again. When he tilted his chin, she knew he did.

"I'm strong enough to build my own life, Brody. To make it with you, while you're by my side. Or while you're away, serving our country. I'm even strong enough to survive without you." She had to stop and swallow the tears that threatened to choke her words. "You're my hero. And I'm strong enough to be yours."

For a brief moment, Brody looked so vulnerable. His gaze was soft and his smile sweet. He leaned down, resting his forehead on hers, and closed his eyes. A heartbeat later, he brushed a gentle kiss over her lips.

"I love you," he whispered. "Forever. I think I've loved you forever."

Too happy even for tears, Genna offered an ecstatic smile. She brushed her fingers over his cheeks, then sighed.

"I love you, too. Just as much, and for just as long. You really are my hero, Brody. You always will be."

"Lane."

Brody held Genna's gaze for a long, heart-melting second longer. Then, transforming before her eyes, he came to attention, did an about-face and saluted.

"Sir."

"Report for duty Monday morning at oh-six-hundred."

Genna pressed her fingers to her lips, trying not to cry. She'd never thought she'd be so happy to hear that the man she loved was committing to spend a huge amount of time away from her. But she'd never thought she'd love someone like Brody, either.

"Yes, sir."

His face blank, Blake returned the salute. Then he flashed Genna a quick smile and a wink before rejoining his grinning wife.

Brody waited until they were out of earshot before turning back to take Genna's hands.

"So. I have to go back to work," he said quietly. He brought one hand, then the other, to his lips to brush each with a soft kiss. "For the next month, at least, I'll be based in Coronado. I can put in a request for military housing instead of the barracks. Or I can come back here and visit on weekends for a while. Until you decide what you want to do."

"What do you want me to do?"

"Whatever makes you happy."

"You," she said simply. "You make me happy."

And there it was.

Genna was smart enough to recognize happy ever after when she was staring right at it. And wise enough to know that while it wasn't always going to be easy, her life with Brody was going to be amazing.

Her lips met his, their kiss as sweet as their declarations. They were going to live happily ever after.

* * * * *

"This is all about business..."

Sabrina licked her bottom lip and Billy had the urge to lean down and catch the plump flesh between his teeth and nibble. "My business. FindMeACowboy.com."

"Sounds highly illegal."

A grin tugged at her full lips. "It's a dating service."

"Why cowboys?"

"Because they're generally hard workers, trustworthy, loyal." She arched an eyebrow at him. "Have you ever thought about meeting someone online?"

"I meet plenty of women as it is, and I barely have time for any of them. I ride bulls for a living, and I'm this close to my first championship."

"Yet here you are dancing with me." Despite the stiff way she held herself, there was just something about the way she looked at him with those deep blue eyes that said she was hungry for more than she wanted to admit. "One would be inclined to think you're looking for someone."

"Maybe, but this isn't about a date."

"What is it about?"

"It's about sex, darlin'." Billy pulled her closer, plastering them together from chest to thigh, holding her securely with one arm around her waist.

"Lots of breath-stealing, bone-melting sex..."

TEXAS OUTLAWS: BILLY

BY
KIMBERLY RAYE

Published in Great Britain 2014
by Mills & Boon, an imprint of Harlequin (UK) Limited,
Eton House, 18-24 Paradise Road, Richmond, Surrey, TW9 1SR

© 2014 Kimberly Groff

ISBN: 978 0 263 91227 2

14-0214

Harlequin (UK) Limited's policy is to use papers that are natural, renewable and recyclable products and made from wood grown in sustainable forests. The logging and manufacturing processes conform to the legal environmental regulations of the country of origin.

Printed and bound in Spain
by Blackprint CPI, Barcelona

USA TODAY bestselling author **Kimberly Raye** started her first novel in high school and has been writing ever since. To date, she's published more than fifty novels, two of them prestigious RITA® Award nominees. She's also been nominated by *RT Book Reviews* for several Reviewer's Choice Awards, as well as a career achievement award. Currently she is writing a romantic vampire mystery series that is in development with ABC for a television pilot. She also writes steamy contemporary reads for the Mills & Boon® Blaze® line. Kim lives deep in the heart of the Texas Hill Country with her very own cowboy, Curt, and their young children. She's an avid reader who loves Diet Dr Pepper, chocolate, Toby Keith, chocolate, alpha males *(especially* vampires) and chocolate. Kim also loves to hear from readers. You can visit her online at www.kimberlyraye.com.

This book is for Josh.
You've turned into a fine young man
and I couldn't be more proud of you!
Go Tarleton Texans!

_1_

PRO BULL RIDER William Bonney Chisholm had a hard-on the size of Texas.

He stood smack-dab in the middle of the kick-off dance for the Lost Gun Fair and Rodeo, a three-week-long event taking place at the fairgrounds on the outskirts of town. The band had started up. Couples two-stepped across the dance floor. The pungent scent of beer and livestock teased his nostrils. Cigarette smoke cluttered the air.

Easy, bud. Easy.

He shifted and damned himself for being such a sucker for the opposite sex. Blondes, in particular.

He'd fallen hard and fast years back the first moment he'd set eyes on Tami Elder's Malibu Barbie. Tami had taken riding lessons at the ranch where Billy and his two older brothers had grown up. They'd been taken in by rodeo star Pete Gunner after their crook of a father had died in a house fire. Since Billy's mother had passed years before that and the Gunner spread was an all-male domain—home to the infamous Lost Boys, a cracker-jack group of young riders trained and honed by pro bull rider Pete Gunner himself—the only female Billy had ever kept company with had been a paint horse by the name of Lula Bell.

Until Tami had started coming out to the ranch every Sunday. He'd done his best, like any ten-year-old boy when faced with a cootie-carrying girl, to make her life a living hell. He'd shot spit wads while she'd rubbed down her horse and fired his water gun at her while she'd trotted around the corral.

He'd hated her, and she'd hated him, and all had been right with his male-dominated world. Then one hot summer afternoon, everything had changed. That had been the summer he'd turned eleven and spied his oldest brother, Jesse, kissing Susie Alexander, the local rodeo queen.

Kissing, of all things.

Billy had been hurt, then he'd been mad, and then he'd glimpsed an actual tongue and he'd been damned interested. For a little while. Then he'd been mad again and he'd raced off to gather some chinaberries for his slingshot. To see how many shots it took to get his brother away from Miss Travis County.

He'd been up in a nearby tree counting his berries when Tami had finished her riding lesson. She'd slid off the horse and wandered over to the tree, her doll case in hand, to play until her dad finished talking to the riding instructor. He'd meant to shoot off a few practice shots at her, but then her dad had called her over. He'd climbed down and had been about to stomp the day-lights out of her Barbie when he'd realized that it wasn't just any old Barbie.

It was a naked one.

Just like that, his belief system had done a complete one-eighty. One glance at all those interesting curves and that long blond hair and those deep blue eyes, and he'd started to wonder at the possibilities when it came to the real thing.

Yep, he loved blondes.

The trouble was, the pretty little thing standing near the bar was a brunette.

His gaze swept from her long, wavy brown hair pulled back in a loose ponytail to the shiny tips of her black stilettos, and back up again. She looked noth-ing like the other buckle bunnies crowding the dance floor. No itty-bitty tank tops or scandalous Daisy Duke shorts. Instead, she wore a black skirt that accented her tiny waist and a sleeveless black blouse that fell softly against a modest pair of breasts. There was nothing vo-luptuous about her. Nothing outright sexy.

Ah, but there was something about the way she stood there, her back so stiff and straight, her lips parted slightly as she sipped from a red plastic cup, that made his adrenaline pump that much faster.

She was a yuppie through and through. Out of her el-ement, given the three-inch heels and what he would be willing to bet was wine in her glass. Probably a big-city reporter who'd gotten stuck covering the local rodeo.

He would have figured her for one of the big-time

reporters who'd been in attendance to cover the "Where Are They Now?" episode of *Famous Texas Outlaws,* a documentary that had featured his father and the crime that had brought a wave of notoriety crashing down on the small town of Lost Gun, Texas. The original episode had aired just six years after his father's death, and the "Where Are They Now?" follow-up just two short weeks ago.

But most of the press had all cleared out, making way for the influx of rodeo riders and fans who'd come from all over the state for the best little rodeo in Texas.

Still, she had that big-city look about her.

She didn't belong here, and damned if that didn't pique his curiosity. A man could only drink black coffee so many mornings before he started hankering for something different. Maybe a few packets of sugar to sweeten things up. Or one of those fancy lattes with all the whipped cream.

A vision hit him, of her naked beneath him, whipped cream covering the really interesting parts, and his groin throbbed. He shifted, eager to give himself a few precious inches of breathing room. No such luck. He'd been training for weeks, straddling the celibacy horse in order to maintain his focus. Tomorrow was his chance. His first shot at riding his way straight into the champion's seat. His brother Jesse, the current PBR champ, had just announced his intention to marry the love of his life and start a business breeding his own bucking bulls. After sweeping the preliminaries with perfect scores just a few days before, he'd decided to pull out of the local rodeo. He was ready to step down from professional bull riding completely and turn his attention to something more long-term. Which meant every bull rider from here to kingdom come was gunning for that top spot.

But the winner's seat belonged to Billy.

He'd waited too long for this shot, worked too hard. He wasn't letting anything mess it up and he wasn't letting anyone beat him.

All the more reason to turn and get while the getting was good. Billy had come out tonight to have a few beers and relax. To lose the nerves.

He'd had a shitty training session today and all because he was wound tighter than a rattlesnake about to strike. He'd gone four days without a decent night's sleep. Four days of tossing and turning and visualizing the semifinals coming up in eight days. He needed a good strong ride to push him into the finals. And he needed *great* to actually win.

And he had to win.

Because even more than the title, Billy had several sponsorships riding on this next win. Big money all looking to back the next superstar since they were losing Jesse. And if there was one thing Billy liked, it was money. Before Pete had taken him in, Billy and his brothers had grown up dirt-poor without a pot to piss in. Their dad had spent his time drinking himself into a stupor and looking for the next big score instead of taking care of his three boys. That had meant cheese sandwiches for dinner every night.

When they'd had dinner, that is.

There'd been too many times when they'd had nothing at all. No food on the table. No shoes on their feet. No decent clothes on their backs. No bed to lay their heads. He and his brothers had spent more than one night in the backseat of their dad's broken-down Chevy because the old man had gone on a drinking binge, thanks to some moneymaking heist gone wrong.

Billy had been young at the time, only eight when Silas Chisholm had died in that fire after the biggest score of his life had earned him two minutes of fame and a feature spot in the hour-long *Famous Texas Outlaws*.

More like *Stupid Texas Outlaws*. The old man had been celebrating with a case of white lightning that had made him more than a little careless with a lit cigarette. He'd set himself on fire and taken the money with him.

At least that's what everyone thought.

Billy ignored the mess of questions swimming in his head. Questions that had just started to surface, thanks to a surge of new interest sparked by the anniversary of the documentary and his oldest brother's crazy intuition.

Jesse had dropped the bomb just a few days ago that he felt certain the money was still out there and that Silas had had a partner in the heist. His older brother had even uncovered said partner's identity.

Not that Billy gave a shit about any of it. He was more content to let sleeping dogs lie. To stop trying to dig up the past and just leave it six feet under where it belonged.

He wanted to forget those early days. The cold upholstery beneath his cheek. The hunger eating at his gut.

The uncertainty knocking in his chest. And the bitter fact that out of all three boys, Billy was a chip off the old block. The spitting image of his father.

The same hair.

The same eyes.

The same, period.

Like *hell*.

He might look like the old man, but he wasn't following the same miserable path. He was going to ride his ass off, impress as many sponsors as possible and bring home a win.

Hopefully.

He stiffened against the niggling doubt and took another drink of his beer.

He needed to get out of his head and breathe for a little while. Maybe talk shop with the other contestants and see who posed the biggest threat. He had an idea, since he'd been following all of his fellow contenders, but still. It was good to see them face-to-face, to look deep into their eyes and see the drive. The determination. To see who messed up tonight by drinking too much, or staying out too late, or carousing with too many women. All three were distractions better avoided.

Which was why Billy sure as shootin' wasn't out tonight looking to get laid. No matter how much he suddenly wanted to.

Hell, no.

He tugged at the top button of his shirt and tossed down another swallow of Coors Light. Neither did much to cool the fiery lust burning him up from the inside out. Tossing down another long swallow, he turned his attention to the old cowboy standing next to him.

Eli McGinnis was the grandfather that Billy had never had. He looked as if he'd stepped straight out of a Larry McMurtry novel with his snow-white slicked back hair and a handlebar mustache that curled up at the ends. He wore a plaid Western shirt starched within an inch of its life, a pair of Wranglers and a knowing expression that said he'd been there and done that a dozen times over. An old rodeo cowboy, he'd been a permanent fixture at the Gunner spread for as long as Billy could remember. A mentor to all of the Lost Boys, Billy included. Eli had also been instrumental in Billy's success on the rodeo circuit. The old cowboy had been handing out advice and badgering him into hanging on just a little longer, a little tighter, a little *more,* for years now.

"…make sure your hand's under the rope real solid before you even think about giving the signal."

"Got it."

"And keep your back bowed, but not too bowed."

"Will do."

"And get your eyeballs back into your head."

"Already done—" The comment cut off as Billy's head snapped up. He stared into the old man's knowing gaze. "What the hell are you talking about, Eli?"

"That uppity-up over yonder." Eli motioned across the sawdust floor. "If you keep staring at her like that, she's liable to burst into flames right here and now."

"You're losin' it, old man. I'm doing no such thing. My mind's all about tomorrow."

"True enough, but to get to tomorrow, you've got to make it through tonight."

"What are you trying to say?"

"Landsakes, do I have to spell it out for you?" He gave Billy a nudge. "Get your ass over there and dance with the woman. Otherwise, you'll keep wonderin' and that sure as shit's gonna kill your concentration and lead to another sleepless night. Better to blow off some steam and get your mind off everything for a little while."

"I thought it was better to avoid any and all distractions."

"Yeah, but if that isn't working out too well, you have to move on to plan B."

"Which is?"

"Just get to it and get it out of your system."

Billy glanced across the dance floor, his gaze colliding with the hot brunette's. The air rushed from his lungs in that next instant, and for a split second he forgot to breathe.

A crazy reaction. But then that's what happened when a twenty-six-year-old, red-blooded male in his prime went without sex for four months and six days and two hours and twenty-nine minutes.

Lust.

That's all it was.

And nerves.

Tomorrow was big. The first official day of training for the semifinal round that would, hopefully, lead him straight to the finals. The press would be there. The rodeo officials. The fans. All watching and speculating.

It made sense he'd be a little nervous. Not scared, mind you. More like anxious. Excited.

He sure as hell wasn't getting all worked up because of the way her eyes sparkled and her lips curved into a smile.

A *smile,* for Christ's sake.

"Maybe you're right," he heard himself say. "Maybe I should just get to it."

"The sooner you start, the sooner it ends." Eli nodded. "Then you can get focused again and forget all about those long legs and that tiny little waist and those really big—"

"Enough," he cut in. "I get the point."

"Then stop talking and start walking."

"Yes, boss." He left the old man grinning after him and headed across the dance floor.

2

SABRINA COLLINS NEEDED a cowboy in the *worst* way.

One hundred and fifty of them to be exact, which was the *only* reason she'd agreed to leave her L.A. apartment and head for a place like Lost Gun, Texas.

The small town played host to one of the biggest rodeos in the state, which had started a few days ago with several preliminary events. The official start, however, was tonight's dance. While the town was little more than a map dot, for the next few weeks it would be *the* place to be for rodeo fans across the nation. Particularly the male variety.

On top of that, the town had gained recent notoriety thanks to a documentary featuring famous Texas outlaws. Lost Gun had started out over one hundred and fifty years ago as a haven for outlaws and criminals, and so it had been a natural pick for the documentary crew who'd not only played up the town's history but also focused on a crime committed by one of Lost Gun's very own who'd robbed a local bank and then bit the bullet in a house fire. The money had supposedly perished in the fire, but the television host had raised enough questions to make viewers think that the treasure might still be out there. The town had been a go-to spot for fortune seekers ever since.

Not that Sabrina was interested in a bunch of treasure hunters.

She wanted cowboys. Hot, handsome, *real* cowboys.

Just like the one headed straight for her.

He had short blond hair and chiseled features. The faintest shadow of a beard covered his strong jaw. A white cotton T-shirt—the words *Cowboy Tuff* blazing in red letters across the front—framed his massive shoulders and hugged his thick biceps. Worn, faded denim cupped his crotch and molded to trim hips and long, muscular legs. His scuffed brown boots had obviously seen better days, but then that was the way every cowboy worth his salt liked them.

She could still remember the boys back in her smalltown high school, a map dot in East Texas that wasn't so different from this one. The boys back home would rather duct-tape their favorite boots than give them up for a shiny new pair.

There was no duct tape in sight, but this guy still looked every bit as wild as any wrangler she'd left behind when she'd rolled out of Sugar Creek and headed for UCLA.

Sabrina's fingers tightened around the plastic cup in her hand and a shiver of excitement worked its way up her spine.

Because he was a cowboy and another name to add to her currently growing database.

She certainly wasn't feeling all tingly because of the way he looked at her. As if he wanted to take several slow bites and savor each one.

No biting.

No savoring.

No.

She pulled a business card from her purse that listed her email address and her cell phone number.

Numbers. It was all about the numbers.

That's what Mitch, team leader for the investment firm, had told her when she'd approached them about fronting the start-up cash for a new online-dating service that specialized in Western singles. The service was the brainchild of Sabrina and her two college roommates, Livi Hudson and Katherine Ramsey. Since Sabrina knew how to write, she'd penned the business model, while Livi focused on the marketing and Kat handled the actual web design. The idea had grown out of yet another bad breakup for Livi, followed by a night of apple martinis and *Bonanza* reruns.

Forget the bank executives and the grungy tattoo artists and the egocentric personal trainers. Livi wanted a real man. A man's man.

A cowboy.

And if she wanted one, then there had to be a ton of other women out there who did, too, right?

Sabrina hadn't been as convinced, but money talks and polls on Facebook and Twitter had convinced her that Livi's idea might be just the ticket to becoming her own boss.

The three had set up a website, done some soft-launch testing at various singles events and now it was time to put up or shut up. If they could prove to potential investors that they could stock their database with an adequate number of profiles, both men and women, then Southern Money International would front the initial capital needed to officially launch FindMeACowboy.com. They'd given the trio three months to build their singles database.

That had been two months and two weeks ago and while Sabrina and her besties had managed to sign up a decent number of females, they were falling a little short when it came to eligible males.

Men were crucial.

Tall, strong, Stetson-wearing men.

With time running out, Sabrina had had no choice. Kat had stayed back in L.A. to fine-tune the website and finish entering profiles while Sabrina and Livi had headed to Texas. It was Lost Gun or failure.

"Listen, I know this isn't your favorite place, but how bad can it be?"

Sabrina cast a sideways glance at the petite redhead standing next to her at the bar.

Livi shrugged. "Okay, so we're talking bad with a capital *B*. You hate small towns and we're in a small town. Still—" she cast a glance around "—it's kind of fun. I always wanted to learn to two-step."

"And I want to be the next Woodward and Burns."

Or at least, she had back when she'd been a freshman

taking her first journalism class and the real world had been four years away. But entry-level journalist positions were hard to come by, and if she did manage to land one, she wouldn't make enough to cover her rent, much less pay back the mountain of student loans.

Which is the reason that she'd taken a slight vacation from hard-core journalism to write fluff pieces for a few local tabloids and work on FindMeACowboy.com. The fluff coupled with the dating service would pay the bills and then some. Meanwhile, she would keep writing for the few blogs that actually liked her work and build her résumé. She was already brainstorming a new piece— an in-depth look at the bank robbery that had put Lost Gun on the map. Who knew? Maybe she could find a new twist regarding the missing money. She was here, after all. She might as well ask around.

In the meantime, she was going to sign up as many cowboys as possible and get the hell back to the city just as soon as she filled up her database.

"I feel like dancing." Livi's voice pulled her from her thoughts. "I'm going to head over to that table and ask one of those hunks to dance." She indicated a handful of good-looking men in starched Western shirts. "And then I'm going to sign him up and find him the love of his life."

Sabrina smiled as Livi made a beeline for the group. The expression died a heartbeat later when she heard the deep, seductive voice.

"What's the fun in that?"

"Excuse me?" She cast a sideways glance at the hunky cowboy she'd spotted earlier.

Up close he was even more mouthwatering.

"Love." His eyes glittered a hot, potent violet. His lips curved in a sexy smile. "Life isn't about love. It's about lust."

"Is that so?"

He shrugged. "Lust makes the world go 'round."

"So sayeth a commitment-fearing man."

"I don't fear commitment, sugar." He shrugged. "I just don't see the point in it."

"And you are?"

"William Bonney Chisholm—" he touched a tanned finger to the brim of his Stetson and tipped it toward her "—but folks around here just call me Billy."

"As in *the* Billy Chisholm?" Her mind scrambled, recalling bits and pieces from the posters plastered around town and the commentaries airing on the local radio stations. "The bull rider?"

A grin spread from ear to ear. "You've heard about me."

"Actually, I've heard about your brother. He's the current pro bull-riding champion, right?"

"For now. But he's getting slow and preoccupied and I can guaran-damn-tee that another win isn't in the cards for him."

"How can you be so sure?"

"Because he sold out in the name of love and now his concentration's for shit. The only plus is that he smartened up and ran for the hills before he embarrassed himself." He arched an eyebrow. "What's your name?"

"Sabrina Collins."

"You a reporter?" he asked, which made sense since the place was crawling with them.

"I wish." The words were out before she could stop them. She stiffened. "What I mean is, I do have a journalism degree, but I'm not here for that." She handed him her business card. "I'm with FindMeACowboy.com. We're an online-dating service for cowboys and cowgirls, and anyone wanting to meet either one. You'd be perfect for our website."

"What about a dance? Would I work for that?"

Her gaze went to the crowded dance floor filled with sliding boots and swaying Wranglers. "I've never really danced to country music."

He winked. "There's a first time for everything." He touched her and her heart stalled.

And then his strong fingers closed around hers and he led her out to the dance floor.

3

BILLY HAD RUBBED bellies with more than his fair share of women over the years. But none had ever felt as soft or as warm as Sabrina Collins.

The notion struck him the moment he pulled her close and felt her pressed up against his body. He trailed his fingertips down the side of her face, under the curve of her jaw, down the smooth column of her throat, until the silky fabric of her blouse stopped him.

"You don't look like much of a rodeo fan," he murmured.

She shrugged. "Rodeos I can do without. Cowboys are a different matter altogether. I need as many as possible."

"I've heard a lot of pickup lines, but that's a first."

"Don't flatter yourself." She licked her bottom lip and he had the urge to lean down and catch the plump flesh between his teeth and nibble. "This is all about business. My business. FindMeACowboy.com."

"Sounds highly illegal."

A grin tugged at her full lips. "It's a dating service."

"Why cowboys?"

"Because they're generally hard workers, trustworthy, loyal."

"You don't sound one hundred percent convinced." There was a cautious air about her and she seemed to stiffen as he stared down at her.

"It doesn't matter what I believe." She shrugged. "It's about the three thousand, four hundred and seventy-two women that we polled last year. So?" She arched an eyebrow at him. "Have you ever thought about meeting someone online?"

"No."

"Why not?"

"Because I meet plenty of women as it is, and I barely have time for any of them. I ride bulls for a living and this is my year. This rodeo is the first step to my very own championship in the fall. I don't have time for dating."

"Yet here you are dancing with me." Despite the stiff way she held herself, there was just something about the way she looked at him with those deep blue eyes that said she was hungry for more than she wanted to admit. "One would be inclined to think you're looking for someone."

"Maybe, but this isn't about a date."

"What is it about?"

"It's about sex, darlin'." He pulled her closer, plastering them together from chest to thigh, holding her securely with one arm around her waist. "Lots of breath-stealing, bone-melting *sex.*"

Billy's words slid into her ears, coaxing her to soften in his arms the way the warm heat of his body urged her to relax and let her guard down.

Fat chance.

The last thing she needed was to wind up in bed with a cowboy. For all her determination to find as many hunky, Wrangler-wearing hotties as possible, she wasn't looking for one for herself. Sabrina Collins didn't do cowboys. She'd seen firsthand just how unreliable they could be, and she certainly wasn't interested in spending the rest of her life with one.

Then again, Billy Chisholm wasn't exactly proposing marriage.

"You smell like cotton candy," he murmured, his rich, deep voice sizzling over her nerve endings.

"A cotton-candy martini. The out-of-towner special over at the bar. About the sex thing, I'm really not interested."

"Why?"

"I beg your pardon?"

"Don't you like sex?"

She gave him a pointed stare. "Maybe I don't like you."

"Sugar, you don't even know me. I'm a great guy. Awesome." The teasing light in his eyes eased the stiffness in her muscles and she felt the flutter of butterfly wings in her stomach. A good sign if she'd just run into a nice-looking guy at her local Starbucks. But Billy Chis-

holm wasn't your average Joe and she wasn't letting herself get sucked in by his Southern charm.

Still. He talked a good talk. She arched an eyebrow.
"Awesome, huh?"

"In bed and out."

"Most men who walk around talking about how awesome they are in the sack usually aren't much to talk
about."

"I guess you'll just have to find out for yourself."

She wanted to.

Her hands crept up the hard wall of his chest, her
arms twined around his neck and she leaned closer.

His heart beat against her breasts. His warm breath
sent shivers down the bare column of her neck. His
hands splayed at the base of her spine, one urging her
even closer while the other crept its way up, as if memorizing every bump and groove, until he reached her
neck. A few deft movements of his fingers and the tight
ponytail she wore unraveled. Her hair spilled down her
back.

His hand cradled the base of her scalp, massaging for
a few blissful moments, making her legs tremble and
her good intentions scramble.

For the next few moments, she forgot all about her
website and the all-important fact that she was supposed
to be working right now.

She tilted her head back and found him staring down
at her, as if he wanted to scoop her over his shoulder
and haul her home to bed.

She had a quick vision of him wearing nothing but his

cowboy hat, looming over her, his muscles gleaming in the moonlight as he loved her within an inch of her life.

And then walked away the next morning.

And that was the problem in a nutshell.

Sabrina had been there and done that. After she'd left home at eighteen, she'd been hellbent on not falling in love, and so she'd focused on lust. She'd indulged in too many one-night stands during those slutty college years, and beyond. Until she'd watched one of her roommates, Kat, meet the man of her dreams and fall in love. That had been two years ago when Kat had been a kindred spirit. A faithful believer in one-night stands just like Sabrina. Until she'd met Harry. He was an accountant by trade and living proof that there were a few good men out there. He didn't lie or cheat or try to charm his way out of a difficult situation. He relied on honesty and integrity and he made Kat feel like a queen.

Sabrina wanted a Harry of her own and so she'd stopped wasting her time with one-night stands.

Sure, she liked sex, and she sure missed it after eleven months of celibacy—the amount of time since her last relationship—but she also liked camaraderie. She wanted a man to make her pancakes the next morning. A man who called if he was running late after work. A man who wouldn't turn tail and run at the first sign of commitment.

A man who could give her more than just a really great orgasm.

Not that she minded a really great orgasm. But she preferred the friendship that came with an actual relationship. And when she wasn't in a relationship like now? She had a vibrator that could deliver without all the awkwardness that followed a brief sexual encounter.

No fumbling for clothing or making promises that would never be kept. A vibrator was simple. Easy. Honest.

"I really don't think this is a good idea. If you'll excuse me…" She didn't wait for a response. She darted away from him and left him staring after her.

His gaze drilled into her, and it was all she could do to keep from running back and begging him to give her the ride of her life.

He could. She knew it. She felt it.

She headed for the rear exit. Out in the parking lot, she climbed behind the wheel of her ancient Bonneville. She gave one last look at the exit door, half expecting, half hoping that he would come after her. He didn't, and a swell of disappointment went through her, quickly followed by a wave of relief.

The last thing, the very *last* thing she needed in her life, was to fall into bed with the exact type of man she'd sworn off of years ago.

Her father had been a cowboy. A charming, salt-of-the-earth type, who worked from sunrise to sunset and never complained. But while he had a strong work ethic, his moral code had desperately lacked. He'd had an easy grin and a weakness for loose-looking women. He'd cheated on Arlene Collins regularly, always smooth-talking his way back into the house after a night of carousing with every female in their desperately small town. Arlene had forgiven him, catered to him, loved him, in spite of his good-for-nothing ways. She'd been a minister's daughter who'd taken her vows very seriously. Therefore, she'd stuck by him through all the bad times, eager to keep her marriage together and make it work. But she'd never really been happy because Dan Collins hadn't been a forever kind of man. He'd been the play-the-field, charm-you-out-of-your-panties sort. The one-night-stand kind.

Just like Billy Chisholm.

Sabrina wasn't making the same mistake her mother had. At this point in her life, she was done with *just sex*. When she invested herself in a man, it would be one who would—could—love her and only her. A man who wouldn't spend every Saturday night cruising the local honky-tonk, picking up women, propositioning them.

Eventually, that is.

At this point in her life, she was busy with her career, dedicated to making her online-dating service a huge success. She needed a big payoff so that she could pay off her student loans, get herself out of debt and get on with her life. As a serious journalist. The website would give her the financial stability she needed right now. That's why she was here in Lost Gun—for the money. Not to find a date, much less a one-night stand.

Especially a one-night stand.

Sabrina didn't do one-nighters. And she most certainly didn't do cowboys.

Not now. Not ever.

No matter how much she suddenly wanted to.

HER CAR WOULDN'T START. The truth sank in after Sabrina cranked the engine a record ten times, until the loud grumble turned into a faint series of clicks that filled her with a sense of dread.

It wasn't the first time it had happened. The car was over ten years old. A clunker she'd inherited from her grandfather before leaving town all those years ago. While she did her best to keep up the oil changes and take care of her one and only means of transportation, she'd found herself stranded here lately more times than she could count. She needed a new car. Even more, she needed the money to afford a new car. She rested her forehead on the wheel and cursed the pile of junk for several seconds before gathering her resolve and popping the hood. Outside, she lifted the heavy metal, grabbed a rag she kept stashed in the front grill and started checking her battery connections.

Corrosion had built up and she damned herself for not shelling out the hundred bucks to buy a new one before leaving L.A. But she was on a budget. One that barely allowed for the secondhand shoes on her feet and the designer skirt she'd picked up at a thrift store in Holly-wood. Clothes that made her feel like a million bucks even though her bank account reflected anything but. Still. If she'd learned anything from marketing guru Livi, it was that success was all about projecting a certain image. About building a brand.

And her brand as a high-powered executive for the next big website did not involve shoving her face under a hood and praying for divine intervention.

She thought about going back inside and hunting down Livi. Her friend, never short on cash thanks to a decent trust fund from her parents, had picked up her own rental car when they'd arrived in town so that they could split up and cover more territory. The rental wasn't anything extravagant—this was Lost Gun, after all—but it ran. They'd met here at the kick-off dance after Sabrina had spent the day at the fairgrounds while Livi had visited a nearby working ranch rumored to employ the hottest ranch hands in the entire county. Livi would give her a lift back to their motel.

Sabrina weighed her options. Calling or texting were both out because Livi was notorious for ignoring her phone when in the arms of a hot, hunky man. That meant Sabrina would have to go back inside and risk running into Billy Chisholm again.

She ditched the idea and fiddled a few more minutes with the connections. Sliding behind the wheel, she cranked the engine again.

Click. Click. Click.

"It's flooded," Billy's deep voice slid along her nerve endings and put her entire body on instant alert. He leaned down, his handsome face filling up the driver's window. The scent of clean soap and raw, sexy male teased her nostrils. "I hate to break it to you, but you're not going anywhere anytime soon."

She blew out an exasperated breath and reached for her cell phone. "I guess it's time to call a tow truck."

"Good luck."

She eyed him. "What's that supposed to mean?"

"That there's only one tow truck in town, sugar, and it belongs to George Kotch," he murmured as if that explained it all. When she didn't seem the least bit enlightened, he added, "He's about a hundred years old and tires out real easy." He glanced at his watch. "It's already after ten. By now, he's already eaten his bowl of ice cream, taken out his dentures and called it a night. Hell, he's probably been asleep a good five hours or so."

"Lovely," she muttered.

"On the bright side, he's up at the crack of dawn. He'll surely have you out of here and over at the filling station by the time they open. You'll get first dibs in the garage."

"Lucky me. What about a cab service?"

He shook his head. "Red's got a thing for TV. Started with soap operas and progressed to late night TV."

"Good Samaritan?"

His grin was slow and extremely sexy. "At your service."

"You want to give me a ride?"

His grin grew wider. "In the worst way."

"Why do I get the feeling you're talking about more than just driving me somewhere?"

"Because I am." His expression grew serious and his eyes glittered. "I want you and I'd bet my next buckle that you feel the same even if you don't seem all that anxious to admit it." He glanced around at the parking lot full of cars. Yet there wasn't a soul around. Everyone was back inside, dancing and drinking it up. "Seems like fate if you ask me. You run off in a tiff and bam, the car won't start. Maybe someone upstairs is trying to tell you that I'm not such a bad guy."

"No, you're a cowboy." Which was worse. Much worse.

At the same time, there did seem something almost inevitable about the way he'd shown up right when she needed a hand. That, and he was right. She did want him. More than she wanted her next breath. Her last relationship had been nearly a year ago and she'd been flying solo ever since. She craved a little physical contact in the worst way. So much so that she found herself thinking about him and the way he smiled and smelled and looked so indescribably good. And all when she should have been thinking about the website and how they were going to make their quota.

Yep, she had a craving, all right. One that wasn't going to go away unless she satisfied it in a major way.

"I'm staying at the Lost Gun Motel," she heard herself murmur.

Something dark and dangerous and oh so mesmerizing sparked in his violet eyes. "Well, what do you know? So am I." He opened the car door. "My pickup's just right down the row." His grin faded and a look of pure determination carved his expression. "Let's go."

Warning bells clamored in her head, but the only thing she seemed conscious of was the frantic beat of her heart.

The excitement.

The anticipation.

The need.

"Just so we're clear," she managed to say despite the heat zipping up and down her spine, "this is just sex. We won't be exchanging phone numbers or going out on a date or anything like that."

He nodded. "That's the last thing I want."

"I'm not interested in getting to know you as a person. This is just physical."

He nodded. "Purely physical."

She squelched an unexpected rush of disappointment at his words and concentrated on the trembling in her hands and the desire coiling in her belly. "Then lead the way."

4

BILLY CHISHOLM'S HANDS actually trembled as he shoved the key into the lock of the Lost Gun Motel, a clean but ancient establishment just off the main strip of town. It had been a long, long time since he'd been this worked up. This hot. This hard. This…anxious.

The knowledge would have been enough to send him running for the next county if the circumstances had been different—if Sabrina had been any of the dozens of marriage-minded women who'd been in hot pursuit since his oldest brother had found the love of his life and gone off the market.

Now Billy was the resident bad boy, which wasn't a bad thing on account of he liked being bad. He liked making noise and breaking rules and living life.

He liked the rush from all three.

At one time, so did every available woman in town. The trouble was, where they'd once wanted a good time back in high school, they now wanted a walk down the aisle. Marriage. *Kids*.

They wanted Billy Chisholm to grow up, man up and settle down, and each and every one thought she'd be the one to make it happen. To rope, tie and tame him before he knew what was happening.

Not this cowboy.

He liked being single. Hell, he loved it. He didn't have to answer to anyone. To worry about anyone. To hurt anyone.

He was the offspring of the most irresponsible man in the county. Silas Chisholm had been a two-bit criminal who'd pulled off the most impressive heist in the county, before pissing it away because of a case of white lightning and a lit cigarette. And all without a thought for his three young sons. The man had been selfish. Unpredictable. Unreliable.

Bad to the bone.

And out of all three boys, Billy was just as bad.

But while he looked like Silas, and even acted like him on occasion, he also knew what it felt like to be on the receiving end of someone else's bad decisions, and so he'd made up his mind to never, ever put someone else in that position. The last thing Billy Chisholm would ever do was get himself lassoed by any one woman.

Even one as hot and sexy as this one.

But Sabrina Collins didn't want to marry him. With her high heels and tasteful clothes and reluctant demeanor, she was as far removed from Lost Gun as a woman could get. She had big city written all over her, even if she did drive a clunker. Even more, she was a stranger. A single stranger. And judging by the way she licked her lips, she wanted the same thing from him that he wanted from her—sex.

He pushed open the door, stepped back and let her precede him inside. He expected more of an exotic fragrance from her, given her big-city appearance and the whiff of cotton candy he'd caught back at the dance courtesy of the flowing martinis. The scent had long since disappeared. Instead, the warm scent of apples and cinnamon filled his nostrils as she eased past him. She smelled like sweet, fresh-from-the-oven apple pie, and his nostrils flared. A warning sounded somewhere in the back of his brain, but it wasn't loud enough to push past the sudden hammering of his heart. A bolt of need shot through his body and his muscles bunched. He barely resisted the urge to haul her into his arms, back her up against the wall and take her hard and fast right there under the bare porch light, the june bugs bumping overhead.

He fought the crazy urge because Billy Chisholm didn't do fast and furious. He didn't lose his head where women were concerned. He stayed firmly in the saddle, calm and controlled.

Laying a woman down on a soft mattress, peeling away the clothes one piece at a time and taking things slow. That was the way to go. The way he always went, because losing his head wasn't part of the proposition. A man said things he didn't mean when he lost his head.

He followed her inside, closing the door behind them. A click sounded as she turned on a nearby lamp. A pale yellow glow pushed back the shadows and illuminated the interior. The room was far from fancy, but it was neat and clean. An unfinished pine dresser sat in the far corner, an ancient-looking television rested on top. A king-size bed took up the rest of the space. Calico curtains covered the one window near a window air-conditioning unit. A matching comforter draped across the bed. The slightly scarred hardwood floor gleamed from a recent polishing. He had his own place outside of town—just a small cabin he'd been building over the past year—but during rodeo time he hated to waste his time driving back and forth, and so he'd opted to rent a room here.

"It's not the Crown Plaza, but it should do."

"I've never stayed at the Plaza." She licked her lips again and he had the gut feeling that she'd never done this sort of thing before. And then his gaze caught hers and he knew deep down that this was, indeed, a first for her.

Not a one-night stand. No, she seemed to know her way around when it came to that.

The first had more to do with him. She'd never done this with a man like him before.

"You're not usually into cowboys, are you?"

"Never." His blood rushed even faster at her admission. A crazy reaction because Billy wasn't in the habit of being the first anything when it came to women. Be it the first cowboy or the first one-night stand or the first man to actually cause an orgasm. Rather, he steered clear of any situation that might set him apart in a woman's mind and make him more than just a really good lay.

He stiffened, his fingers tightening on the room key. "Maybe this isn't such a good idea."

"You're right about that." The hesitant light in her gaze faded into a wave of bright blue heat as she stepped closer. "It's not good at all." Another step and her nipples touched his chest. "You're so *not* my type."

Before he could blink, she shifted things into high speed, pressed herself against him and thrust her tongue into the heated depths of his mouth, kissing him, devouring him, shaking his sanity and his precious control.

Before he could think, his body reacted. His hands went to her tight, round ass, and he pulled her even closer. He rubbed his throbbing erection against the cradle of her pelvis. His fingers bunched material until he reached the hem of the skirt and felt her bare flesh beneath. Her thighs were hot to the touch. Soft. Quivering.

Holy shit.

Urging her backward, he eased her down onto the bed. He captured her mouth in a deep, intense kiss that lasted several heartbeats before he pulled away and stepped back. He drew a much-needed breath, determined to get himself in check and hop back into the driver's seat. He pulled his T-shirt over his head and tossed it to the floor. He unfastened the button on his jeans and pushed the zipper down. The pressure eased and the edges gaped and he could actually breathe for a few seconds.

Until she pushed to a sitting position and leaned forward.

Her fingers touched the dark purple head of his erection where it pushed up above the waistband of his briefs. The air lodged in his throat and he ground his teeth against a burst of white-hot pleasure. Her touch was so damn soft and he was so hard and...

He needed to touch her.

To see her.

He reached for the hem of her blouse and pulled it up and over her head. One dark nipple pushed through the lace-patterned cup of her black bra. He leaned over and flicked his tongue over the rock-hard tip. She gasped and he drew the nub deeper into his mouth, sucking her through the flimsy covering.

Her fingers threaded through his hair and held him close. He relished the taste of her flesh for several heart-pounding moments before he pulled away. He gripped the cups of her bra and pulled them down and under the fullness of her breasts. The bra plumped her and her ripe nipples raised in invitation.

When he didn't lower his head and suckle her again, she reached for him. "What are you waiting for?"

"Easy, darlin'. We'll get to it." But not yet. He meant to take his time. He always took his time and now was no different.

She was no different.

Even if she was softer and warmer and sweeter than any woman he'd ever been with.

He unzipped her skirt and peeled it from her body

in a slow, tantalizing motion that stirred goose bumps in her soft flesh. Trailing his fingers back up the way they'd come, he hooked his fingers at the thin straps of her panties and followed the same path down her long legs. When he had her naked, with the exception of the bra pulled beneath her luscious breasts, he leaned up and let his gaze sweep the length of her.

She was definitely not from around here, he realized when his attention settled on the barely-there strip of pubic hair that told him she'd been waxed at some big-city salon rather than the local Hair Saloon.

"Did you get this back in L.A.?" He trailed a finger down the barely-there strip of hair and watched her tremble.

"Yes."

"I like it." He traced the slit that separated her lush pink lips and a groan trembled from her mouth. Her legs fell open and the soft pink flesh parted for him.

He dipped his fingertip into her steamy heat and watched her pupils dilate. Her mouth opened and she gasped. And then he went deeper, until her eyes fluttered closed and her head fell back. He worked her, sliding his finger in and out until her essence coated his flesh and a drop trickled over his knuckle.

Hunger raged inside him and he dipped his head, flicked his tongue over the swollen tissue and lapped up her sweetness.

At the first contact of his mouth, she arched up off the bed and her hands tangled in his hair. He tasted her, savoring the bitter sweetness and relishing the soft, gasp-

ing sounds coming from her trembling lips. He swirled
his tongue around her clitoris and felt the tip ripen for
him. She whimpered as he sucked the sensitive nub into
his mouth and nibbled until she tensed beneath him. Her
fingers clutched at his hair in a grip that was just short
of painful. The sensation fed his ravenous desire and
made his breath quicken. He stroked her once, twice
and her breath caught on a ragged gasp.

"Please. Just do it. Do it now."

He gathered his control and pulled away, determined to make it last for both of them. But then his
gaze collided with hers and he saw the fierce glitter in
her eyes—a mix of desire and impatience and fear—
and he had the strange feeling that there was more than
just an orgasm hanging in the balance.

As if she feared the morning after even more than
he did.

Good.

At least they were both on the same page.

That meant if one of them lost perspective for whatever reason, the other could push them back on track.
It was all about tonight.

This moment.

Nothing more. He snatched up his jeans and retrieved
a condom from his pocket. After sliding on the latex,
he settled between her legs. Bracing himself, he shoved
his penis deep into her wet heat in one swift thrust that
stalled the air in his lungs.

He gripped her lush hips, his tanned fingers digging into her pale flesh as he plunged into her again.

She closed her eyes, lifted her hips and met each thrust until he couldn't take it anymore. His cock throbbed and filled and he was right there. He thrust again and the pressure built.

Pleasure fogged his brain and before he could stop himself, he reached down between them and parted her flesh just above the point where he filled her. He caught her swollen clitoris between his thumb and forefinger and squeezed lightly.

She moaned and her body convulsed around him and he knew she'd tumbled over the edge. He buried himself deep one last time and followed. He held her tight and relished the way her inner muscles milked him.

Finally, his hold loosened and he collapsed onto his back. He reached for her, tucking her against his body and losing himself in the frantic pounding of his heart.

Fear hammered at the edges of his brain, but he wasn't going to let it in. Not just yet.

There would be plenty of time later to beat himself up over the fact that he'd lost control for a few precious seconds and, in the process, violated every promise he'd ever made to himself when it came to women and sex.

Plenty of time.

But right now… Right now he just wanted to close his eyes and hold her close. Just for a little while.

GET UP. THAT'S what Sabrina told herself the minute she heard the soft snores coming from the man next to her.

Get up.

Get out.

Get moving.

While she didn't have to worry about alarming Livi if she failed to make it out of Billy's room before daybreak—she and Livi had opted to get separate rooms since they were splitting up most of the time to work more territory—she'd still promised to meet her first thing in the morning for breakfast.

Even more, she had a column to finish for one of the blogs she regularly wrote for. The name of the column? "Oh, No, She Didn't." It was a weekly tell-all on female celebrities and their outlandish behavior that she penned for a tabloid website out of Los Angeles. A far cry from CNN or Fox News, but the site paid a small fee per word and at least she was actually getting paid to write something. Heaven knew she had a stack of journalism pieces she'd written on spec that would never see the light of day. Commentaries on the state of the nation, a story on the outrageous salaries paid by the L.A. County Water Department, and even a twenty-page analysis on the anti-gluten craze. Anything she'd felt might draw some interest, she'd penned and sent in to every newspaper and website she could think of. And the most she'd gotten back was a few comments saying her writing was good, but they needed material that was groundbreaking. A fresh angle. A cutting edge story that would sell copy. And so she'd stuck with her one sure writing gig—the column for the tabloid site. A paycheck, however small, at least made her dream seem legitimate, even if it didn't pay the bills.

She thought of the bank robbery that had put Lost

Gun on the proverbial map. The story had been big news back in the day, but she didn't know nearly as much as she needed to in order to start thinking about an angle. An easy fix, of course, thanks to Google. A few articles would put her up to speed and maybe spark some ideas for a new look at the story. But first she needed facts.

Who? What? When? Where?

Billy's arms tightened around her and suddenly the last thing she wanted to do was spend the rest of her night chained to her computer, checking facts or slogging another story about yet another actress who'd ditched rehab and gone on a party spree.

No, what she really wanted was to stay right here and snuggle down into the warmth wrapped around her.

All the more reason to get up.

The last thing she needed was to fall asleep and risk an awkward morning after. While she'd fallen out of practice thanks to her change of heart, she'd still had enough one-night stands to know that she didn't want to get stuck facing Billy Chisholm the morning after.

She had no doubt he would tell her thanks and hit the road faster than she could blink. He'd made his intentions crystal clear, and so had she. She didn't want more. At least, not from him.

Now if he'd been any other man…

Maybe a bank executive or a photojournalist or anyone but a Stetson-wearing bull rider. Then she might have thought about getting to know him.

But she already knew more than enough.

Billy Chisholm wasn't her type.

She knew that, but with him so close, the scent of sexy male filling her head, she had the gut feeling that she wouldn't be all that happy to see him go.

The thought struck and she gave herself a mental kick. She didn't have to think about him walking out because she intended to walk out first.

Soon.

At the same time, it had been such a long day and she really was worn out. Exhausted. Might as well take advantage of the warmth and close her eyes for just a few seconds. A cat nap.

Then she was up and out of there.

Guaranteed.

5

"WHERE THE HELL are you?" Livi's frantic voice carried over the line the minute Sabrina answered her cell phone. "You're not hurt, are you? Oh, crap, you're not dead, are you?"

"Yes, and I'm speaking to you from the hereafter."

"Very funny. Seriously, I all but freaked when I woke up this morning and realized you hadn't come back to the motel room."

"Morning?" Sabrina blinked against the blinding light pouring through the open curtains, and panic seeped through her. It *was* morning.

She'd slept with Billy Chisholm.

Slept slept.

There'd been no creeping out before dawn. No "Thanks, but gotta go." Or "I really appreciated it, but have a nice life." No, she'd snuggled right up next to him and closed her eyes and now the sun was up and she was late.

"*So?*" Livi's voice pushed past the panic beating at her senses. "How was it?"

"How was what?" She glanced at the clock on the nightstand. It was eight-thirty in the morning. Not only had she fallen asleep, but she'd slept past her usual 7:00 a.m. And all because of a man.

A cowboy.

"Did you get lucky?"

More like *un*lucky. Of all the available men in town—the reporters and the out-of-town fans—she'd hooked up and fallen asleep with a homegrown, certified, grade A *cowboy.*

"Well?" Livi prompted.

"I really need to go."

A thought seemed to strike and her friend's voice rose an octave. "You're not still with him, are you?"

Was she?

Her gaze ping-ponged around the room, looking for boots or clothes or *something* before stalling on the open bathroom door. She strained her ears for some sound, but there was no water running. No footsteps. Just the distant sound of a vacuum cleaner humming from a few rooms down.

"Of course not." She ignored the disappointment that niggled at her, pushed the blankets to the side and scrambled from the bed. She grabbed her undies, which lay on the floor a few feet away. "I'll meet you in a few minutes. Where are you?"

"The diner next door to the motel, remember? That's where we agreed to meet."

"Oh, yeah."

"Cowboys have to eat, right?" Livi went on. "Plus, they've got the best coffee in town and you know how I need my coffee. Lots of coffee."

"Save a few cups for me. I'll be there in ten."

She spent the next few minutes plucking her clothes up off the floor and damning herself for forgetting the all-important fact that she'd agreed to a one-night stand only. The key word being *night*. She'd had every intention of being the first one to hit the road after the deed had been done, the first one saying goodbye, walking out, calling the shots.

She certainly hadn't meant to close her eyes. To get too comfortable. To forget for even a split second that cowboy Billy was not the morning-after type and that, even more, neither was she.

Luckily that all-important fact hadn't slipped *his* mind.

She spared a quick glance around the room. There was no suitcase. No personal items scattered across the dresser. No clothes hanging in the closet. And definitely no note. He'd taken everything with him as if he meant to never come back.

And the problem is?

No problem. Sure, she preferred being the one out the door first, but at least he'd had the good sense not to linger and make things that much more awkward.

Anxiety pushed her that much faster and she pulled on her clothes quickly. She was getting out of here now, and she wasn't going to think that maybe, just maybe, it might have been nice if he'd at least said goodbye.

Forget worrying over one measly cowboy. She had one hundred and fifty-two to think about.

Slipping out of the motel room, she ignored the knowing smile on the maid's face as she rushed down the walkway and rounded the corner toward her own room. A quick shower and change, and she would hit the soda machine next to the ice maker before the diner. She wasn't facing Livi and a room full of Stetsons until she'd calmed down completely. To do that, she needed sugar. Lots of sugar.

A soda. Maybe a bag of M&Ms.

Forget a fully stocked minibar for the source. The Lost Gun Motel was like any other small-town inn she'd ever known.

That meant vending machines instead of minibars. Homegrown soda fountains and pharmacies instead of McDonald's or a CVS. A family-owned general store instead of the brand-name, big-box type.

Sure enough, she rounded another corner and spotted an old Coke machine stuffed with glass-bottled sodas. A crate sat next to the rusted-out monster, the slots half filled with empties.

Her gaze snagged on an Orange Crush and she could practically taste the sugary sweetness on her tongue. As if it had been just yesterday that she'd given up her favorite drink, instead of eight years. The day she'd turned eighteen and left town in her granddaddy's ancient Bonneville.

She'd never looked back since.

She'd never wanted to.

The soda had been just as bad for her as the small-minded hometown where she'd grown up, and so giving it up had been a no-brainer. She'd switched to lattes and bright lights and a great big city full of zillions of people who didn't know what a big pile of unreliability her father had been. There were no knowing looks when she walked into the corner drugstore. No one gossiping behind her back when she went into the nearest Starbucks. In L.A. she was just one of the masses, and she liked it that way. She liked her privacy.

Which was why she'd stayed away from home all these years.

Since her mother had dropped the bomb that she was getting married—again—to a local wrangler from one of the nearby ranches, despite the fact that she'd walked that road once before. Arlene had obviously learned nothing the first time with Sabrina's father. He'd been a ranch hand. Worth his salt when it came to horses, but worthless when it came to being a good husband and father. He'd cheated on her for years before finally running off with a barmaid from the local honky-tonk when Sabrina had been thirteen.

Her mother had been devastated. She'd cried for months, then she'd spent the next few years telling herself that he was coming back, that it was just temporary. Eventually, she'd faced the truth. Not that it had done any good. She'd turned around and hooked up with loser number two. Different time. Different man. Same story.

Sabrina hadn't been in any hurry to watch a repeat of the past. When her eighteenth birthday had rolled around, she'd packed up and left her mother, her mother's new cowboy and her small-town life in the dust.

Her resentment toward Arlene and her cheating father had faded over the years, but she'd never been able to bring herself to go home. To the same double-wide where she'd listened to her mother cry herself to sleep night after night after Sabrina's father had walked away. The place had never felt like home.

It never would, so there was no sense rushing back and pretending. Instead, she'd accepted the truth and turned her back on Sugar Creek like a piece of gum that had lost its flavor.

Sure, she'd seen her mother a few times over the years, but always on neutral ground. Arlene had flown out to California once. They'd met in Vegas another time. Colorado for Christmas a few years back.

She'd heard through the grapevine that her father had ended up single again, working on a horse ranch in Montana. Not that she cared. The day he'd walked away from her had been the day that he'd died in her mind, and so she had no desire to see him.

But as much as she hated him, she owed him, as well. He'd at least taught her one important thing—to never, ever fall for the same type of man.

A man who didn't know the meaning of the word *commitment*.

Which was why she was chalking last night up to a

good time. A temporary good time that was now over and done with.

No matter how much it had felt otherwise.

She slipped inside her motel room and spent the next few minutes getting dressed, before she heard a knock on the door.

"Maid service," came the voice from the other side a split second before the hinges creaked and the knob twisted. A woman with bleached-blond hair and too much red lipstick came up short in the doorway. "It's nearly noon," the woman said as she noted the towel wrapped around Sabrina. "Folks are usually up and about by now."

Folks, as in the locals. But Sabrina wasn't a local, which meant she fell into the same class as a communist/sociopath/deviant puppy kicker. Small towns like Sugar Creek and Lost Gun were close-knit. Folks didn't take too kindly to outsiders, and they certainly didn't trust them. Which was why Sabrina made a point to give Olive—according to the name tag—a big smile before retreating to the bathroom to get dressed, and an even bigger tip when she grabbed her purse to leave fifteen minutes later. Not that it made her any less of a communist/sociopath/deviant puppy kicker. It just meant that she wouldn't have to beg for an extra set of towels. And maybe, just maybe, she might get an additional name or two to pursue for her database.

"So he's the hottest single male in town?" she asked Olive a few minutes later, after complimenting her lipstick and matching nail polish, and slipping her another five.

The woman shrugged as she smoothed Sabrina's sheets. "I don't know about hot, honey, but Martin Trawick is surely single, now that his fifth divorce is final, that is."

"He's been married five times?" Unease rolled through her.

"Six, actually, but we don't count the first one on account of it was old man Talley who officiated and he ain't an actual clergyman. Just tells folks that so's he can get the clergyman's discount special at the diner. It's an olive-loaf sandwich with fresh pickle chips. Anyhow, Martin is always looking for his next wife. He'd probably be tickled to sign up for your service."

Okay, he wasn't prime grade A marriage material. At the same time, they weren't promoting an actual *marriage* service. She and her roommates had invested a lot of time in their mission statement, which outlined their venture—namely, an interactive website where women could go to meet, not marry, cowboys. Which meant the only criteria she had to establish was that any prospective candidate was a Wrangler-wearing, cowboy-hat-tipping, boot-stomping country boy.

"What does Martin actually do for a living?"

"Owns a pecan farm outside town. Actually, he owns a sixth of the pecan farm on account of he had to split it with each of his exes, but he's still got a good hundred acres of his own."

Okay, he wasn't a pro bull rider, but he *was* country. *Check.*

"Does he wear boots?"

"You're in Lost Gun, sugar. Who doesn't wear boots?"

Check.

"How about a cowboy hat?"

"I reckon when he's out tending pecans and it's hot."

Check.

Sabrina smiled. "Where can I find him?"

6

"Now, that's what I'm talking about!"

Eli let loose a loud whoop as Billy climbed to his feet and dusted off his backside. Meanwhile, several wranglers chased the bull he'd just ridden for eight seconds toward the gate leading to the holding pen.

"If you ride like that in the semifinals on Saturday, you're sure to zip straight through to the finals."

If.

The word hung in the air because as much as Billy's pride told him he was a shoo-in, he knew better. While he knew he had the talent, other factors came into play when it came to a successful ride. With all the publicity from the *Famous Texas Outlaws* episode, Billy had been tense. Sleep deprived. Anxious. Even if he was damn good at hiding it.

Still, his numbers had been down in the preliminaries and while he'd had a good ride, good wasn't enough.

To make it to the Lost Gun finals, he had to be great.

And to make it all the way to the finals in Vegas in November?

He had to be flawless.

"That was damn near perfect," Eli said as he clapped Billy on the back and followed him out of the corral. Die-hard fans packed the training facility and cameras flashed left and right.

"Way to go, Billy!"

"Awesome ride!"

"You're the best!"

The comments came at him from all angles and fed the excitement already pumping through his veins.

Not that Billy was letting the praise go to his head. He knew that the past eight seconds meant nothing if he couldn't pull it off again on Saturday in front of the judges. That meant the next week of practice had to be this good. Or better.

Fat chance.

The doubt trotted into his head before he could close the gate, and unease settled low in his belly. Not because his success just now had anything to do with a certain brunette. Sure, the sex had relieved his tense muscles and given him the best sleep he'd had in a helluva long time, but she could have been anyone.

"Whatever you did last night, you better make damn sure you do it again." Eli retrieved a bottled water from a nearby cooler and handed it to Billy. "Rinse and re-peat, buddy. Rinse and repeat."

If only.

He ignored the crazy thought and made his way

around the chutes toward the cowboy who waited on the other side of the railing.

His brother Jesse wore a serious expression that said *major badass*.

But Billy wasn't the least bit intimidated. At six foot three, Jesse had only an inch and a half on him. And when it came to attitude? Billy put the *b* in badass.

"Not too shabby," Jesse remarked when Billy reached him. "I might have taught you something, after all." He grinned and his violet eyes twinkled.

The same eyes that stared back at Billy in the bathroom mirror every morning. But while they had the same eyes and a similar build, that's where the likeness ended. Billy had sun-kissed blond hair, an easy smile and a shitload of Southern charm.

Jesse, not so much.

He'd always been the serious one, sick of his past and eager to leave it behind for something bigger and better. Which was why it had surprised everyone when Jesse had announced last week that he was not only staying in Lost Gun permanently but rebuilding on the old property that had once housed the one-room shack where they'd grown up.

The reason for his sudden change of heart?

The petite blonde standing on the opposite side of the corral, snapping pictures of the various bulls and riders as they exited the chute.

Jesse and Gracie Stone had had a thing for each other back in high school. A fire that had burned so fierce and bright that neither time nor a blanket of stubbornness had managed to smother. They'd kept their distance up until a few weeks ago when Gracie had warned Jesse about the renewed interest in Silas and the "Where Are They Now?" episode that had been about to air. One face-to-face and *bam,* the flames had reignited and blazed that much hotter. They were inseparable now. They'd moved into Gracie's house over on Main Street while they built their very own place on the ruins of Silas Chisholm's old house.

The news couldn't have come a moment too soon for Billy. While Jesse had been eager to forget the past, Billy had always been more inclined to remember.

To keep in mind the unreliable man his father had once been, and even more, to keep a tight hold on the man he knew lurked deep inside himself.

"You're my blood," he'd heard Silas say too many times to count. *"Just 'cause you think you're so high and mighty, don't make it true. You'll see. I ain't cut out for the nine-to-five life, and neither are you. There are too many options out there. Too many ways to make it really big to waste your time with some penny-ass job."*

The words had been spoken to Jesse, who'd been thirteen at the time and the caretaker to his two younger brothers, but Billy had been the one to take the statement to heart.

Silas Chisholm had never been able to settle down and straighten up his life. There'd been no finding a steady job and building a home for his boys and meeting a nice woman to share his life with. He'd been a low-life who'd floated from one two-bit crime to the next,

always looking for the next big thing. A better opportunity. A bigger payoff.

Ditto for Billy.

Not the crime, part. Hell, no. He was one hundred
percent legit and damn proud of it.

It was his inability to commit in his personal life that
made him a chip off the old block. It had started back
in kindergarten when he hadn't been able to choose
between the monkey bars and the slide, and continued
through middle school—baseball or football?—and high
school, where he'd accepted not one, but four invitations
to his senior prom.

Even now, he couldn't seem to pick a shade of blue
for the tile in his new bathroom, or figure out whether
to add an extra bedroom to the cabin or a man cave. He
could see the value in both, the payoff, and that was the
problem. Billy hated to narrow his options. To miss out
on something better. To *commit*.

Now, bulls were different.

They were the only thing he managed to focus on,
to follow through with, to go balls to the wall without
a second thought. A championship was the one thing
he wanted with a dead certainty that he'd never felt for
anyone or anything.

Until last night.

He nixed the crazy thought and ignored Eli's voice
echoing in his ear. *"Rinse and repeat."*

Like hell.

He'd made it out of the motel room this morning
without a confrontation or the dreaded "Call me, okay?"

Uh, no.

Last night had been just that—*last* night. *One* night. End of story.

"If you ride like that in the semifinals," Jesse went on, drawing his full attention, "you just might land yourself a spot in the final round."

"There's no *if,* bro," Billy said with his usual bravado. "I *will* ride like that. That purse is mine, and so is your title."

"I hope so, but all the positive affirmation can't change the past few days and the fact that you sucked big-time in the first go-round." Jesse shook his head. "What the hell happened?"

"I was running on fumes. Tired. Stressed. You know how it is."

"And now?"

Billy shrugged. "I finally got a decent night's sleep is all."

Jesse arched an eyebrow. "Jack Daniels or a double dose of Sleepy Time?"

"Don't I wish." Jesse arched an eyebrow and Billy shrugged. "You don't want to know. Listen, are you really serious about tonight?" He shifted the subject to the voice mail Jesse had left for him earlier that day. "You want me out at Big Earl Jessup's place?"

Jesse nodded. "At sundown. And if you see Cole, make sure you remind him. I left a voice mail, but he's got semifinals today in bucking broncs, so he probably hasn't checked his messages."

Billy eyed him. "You going to tell me what this is all about?"

"Tonight." Jesse motioned to the bull being loaded into a nearby chute. "You'd better get back to work." He winked. "You need all the practice you can get."

But it wasn't practice that Billy desperately needed.

He realized that as he spent the rest of the day busting his ass atop the meanest bulls in the county. His skill, his technique, his drive—it was all there. In spades. He'd just been too tired to shine.

No, what he *really* needed was another six hours of uninterrupted sleep courtesy of a certain brunette with a vibrant pink-and-white Hello Kitty tattoo on the slope of her left breast.

Not that he was admitting as much.

Any woman, he reminded himself. He'd been so hard up that any woman would have had the same effect.

And he knew just how to prove it.

"AND I WANT A MAN with dark hair and blue eyes. And he has to be at least six feet. And have all his own teeth. And no bunions. And I need him by next Saturday night, 7:00 p.m., sharp," announced the elderly woman who'd hobbled up to Sabrina's table at the Fat Cow Diner.

The woman wore her silver-white hair in a short bob, her round body stuffed into an aqua tracksuit and white tennis shoes. "The rodeo committee is hosting their Senior Sweetheart dance and I need a date," she went on. "They do it simultaneous with the bull-riding semi-finals on account of no one down at the senior center can watch the event on account of all the pacemakers and stents and they need every available EMS worker focused on the riders in case they get hurt. The name's Melba Rose Cummins, like the diesel engine but no relation. I'm a shoo-in for queen." She indicated the silver pin attached to the collar of her jacket. "I was princess last year and princess always wins queen second time around."

"Unless you're Shirley Hart," chimed in the woman standing next to her. She had the same silver-haired bob—a testimony to the weekly special over at the Hair Saloon—but she wore a hot-pink tracksuit that hung loosely on her thin frame. "Poor Shirley won princess six years in a row on account of she had bad eyesight and refused to wear her glasses onstage. Kept walking into the podium during evening wear and knocking over the mic stand, which totally killed her score. But she finally saved up her social security checks and got herself some of that fancy LASIK surgery." She shook her head. "Poor thing was so sure that seven would be her lucky number. But then she up and had a heart attack. Keeled over two weeks before the competition and that was that."

"Nobody wants to hear about poor Shirley," Melba said. "This is about me."

The pink track suit shrugged. "All's I'm sayin' is if that had been me and I woulda spent that kind of money, I would have made sure they had my eyes open when they laid me to rest. My name's Louise Talley, by the way."

"Here's the address where I need him to pick me up," Melba handed over a slip of paper that smelled like a mixture of mothballs and dry-cleaning fluid.

"I'm sorry," Livi started, "but we're not an escort service. We run a website for women looking to meet cowboys."

"I don't care if he's a cowboy as long as he's in good shape," Louise said.

"That's nice, but we can't guarantee someone to pick you up next Saturday night—"

"He can meet me there," Melba cut in. "Just make sure he wears a tie. He'll have to walk me across the stage." She reached for her white patent-leather purse. "Cash or credit?"

"We can't—" Sabrina started, but Livi held up a hand.

"Cash."

Melba unearthed a coin purse and stared at the two dollar bills inside. "I'm afraid I'll have to go to the ATM."

"We'll be here waiting."

"What are you doing?" Sabrina asked when the two old women had disappeared.

"Getting rid of them."

"But they'll come back."

"And we won't be here." She motioned to the waitress. "Check, please. This place is a dead end," she told Sabrina. "Let's head over to the rodeo grounds. Maybe we'll have better luck there."

"That seems kind of rude."

"You know what's rude? The fact that we've explained our business over a zillion times and we keep getting these ridiculous requests. It says right on the pamphlet—meet the cowboy of your dreams. Meet. Not date. Or marry. Or molest. All we do is set up a meet."

"Maybe we can at least find her a prospect before next week. The actual date would be up to him at that point."

"Are you kidding me? We've got bigger fish to fry. I only managed to snag three profiles this morning. That coupled with the two I picked up last night leaves one hundred and forty-seven more. At this rate, we'll be over a hundred shy by our deadline. We have to speed up, not slow down and play escort service for the Lost Gun seniors."

"You're right." But that didn't mean Sabrina wasn't going to at least keep her eyes open for a prospect. She told Melba Rose as much when she caught her coming out of the feed store next door, cash in hand. "I can't make any promises, but I'll try."

"That's good enough for me." Melba made to hand her the cash, but Sabrina waved it away. "If I come up with someone, you can pay the usual posting fee after the fact."

"Next Saturday at seven," Melba reminded her. "And I'm negotiable on the teeth."

"That's good to know."

7

"WHAT EXACTLY ARE we doing out here?" The question came from Cole, Billy's older brother, as they stood in the middle of a huge pasture located behind Big Earl Jessup's worn-looking house.

Big Earl was a throwback to the good old days when moonshine was just as much a commodity as the cattle grazing in the nearby pastureland. He'd gained notoriety for his white lightning moonshine and his eccentric method of cooking—namely in his deer blind.

Those days were long gone, however, and his great-granddaughter was now cooking up the family recipe in the nearby garage. At least that was the rumor circulating around town, along with several jars of premium, grade A liquor.

At ninety-three, Big Earl spent his days in front of the TV with a tube of Bengay to soothe his severely arthritic joints. He lived just outside of town on several acres guarded by the pair of pit bulls currently tied up on the front porch. The sun had just set and darkness blanketed the area. The only light came from the windows of Big Earl's house and the lantern in Jesse's hand.

"The money's here," Jesse announced.

Billy's curiosity piqued and he spoke up. "Silas buried it here?"

"Actually, Big Earl buried it out here. He was Dad's partner. A silent partner. It turns out that Big Earl was on the construction crew that built the savings and loan some fifty-five years ago. He knew the place like the back of his hand, but he was too old to actually pull off a heist. Instead, he planned the robbery and Dad executed it. The plan was to hide the money and lay low for a while before spending any of it. But then Dad died and they featured him in *Famous Texas Outlaws* and the time never seemed right, so Big Earl was afraid to dig up the money. And then his old-timer's set in and now he can't actually remember where he buried it. He knows it's somewhere out here, in the middle of a tall stretch of grass."

Billy glanced from side to side. "This pasture's a good twenty acres each way."

"I know. That's why I need you two to help. I can't cover all this ground by myself."

"Can I ask a dumb question?" Cole held up a hand. "Why don't we tell the sheriff and let them get out here and dig the money up? It's not like we had anything to do with it."

"No, but we might as well have. If we hand over the info to the sheriff, the entire town will think we knew all along. But if we give it back ourselves, maybe we can prove once and for all that we aren't anything like Silas Chisholm. He took from this town, and now we're going to give back." He tossed a shovel at Billy. "We're going to dig every night up and down this pasture until we hit pay dirt. It might take a few days. It might take a few months."

Billy shrugged. "I guess hauling an excavator up here would attract too much attention."

Jesse nodded. "If anyone gets wind that the money might be here, there will be gold diggers from here to Houston looking for that money. We have to keep this between us and do it ourselves."

"How long are we supposed to dig tonight?" Cole asked. "Not that I don't want to dig. I'm totally on board with the plan, I just didn't figure on being up here all night."

"Don't worry. You'll be out in time for a booty call. Which Barbie is it this time?"

"None." Cole shook his head. "Jimmy and Jake hooked up with Crystal and April and they're now officially off the market."

Jimmy and Jake Barber were the last two members of the Lost Boys. They were twins who competed on the team roping circuit. They'd always been players when it came to the ladies, but it looked as if they're carousing days were fast coming to a close.

"Jimmy and Jake are getting serious?" Billy arched an eyebrow.

"Last I heard," Cole replied.

"And what about Barbie sister number three?" Jesse

asked. "You thinking about making an honest woman of her?"

"Hardly. Nikki Barbie may look as good as her sisters, but she's not nearly as much fun." Cole shrugged. "Besides, I met someone today." He grinned. "A lot of someones. There are girls coming out of the woodwork at this rodeo and I aim to make the most of it."

Jesse eyed Cole. "Love at first sight?"

Billy grinned. "Safe to say it's lust at first sight."

Cole shrugged. "Lust is good."

Jesse motioned to Cole. "Don't worry, you won't miss your booty call." He turned to Billy. "What about you? You got a midnight rendezvous planned?"

If only.

Billy stifled the thought and gripped the shovel. "Let's just get this done." And then he started to dig.

"IF I SEE ANOTHER female, I'm going to slit my wrists," Livi said the next day as she collapsed in the chair next to Sabrina. It was Sunday—over twenty-four hours since she'd met Billy Chisholm on Friday night—and the fair was in full swing.

She stared at the crowds milling about the rodeo arena where they'd set up their booth. While there were plenty of single males walking here and there, none of them were falling all over themselves to fill out a profile. No line around the corner like the nearby funnel cake stand. No whoops and hollers like the kissing booth across the way. "This obviously isn't working. You man

the table and I'll go see if I can stir up some business."
She stood and grabbed a stack of flyers.

"Where are you going?"

"The animal pens. There are a ton of hands on duty over there."

"They're all working. I doubt they'll want to stop to fill out a questionnaire."

"They will if I'm offering an incentive." Livi pulled a white bakery box from beneath the table.

"What are those?"

"Seductive Strawberry cupcakes. A lady over at the diner makes them. The place was full of old geezers from the local VFW hall all going nuts over these. There was a line clear out the door. I figure if they can stir up the old guys, they might help out with the younger ones. I bought a full dozen. I'm thinking this will nab at least twelve men. Twenty-four if we cut them in half."

"Five minutes and writer's cramp for half of a Seductive Strawberry cupcake. Sounds like a fair trade."

"Hey, I'm desperate. And desperate times call for desperate measures. See what you can do to get more men to stop here. Undo a few buttons." She motioned to Sabrina's blouse. "Or hike up the skirt."

"Why don't I just strip down to my underwear and do a table dance."

"Great, but make sure to peel off the granny panties first." Livi winked and disappeared.

She was *not* doing a table dance. Not yet, at least.

She pulled out more flyers, grabbed her clipboard and rounded the table. If she couldn't lure the remaining one hundred and twenty-seven eligible cowboys still needed over to her table for information, she would take the information to them.

She spent the next hour walking the aisles and approaching every available man. And a few not-so-available ones who hadn't been wearing their wedding rings. She'd been cussed at (*Mrs.* Tammy Johnson, wife of thirty-something Max Johnson, whose three daughters were showing goats in the arena next door) *and* kicked (*Mrs.* Denise Carter, wife of Harley Carter, a professional steer wrestler and competition eater signing autographs over in the barbecue tent), and all in less than ten minutes.

"I'm really sorry," Sabrina called after the blonde as pain radiated up her calf. "He's not wearing a wedding ring."

"He doesn't have to. The entire town knows he's mine. Now you do, too."

"It was an honest mistake," she tried again, but the woman had already rounded the corner.

"Don't let Denise bother you," came a voice from behind. "She's got somewhat of a temper."

Sabrina turned to see a seventyish woman wearing a flower-print dress half covered with a pink apron, a large white box clutched in her hand. Her silvery-white hair was rolled into fat sausage curls and piled high on top of her head. A pair of pink bifocals sat low on her nose. The scent of rich chocolate and cheap hairspray filled the air. "Why, she once threw a package of fish sticks at old Mrs. Shivers for looking at Harley in the checkout line at the Piggly Wiggly. Almost gave her a concussion, too, since the frozen-foods cooler runs a good twenty degrees lower than it should on account of Mr. Ricks—he's the owner—is too cheap to get the darn thing fixed. Name's Sarah Jean Hunt," the woman said, hefting the box to one arm and holding out her hand. "I own Sarah's Sweets. It's the one and only bakery in town."

"Sabrina Collins. I'm with—"

"FindMeACowboy.com," Sarah Jean finished for her. "I heard. The whole town's heard. You guys are here to sign up cowboys for your new website. Talk about exciting stuff."

"Your town hosts one of the biggest rodeos in Texas and you were just featured in a *Famous Texas Outlaws* episode. I can't imagine a website start-up is big news."

"To me it is." The older woman drew a deep breath as if gathering her courage. "I'm here to sign up for your hook-up service."

"I'm afraid we've reached our quota on females. We're here in town to sign up more men."

"I know. That's why I brought these." She held up the bakery box. "I sell everything from pies to cream puffs, but cupcakes are my specialty. Your friend bought a dozen of my Seductive Strawberry 'cause all those geezers from the VFW hall like them. But they just like 'em 'cause the strawberry puree I use works better than their Metamucil. If you want to rope in the younger ones, you need to try my Frisky Fudge Fantasy. I use a dark chocolate guaranteed to rev the libido and make any man hornier than a buck during mating season."

"Dark chocolate does that?"

"My dark chocolate does that. Mix it up myself with a secret recipe handed down from my great-grandmother. She used to own a brothel at one time and it's been said the menfolk would come from miles around to sample her goodies. 'Course, most folks think *goodies* refers to something sexual, but I know better 'cause I got all her recipes. Anyhow, if you want to sign up the cowboys around here, just give 'em one of these." She handed over the bakery box. "And there's more where those came from. All I ask in return is that you help me hook up with my very own cowboy."

While Livi had seemed convinced about the cupcakes, Sabrina wasn't nearly as gullible. Not after getting her leg kicked in. "Listen, Miss Sarah, I'd love to help, but—"

"I know I ain't no spring chicken. That's why I need your help. See, I'm not the luckiest when it comes to men. Spent nearly twenty years with a drunk rat bastard who up and died on me and left me with three kids to raise and not one penny of life insurance. Went into business for myself doing the only thing I knew how. I made it, too. The thing is, on account of running my own business and raising my girls, I ain't never had much free time to get out and meet many men. And I ain't really trusted my own instincts after picking such a dud the first go-round." She motioned to Sabrina.

"But you could find me a decent guy. That's what you do, right? Your specialty?"

"Actually, I have a journalism major. Livi, my partner, is the marketing guru who actually designed the meet-and-greet system—"

"But you find the men, right?"

"Actually, we're both here to find the men. Our friend Kat helps out, too, but she's back in L.A. right now working on the website."

"A triple threat." Sarah Jean grinned. "I like it." Hope glimmered in her eyes. "So you and your partner help me, and I'll help you."

No.

That was her first instinct.

She needed to fill her database, not search for one man for one particular woman.

Then again, she wasn't filling anything at the moment. She eyed the whopping two profiles she'd managed to complete in almost as many hours, before shifting her gaze back to Sarah. That, and she'd already committed herself to Melba. What was one more?

The old woman wasn't the ideal twenty-thirty-something they specialized in. Still, she *was* a strong, successful female. Determined and forthright. And she had the whole Mrs. Fields thing going on. Definitely a prize catch for any man over the age of seventy-five.

Provided the men over seventy-five were fishing.

There was only one way to find out.

She smiled at the older woman. "You've got yourself a deal."

HE WAS HAVING shitty luck.

Billy came to that realization after a sleepless Saturday night spent tossing and turning and staring at the ceiling, followed by an exhausting Sunday spent busting his ass at every turn.

"You suck," Cole told him when he took time out from his broncs to watch Billy during a practice ride. "You'll never make it through the semifinals like that."

"That's what I've been telling him," Eli said. "What happened to yesterday? You were so good."

"I had a late night." A fruitless night spent digging for a bunch of money that may or may not exist. At least that was Billy's take on the situation. To top it off, he'd spent the morning at his cabin trying to narrow down the flooring choices for the new bathroom. Hardwood or tile? The question ate at him when he should have had his mind on his ride. He needed to make his mind up so that the contractor could actually finish a job that should have taken three weeks. Instead, they were on month number two. And all because Billy couldn't just pick one.

He could.

He would.

It's just that he liked both.

Just as he'd liked both blondes that had hit on him last night at the local bar. They'd both been attractive, sexy, eager. He could have had either one of them.

He should have had one of them.

Then he wouldn't be sucking so badly now.

That's what he told himself, but deep in his gut, he

knew it wasn't true. He'd slept on Friday night after the sexual encounter with Sabrina not because he'd needed sex, but because he'd needed sex with her. Because he didn't have to worry about the act coming back to bite him because he knew she was temporary.

She didn't want more and neither did he and he was through denying it.

He had to do something. Even if it went against his good judgment.

"Where are you going?" Eli asked when Billy picked himself up off the ground, dusted off his jeans and started for the gate. "You've still got a few hours left of practice."

"I'm tired of busting my ass. I need an insurance policy." And then he headed for the fairgrounds next door and the woman with the Hello Kitty tattoo.

8

SABRINA FOUGHT TO control the trembling in her hands as she headed down the aisle of booths and rounded the corner into the food section. The scent of sweet cotton candy called to her, but she was too determined to get as far away from Billy Chisholm as was humanly possible.

Sure, she'd been attracted to him last night. But that had been deprivation on her part and sexy mystique on his. But she'd explored that mystery in great detail. She'd climbed to the top of the mountain. She'd jumped off the ledge, and so it should have been downhill from there.

It was always downhill from there.

She shouldn't be trembling. Or shaking. Or wanting. Especially the *wanting*.

Hunger yawned deep in the pit of her stomach and she found herself digging out a wad of change for an extra-large cotton candy. A few sugary-sweet wisps melted on her tongue and a rush of *aaaah* went through her.

There. Hunger sated. Now she could think straight

and remember the all-important fact that Billy Chisholm was off-limits. Cowboy non grata. The more distance she kept between them the better.

"Hey, Sabrina, wait up." His deep voice rumbled behind her and she half turned to see him headed down the food aisle, his jeans molding to his body in all the right places.

"Gotta run." She picked up her pace and headed straight for the sign that said Ladies' Room up ahead.

"I want to talk to you."

"There's nothing to talk about. Just write it down on the sheet and I'll get everything entered into the computer. You'll be hooking up with women in no time."

He stopped, but his voice followed her. "Why are you so freaking scared to talk to me?"

The question rang in her ears, pricking her ego and the self-worth she'd fought so hard to cultivate all those years she'd watched her mother hide out in her room every time Sabrina's father had done her wrong. There'd been no confrontation. No standing up for herself. She'd taken it and retreated, and then she'd forgiven him and the pattern had started all over again.

She stopped dead in her tracks and turned on him. "Maybe I'm not scared. Maybe I just have nothing to say to you."

"But I have something to say to you."

"Maybe I'm not interested in talking to you." She tried to sound nonchalant, but it was next to impossible when she caught a whiff of his scent. The enticing aroma of leather and male and that unnameable something that made her think of soft cotton sheets and the moonlight peeking past the curtains of his motel room... Forget it. Forget him. Forget the night before last. *Forget*.

She tried for a steadying breath. "Look, I realize that you're very popular around here, but unlike the other females in this town—" she motioned to the group of women near the funnel cake stand, their gazes hooked on Billy "—I'm not interested in being one of your groupies."

"Really?"

"Really."

"You know what I think?"

"I couldn't care less."

"I think," he said, stepping toward her, "you're pushing me away on purpose because you really are scared."

"There goes that word again." She gathered her courage and focused every last ounce on holding her ground. Last night she hadn't been prepared to resist him, hadn't been armed against his sexy grin and his sparkling eyes and his honey-dripping drawl. But she was ready now. *Bring it on, cowboy. Bring. It.* On.

"Walking away doesn't mean I'm scared," she said. "It means I'm just not interested."

"Is that so?" He stared at her, his eyes bright and mesmerizing. His lips hinted at the faintest of grins and his gaze dropped, peeling away her clothes and caressing every bare inch.

Her skin tingled and her heart stalled.

Okay, maybe she wasn't prepared for this.

For *him*.

She feigned a smile. "They call it a one-night stand for a reason. It means one night and it's over."

"I know what it means."

"Then stop stalking me."

"You don't have to be afraid."

"For the last time, I'm not afraid of you."

"Not me, sugar." He took another step, closing the distance between them. "Us." The word trembled in the air between them.

"There is no *us,* or did you miss the whole one-night-stand explanation?"

"We're good together."

"We *were* good together. That night. I was horny. You were horny. I'm no longer horny. So that's the end of it. And if you're looking for more, that's great. I'll get your profile entered into my system and I'm sure you'll find a zillion girls to hook up with. You might even find Miss Right—"

"I'm not looking for a wife. Or a relationship." He hesitated, as if suddenly unsure. Something tugged at her heart. "I slept for the first time in a long time, I actually slept for a few solid hours. Since sleep is imperative to a good ride, I was hoping we could work something out."

"Wait a second." She tried to process his words. "You want to have sex with me again because I put you to sleep?" Not because she'd rocked his world or did that little twist with her hips that had sent him to the moon and back. "*Sleep?* Seriously?"

"I know it sounds crazy, but you don't know how

worked up I've been. I haven't slept a solid three hours in weeks." He ran a hand through his hair and she noted the weary light in his eyes. "I've got the semifinals this weekend. If I have a good showing, that'll mean the finals." His gaze locked with hers. "I had the best practice of my life yesterday." He shrugged. "I figure the night before had something to do with it, so I want a repeat."

"So go forth and hook up again." She motioned to the group of women still gathered near the stand. "Take your pick."

He grabbed her arm and hauled her around the corner behind one of the shopping booths.

"What are you doing—" she started, the words drowning in the lump in her throat as he invaded her space.

"Taking your advice." He swung her around to face him. "I pick you."

She stared up at him, wishing he wasn't so tall, so handsome, so...close. "I'm not ripe for picking."

His eyes darkened and she realized she'd said the wrong thing...or the right thing, depending on the part of her doing the thinking. From the heat pooling between her legs, she'd bet money it wasn't her head.

"I'd say you're plenty ripe, sugar." His thumb grazed the nipple pressing against her blouse, and heat speared her. "Ripe *and* juicy, and damn near ready to burst."

"That's not what I meant." She fought for an extra breath to send a much-needed jolt of oxygen to her brain. "From what I've seen, there are dozens of women around here eager for a chance to help you out. Why don't you go make your offer to someone who might actually be interested?"

"Because they've all got one thing on the brain— a wedding ring. This is a small town, sugar. The local girls aren't thinking about having a good time. They're more worried about what time you're going to call them tomorrow. And whether or not you're going to ask them to the church picnic. And when you're going to order the ring and pick out the crystal."

"There's nothing wrong with a nice piece of Waterford."

"Except that I'm more a Dixie cup kind of guy."

"Meaning?"

"I don't want to lead anybody on. I'm busy and I'm not the least bit interested in an actual relationship."

"So make that clear up front."

"Been there and done that."

"And?"

"It lasted one week. The day before I was set to leave for a rodeo up in Montana, her daddy showed up with a shotgun and a preacher. He wanted me to make an honest woman of her."

"What did you do?"

"I told him no and now I can't fly without a strip search. I took two buckshot fragments in the ass."

"You did not."

"It was easier just to leave it in than let a surgeon dig it out." He shook his head. "One-night stands don't happen well in a small town. And since I don't have time to drive up to Austin, I'm stuck here."

"So you want to have sex with me again because I'm an outsider and I'm convenient."

"And damn sexy." He touched her then, skin to skin, the tip of one finger at her collarbone, and her heart jumped at the contact. "You're something when you get all worked up."

Before she could form a reply, he dipped his head and kissed her.

Billy Chisholm tasted even better than she remembered. Hotter. More potent.

His hand cupped her cheek, the other splayed along her rib cage just inches shy of her right breast, his fingers searing through the fabric of her blouse. His mouth nibbled at hers. His tongue slid wet and wicked along her bottom lip before dipping inside to stroke and tease and take her breath away.

Now, this…this was the reason she'd walked away from him a few minutes ago. Because she'd been a heartbeat shy of crawling over the table and pressing herself into his arms and begging for another kiss.

And Sabrina had no intention of begging any man for anything. Especially a too-big-for-his-britches cowboy with a sexy smile and purposeful lips. He was off-limits…

The thought faded as his fingers crept an inch higher, closer to her aching nipple, which bolted to attention, eager for a touch, a stroke, something—anything.

His fingers stopped, but his mouth kept moving, his tongue stroking, lips eating, hungry…so hungry. His intent was pure sin, and Sabrina couldn't help herself; a moan vibrated up her throat.

He caught the sound, deepening the kiss for a delicious moment that made her stomach jump and her thighs quiver, and left no doubt as to the power of the chemistry between them.

"I'm sorry about your ass, but I really don't think this is a good idea," she murmured, dazed and trembling when he finally pulled away.

He leaned in, his breath warm against her ear. "Actually, sugar, I think it's the best idea I've had in a hell of a long time." His words made her shake and quiver all the more.

Shaking? Quivering? Over a cowboy?

This cowboy, a voice whispered, that same voice that had warned her off him the minute she'd spotted him across the arena. The voice that had urged her to cut and run when he'd approached her table.

Because no way was Sabrina going to fall head over heels for a Stetson-wearing, Wrangler-rocking cowboy.

At the same time, it wasn't as though Billy had moved in next door and she had to resist temptation day in and day out for God knew how long. It was two weeks, and that was only if he made it to the finals. Fourteen days at the most.

She could keep her head on straight and her heart intact for two weeks, DNA be damned.

Sure, her mother had a weakness for cowboys, but she'd been stuck in Sugar Creek, surrounded by them. There'd been no way out for her mother, who'd worked a minimum-wage job all her life and so, of course, she'd fallen victim to Sabrina's father's charms.

His lies.

His conniving ways.

But Sabrina had a clear-cut exit plan with Billy. That, and she had obviously yet to make up for the past months of deprivation since her last relationship. It was the long, endless dry spell making her so hot for Billy Chisholm. She had no doubt. Once she made up for that deprivation, the attraction would fade and she would stop forgetting that he was the very type of man she *didn't* want. A little sex in this case would definitely do her good.

And a lot of sex would be even better.

"No strings attached, right? You're not going to expect me to make pancakes or hold your hand at the Dairy Freeze or iron your shirts?"

"I'm in training. That means lots of protein for breakfast and no ice cream. And I get all my shirts dry-cleaned." His gaze met and held hers. "We spend the nights together. That's it."

"And then you go your way and I go mine?"

"That's the plan."

"All right, then." Her gaze locked with his and her heartbeat kicked up a notch. "I'm in."

"EVERYONE, I'D LIKE to welcome a special guest to the Lost Gun Senior Center. This is Sabrina Collins. She's in town for the rodeo festivities," said the petite blonde who read the pitch Sabrina had handed her when Sabrina had walked into the sprawling brick building and asked to pass out some free T-shirts and mugs to the residents. "Miss Collins is here all the way from Los Angeles, California. She's here promoting her new website, FindMeACowboy.com."

A murmur went through the group of women that filled the small recreation room.

"I'd like to find me a cowboy, that's for sure," murmured an elderly woman with brightly colored red hair. She wore a flower-print pantsuit and bright white tennis shoes.

"You'll have to get in line behind me," said yet another woman. She had white hair and wore enough blue eye shadow to make a Vegas showgirl envious. "I've been widowed the longest, so I get first dibs."

"That's a lie, Dolores Rankin. I've got you beat by at least three days on account of I lost my Joe on Good Friday and your Milton didn't bite the dust until Easter."

"Joe slipped into a coma on Good Friday."

"Same thing."

"Is not."

"Is too."

"Now, now," said the blonde. "Let's try to be on our best behavior, ladies. We've got company." The woman, Susan Swanson, according to her badge, smiled and gave Sabrina an apologetic glance. Susan was the recreation coordinator for the center, as well as the head coach for the senior ladies' softball team, Old Chix with Stix. The last bit of info came from the brightly colored pink T-shirt she wore. The front depicted a swinging bat and the phrase *You're never too old to open up a can of whup ass,* while the back held the names and positions of the various team members.

"You just think your perm don't stink," said the redhead, "'cause you're a pitcher. But I'm one fastball away from knocking you out for good."

"You and what joint replacement?" Dolores arched one penciled-in eyebrow.

Red's face crinkled into a thousand tiny lines as she frowned. "What is that supposed to mean?"

"That you creak more than the rusted-out barn door on my old farm."

"I do not."

"Do too."

"Ladies," Susan chimed in again. "I'm sure Miss Collins didn't come here to listen to a bunch of bickering. She's got some freebies for us, isn't that right?" Sabrina nodded and Susan glanced at her watch.

"And cupcakes, too." Sabrina held up a bakery box, courtesy of Sarah and their newly formed alliance. "Chocolate and red velvet."

Another excited murmur floated through the crowd, this one even bigger than the first.

Maybe the baker did know her stuff.

"Yum," Susan murmured. "Can I have one of those?"

Sabrina nodded and handed over a Chocolate Ecstasy.

"I'll leave you to it then," the woman said around a mouthful. "I've got charades starting in the east wing in a few minutes."

Sabrina eyed the roomful of women quickly closing in on her. "Any men in the east wing?" She gave Susan a hopeful glance, but the woman had already started for the door.

"Only the Morgan sisters," Red chimed in as she came up to the card table where Sabrina had set up her display of goodies. "They're not actually men, but they tell everybody that they're bisexual."

"They only do that because they think it makes them more interesting to the opposite sex," Dolores chimed in, wedging in next to Red. "I'll take a red velvet. And a shirt and a mug." She pointed to the stand-up display depicting the shadow of a cowboy, hat tipped low, and the caption *Looking for a real man?* "And I'd like to fill out one of them profiles, too."

"Sure thing." Sabrina handed over the items, along with a clipboard with a questionnaire. While she'd promised Livi to turn down any more female profiles, she didn't have the heart to turn away Dolores. Or the dozen or so other women who crowded around her. Not when they looked so eager. And lonely.

Still, her real objective was to find some eligible widowers for Melba and Sarah Jean.

That, and she was doing anything and everything to keep her mind off the coming evening and the fact that she'd agreed to meet Billy at the motel at ten for night one of their agreement.

Her nipples tightened at the notion and excitement zipped up her spine. Too much excitement, considering she'd already slept with him.

But that was the point entirely.

She was going back for seconds when she never allowed herself a second rendezvous. There were no seconds when it came to her weakness. Yes, she indulged because she couldn't help the attraction, but she didn't give it a chance to morph into more.

There were no follow-up dates. No phone calls or text messages or contact of any kind. She kept it simple and brief and safe.

Until Billy.

He'd thrown a wrench into her entire system, not that she was going to let him throw her off track entirely. It was just a matter of keeping her perspective and remembering that this was a mutually beneficial arrangement.

That meant no primping for tonight or worrying over

what she was going to wear or if he was going to be on time.

She'd done all three for all of a half hour after she'd parted ways with Livi. Her partner had gone back to her room to work, while Sabrina had spent thirty minutes feeling like a virgin before her first real date. She'd finished up at the fairgrounds an hour ago with a whopping thirty cowboys to add to their database. While she still needed to scan in the profiles and send them to Kat for entry, she knew that would only take a half hour at the most.

And so she'd come here, desperate to do anything and everything to keep her mind off the coming evening and off Billy and her crazy reaction to him, and do something productive.

Yeah, right, a voice whispered as she accepted profile after profile. All the right age range, but the wrong sex.

"Is this an all-female home?" she asked after adding another profile to her growing stack. "No offense, but I was sort of hoping to find a few senior men."

"Aren't we all, sugar," said the short, round eighty-something with tight silver curls and thick glasses who reached for a mug. "Aren't we all."

SHE FINALLY FOUND a man.

Sabrina gave herself a mental high five as she rounded the corner with a few leftovers in her bakery box, headed toward the dining hall, and ran smack-dab into a silver-haired man wearing a blue polyester golf shirt and plaid walking shorts.

"Watch where you're going," he growled. "Why, you damn near ran me down."

"I'm so sorry." Sabrina grabbed the magazine he'd been carrying, which had taken a nosedive during the collision. "Let me make it up to you." She held up the box. "I've got cupcakes."

"Sarah's cupcakes?"

"You know her?"

"Who?"

"Sarah."

"She's an actual person?" He shrugged his narrow shoulders. "I just know about the cupcakes. Thought they were a brand. Like Hostess or something."

"She owns a bakery over on Main Street."

He shrugged again. "I don't get out much."

Which meant they'd never met. Which meant that maybe, just maybe, she'd hit pay dirt.

"You like red velvet?" she asked.

"You trying to send me into a diabetic coma? I don't eat sweets."

Bye-bye, Sarah.

"I like Cheetos," he went on. "Now, *there's* a snack."

Sabrina glanced around and caught a glimpse of the vending machines down the hall. "Then let me buy you a snack."

He eyed her, his pale blue eyes wary. "*You* want to buy *me* a snack? What's this?" He glanced around. "One of those hidden-camera shows or something for that there YouTube my grandson is always carrying on about?"

"No hidden camera. I just want to make up for almost running you over. That, and I'd like to tell you about my website."

"You selling something?" he asked after he let her steer him around the corner toward the vending machines.

"Not a thing." She sat her bag on one of the round tables clustered next to the machines. "Puffy or crunchy?"

"The puffy ones on account of the crunchy hurt my dentures."

She sent up a silent thank-you that Melba had agreed to be negotiable on the teeth issue.

"One bag of puffy Cheetos coming right up." She unearthed some change from her purse and fed the quarters into the machine. A few seconds later, she set the bag of chips and a Diet Fresca in front of the man.

"My name's Sabrina Collins."

"Lyle Cornflower. So if you ain't selling anything, why else would you have a website?" His expression grew serious. "You one of them bloggers?"

"No."

"Communist?"

"No."

"'Cause I know how it works. The government sends you people in to rant about all the stuff you think is wrong just to distract us from all the stuff that *is* wrong. Before you know it, the bigwigs swoop in and raise taxes and no one's the wiser."

Lyle hadn't paid taxes in a few decades, but Sabrina

didn't point that out. He was on a roll, the color in his cheeks blazing, and she couldn't help grinning.

"I can promise I'm not creating any diversions for the government."

"Why else would you have a website?"

"My business partners and I created a meet-and-greet site called FindMeACowboy.com. I wrote the business model. I'm here in town to sign up single men for the website."

"A matchmaking website?"

"Something like that. I'd like to add your profile to our growing list of men."

"I ain't no cowboy."

"Not now—" she arched an eyebrow "—but maybe once upon a time?"

"I did ride a horse once. Damn near broke my neck."

"Close enough." At least for Sarah and Melba, and that's who Sabrina was trying to match up at the moment. She pulled a pen and paper from her bag.

"You really want to find me a woman?"

"Hopefully, if your profile matches up with someone in particular. Then she can email you and you can email her, and see where it goes from there. Why, you might even have a date by next Saturday."

"For the Senior Sweetheart dance?"

"It's possible."

He shook his head. "Not no, but hell no. I already turned Melba Rose down for that and she still won't stop bugging me. You know she hates Cheetos? She even petitioned the center to take them all out of the vending machines."

"Maybe she doesn't realize they're your favorite."

"She ought to. I'm eating a bag every night when she stops by my room to see if I want to watch late-night TV with her. I say no, but she keeps coming back. She's just trying to get in my craw and catch me off guard. She has to get my signature on the petition or they won't take them out. I'm the last holdout."

Forget Melba. There was always Sarah Jean.

"Okay, we know you like Cheetos. How do you feel about cupcakes? Or pies? I'm a cream-puff girl myself."

"I'm a diabetic."

Hey, at least she'd tried.

"Say, is it seven already? My show is on." He grabbed a mug and pushed up from the table, and then he hobbled off toward the main room and the sound of CNN blazing on television.

"I say we head for the bakery and snag a cream puff." The deep voice sounded behind her and she whirled around into a rock-hard chest. Strong, familiar hands came up to steady her. Billy's husky laughter rumbled in her ears. "Easy, sugar."

"Don't do that."

"Do what?"

"Sneak up on me like that." Her gaze collided with his and her stomach bottomed out. "How long have you been standing there?"

"Long enough to know you'll do anything for a cream puff."

"I won't do anything, although I have been known to drive an extra ten minutes to indulge myself. But not very often. What are you doing here?"

"Looking for you." He glanced around. "What are you doing here?"

"I promised Sarah Jean and Melba Rose that I would find them cowboys. Melba, in particular, needs one by next Saturday night."

"And you thought Lyle Cornflower fit the bill?"

"He's the right age."

"He plays golf every Sunday with the church golf team. Cowboys don't play golf."

"So what do you want?"

"This." He leaned down and claimed her mouth for a deep, stirring kiss. "We have a deal, remember?"

"One that doesn't start for another few hours," she murmured, once she managed to drag some air into her lungs.

"I finished up early."

She braced herself against the rush of excitement and ignored the urge to touch her hair to see if everything was in place. This wasn't a date and she wasn't a virgin.

"Let's go. I thought we could get some dinner."

"I can't. I mean, you might have finished up early, but I still have a few things to do." She gathered up her purse and her bag full of leftover freebies. "I still have a few stops to make."

"Seriously?"

She nodded and then she turned on her heel and headed for the door as fast as her heels could carry her.

Because the last thing she intended to do was to have dinner with Billy Chisholm. This wasn't about dinner.

It was sex. Nothing more.

At least that's what she kept telling herself.

SHE WAS ALMOST THERE.

Sabrina clutched the edge of the sheet, her knuckles white, as she stared at the motel room ceiling a half hour later. Her nerves still buzzed. Her legs trembled. Her heart beat a frantic rhythm.

And all because of that brief, fleeting kiss at the senior center.

One measly, tired kiss.

Which meant she was even more deprived than she'd first thought.

And even more determined to work herself up so she didn't blow like Old Faithful at the first instant of contact.

She let the images from their first night together replay in her head. The impression his fingertips had made against her heated skin. The rasp of his jaw against the tenderness of her breasts. The warm press of his lips against the side of her neck. The touching…

Yes, the man had one hell of a lasting touch. That's what had her so worked up now. A kiss was just a kiss. Nothing special. Even if it had come from Billy Chisholm.

Especially because it had come from Billy Chisholm.

But the anticipation…

That she needed to get a grip on right now. Before he knocked on the door.

An orgasm. That's what she needed right now. And so she did what any healthy, red-blooded female would do. She trailed her fingers south.

Oddly enough, it didn't feel quite as good. Her hands weren't callused, her skin raspy, or her touch quite as purposeful as…

She frowned and stepped up the action, moving lower to the tender flesh between her legs. She closed her eyes and tried to picture Brad Pitt à la *World War Z*. The guy was an oldie but a goody. Unfortunately, the image just wouldn't come. Instead, she saw Billy looming over her, driving into her, and this time his moves were perfect. She came quickly, clamping down on her bottom lip to contain the scream and the screech and… *Aaah.*

Delicious sensation gripped her for a few blessed moments and she slumped back, welcoming the satisfaction sure to follow. The rush of warmth she'd felt during their night together. The punch of *oomph* that had drained the tension from her body and left her limp and lifeless and completely sated.

If only.

Instead, she still felt edgy. Nervous. Needy.

Crazy.

She ignored the strange emptiness that lingered deep inside and focused on the positive; the clenching and unclenching between her legs, the trembling of her body, the numbness in her toes and the all-important fact that while she might still be waiting, she wasn't waiting *and* wanting.

Okay, so maybe she still wanted him, but it wasn't the all-consuming, rip-off-your-clothes-right-here-and-now want she'd felt five minutes ago.

This, she could handle.

10

SABRINA HAD BEEN naked in front of her fair share of men, but none had ever made her stomach quiver or her hands tremble the way they were right now.

It was two hours later and Billy had just shown up at her motel room. He stood just inside the doorway while she faced him and tried to remember that this was no big deal.

He was no big deal.

Her fair share, remember? She'd been there and done that, but not once had she ever felt the way she did right now with Billy Chisholm's powerful body filling up the doorway and his hot-as-a-Texas-summer gaze scorching her from her head to her toes and back up again.

He made her feel so excited and anxious and needy.

No.

She didn't need Billy Chisholm, or any man like him. She simply wanted him physically. Right now. This moment.

Temporarily.

She forced her thoughts away from her fluttering stomach and shifted her attention to the six feet plus of warm male who hadn't so much as budged an inch since he'd caught sight of her.

At least his feet hadn't budged.

Her gaze lingered on the very prominent bulge beneath his jeans. Her throat went dry and she licked her lips before she could think better of it.

"Come over here and do that, sugar."

Her gaze snapped to his, to the sexy slant of his lips and the knowing light in his eyes, and she was left to wonder if she'd just imagined the flash of raw desire she'd detected when he first entered the room. A look that told her she was much more than a convenient way to spend his unchecked lust.

Right. She was as far from Billy's ideal as a woman could get, and he was far, far, far from hers. He wanted a one-night stand only.

"Well?" he drawled.

"Well, what?"

"Why don't you stop giving your bottom lip all that attention and come over here and give me some?"

"Why don't *you* come over here?"

He didn't say a word. Just stared at her with those hot eyes and that ever-widening grin, as if she'd unknowingly delivered the punch line in some private joke of his.

"What are you thinking?" she demanded before she could stop herself.

"That you're about the most stubborn woman I've ever had the misfortune to meet up with."

"I am not stubborn, and for your information, it hasn't been a picnic meeting up with you. You're stubborn yourself, and infuriating and frustrating and irritating and—"

"You look good enough to pluck from a tree and eat nice and slow." He stood barely a hand span from her. Filling up her line of vision. Drinking in all her oxygen. Zapping her common sense.

She licked her lips as her gaze riveted on his mouth. He really had a great mouth, with firm, sensual lips that made her skin itch and her insides tighten in anticipation. "It's really hot in here." She blew out a breath and fought for another. "Can we just get to it?"

He stared at her long and hard, his grin faltering for a quick second when his gaze dropped to drink in the rapid rise and fall of her chest. *"Hurry up and get to it?"* He reached out and caught a drop of perspiration as it slid down the valley between her breasts. His touch lingered and her heart thudded a frantic rhythm against his fingertip. "We'll get to it, darlin', but there won't be anything hurried about it."

And then his mouth touched hers.

Sabrina Collins had the sassiest mouth Billy Chisholm had ever heard on a woman, all right. And the sweetest he'd ever tasted. Her lips parted at the first moment of contact, and for several heartbeats Billy actually forgot that he liked his kisses slow and teasing.

There was nothing slow about the way he stroked his

tongue along the length of hers and plunged deep into her mouth. Nothing teasing about the purposeful way he ate at her lips, as if she were his only sustenance and he'd gone far too long without.

He had.

That was the only thought that drew him back to reality and helped him resist the sudden urge to bend her over in that next instant and sink as deep as possible into her soft, warm body, until he forgot where he ended and she began. Until he forgot everything—the upcoming ride and the pressure to step up and take his brother's place—everything, save the woman in his arms and the need heating his blood.

Slow and easy.

He gathered his control and fought for a leisurely pace because as much as he wanted Sabrina Collins, he wanted that PBR buckle, and that meant getting a good workout right now.

The kiss softened as he suckled her bottom lip and wrung a frustrated moan from her.

He slid his hands up her arms, over her shoulders, learning her shape, the dips and curves near her collarbone, the soft, satiny slopes of her breasts.

He lifted her onto the desk, parted her long legs and stepped between her thighs. Her heat cradled the rock-hard erection pulsing beneath his jeans. He thumbed her nipples and caught her cry of pleasure with his mouth, the sound exciting him almost as much as the knowledge that he was finally going to slake the lust that woke him every morning, his body taut and throbbing after a restless night spent dreaming and wanting.

He gave up her lips after a deep, delicious kiss to nibble down her chin, the underside of her jaw. He licked a fiery path to the beat of her pulse, and teased and nibbled at the hollow of her throat until she gasped. Then he moved on, inhaling her sweet, fragrant smell, savoring the flavor of her skin. An echoing flame leaped through him, burning hotter, brighter...

Easy.

He leaned back long enough to drink in the sight of her, her head thrown back, her eyes closed, her breasts arched in silent invitation. Dipping his head, he took a slow, leisurely lap at her nipple. The tip quivered, expanded, reached out and begged for more. He licked her again, slow and easy and thorough, before drawing the flesh deep into his mouth and sucking long and hard. A moan vibrated up her throat and she gasped, grasping at his shoulders.

The grasping he could handle. It was the way she wrapped her legs around his waist and rubbed herself up against his aching length that scattered his common sense. He felt her heat through the tight denim. Anticipated it.

Her desperate fingers worked the button of his jeans, then the zipper. It stuck for a heart-pounding moment, the teeth stretched too tight over his straining length. A swift yank, a frenzied *zippp* and he could breathe again.

One silky fingertip touched the swollen head of his

erection peeking up at the waistband of his underwear, and the air lodged in his throat. So much for breathing.

He caught her head in his hands, his fingers splaying in her hair, anchoring her for the long, deep probe of his tongue.

"Billy!" A knock on the door punctuated the shout, the noise piercing the passionate fog Billy found himself lost in. He stiffened, breaking the kiss to gasp for air as footsteps sounded on the walkway outside.

Sabrina's forehead furrowed and her eyelids fluttered open. "What's wrong?"

Before Billy could answer, he heard Cole's voice again on the other side of the motel room door. "Hey, Billy! You in there? Listen, I was minding my own business at the rodeo arena when I ran into that reporter Curt Calhoun. You know, the one who did the follow-up episode on *Famous Texas Outlaws*. Seems he's still poking around. I gave him a statement, but he said he wants to talk to you. Billy? I know you're here, bud. Your truck's in the parking lot." The words trailed off as the knob twisted, the door creaked.

Billy fought with his zipper, but he didn't have enough time. The best he could do in the name of decency was yank his T-shirt down over his open fly as he whirled, Sabrina's nude body hidden behind him.

"There's a shitload of reporters waiting to get a statement from the bull riders and—" The words stumbled to a halt as Cole's gaze hooked on the bare knee peeking past Billy's jean-clad thigh. He looked puzzled for an eighth of a second, before a knowing light gleamed in his violet eyes. "Sorry, man. I—I didn't know you had company."

Billy tried to ignore the soft hands resting against his shoulder blades, the warm breath rushing against the back of his neck. "They want an interview now?"

"Who?" Cole shook his head as if to clear the cobwebs. "The reporters? Yeah. There're three in the motel lobby, not counting Calhoun who's on his way right now. I told 'em you'd be along any second, but I'll just let them know the timing is bad. Maybe they can catch you tomorrow." Just before the door clicked shut, Cole said, "You just go back to what you were doing and I'll get rid of them."

The best advice Billy had heard in a helluva long time. That's what his throbbing body said, but his conscience, his damn conscience, kept him from turning and taking Sabrina in his arms.

"Who is Curt Calhoun?" she asked quietly as he fought for a deep, calming breath.

"A reporter. *The* reporter who put together the *Famous Texas Outlaws* episode that features my dad."

"Your dad?"

He expected a lot of things from Sabrina, namely the slide of her arms, the touch of her fingertips, a whispered "Let them wait." She wasn't a woman to take no for an answer when she wanted something and she obviously wanted him. But he didn't expect her to pull away from him.

"Maybe you ought to go see what they want." Her

hands grasped the gaping edges of his jeans. Soft fingertips grazed his erection as she slid the button into
place and tugged at his zipper.

His hands closed over hers, helping her until the teeth
closed and he was rock-hard and throbbing beneath the
denim once again. As if the action had tried her patience as much as his, he heard the deep draw of her
breath. Relief.

"You go on," she told him. "I'll wait here."

Billy wasn't about to argue. He started walking, conscious of her eyes on him and even more aware of the
need gripping his insides. It would be so easy to turn
back to her, to forget about Curt Calhoun the other reporters who would guarantee him top-notch media cov-
erage for the upcoming rodeo.

Too easy.

He kept walking.

Besides, as eager as he was right now, he wouldn't
last a decent minute. Sabrina would be flat on her back
and he'd be inside her for less than a heartbeat, and Billy
didn't want that. He liked his loving long and slow and
fierce. He'd never had much of a fondness for quickies.
He abstained for months on end when he was in training, and so when he indulged, he liked to make the most
of his time. To commit every breathless sigh, every soft
moan to memory.

He liked things slow and he wasn't about to change
his mind on account of a bad case of lust.

Not now. Not ever.

HIS DAD WAS Silas Chisholm. *The* Silas Chisholm.

The truth crystallized as Billy's words echoed in Sabrina's ears.

He wasn't just Billy Chisholm the up-and-coming bull rider. He was one of Silas Chisholm's three sons. Her heart pounded in her chest at the realization because Silas had been one of the biggest stories to ever come out of a small town.

A career-making story.

If she could find a fresh angle, that is.

She wasn't sure if there was one, but it warranted some serious thought and so she'd let Billy walk away when the only thing she'd really wanted to do was haul him close, to hell with any reporter.

She'd run across Curt Calhoun's name in connection with Silas when she'd started her research last night. Calhoun had hosted the original *Famous Texas Outlaws* story, as well as the recent "Where Are They Now?" episode that had aired only a week or so ago. But he hadn't packed up and shipped out after the episode.

No, he was still here. Still digging.

Because there was more information still to come to light?

Maybe, and it was that maybe that sent a burst of excitement through Sabrina and had her scrambling to right her clothes after Billy disappeared.

A few tugs and she headed straight for her computer. Opening a document file, she started brainstorming a list of questions that she meant to ask Billy. Tactfully, of course. She'd seen his reaction tonight and so she had no doubt that he wouldn't be too keen on her fishing for information, let alone writing a story about his past.

If there was a story.

The doubt echoed and she considered the possibility that maybe it was over and done with. Maybe Curt Calhoun was hanging around for a different reason altogether, a new story that had nothing to do with the late Silas Chisholm, or maybe he had new suspicions that were just plain false.

There was only one way to find out.

She was going to keep her eyes and ears open, and dig for information whenever she had the chance. That, and she couldn't shake the niggle in her gut that told her something was up.

More than just Billy's libido.

Particularly when he didn't head back to her room when he finished up with the reporters.

Instead, she heard the grumble of his truck and the spew of gravel as he pulled out of the parking lot and disappeared for the rest of the evening.

Even more than suspicion, disappointment ricocheted through her and she resigned herself to the possibility that he'd changed his mind.

Hours passed before he finally proved her wrong and knocked on her door just this side of midnight.

"What took you so long?" she asked, her heart racing and her body trembling. From excitement and anticipation and relief. Both heightened because Billy wasn't just a way to break her dry spell. He was her ticket to a real story.

No way was she so worked up because she'd thought for those few hours that he truly had changed his mind, and she'd been nervous. No. *Way.*

"I had some business to take care of with my brothers." He arched his back as if his muscles ached and exhaustion tugged at him.

She lifted an eyebrow. "What kind of business?"

"A favor for Jesse. He's got this cockamamy idea…" His words trailed off and he shook his head, as if he'd said more than he wanted to. As if he'd wanted to say more. "It doesn't matter now." He wiped a hand over his face before his attention shifted to her and a hungry light fueled his eyes. "What do you say we get out of here?"

"But I thought we were going to do it—"

"We are," he cut in, closing the distance between them, his lips finding hers. "But not here. I don't want to risk another distraction."

Neither did she. She wanted him all to herself.

For sex, that is. And information. And that was it.

At least that's what she was telling herself.

She nodded, and then she grabbed her purse and followed him out to his pickup truck.

11

BILLY MEANT TO get busy at the motel.

At least that was the idea that had been cooking in his head since they'd first agreed to get together again. A nice, neutral room at the local motel just like the one they'd used during their first encounter.

But then Cole had shown up. And a bunch of reporters. And he'd found himself stuck in the lobby for way too long since Curt Calhoun had insisted on walking down memory lane and bugging him about his dad.

No comment.

That was his standard response. While Billy had no problem talking about the past, he didn't want to give the media any more fuel for gossip than they already had. And for whatever reason, Curt Calhoun had a bug up his butt.

The man should have left last week like all the others who'd gathered in Lost Gun for the "Where Are They Now?" episode. Instead, he was hanging around, asking more questions, as if he knew that something was up.

As if he knew about the money.

Like hell.

Nobody knew except Billy and his brothers, and Big Earl and his great granddaughter, Casey. And Big Earl surely wasn't talking. He could barely remember his name half the time now. And Casey? She wasn't the social type. Even more, Jesse had promised her a sizable reward if she helped them uncover the money while keeping her mouth shut.

Billy pushed the thoughts out of his head and concentrated on the task at hand—finding some much-needed privacy with Sabrina.

He was too preoccupied. Too uptight. Too damn tired.

He needed some sleep.

But first he needed her.

Now.

So he'd opted for the quickest solution instead of hauling butt all the way out to the interstate and over to the next county. He'd turned off the main road and driven here.

For convenience' sake, of course.

It wasn't because he wanted her to see his cabin, to actually like it. And no way was it because he'd been fantasizing about seeing her in his bed for the past few days. And nights. And every moment in between.

This, he told himself again as he stared at the newly built cabin visible just beyond the break between two towering Texas pines, was nothing more than pure convenience.

"This isn't a motel," she said, her gaze following his.

"What was your first clue?" Billy killed the engine and climbed from the front seat.

"All right, smart-ass." Her voice followed him and he grinned.

"It's not much," he said as he rounded the front and reached her door. "Just something I've been building in my spare time." He helped her from the passenger seat and started walking toward the cabin. "It's still a work in progress, but the walls are up and it has all the bare necessities to get us through the night. Lights and running water and a shower and even a working kitchen—"

"It's really big." Her voice carried after him as she followed him down the path.

"—and the toilet is fully functional—"

"And isolated."

"—and there's a king-size bed with fresh sheets and—"

"And really beautiful."

"—and there's a fireplace in the living room, not that we want a fire this time of year, but— What did you just say?" He stopped and turned on her so fast she bumped into his chest.

"I said it's beautiful." She touched one of the hand-carved beams, and her gaze met his. "It's amazing that you actually did all of this yourself. You did great work."

A strange warmth spread through him, a feeling he quickly pushed back down as his gaze dropped to her shoes.

Her attention followed his and she picked up her feet,

dislodging one of her three-inch stilettos, which had sunk in the soft ground. "Beautiful, but muddy."

"We could drive back into town if it's too rustic for you. Not that the motel is all that much better, but at least there are people around. The Dairy Freeze is nearby."

She cast a glance past him and something strangely close to fear flashed in her eyes before fading into hard, glittering determination. She planted her hands on her hips. "I'm not interested in an ice cream."

His eyes glittered. "Is that so?"

"You bet your cowboy hat. We made a deal and it's time we get started."

Before he could so much as blink, her free hand reached out and gripped his collar. And she hauled him close for a spectacular kiss that overshadowed anyone and everyone in Billy's past. He forgot every woman, every encounter, *everything* except Sabrina and what she was doing to him with her lips.

SEX, THAT'S ALL THIS WAS, Sabrina told herself, throwing herself into the single act of kissing Billy Chisholm, desperate to ignore the strange feelings that had assailed her the moment they'd rolled to a stop in front of the cabin—the sprawling, still-under-construction cabin with the hand-carved porch swing hanging out front and a dusty old saddle draped over the porch railing and several old fashioned milk cans overflowing with sunflowers. One look at the swing and she'd had the sudden vision of herself, barefoot and pregnant, rocking back and forth, a sunflower stuffed behind one ear, Billy planted next to her—

No.

No, no, no, no, *no*.

Not the barefoot and pregnant part. It was the man himself she was objecting to. The wrong man. A cowboy.

The cowboy.

Fat chance.

She'd vowed off cowboys a long time ago when she'd watched her mother wait up for her father night after night. She'd loved him so much and he'd used that emotion against her. No matter how much he'd cheated on her, he'd always managed to sweet-talk his way back into her good graces. He'd smiled and teased and charmed and made promises he'd had no intention of keeping, and *bam,* everything had been perfect. Until the next night when he headed back out to the honkytonk and started carousing all over again.

He'd used her mother. Worse, the woman had let him. She'd known what he was up to. The whole town had. Still, she'd let him get away with it because she'd been powerless to stop it. Weak. Spineless.

Then and now.

Her mother was back at it with yet another cowboy, letting him use her because she feared letting go of the ideal that she'd built up in her head. She feared losing her *real* cowboy for good.

Not Sabrina.

She was working Billy Chisholm out of her system

and killing the whole cowboy ideal right here and now. And she was not—repeat, was not—falling for him the way her mother had fallen for her father, no matter how many porch swings he had hanging outside his cabin. Or how many sunflowers—her favorite flower as a matter of fact—he stuffed into those milk cans. Or how good he kissed. Or how he pulled her close and rubbed the base of her spine with his thumb until she wanted to purr. Or how he held her close, his arms solid and strong and possessive, as if she actually meant more to him than a few moments of pleasure.

This wasn't about forever. It was about this moment, this kiss, *this...*

For the next few moments, she drank in the taste and feel of him, ran her hands up and down his solid arms, relished the ripple of muscle as he cupped her buttocks and pulled her closer.

He rocked her, his hardness pressing into her and heat flowered low in her belly, spreading from one nerve ending to the next until every inch of her body burned.

She moaned into his mouth and, without breaking the kiss, he swung her into his arms and headed for the cabin.

A few seconds later, her feet touched down in the bedroom. The walls were still raw and unfinished, just bare frame filled with insulation, except for one. Floor-length windows spanned from corner to corner, overlooking the surrounding forest and a small creek that shimmered in the distance. A king-size bed, piled neatly with colorful quilts, sat in the middle of the room, looking out of place amid the surrounding chaos of wood and tools. Beams crisscrossed the ceiling, framing a tarp-covered soon-to-be skylight. Sawdust covered the floors, and as much as Sabrina liked the soft floral scent of her potpourri-scented bedroom back in L.A., she found herself inhaling, filling her lungs with the sharp aroma of fresh air and Texas pine and Billy.

She pressed herself up against him again, the need building until she clawed at his shirt. He caught her wrists and pulled back, his grin slow and wicked and dangerous.

"Easy. We've got all night, sugar."

"We've got a few hours," she said as she unfastened her skirt and let the material pool at her ankles. "I have to put in an appearance at the dance tonight, so you'd better start undressing."

"If you want to dance, sugar, I can accommodate you right here." His bright, heated gaze slid from hers to roam down her body—her parted lips and heaving chest and quivering thighs—and back up again.

"I'm not going there to dance. I'm going to work. I need more men."

"Not tonight you don't. Tonight all you need is me. Us." The hands that slid from her shoulder to her collarbone, and down, were strong and sure and possessive.

As if he was branding her his and only his.

Just as the thought struck, he touched the tip of her nipple through the thin fabric of her blouse. The ripe tip throbbed in response and she barely caught the whimper that jumped to her lips.

He pressed a kiss to her lips then, coaxing them open with his tongue before delving deep for a long, heart-pounding moment. "Don't hold back," he murmured when he finally pulled away. "I like to hear you."

He parted her blouse and touched her, his hot fingertips tracing the edge of her bra where lace met skin, and she forgot everything except the need churning inside her.

Sabrina closed her eyes and tilted her head back, arching her chest forward. Strong fingers stroked her nipples through the lace for several long moments until she gasped.

A deep male chuckle warmed her skin a heartbeat before his hot mouth touched her neck, licking and nibbling as his hands worked at her bra clasp. A few tugs and the lace cups fell away.

She all but screamed at the first stroke of his callused thumb over her bare breast. The next several moments passed in a dizzying blur as he plucked and rolled her sensitive nipples, until they were red and ripe and aching for more.

His hands slid down her rib cage and warmed her stomach. A deep male growl vibrated up his throat when his hands slid into her panties and found her wet and ready. One fingertip parted her swollen flesh and dipped inside.

She cried out, grabbing his shoulders, clutching fabric as she fought to feel his bare skin against her own.

He leaned back far enough and let her pull the material up and over his head. She tossed the T-shirt and went for his jeans, but he'd beaten her to the punch, his tanned fingers working at the zipper.

Metal grated and the jeans sagged onto his hips. He stepped back far enough to push them down and kick them free until he stood before her wearing only a pair of black boxer briefs. He was rock hard beneath the clingy black cotton. A heartbeat later, the full length of him sprang forward, huge and greedy, as he pushed his underwear down and kicked it to the side.

But it wasn't the sight of him naked and tanned and fully aroused that took her breath away, it was the heat burning in his gaze, making his eyes a bright, mesmerizing violet.

Her hands went to her open blouse, but he pushed her fingers aside to peel the shirt and bra away from her flushed skin.

"Aren't you forgetting something?" she breathed when he made no move to remove her last item of clothing—a pair of slinky bikini panties cut high on the thighs.

"Soon," he murmured. He cupped her, his palm warm through the thin covering.

An ache flowered low in her belly. "Soon isn't soon enough. I want to feel you. Now." Anxiety zipped up and down her spine, along with a ripple of unmistakable fear.

Because she didn't *want* to want him so deeply. So desperately. Billy Chisholm was a cowboy.

If only that thought didn't turn her on even more.

12

He dipped one finger past the elastic, into the steamy heat between her legs. He stroked and teased and a sweet pressure tightened low in her belly.

"Then it's settled. You're not working tonight." For emphasis, he slid his finger into her slowly, tantalizingly, stirring every nerve to vibrant awareness until he was as deep as he could go, and then he withdrew at the same leisurely pace.

Advance, retreat, until her heart pounded so hard and her breath came so fast, she thought she would hyperventilate.

She was close.

So close…

"Not yet," he murmured, withdrawing his hand before dropping to his knees in front of her.

He touched his mouth to her navel, dipped his tongue inside and slid his hands around to cup her bottom for a long moment before moving his mouth lower. His tongue dipped under the waistband of her panties. He licked her bare flesh before drawing back to drag his mouth over her lace-covered mound. His lips feathered a kiss over her sensitive skin, and her legs buckled. Her hands went to his bare shoulders to keep her from falling.

A warm chuckle sent shivers down the inside of her thighs before he lifted his head and caught the waistband of her underwear with his teeth. He drew the material down, lips and teeth skimming her bare flesh in a delicious friction that made her want to scream. Her entire body trembled by the time she stepped free.

"My turn."

"I don't have any underwear on." He pushed to his feet and faced her.

"I'll improvise." She knelt and kissed his navel, swirling her tongue and relishing the deep male groan that vibrated the air around them. She grasped him in her hand, running her palm down the length of his erection. He was hot and hard and she did what she'd been wanting to do ever since she'd seen him standing there completely nude. She took him into her mouth and laved him with her tongue as a low hiss issued from between his lips.

He grasped her head, his fingers splaying in her hair, guiding her, urging her—

"Stop." The word was little more than a groan before he pulled her to her feet and tumbled her down onto the bed.

She watched as he withdrew a foil packet from his jeans pocket and put on a condom in record time.

"I thought you wanted slow and easy," she said as he settled himself between her thighs, his penis pressing into her a decadent inch.

"It'll be easy," he promised. "I'm just not so sure about the *slow* part." Before she could comment, he pressed her thighs wider, grasped her hips and slid into her with one deep thrust.

He stilled for a long moment, letting her feel every pulsing vibrating inch of him as he filled her completely.

She closed her eyes, fighting back the sudden tears that threatened to overwhelm her. This was crazy. This was all about feeling good, not about *feeling*.

That was a lesson her mother had never been able to learn. That sex wasn't love and that a man good with his body wasn't necessarily as skilled with his heart.

"Are you okay?" His voice was soft and deep and so tender she had to fight back another wave of tears.

Tears, of all the silly, ridiculous, *emotional* things....

She swallowed and forced her voice past the lump in her throat. "Stop talking and just ride, cowboy. Just ride."

His mouth opened and she thought he was going to make a smart comeback, but then he dipped his head and his lips closed over her nipple. Thankfully. She needed a distraction from the strange feelings threatening to overwhelm her.

All thought faded into a wave of delicious pressure as he suckled her long and hard, his erection pulsing inside her. The sensation of him drawing on her breast and her body drawing on his was a double whammy. Twice as delicious. As distracting.

He moved, pumping into her, pushing her higher—stroke after stroke—until she cried out, her nails digging into his back as she climaxed.

Several frantic heartbeats later, her eyelids fluttered open just in time to see him throw his head back, his eyes clamped tightly shut. He thrust deep one final time and stiffened, every muscle in his body going rigid. Her name tumbled from his lips, riding a raw moan of pure male satisfaction.

He collapsed beside her and gathered her close, pulling her back against him in spoon fashion. His chest was solid against her back, his arms strong and powerful around her. Warmth seeped through her, lulling her heartbeat for the next several minutes as their bodies cooled.

Her gaze went to the floor-length windows and the sparkling lake just beyond. The light of the full moon danced across the shimmering surface.

"Wow," she breathed, the word so soft and hushed she marveled when she heard his deep voice in response.

"You should see it late at night when the moon is full."

"How did you ever find this place?"

"My oldest brother, Jesse, found it a long time ago. He was hiking up here in the woods one time and stumbled on this old, abandoned hunting shack. It wasn't much. Just a tin roof and four walls, but it was quiet and calm. We used to come up here to get away from our father whenever he drank too much." His gaze brightened for a split second. "We spent way too much time here."

"So your dad was an alcoholic?"

"That was his second calling. He was a criminal first and foremost. He robbed one of the local banks."

"Your dad is Silas Chisholm," she murmured, her heart pounding in her chest at the mention of the man. This was it. Her chance to ask him about his past. About that night.

"What about your mom?" she voiced one of the dozens of questions now running through her brain. Not nearly the most provocative, but then she was trying to play it smart and slow. If she started drilling him, he would more than likely freeze up or tell her to take a hike. Neither possibility was one she wanted to risk. "Where was she during that time?"

"She took off when I was a few months old. She died a few years later in a car wreck." He shrugged. "I didn't really know her. What about you? Where are your parents?"

Divert and keep prodding. That's what her head said. Ask him another question. Get him talking more.

At the same time, she didn't miss the curiosity in his gaze, the interest, as if her reply truly mattered to him. "I just have my mom," she heard herself say. "She lives in a little town about a half hour outside of Houston. My dad wasn't the faithful type. He'd cheat. My mom would kick him out. Then she'd take him back. Then it would start all over again. About ten years ago, he cheated again, but my mom didn't have the chance to take him back. He walked out for good and never came back." She expected the mention of her father to stir the usual anger and fear and loneliness, but with Billy's arms around her and his lips so close to her ear, she didn't feel the same twist of hurt. She felt warm and wanted and content, and she realized in a startling instant that she liked having Billy curled around her as much as she'd liked having him deep inside.

Maybe more.

"I really need to get dressed," she blurted, desperate for a quick exit strategy from the crazy feelings and the all-important fact that for those few seconds as she'd talked about her father, she'd forgotten all about her story.

Before she could blink, she found herself flipped onto her back. Billy glared down at her for a long moment as if the comment actually bothered him. Ridiculous, of course, because nothing she said or did seemed to really shake that charming, controlled demeanor.

Until now.

His expression eased, quickly killing her theory as a slow, sensual smile crept across his lips.

"Nah, sugar. That," he said, pausing to kiss her Hello Kitty tattoo and one pert nipple, "was just the warm-up." He slid down her body, his large hands going to the inside of her thighs. He spread her legs wide and scorched her with a heated glance before reaching for the ice-cold beer sitting on the nightstand. Popping the top, he took a long swig before dribbling just a hint into her belly button.

The cold liquid tickled its way across her skin and she shivered. But not from the temperature. From the determined look in his eyes.

"The main event starts now." And then he dipped his head and lapped at the golden liquid with his tongue, providing a much-needed diversion from the tender feelings coiling inside her.

She didn't want tender. She wanted wild and wicked and hot, and over. That's what she really wanted. To be done with him. To move on.

Physically that is.

The trouble was, she wasn't done with him. Not yet, anyhow.

Not. Just. Yet.

13

SHE WAS NOT going to watch.

That's what Sabrina told herself as she drove back to the motel after yet another exhausting day at the rodeo arena.

So what if it was Saturday? The day of the semifinals? The ride that would dictate whether he went to the next level?

Whether *they* went to the next level and continued with one more week of their arrangement, or called it quits tonight.

She stifled the anxiety that rolled through her. If it ended, it ended. All the better. She was already having enough trouble getting herself out and about before he opened his eyes. Sleeping in would be a good thing. Welcome.

No, she wasn't watching.

Not only couldn't she care less if tonight ended their temporary arrangement, but she certainly didn't want to see him in his element. It was one thing to know she was sleeping with a bona fide cowboy and quite another to see the proof for herself.

At least when he touched her in the dead of night she could pretend that he was as far from her Not Happening list as a man could get. She could even picture him in a three-piece suit or a policeman's uniform or something equally acceptable. In the dead of night, he could be any man.

But seeing him thrashing about on a thousand-pound bull would only confirm what she already knew deep in her gut.

No, she wasn't watching.

She scanned in the profiles she'd collected that day and emailed them to Kat for entry into the database. She did some online research on Silas Chisholm and the bank robbery. Oddly enough, the research didn't stir the usual ideas when it came to a story. The more she discovered, the more she thought about Billy. But not about his childhood or the crime or a great angle to pursue for the story. Instead, she found herself thinking about the man he'd become. A man so different from his sorry excuse for a parent. Billy was kind and brave and honest and—

Ugh, she needed to think about something else. Anything else.

She gave up the research and turned her attention to Sarah. She and Livi were making slow and steady progress signing up cowboys, and while she knew she should devote her time and energy to that, she couldn't stop thinking about the bakery owner. The woman was

lonely. Sabrina had seen it in her eyes. The same loneliness she'd seen in her own mother's eyes every time
Sabrina's father had walked out the door, which was
why she'd agreed to help the woman in the first place.
And so she spent the next few hours going over various
date possibilities, including Harwin who called bingo
at the VFW hall. While he ran his own plumbing company and spent most of his time in overalls and tennis shoes, he had been voted Hottest Bachelor Over
Forty at last year's Fourth of July picnic, which earned
him a personal evaluation. While he wasn't much in
the looks department, he'd earned the title—which had
been voted on by the single members of the ladies' aux-
iliary—somehow.

Maybe he was the legendary lover Sarah was looking for.

She eyed the photo she'd found on Google depicting
him midcall at last week's bingo night. Receding hair-
line. Beady eyes. Double chin.

Maybe not.

Still, she had to see for herself.

Her mind made up, she went back to doing anything—everything—except turning on the TV. She took
a shower. She painted her nails. She painted her toenails.
She ate three Reese's peanut butter cups *and* a Snickers.

Okay, so maybe she'd watch for just a few minutes.

The thought struck as she swallowed the last bite of
peanut butter and chocolate. She should have known
nothing good ever came from a triple dose of chocolate,
but desperate times, as the saying went.

The ancient TV fired to life, the screen rolling and pitching as Sabrina flipped through the channels. She hit the local station and *bam,* the rodeo arena filled the screen. Thousands of screaming fans loaded the stands and in the center a bull kicked and pitched, desperately trying to throw cowboy number 13.

Her gaze went to the leaderboard in the background and Billy's name, which sat next to the number 22. Each cowboy went three rounds, then the scores were added together and averaged for a final tally. Her gaze drank in the two scores posted. He still had number three to go.

Three more cowboys—all of whom hit the dust before the buzzer sounded—and Billy was up.

Sabrina perched on the edge of the bed, her heart in her throat as she watched the chute open. The bull pitched forward, but Billy held on tight.

One thousand one.

Another vicious twist and he jerked to the right.

One thousand two. One thousand three.

The bull reared up and Billy leaned forward.

One thousand four. One thousand five.

Another twist and Billy went to the side.

And then the damnable TV flickered and the screen went blank.

"ARE YOU OKAY?" Sabrina demanded the second she hauled open the door to her motel room.

It was one in the morning and Billy hadn't even had a chance to knock. She'd obviously been waiting for him.

Worried about him.

A burst of warmth went through him and he barely ignored the urge to haul her into his arms and bury his face in her sweet-smelling neck. But hugging for the sheer closeness wasn't part of their arrangement. That, and his shoulder hurt like a son of a bitch, despite a triple dose of ibuprofen the rodeo doc had given him and two hours spent in the training room with an extra-large ice pack.

"Hello to you, too." He moved past her into the small motel room and tossed his hat onto the dresser. "I'm a little bruised up but I'm okay." He couldn't help his grin as reality hit him. "You watched me ride."

"Not on purpose." She shrugged as if trying to dismiss the truth. "I was looking for *Cupcake Wars* and there you were." Her gaze met his and he saw the worry swimming deep. "But then the TV messed up before your last ride ended. I saw you go to the side and then the screen went black." Concern fueled her voice. "What happened? Did he throw you?"

"Damn straight he did." He sank onto the edge of the bed. "But I managed to hang on anyway."

"That's great."

"Not so great. Hanging on sideways doesn't exactly command a high score. I lost major points for losing my seat, but I still hit the buzzer."

"And?"

A grin pulled at the corner of his mouth. "And I made the finals."

"That's great!" She smiled, and damned if the sight didn't make him forget the pain in his shoulder for those next few moments as the realization of what that meant sizzled in the air between them. "I mean, um, that's great for you," she rushed on when his own grin widened. "You're one step closer to your dream."

"Damn straight." He leaned down to pull off his boots, and his shoulder cried with the motion. He winced and caught his breath.

She was beside him in that next instant. "What's wrong?"

"Damn bull pulled my shoulder out of socket." He noted the sudden brightness of her gaze and something softened inside him. "But I'm fine now. Sore, but everything's back where it needs to be."

"Maybe you ought to soak in the tub, or at least climb into a hot shower."

He shook his head. "I already had a shower. All I really want to do now is get into bed."

She nodded and helped him pull off his boots. A few seconds later, his clothes lay in a heap next to the bed. He crawled between the sheets and sank into one fluffy pillow while she shed her clothes and crawled into bed next to him.

She looked so soft with her hair mussed and her face free of most of the makeup she usually wore, and something tightened in his chest.

She wasn't the most beautiful woman he'd ever been with. Logically, he knew that. But damned if he could recall even one that was sweeter or more perfect than the woman next to him.

The realization sent a wave of panic through him and

he kissed her roughly on her full lips and rolled over, putting his back to her before he gave in to the urge to lose himself in her tight, hot body.

"What are you doing?"

"Going to sleep," he grumbled into the pillow.

"But you can't sleep. I mean, I know you had a close call and all, but you're okay. You are okay, right? That bull didn't stomp any important parts, did he?"

He couldn't help the smile that tugged at his lips. "Nothing below the waist, if that's what you're worried about. I'm just exhausted."

And scared shitless because not once had Billy been so focused on any one woman. Ever.

And not just for the past few seconds.

Her image had haunted him all evening while he'd walked the rodeo arena and watched the other contestants. When he'd climbed onto the bull for a ride that would make or break his career. When he'd hit the dust after hanging on for dear life. Especially when he'd hit the dust.

For a few seconds as the pain had gripped his body, he'd thought that maybe that was it. That he was biting the dust once and for all. And instead of thinking what a damn shame it would be because he was this close to nabbing his own championship, he'd thought of her.

Her sweet face. Her sexy body. *Her*.

Not that it would last.

Billy had been there and done that, and while it felt really good right now, he knew it would end. It always ended.

Better to put a little distance between them until his head was screwed on straight again. The fall he'd taken after the buzzer. That's what had knocked his senses loose. That was why he was thinking such foolish thoughts, like how he wanted to curl up next to her and nuzzle her neck even more than he wanted to slide into her hot, tight body.

Holy crap, that bull really had jarred something loose upstairs.

That, and he really *was* tired. Every bone in his body hurt. His head throbbed. No wonder he wasn't thinking straight.

"Sweet dreams," he murmured.

"Maybe for you," she grumbled as she rolled the other way.

Billy closed his eyes and drew in a deep breath, the effort stirring a sharp pain, thanks to his bruised ribs. He sucked in another deep breath and bit back a groan.

She didn't move for a long moment, but then the mattress dipped as she turned over and scooted up next to him.

In the back of his mind, an alarm bell went off, but the pain was still needling him and so he didn't heed the warning. He felt the soft press of her lips on his temple and his heart stopped for a long moment. The familiar scent of warm woman and fresh peaches filled his nostrils and soothed the throbbing at his temples. Her arm slid around him and her fingers lightly stroked his rib cage, and it was the last thing he remembered before falling asleep.

14

WITH EACH DAY that passed, Billy was finding it harder and harder to remember that this was just sex. Temporary.

Because it felt more permanent than anything else in his life. More right. He found himself looking forward to the little things. Counting on them. Seeing her smile when he kissed the tip of her nose. Holding her until the crack of dawn. Listening to her off-key singing in the shower. *Liking* her off-key singing in the shower.

Sabrina Collins was the last woman he needed to fall into like with. She was out of here in less than four days. She'd made no false promises, left no room for maybe.

Soon their arrangement would be over and she would be long gone, and Billy could get back to his career and finishing up the additions to his cabin and the stuff that really mattered.

Not the crazy feelings pushing and pulling inside him. It was time to switch those off and simply enjoy his last few nights with her.

At the same time, he couldn't help wanting her to feel the same way. To miss him when he climbed out of bed in the morning, to look forward to his company every night, to want to see him in a capacity that didn't involve getting naked.

Hell, maybe she already did.

The thing was, there was no way to really know because the sex was muddying the waters. She might already like the little things as much as he did. She might like him.

Enough to stay?

He wasn't sure, but there was only one way to find out.

"WHAT IS ALL THIS?" Sabrina stood at the island stove, in the middle of Billy's newly renovated kitchen, surrounded by pots and pans and black granite countertops cluttered with all the ingredients for Billy's infamous Hell, Fire & Brimstone Chili.

"I make it for the cowboys every year before the finals. I competed once in the actual cook-off when I was sixteen—Eli made me since I was too young to ride and he was trying to get me more involved at the arena—and it was such a huge hit that I still cook up a mess every year and drop it off at the rodeo grounds for the workers. It's my own recipe," he'd told her earlier that afternoon when he'd stopped by her booth at the festival to tell her they would have to postpone tonight's rendezvous. He had too much to do to get enough chili ready for thirty rodeo hands by tomorrow morning. All night. That's what he'd said.

Unless she wanted to help him. They could get it done in half the time and get on with the sex.

And so she was here, smack-dab in the middle of her worst domestic nightmare, because Sabrina had never been much of a cook. She'd never wanted to be after watching her mother slave away for her father, who'd never appreciated it.

But this wasn't cooking for the sake of pleasing some ungrateful cowboy. This was just part of her arrangement with Billy.

At least that's what she told herself as she moved about his kitchen while he stood at a nearby countertop and seasoned a mountain of ground beef. He'd pulled his shirt tails free of his jeans and unfastened the top buttons of his Western shirt. The vee afforded her a glimpse of silky chest hair and tanned skin.

Her stomach tingled and her nipples tightened and all was right with her world.

Sex.

That's all it was between them. It wasn't as if she liked standing next to him, working side by side, as a slow, twangy country song drifted from a nearby radio. It was all about the heat that raged between them. The intense lust. The overwhelming physical attraction.

She held tight to the thought as she rinsed the uncooked pinto beans and dumped them in a large pot. Thankfully, she could feel his eyes following her as she filled the pot with water and left the beans soaking, to turn her attention to the stove. Her skin prickled with awareness as he moved next to her and fed the seasoned meat into another pot before kicking up the heat. Her nipples tingled. Her tummy quivered.

He turned and his arm brushed against her breast. A tiny thrill of excitement zipped up her spine. He stared deep into her eyes and for a split second, she felt him lean forward. His warm breath brushed her lips and she closed her eyes. This was more like it. They could forget all this domestic crap and get to the really good stuff. He was going to kiss her—

"I've got a few more pots in the car," he murmured before planting a kiss on the tip of her nose. "Hold down the fort. I'll be right back."

Her nose. He'd kissed her nose, of all things.

Her skin tingled and a strange warmth stole through her. Okay, so it was nice, but still. It wasn't what she'd expected.

The sound of his footsteps drew her from the emotional push-pull. Her eyes popped open in time to see him disappear outside and she found herself alone.

Her chest hitched at the thought. A ridiculous reaction because the solitude gave her a few minutes to pull herself together and remember that she wasn't here for *nice*.

She drew a deep, shaky breath and reached for a nearby spoon to stir the meat that was slowly starting to brown.

She spent the next few minutes stirring and trying to

convince herself that she hated every second. Even if the meat did turn the most perfect shade of sizzling brown.

"It looks good."

The deep voice stirred the hair on the back of her neck and sent a jolt of awareness through her. Her hands trembled and her grip on the spoon faltered. It fell into the pot and landed with a splat on top of the pile of beef.

Billy's deep chuckle sent a tingle through her body. "I usually add cayenne at this point." He eyed the sinking spoon. "Trying something new?"

"Maybe." She scooted a few feet away toward the utensils drawer. "Do you always sneak up on people?" She tossed him a sideways glance as she rummaged for a pair of tongs.

His eyes twinkled and his sensuous mouth crooked. "Are you always so touchy when you cook?"

"I don't cook very much." The words were out before she could stop them. This wasn't about having a conversation. It was about getting to the good stuff. The physical stuff. "My mom tried to teach me, but I was never very interested. In my mom, not the cooking." The words were out before she could think better of them. "I pretty much taught myself. Jesse never could cook to save his life, and Cole was always too busy chasing women."

"And that never kept you very busy?"

His grin was slow and wicked and her heart skipped a beat. "I never had to do any chasing, sugar. They come running after me."

Before she could stop herself, she popped him with a

dish towel and his grin faded into a look of pure shock. "What the hell?"

"You're too cocky for your own good," she said, turning back to the pot of meat. She retrieved the spoon with the tongs and set them to the side. "Somebody needs to bring you down a notch or two."

"So why didn't you like being in the kitchen with your mom?"

"I thought we changed this subject."

"You brought it up."

"My mom is the type of woman who bends over backward for any and every man in her life. She bent and they let her. They used her."

"Your dad, too?"

"My dad was the worst. She was with him the longest. She did everything for that man, but it wasn't enough to keep him at home. To keep him faithful. He walked out on us when I was thirteen years old. My mom's been looking for his replacement ever since. The trouble is, she keeps finding him and the pattern repeats all over again."

Her mind rushed back to the past and she saw her mother standing in the kitchen, slaving over her father's favorite red velvet cake. She'd made four batches of cooked white frosting before she'd managed to get it right, and all for nothing. He'd never even come home from work that night. Instead, he'd gone straight to the local beer joint and spent the night with some barmaid.

He'd come home smelling like Emeraude and Aqua Net the next morning and her mother had simply sliced the cake and served him a slice as if he was fresh out of the shower after a hard day's work.

"I'll never kill myself for a man like that." She didn't mean to say the words, but they came out anyway.

"You shouldn't have to."

She turned then and her gaze caught his. Sympathy gleamed so hot and bright in his eyes and a sudden rush of warmth went through her. A feeling that had nothing to do with the lust that burned between them and everything to do with the fact that Billy Chisholm actually understood her feelings. Even more, he was on her side.

Yeah, right.

"So, Eli taught you to cook?"

"Sort of. He taught me to just throw it all together and see what happens. I practiced on my own to come up with this recipe." He grabbed a bottle of garlic and handed it to her. "Add a little bit of this."

She grabbed the spice, popped the cap and shook once, twice, a third time.

"That's not enough," Billy's deep voice whispered into her ear as he came up behind her. One hand slid around her waist while the other closed over hers.

"You don't have to do this." *What the hell?* a voice whispered. This was exactly what he needed to do. To get them off the topic of mothers and brothers, and back onto the real reason she was here—sex.

She knew that. But her heart beat double time anyway, as if there was much more at stake than a little mattress-dancing.

The fingertips that held her frantic grip on the garlic

powder slid down until his thumb massaged the inside of her wrist. The heat from the bubbling chili drifted up, bathing her face and making her cheeks burn. Air lodged in her chest and she couldn't seem to catch her breath.

"Give it another shake," Billy murmured, the words little more than a breathless whisper against the sensitive shell of her ear.

She wanted to say something, to argue the point, but she couldn't seem to find the words.

"That's it." His thumb slid from the inside of her wrist, up her palm, leaving a fiery trail. "Now you're cooking like a real champion."

Boy, was she ever.

She became instantly aware of his hard male body flush against hers, her bottom nestled in the cradle of his thighs. His erection pressed into her, leaving no doubt that he was turned on.

Extremely so.

Her mouth tingled and she had the insane urge to turn into the warm lips nuzzling her ear.

A perfectly natural reaction, given the situation. A perfectly physical reaction.

Yet there was more at stake at the moment.

She felt it in the double tap of her heart. In the strange fluttering in the pit of her stomach. Both physical reactions. The thing was, she'd never felt either with any man before. Cowboy or otherwise.

Because Billy wasn't just any man.

He was *her* man.

The thought struck and before she could drop-kick it out of her mind, she turned.

And then she wasn't just thinking about kissing him, she was actually leaning forward, sliding her arms around his neck and pressing her lips to his.

15

SHE WAS KISSING HIM.

Billy felt a split second of panic as her lips parted. Her tongue touched, swirled and teased. She didn't hold anything back.

Which meant he should have reined in his response right then and there. This wasn't about sex. It was about like. About spending time together and figuring out if she felt even half of what he did.

At the same time, there was something desperate about her touch. As if this kiss was different from all the others they'd shared over the past few days.

The thought intoxicated him even more than the sweet taste of her lips. He planted one hand on the back of her head, tilted her face to the side and kissed her with everything he had.

He nibbled her bottom lip and plunged his tongue deep, exploring, searching. When he couldn't breathe, he slid his lips across her cheek and along her jaw. His mouth slipped to her neck and he pushed her hair to the

side, inhaling her sweet scent. She smelled of peaches
and warm, feminine skin. He breathed her in for a long,
heart-pounding moment and closed his eyes. He thought
of all the things he wanted to do with her.

Everything.

He ached to see her soapy and wet in his shower.
Naked and panting against his sheets. Smiling and
laughing across the breakfast table—

He killed the last thought and concentrated on the
lust that rolled through him like a ball of fire that dive-
bombed south. He edged her sideways until they were
clear of the stove, then bent her back over the countertop and captured her lips again.

He fed off her mouth for several long moments, tasting and savoring, before nibbling his way down the sexy
column of her throat.

His penis throbbed, and it was all he could do to
keep from shoving his zipper down, parting her legs
and plunging fast and sure and deep inside her hot,
tight body.

Now. Right. Friggin'. *Now.*

He wouldn't.

He didn't want just sex anymore. He wanted to know
that she felt something more.

Love?

Hell, he was the last person to even know what love
was. He'd never been in love. He'd spent his younger
years barely surviving, and his teenage years trying
to do more than just survive. He'd never had time for
more than sex.

He didn't have time for it now.

But he wanted it.

Not that he wanted her to fall madly in love with him or anything crazy like that. He just wanted to know that she at least felt *something* for him.

And that meant slowing down enough to give her time to feel. To think. To want.

He slammed on the brakes and concentrated on the small cry that bubbled from her lips when he licked her pulse beat. He liked pleasing her, so he held tight to his control and paced himself. With each touch of his lips, she sighed or gasped. The sounds fed the desire swirling inside him.

When he reached the neckline of her dress, he traced the edge where her skin met the material with his tongue and relished the breathy moan that slipped past her full lips. His hands came up and he touched her, a feather-light caress of his fingertips over the soft fabric of her dress. He traced the contours of her waist, her rib cage, the undersides of her luscious breasts.

He slid his hands up and over until he felt the bare skin plumping over her neckline. Heat zapped him like a live wire and his pulse jumped. He tugged at the bodice. Buttons popped and her luscious breasts spilled over the top.

Grabbing her sweet round ass, he lifted her, hoisting her onto the countertop. He stepped between her legs and caught one ripe nipple between his lips. He suckled her and she arched against him.

He pushed her back down, still sucking as he caught

the hem of her dress. He shoved the material up until he felt the quivering flesh of her bare thighs.

He didn't mean to touch the softest part of her, but suddenly he couldn't help himself. He slid a finger deep inside her slick folds and her body bucked. He drew away from her swollen nipple and caught her delicious moan with his mouth. He plunged another finger inside, wiggling and teasing.

He wanted to feel every steamy secret. Even more, he wanted to taste her.

Tearing his mouth from hers, he worked his way down, kissing and teasing and tasting until he reached the dress bunched around her waist. He glanced up and his gaze caught hers for a brief moment before he dipped his head.

He licked the very tip of her clit with his tongue and she shuddered. She opened wider, an invitation that he couldn't resist. He trailed his tongue over her clit and down the slit before dipping it inside.

She was warm and sweet and addictive, and suddenly he couldn't help himself. Hunger gripped him hard and fast. He sucked on the swollen nub and plunged his tongue inside until her entire body went stiff.

"Come on, baby," he murmured. He gripped her thighs and held her tight. "Let go."

A few more licks and she did. A cry rumbled from her throat and tremors racked her body. He drank her in, savoring her essence until her body stilled.

Then he pulled away and stared down at her.

"Please. Just do it. Do it now," she murmured, her

eyes closed, her face flushed. Her chest rose and fell to a frantic rhythm that made his groin throb and his entire body ache. She was so beautiful. So damn sweet. He wanted her more than he'd ever wanted any woman.

But even more, he wanted her to want him more than she'd ever wanted any other man.

"I think the chili's burning."

Her eyelids fluttered open. "What?"

He took a huge drink of oxygen and forced his hands away from her. "I need to turn the heat down."

Boy, did he ever.

"Chili? You're worried about the chili?" Her gaze swiveled toward the stove and the stream of smoke that funneled from the gigantic pot. "Oh, no." Her cheeks fired a brighter red as she shoved at the hem of her skirt and tugged up her bodice.

City gal Sabrina Collins blushing, of all things. It was definitely a first. He liked it. He liked it a hell of a lot.

What he didn't like was that she'd scrambled away from him faster than he could blink. As if she'd just realized she'd made a big, big mistake. One that had nothing to do with the smoke that slowly filled the room.

"I've got an early meeting tomorrow," she said as he turned his attention to the stove. "I really should go."

"Duty calls."

"I know I'm supposed to help so we can get busy later, but—what did you just say?"

He winked. "If you have to leave, you have to leave."

"That's okay with you?"

"I'd rather you stay and help me finish this batch, but I know you've got a lot on your plate."

"But our arrangement—"

"—will wait." He arched an eyebrow. "You can wait, can't you?"

"Um, yeah. Sure. I just thought you needed some sleep."

"I'm sure I'll be pretty tuckered out after all this chili. I'll take a rain check tonight."

"Well, all right then." She turned and snatched up her purse. "I'll just head out."

"Sweet dreams," he called after her.

"Yeah, right," she muttered, and a rush of satisfaction went through Billy. He'd won tonight's battle.

Now if he could only win the war.

THEY WEREN'T HAVING SEX.

It had been two days since the chili incident and other than a few hot kisses and some heavy petting, she wasn't any closer to working Billy Chisholm out of her system. She needed the real deal for that.

At least that's what she was telling herself.

She needed him inside her and her wrapped around him and she needed an orgasm. A major, mind-blowing orgasm during the actual deed. The preliminary stuff… It just wasn't the same thing.

At least that's what she was telling herself.

Because no way was she so wound up because she was nervous. Afraid. She had only two days left in Lost Gun before the rodeo finals and no doubt that she would add the last twenty cowboys to her list and meet her goal. Twenty-one counting Billy, who'd promised she could sign him up when all was said and done.

She certainly wasn't so antsy because she didn't want to sign him up. Because she wanted him for herself. For the next two days and beyond.

Real sex.

That was all she needed to relieve the tension in her shoulders and ease the anxiety knotting her stomach. She held tight to the truth as he ended the heavy-duty petting session that had started the minute she'd arrived on his doorstep late Friday night, after a long day at the festival and enough profiles to push her that much closer to her goal.

All the more reason she should have headed to the saloon to celebrate with Livi. They were going to make it, to secure their funding.

But Sabrina wanted more. She hadn't given up on her story, even if all of the research she'd done on Silas Chisholm made her want to wrap Billy in her arms and hug him for all the grief he'd suffered thanks to his father. A story was a story. If she ever wanted to make it as a real journalist—and she did, even if it wasn't half as much fun as she'd anticipated—she had to learn to separate her emotions from the situation. She would. She would never have another opportunity like this one. Billy had seen the fire. He'd been an actual eyewitness to the events that had unfolded that night. He was her inside track on the story of a lifetime. One she desperately needed if she ever wanted to move beyond running a web hook-up service. She needed this story. Even more, she needed sex. And so she'd headed up to Billy's cabin instead.

And straight into his bed.

For about fifteen minutes, she felt convinced her dry spell was about to end. But then he pulled away, kissed her one last time with enough passion to make her hormones cry, and then he rolled over to go to sleep.

Sleep.

Seriously?

She tossed and turned and did everything she could to keep him up, but then he slid an arm around her and pulled her back flush against his body. Her hopes soared one last time, but then she heard the deep snore directly in her ear.

"Really?" she muttered, barely resisting the urge to pinch the hell out of his arm.

But the solid muscle wrapped around her did feel good and she found herself relaxing a little. Enough to stop contemplating revenge plots and actually close her eyes for a few moments. It *had* been a long day and this was sort of nice, too.

Not that she was falling asleep.

SHE FELL ASLEEP.

The truth sank in several hours later when her eyes finally popped open and she realized that it was almost five o'clock in the morning.

She'd fallen hard and fast, but he hadn't.

Her gaze went to the empty stretch of sheets beside

her. Obviously he'd been the one to beat a hasty retreat this time and now she was all by her lonesome.

All the better.

That meant she didn't have to worry about picking herself up and getting the hell out of Dodge before he opened his eyes. He'd beaten her to the punch and now she could close her eyes and go back to sleep for a little while. And she certainly wasn't going to wonder where in the world he'd run off to at five o'clock in the morning. Probably some early-morning training session. Or some interview with PBR executives. Or maybe he was helping out at the Gunner Ranch until Pete and his new wife returned.

Not that she cared.

She rolled onto her right side and punched the pillow a few more times before snuggling back down. There. She was going to close her eyes and she wasn't going to remember the tenderness in his eyes when he'd fed her a taste of chili the night before. Tenderness? Yeah, right. That had all been part of the foreplay, which had been part of the sex.

That's all last night had been.

Even if it had felt like an actual date.

She nixed the thought. A date implied like, and no way did he like her. And she certainly didn't like him.

Her chest tightened and her eyes popped open. She rolled onto her left side, scrunched the pillow under her head and snuggled down. There. Now she was going to close her eyes, and she wasn't going to remember the way he'd pulled her close the minute they'd hit the sheets and held her as if she was the most important thing in his life—

Her eyes popped open again and she rolled onto her back.

She sat up and climbed out of the bed. A few steps and she found herself in the hallway. The hardwood floor was cool beneath her bare feet, but it did nothing to ease the fire burning inside her as she walked toward the kitchen. A glass of ice water would do the trick. Or maybe she could stick her head in the fridge until she started to calm down and think rational thoughts.

Like how excited she was that she was *this* close to meeting her quota and getting the hell out of Lost Gun for good.

At the same time, she still hadn't managed to put together a decent story about the death of Silas Chisholm. Even more, she hadn't managed to find a date for Melba Rose and she was no closer to hooking up Sarah Jean from the bakery and—

Seriously?

She wasn't a matchmaker. She was a journalist biding her time until she got her big break. Melba and Sarah would just have to find their own men because she had ten more cowboys to sign up and a story to write before she left town.

And she *was* leaving.

"Can't sleep?" The deep, husky timbre of his voice met her the minute she reached the doorway to the kitchen.

She found Billy standing at the kitchen counter. The

sight of him wearing nothing but a pair of snug, faded jeans stalled her heart for a long moment. Soft denim molded to his lean hips and strong thighs, and cupped his crotch. A frayed rip in the denim on his right thigh gave her a glimpse of silky blond hair and tanned skin and hard muscle and... *Oh, boy.*

She'd seen him without a shirt before, but she hadn't really *seen* him. She'd always been too anxious to get to the main event to really take a long, leisurely look, and too determined the morning after to ignore him.

He had the hard, well-defined physique of a rough-and-tough bull rider. Broad shoulders. Muscular arms. Gold hair sprinkled his chest from nipple to nipple before narrowing into a thin line that bisected his six-pack abs and disappeared into the waistband of his jeans. Her gaze was riveted on the hard bulge beneath his zipper for several fast, furious heartbeats before shifting north.

"Hungry?" he asked.

She swallowed. "You have no idea."

"Me, too." He held up a forkful of pancakes. The aroma of melted butter and sweet syrup hit her nostrils. Her stomach grumbled and he grinned. "I've got a big stack if you want some." She didn't miss the heat that simmered in the bright violet depths of his eyes, which made her all the more confused as to why he'd stopped before the main event last night.

He obviously wanted her.

She could see it.

Feel it.

But then his gaze darkened and he stiffened, as if he'd just remembered some all-important fact.

"Come on and I'll get you a plate," he offered.

Pancakes, a voice reminded her. *As in breakfast. As in the morning after.*

But it was still dark out and she was too hungry and, besides, they hadn't actually done the deed last night, which completely killed the notion of a morning after.

"They're homemade," he added. Determination gleamed hot and bright in his gaze, along with a glimmer of possessiveness that said he'd just climbed onto a monster bull for the ride of his life, and he had no intention of letting go.

Not now.

Not ever.

And damned if that notion didn't excite her even more than the prospect of hot, breath-stealing sex.

She smiled. "Let's eat."

16

BILLY HAD NEVER been a big believer in luck. Good fortune came through hard work and talent, and when things went wrong, there was usually a damn good reason behind it. Lack of motivation. Fear. Laziness.

He'd learned that from Pete and his older brothers.

A man made his own luck. It never just waltzed in on its own.

But as he watched Sabrina walk into his kitchen, he couldn't help but reevaluate his position. He fully expected her to turn and run, the way she did every morning. Yet here she was, standing right in front of him wearing nothing but his T-shirt and a look that said she was none too happy about it.

Still, she was here.

And damned if Billy didn't feel like the luckiest man on the planet.

He turned back to the stack of pancakes he'd just made. Grabbing a nearby plate, he fed a few golden cakes onto it. "Syrup?"

"Please."

He grabbed the bottle and poured a hefty amount of brown liquid before handing her the cakes. He watched as she cut into the stack and stuffed a bite into her mouth.

Her features softened and pure ecstasy rolled across her face, the sight like a sucker punch to his gut.

"The chili I could see," she murmured around a mouthful, "but pancakes, too?" Her gaze caught and held his and the air rushed back into his lungs. "I'm impressed."

"Glad to hear it."

"Did your older brothers teach you this?"

"Jesse can barely heat up a frozen waffle in the toaster. And Cole's the fast-food king." He shrugged. "Eli was always the cook in the family."

"My partner and best friend Livi did most of the cooking in our dorm room. Mostly microwave stuff, though. That, or we did takeout."

"What about your mom?"

"She could outcook Rachael Ray, which is why I stay as far from the kitchen as possible." She took another bite and he had the distinct feeling she wanted to change the subject.

"So how long have you and Livi been friends?"

"Since freshman year. I didn't know if I was going to like her at first. We were so different." When he arched an eyebrow, she added, "I know I don't look like it, but I was a small-town country girl at one point in time."

"You say that like it's a bad thing."

"It is. It was." She shook her head. "I hated being from a small town. I hated the fact that we had to drive two hours just to get to a mall. I hated everybody being in everybody's business. I hated that everybody knew what a rat bastard my dad was, while my own mom buried her head in the sand."

"Maybe she wasn't as clueless as you think. Maybe it just didn't matter."

"How's that possible?"

"Maybe she accepted him the way he was." He ate another bite of his own pancake. "My dad was a son of a bitch. There's no denying that. He did some really awful things and my older brothers hated him for it." He shrugged. "I didn't."

"But you were young—"

"That had nothing to do with it. I knew what he was, but it didn't matter. He was still my dad." He shrugged. "Maybe your mom knew, too, but she just accepted it because that's the way he was and she loved him anyway."

"Love had nothing to do with it. She was afraid of being alone."

He shrugged. "I can see that. A single mom on her own seems pretty scary to me."

"Being a mom didn't have anything to do with it. She didn't stay for me. She stayed for her own selfish reasons."

"You sure about that? It seems pretty selfless to sacrifice your own happiness to stay in a bad relationship and try to make it work. To give your kid a real family." When she didn't look convinced, he added, "And sometimes it's just easier to run from the truth than stand and face it."

"Profound words from rodeo's biggest good-time cowboy."

He winked. "Just call me Dr. Phil."

A companionable silence engulfed them for the next few minutes as he watched her finish off her pancakes. A glimmer of sadness lit her eyes and he had the crazy urge to haul her into his arms and hug her tight until the look disappeared.

But he knew if he touched her, he wouldn't be able to stop. It had taken every ounce of strength not to finish what he'd started earlier that evening and his control was shaky at best.

"You're lucky she at least tried," he heard himself say, eager for something to distract himself from the sudden image of her naked and panting beneath him. "My dad never gave a lick about anyone other than himself, otherwise he would have straightened up his life and played by the rules. Folks call him a career criminal, but being a criminal isn't a career. It's a death sentence."

"What really happened that night?"

"He robbed a bank, went home, had too much to drink and fell asleep with a lit cigarette. End of story."

"Where were you?"

"Jesse had this part-time job at the training facility. He used to feed the bulls after school, shovel manure—that sort of thing. Jesse didn't want us going home without him, so he kept us at the training facility. When Silas drank, which was most of the time, he wasn't the nicest guy, and Jesse didn't want him beating the crap out of us."

"He doesn't sound like much of a man."

"He wasn't, but he was still our dad."

"It seems to me, Jesse was more like a dad to you."

Her words eased the tight feeling in his chest just a little.

Because she was right. Jesse had been more of a dad than Silas ever would. More of a man. A good man. Honest. Loyal. Trustworthy.

But then Jesse wasn't a carbon copy of their old man. *It's just hair, bro. You're nothing like him.*

That's what Jesse had told him too many times to count, whenever Billy stared into a mirror and saw his old man in his reflection, but he'd never let himself really believe it.

Until now.

Until Sabrina Collins looked deep in his eyes and said the very same thing.

There was just something about the conviction in her gaze, the sincerity, the compassion that hit a button deep inside him and made him think that he could be different. That he *was* different.

"I look just like him," he said, because old habits died hard and Billy had been reminding himself of the past far too long to stop now. "That's what everybody says."

"So? I look like my great-aunt Mildred, but I'm nothing like her." When he arched an eyebrow, she added, "She's a lesbian. She just moved in with her bingo partner and adopted a new cat. I'm not a cat person either.

I like dogs. Not that I have time for one, but when I do, I plan on getting a blue heeler."

"Heelers are great. Eli used to have a red heeler pup that always hung out at the training facility. Cole and I used to play with him while we were waiting for Jesse to finish up work. That, or we'd play Lego or Hot Wheels. Then we'd all walk home together."

"Were you together the night of the fire?"

He nodded. "Jesse finished up late and we were a good hour past our usual time. Otherwise, that night was just like any other until we saw the flames. We knew it was our house that was burning even before we got close." His gaze caught and held hers. "We just knew."

Ask him.

Ask him when? Where? What? Why? How?

There were so many unanswered questions and this was the chance she'd been waiting for. Her opportunity to get the inside scoop. There had been dozens of reports on what had happened to Silas Chisholm and the money he'd stolen, but no interviews with the actual witnesses. The Chisholm brothers had answered all the police's questions, but they'd never given an actual one-on-one to the press.

And they never would.

Which made this moment all the more valuable.

Billy was talking freely about that night, opening up to her. All she had to do was ask the really tough questions and she could write an exposé that would lead her to a real journalism career and stir up the past for all three of the Chisholm brothers yet again.

And while Billy didn't seem all that upset to be walking memory lane, she didn't miss the tight lines around his mouth or the sudden tensing of his shoulder muscles, or the fear that flickered deep in the depths of his gaze.

For all his bravado, the past pained him. And damned if she could make herself probe the wound.

"Wow," she blurted, stuffing a forkful of pancake into her mouth and killing her one shot. Surprisingly, that fact didn't bother her nearly as much as it should have. Because she wasn't cut out to be a journalist? She didn't know. She only knew that now wasn't the time to figure it out. She had more important things to worry about. Like Billy. And the hurt she'd glimpsed. "These are really good. You have a recipe?"

"No, but I could teach you." He eyed her. "That is, if you want to learn."

And where she'd avoided the kitchen her entire life because it reminded her of her mother, suddenly whipping up a batch of pancakes with hot, hunky Billy Chisholm didn't seem all that bad. Especially since it chased the fear from his gaze and filled it with a hopeful glimmer.

She smiled. "It's about time I learned how to make something other than ramen noodles."

17

"THIS ISN'T PART of our agreement." Sabrina stood on the front porch of Billy's cabin later that morning and stared at the black-and-white horse he'd just walked from the barn.

He tipped his hat back and the devil danced in his gaze. "How's that?"

"For one thing, it's daytime. Morning, to be exact, and I don't do mornings."

"I'll be busy tonight winning this rodeo, so just think of this as a schedule change."

"I wasn't planning on a schedule change, but suppose I go with it. Our agreement still doesn't state anything about riding horses." Or making pancakes, or laughing and talking until the sun came up about his life growing up on the Gunner spread and her life in Sugar Creek. But they'd done it anyway, and she'd enjoyed every moment. "It's all about sex."

"Trust me," he murmured, the early-morning sun bathing him in a bright light that made him seem even darker and more dangerous, "so is this." Billy winked. "We're riding double."

"So we will be fooling around?"

His grin was a slash of white beneath the brim of his hat. "That's the plan."

"Really? Because it's been four days." The grin widened and she stiffened. "Not that I've been, um, counting."

"Actually, it's been four days, three hours and fifty-two minutes." She arched an eyebrow and his expression went serious. "I've been the one counting."

Her heart did a double thump and the butterflies started to flutter low in her belly. "So, um, how exactly is this going to work?"

"Well, I'll be in back and you'll be in front." He let the words hang between them for a long moment. "Use your imagination, sugar."

"What if I fall off?"

"I've never lost a partner yet."

"Meaning, you've done this before?"

"Ridden a horse? Yes." His gaze darkened for a split second and a serious note touched his expression. "Riding double? No. You'll be the first." The look went from serious to seductive. "But I've thought about it a time or two." His eyes twinkled. "Or three."

"And here I thought you spent your time dreaming about PBR titles."

"I did up until I met you."

His words sent a burst of warmth through her that crumbled her defenses. She glanced down at the oversize T-shirt she wore. The soft cotton hit her below the hips. Beyond that, her legs and feet were bare. "I'll have to get dressed—"

"You're fine just like that." He stared at her as if he could see the slinky undies beneath. "The less you have on, the better."

If the words weren't enough to convince her, the hungry look on his face left no doubt that the next few hours would, indeed, be all about sex.

A shiver worked its way through her, along with something else. A rush of hesitation, because despite his words, this wasn't just sex. The past few hours, even the past few days, had changed things between them. Upped the stakes.

"You're not scared, are you?" Challenge fueled his words and lured her down the steps, when every ounce of sanity told her to climb into her car and get while the getting was good. That, and he was smiling at her. And she had a really, *really* hard time thinking straight when he smiled like that.

"Of you? Hardly."

He threw a blanket over the horse's back. "So prove it."

The words hung between them for a long moment before she gathered her courage and closed the distance between them. She planted both hands on her hips and stared up at him. "So how do I do this?"

He held out a hand. "Just put your foot in the stirrup and I'll pull you up."

She slipped her hand into his. "I hope you have a heavy-duty insurance policy that covers passengers."

"No insurance, but I'd be happy to kiss away any bruises if you get hurt." He hauled her up in front of him and nudged the horse.

They jerked forward and Sabrina grabbed Billy's thighs to keep from teetering to the side.

"Easy." The word whispered through her ear as they trotted forward, and Sabrina clutched him tighter.

"I don't think she heard you," she said over her shoulder.

"I wasn't talking to the horse. I was talking to you." He held the reins with one hand, and moved the other to cover her fingers, which dug into his blue-jean-clad leg. "Relax, sugar." He touched her, his fingers warm and strong and reassuring.

They rounded the cabin and started for the open pasture up ahead. For the next several minutes, Billy kept them moving at a steady walk and Sabrina managed to relax her grip.

"This isn't so bad—*whoaaaaa!*" They pitched forward as he urged the horse to a trot.

Her heart lodged in her throat for the first few moments. But soon, she grew used to the steady pace and her body relaxed. Her grip on his thighs loosened until her hands rested easy on either side and she actually started to enjoy herself.

The wind whipped at her face, catching the edge of her T-shirt and sneaking beneath the soft material to tease her bare skin. She became acutely aware of the powerful thighs that framed hers, his chest a solid wall of muscle and strength behind her.

"Why don't you take the reins." The deep voice in her ears caused her to shiver. Without waiting for a reply, he urged the leather straps into her hands and she found herself steering the horse. "Just remember to keep your grip firm but not tight. And don't jerk. You'll scare her if you do that."

"What if I want to stop?"

"We're not stopping until we're done." She had the sneaking suspicion that he was talking about more than just the ride.

A few frantic heartbeats later, he touched her thigh and she knew she'd been right. His palm burned into her flesh and her grip faltered.

Billy's other hand closed over hers, urging her fingers tight around the leather until he had a proper grip again.

"Focus," he told her.

"You try focusing in a thong."

Laughter rumbled in her ears and danced along her nerve endings in a seductive caress that made her entire body tingle. "I guess that would make it a little difficult."

"More like hot. Is your bottom supposed to burn like this?"

"You have to rise and fall with the horse. Feel the motion with your thighs and let it guide you."

She spent the next few minutes doing her best to tune into the horse. But the only thing she seemed aware of was the way Billy's hands splayed on her bare thighs.

His hardness pressed into her bottom, proof that he'd meant every word he'd said—this was about sex.

If only it felt like sex.

"This isn't right," she murmured out loud before she could stop herself.

"You're trying too hard," he told her. "Just feel the animal and think about something else. Think about me and what I'm doing to you."

"You're not doing anything."

"Not yet."

His fingers made lazy circles on the inside of her thigh and Sabrina's insides tightened. The movement continued for an endless moment before he urged the animal a little faster. The horse picked up the pace even more and so did Billy. His fingers swept higher, his touch more intense as he moved beneath the edge of the T-shirt and higher until he was an inch shy of the moist heat between her legs.

"See," he murmured against her ear, his deep voice gliding over her nerve endings. "You're doing it. You're moving with the horse. Can you feel it?"

The only thing she felt was him. Surrounding her. Filling her senses. Her heart pounded and her nipples tingled and she could barely think, much less form a reply.

"Sabrina? Are you with me?"

Boy, was she ever, she realized when his thumb brushed her clitoris through the thin lace of her thong and sensation speared, hot and jagged, through her body.

She would have dropped the reins if Billy's hand

hadn't been fastened around hers, guiding the horse when all rational thought flew south to the pulsing between her legs.

"You're so wet." His word were more of a groan as he dipped a finger beneath the edge of her undies and touched her slick folds. "So hot and wet and…" His voice faded into the pounding of her heart and the buzz of excitement that filled her ears.

She tilted her head back, resting in the curve of his shoulder as she surrendered herself to the ecstasy beating at her sanity and let him take control, of the horse and her body.

He slid a finger deep inside her and the air bolted from her lungs. He moved with the horse and so did she, shifting just so, riding his fingers the way the two of them rode the animal.

Her body grew tight and hot. The pressure built with each stroke, every thrust, until a cry broke past her lips. Her climax hit her hard and fast, like a zap of lightning that shook her to the bone. Shudders racked her. The blood hummed in her ears.

The horse seemed to slow with her heartbeat, until they moved at a slow, easy walk. Sabrina had never felt as relaxed as she did at that moment with Billy's arms around her, his heart beating at a steady tempo against her back.

The sun blazed high in the sky by the time they topped a small ridge and found themselves overlooking an endless stretch of green grass that gave way to a winding creek.

"It's pretty, isn't it?" he said.

"Very. Is this your favorite spot?"

"It used to be. Actually, this is the first time I've ridden over this way since I've been back. My brothers and I used to come out here to fish."

"Before or after you went to live at the Gunner Ranch?"

"Both. At first, we did it because we had to. But even after Pete took us in, I'd still ride up here every once in a while and throw out a line." His arm slid around her waist and held her. "Jesse hates coming out here because he says it reminds him of all those tough times. But I never really saw it like that. This place reminds me of my brothers and how close we always were." He neared the creek and brought the horse to a stop. "Come on." He slid down and turned to pull her after him.

"What are we doing?" she asked as her feet settled in the lush grass.

"Getting wet." He pulled his own T-shirt up and over his head and walked toward the grassy bank.

She followed. "I think I already beat you to the punch."

His grin was infectious. "Then it's time for me to catch up." He unfastened his jeans and pushed them down in one fell swoop until he stood completely naked. He fished a condom from his pocket and sheathed himself in one deft motion before he turned to her. He grabbed her hand and pulled her close to help lift the T-shirt up and over her head. He pushed her undies down, gliding the lace over her skin until it pooled at her ankles and she stepped free. And then he hauled her into his arms for a kiss that sent a flood of moisture between her already damp thighs.

Sweeping her up into his arms, he waded out into the water and walked toward the small waterfall coming off the cliff above.

A heartbeat later, the cool water rushed over them like a soothing shower, killing the heat of what promised to be another scorching Texas day.

But the relief didn't last long because he pulled her close and then they were kissing again, his hard body pressed to hers, his mouth plundering hers. He moved them deeper into the waterfall, beyond the constant stream of water into the small opening that sat behind the curtain of water.

He urged her legs up on either side of him and lifted her, hoisting her up until his thick erection rested between her slick folds. His large hands cradled her bottom as his mouth shifted to her nipple. His hot tongue flicked the ripe tip and her moan split open the peaceful quiet.

He teased the ripe peak, licking her over and over. Soon his lips closed around her areola and he sucked her so long and deep that she thought she would come apart right then and there. She tilted her head back

He worked her up and down his erection, the friction making her gasp.

With one hand braced on his shoulder, she reached down between them with her other and touched him.

He was hot and heavy and she wanted to feel him inside even more than she wanted her next breath.

"Now. Please."

His grip on her buttocks tightened as he lifted her a few inches, braced himself and thrust deep inside.

Billy ground his teeth against the overwhelming heat that gripped his throbbing erection. Holy hell, she was hot. And tight. And juicy. He closed his eyes and drank in a deep draft of air, determined to gather his control.

But he had none left.

What little he had had been spent that morning, making pancakes and doing his damnedest not to touch her. To take her.

He'd wanted to give her some distance, some space to see if she felt the way he did.

If she actually liked him as much as he liked her.

She did.

He'd seen it in her smile when he'd asked how the website was going. Heard it in her voice when she'd told him about Melba and Sarah Jean, and how she really wanted to help both women find that someone special even though they weren't her usual demographic. Felt it when she'd told him how much she appreciated him sharing his secret pancake recipe.

She liked him and while he wasn't one hundred percent certain she was ready to admit it, she still felt it.

And that was enough.

It had to be enough because his time was running out. The realization had hit him when Eli had called to give him the night's line-up for the finals. Tonight.

Tonight was his chance at a local championship, the first step toward making the finals in Vegas and winning the overall championship to become PBR's best. That's what he really wanted. The one and only thing that had ever really mattered to him. But at the moment, he couldn't think beyond the fact that the rodeo ended tonight, and so did their agreement.

And while he hoped like hell she'd come to realize how she felt about him enough to keep seeing him for a little longer, he wasn't going to miss his one sure shot to be in her arms again.

And now she was here, beneath him, pulsing all around him.

She lifted her hips, urging him deeper and he lost his mind. He backed her up against the slick rock wall of the cave and rode her hard, one arm braced on the wall behind her head, the other holding her close as he plunged deeper, faster, until she grasped his shoulders and moaned again.

A rumble worked its way from deep in his chest as he buried himself fast and sure and deep one final time. He bucked, spilling himself while her insides clenched and unclenched around him.

He gathered her close then, holding her tight as his heart threatened to burst from his chest. The water rushed in the background, masking the frantic in and out of his breath as he fought for oxygen. And his sanity.

A losing battle with her so warm and sweet and close.

Losing? Hell, he'd lost the moment he'd first spotted her at the kickoff dance. He'd lost his head.

And his heart.

The realization hit as he drank in another deep breath and tried to think about the rodeo that night and the bull Eli had said he'd drawn. And damned if he could remember exactly which one it was.

Damned if he cared.

Once he'd calmed down long enough to move, he carried her back under the rushing water and out into the waist-deep river. He walked up onto the riverbank and stretched her out on the soft grass. The sunlight spilled over her, bathing her in a warmth that was palpable. Her eyes were closed, her face flushed. Her lips were pink and swollen from his kisses. Her creamy breasts were tight, the nipples a bright rosy pink. A smooth strip of silky hair bisected the vee between legs that were long and slim, her calves shapely, her feet dainty as they rested on the soft green grass.

He'd pictured her like this so many times, so open and naked and *his*. But nothing he'd cooked up in his imagination had been quite as good as the real thing.

This he could touch, smell, feel.

He reached out and traced one nipple.

Her eyelids fluttered open and she smiled up at him. "I think I like this place."

"Glad to hear it." He leaned over and dropped a kiss on the tip of her nose. "Really glad to hear it."

She smiled and the picture she made burned into his memory and made him think that maybe, just maybe, winning the finals wasn't all it was cracked up to be.

This… *This* was what snagging the top prize felt like.

And where he'd recognized before that he felt something different for her, he hadn't grasped just how different until her lips parted and she smiled at him.

Because this wasn't just like.

This was the real thing.

Blinding, dazzling, mind-blowing *love*.

Not that it changed anything.

Because while he knew she felt something for him, he also knew that it wasn't enough to make her stay. While he'd finally accepted that just because he looked like his old man and had a few of his traits, he wasn't the same rat bastard who'd chosen a life of crime over being a father.

He wasn't his dad.

Any more than Sabrina was her mom.

The trouble was, she didn't realize that and there was no guarantee that she ever would.

She was leaving. He knew it. He felt it when she reached up and touched his face, as if memorizing every contour.

And there wasn't a damn thing he could do about it.

18

"BILLY AIN'T HERE," said the old man as he came around the corner of a bull chute at the rodeo grounds later that morning.

It was almost noon on Saturday after the hottest morning of her life.

And the most jarring.

Something had happened between them. Something big.

Billy Chisholm had lost his precious control, and while a small part of her rejoiced, her brain kept telling her that she was in trouble. Big trouble.

Because a small part of her was rejoicing.

Sabrina ignored the strange warmth zipping up and down her spine and concentrated on the old cowboy standing in front of her. "I'm not looking for Billy." She gave Eli an assessing glance. "I'm looking for you."

"Me? Hells bells, what do you want with me?"

"I want you to fill out a profile for my website."

"You might have hypnotized all the other cowboys

around here with that nonsense, but I ain't fallin' for it. Why, it ain't natural to meet a woman on a computer. Whatever happened to good, old-fashioned courtin'? Meetin' at the Piggly Wiggly and gettin' a whiff of her perfume in the vegetable section? Or watchin' her smile while we share a banana split at the Dairy Freeze? Or holdin' her hand while we head for the church picnic? Why, I ain't had a good mess of potato salad since I don't know when."

"You can still do all of that after you fill out a profile. A profile is the first step to meet someone. Then she emails you and you email her and bam, you hit the picnic grounds. Or the Senior Sweetheart Dance," she added, anxiety racing through her as she glanced at her watch. It was Saturday at noon and she had less than seven hours to find Melba a date. She'd gotten the idea for Eli after paying yet another visit to the senior center and realizing that her choices were severely limited. And then she'd thought of Billy and how much he thought of the old man who'd been like a grandfather to him. And just like that, the idea had popped into her head.

"I ain't messin' with no computer." Eli shook his head. "Can't stand the thing as it is. I told Pete not to go all electronic out at the ranch, but he didn't listen. Now every time there's a lightnin' storm, I can't print out an invoice for a decent order of bull semen. Tried writin' the damned thing, but Pete told me it has to be in the system. System, my ass. It's bull semen, for heaven's sake. Nature's moneymaker. It ain't natural that we're all so damned dependent on technology. Why, if a zombie apocalypse wipes us out, we're all screwed."

"What did you just say?"

"I said we're screwed."

"Before that."

"Dependent on technology?"

"After that."

"Zombie apocalypse?"

"Bingo." While Eli seemed like the last person for Melba, that one statement had zapped a connection between them. Even more, Sabrina had a gut feeling that it would work.

"So forget the computer and just let me set you up on an actual date."

"I can do that?"

"Sure. I can take care of all the details. I've got someone perfect in mind. You can pick her up and take her on a real outing. No pictures or email required."

"Who are we talking about?"

"Her name is Melba Rose and—"

"No." He shook his head. "That woman's got a few screws loose and I ain't going to be the one what gets stuck with her at the dance. Do you know she cried last year when she didn't win queen? Broke down and bawled like a baby. No sirree, not me. I ain't gettin' stuck with no crying woman."

"But I have a good source that tells me she's a shoo-in for queen this year. That means no crying."

"Are you freakin' kiddin' me? The happy cryin' is even worse than the sad cryin'. Women 'round here freak out for everything. That's why I been single all these years."

"Well, if that's the way you want it." She shrugged. "But I hear she makes a mean potato salad."

That seemed to get his attention. "She does?"

"Prize-winning," Sabrina assured him, barely resisting the urge to cross her fingers. She hated to lie, but she was desperate. At the same time, maybe she wasn't lying. Maybe Melba did make a mean potato salad. Sabrina grasped at the hope and went in for the kill. "I heard she even took first place over at the Mason County potato festival."

"Mason County? Whereabouts is that?"

Sabrina wasn't actually sure since she'd just made it up, but desperate times called for desperate measures. She'd said it, and now it was just a matter of going with the flow and following through. "It's up around Dallas or Waco or something like that."

"Mason County, you say?" He seemed to think. "Why, I think I went to a rodeo out there once. They host an annual potato festival, you say?"

"*The* potato festival. The biggest in Texas."

"And Melba walked away with first place for her potato salad?"

"And her hash browns."

"You don't say?"

"Cross my heart." She tamped down on the guilt that swore she was a terrible person for getting an old man's hopes up. But then she'd already gotten Melba's hopes up, too, and she couldn't very well let the woman show up stag to her big night. Besides, all she had to do was pick up a few pints of potato salad at a nearby barbecue joint and Eli would be a happy camper.

Two birds with one stone.

"So are you in?"

"So long as we eat before the dance. Potato salad *and* hash browns."

"They'll be ready and waiting."

The Piggly Wiggly didn't have a deli section which meant that Sabrina had all of four hours to make potato salad and hash browns, and deliver them both to Melba's house before Eli arrived to pick her up at 6:00 p.m.

Worse, she'd never cooked up a batch of potato salad in her life. And the hash browns? A great, big, fat *never*. She had no clue how to do either.

But she knew someone who did.

"Hello?" said a familiar voice after Sabrina hit the call button on her cell phone.

"Mom?"

"Sabrina? Is that you?" Surprise morphed into concern and Sabrina's chest tightened. It had been so long since her last phone call and she could only imagine the horrifying possibilities that would prompt a phone call running through her mother's mind. "Is everything all right?"

"Fine. Sort of. I mean, I do have a problem, but nothing bad."

"What is it? What's wrong?"

"I need to make potato salad."

"Excuse me?"

"And hash browns. And I know you know how to do both, so I thought you might help me out."

"You're cooking?"

"Only because of extenuating circumstances," she blurted, eager to kill the hopeful note in her mother's voice. "I don't really *want* to do it, but I promised someone and I need to follow through." That or she could kiss goodbye any hope that Eli would take Melba to the sweetheart dance.

"Well," her mother's voice carried over the line, "I do have a really good recipe."

But then Sabrina already knew that. Her mother had been the queen of the kitchen, busying herself for hours to avoid the fact that she was waiting for a man who didn't have the courtesy to even call.

Waiting.

Or maybe that had just been her way of dealing with the situation. Of trying to hold on when all she really wanted to do was let go.

The thought struck and try as she might, Sabrina couldn't push it back out. She'd never really talked to her mother about the hows and whys of her relationship with Sabrina's father. She'd never wanted to. It had been easier to point the finger at someone else than to realize that maybe her father had left because neither one of them had been worth staying for. Not her mother.

And not Sabrina.

Of course, she was all grown up now. Enough to know that her father had been the one at fault. But back then she'd wondered. And worried. And so she'd made up her mind to change. To put as much distance between herself and the woman on the other end of the phone so that she could honestly say she was nothing like Arlene Collins. She'd wanted to be different. To be the sort of woman that a man could love.

A man like Billy.

She nixed the thought and focused on the phone in her hand. "Why didn't you leave?" she voiced the one question that had haunted her so many nights as an adult.

"Excuse me?"

"I don't understand. All those years you wasted on a man who didn't return your feelings. Why?"

"I didn't waste those years. I spent them raising you, loving you. Maybe I should have left, but I just kept thinking of what my own mother and father always believed—that a child deserved both parents. Good or bad. At least they were there. I just wanted you to have a complete family."

And there it was. Billy had been right. Her mother hadn't stayed because she'd been weak. Because she'd feared being alone. Rather, she'd feared disappointing Sabrina.

"Your father wasn't perfect," her mother went on. "I knew that when I married him, but he always made so many promises. Boy, the man could talk. Of course, back then I thought it was more than talk. I hoped it was more. And so I gave him a chance. I gave our family a chance."

"At your own expense. You were miserable."

"It wasn't so bad. I had you." She heard the tears in her mother's voice and it made her own eyes burn.

"I'm sorry, Mom. Sorry that you tried so hard only to be disappointed."

"The only disappointment is that you don't get around to seeing me more. I miss you."

The words echoed in Sabrina's ears and filled her with a rush of warmth that pushed away the cold resentment she'd felt for so many years. "I miss you, too, Mom," she murmured.

"Well, now," Arlene sniffled as if desperate to hide a rush of emotion, "About that recipe…"

SABRINA PULLED TO A stop in front of Billy's cabin a half hour later and sent up a silent thank-you that he wasn't there. He had a full afternoon before the finals tonight, from meetings with the rodeo commissioner and the board of directors, to a special TV segment featuring the best of the best, which meant he wouldn't be back until tonight.

Sabrina intended to be long gone by then.

Their time together had ended and while she wasn't quite finished with her business here in Lost Gun— they still had to pick up five final cowboys to meet their quota and Sabrina needed to match up Sarah—she was finished with Billy.

Tonight was the finals. The end of the road.

She ignored the depressing thought and focused on pulling all of the groceries from the backseat. Inside, she headed for the kitchen and started prepping her potatoes.

"You're doing what right now?" Livi asked when Sabrina answered her cell a few minutes later.

"I'm helping out a friend."

"You're hooking up those old women."

"No, I'm not." She was *trying* to hook them up. Big difference. "So where are you?"

"At the saloon. I'm about to pop the top on a bottle of Redneck Rosé."

"Since when do you drink Redneck Rosé?"

"Since it's the closest thing they've got to a bottle of champagne. I got the last handful of profiles."

"No way."

"Way. I spent the morning at the donut shop out near the interstate. You wouldn't believe the number of men who eat donuts at six a.m."

"Cowboys?"

"Every single one of them. That hunky booty call of yours sent them over from the rodeo arena."

"Billy?"

"The one and only. They said he paid them ten bucks each to fill out a profile."

"He what?"

"He paid them and while that violates our strict policy of not soliciting, it doesn't count because we weren't the ones dishing out the cash. So it's all good." Her voice rose an excited octave. "We did it, Sabrina. We're going to get our financing."

"That's great."

So why didn't it feel great?

The question niggled at her for the rest of the afternoon, along with the fact that Billy had paid a handful of cowboys to help her out.

Because he was anxious to send her on her way?

That's what she wanted to think, but she couldn't help but wonder if there was more to it than that.

If maybe, just maybe, he'd done it because he knew how important this was to her.

Because he loved her?

She dismissed the crazy thought.

No way did Billy Chisholm love her. Not that she would recognize the emotion if she saw it coming at her like a freight train. She'd never seen it between her own parents. Never felt it herself.

No, he knew their time together had drawn to a close and he was anxious to send her on her way. Paying off a few cowboys had been the easiest way to do it. Which meant she was going to get a move on, follow the recipes her mother had given her, and get the hell out of his kitchen.

And then in less than twenty-four hours, she was going to leave Lost Gun—and Billy Chisholm—for good.

"HE'S GONE." Billy heard Jesse's voice just outside the closed doorway to the dressing area where he was pulling on his chaps. "You can't talk to him."

"But he promised me an interview."

"About the rodeo," Jesse said. "You want to talk about our dad and that's not happening right now."

"So will you talk to me about Silas?" The familiar voice carried inside and Billy recognized Curt Calhoun, the reporter from the "Where Are They Now?" episode. "You can't expect people to seriously believe that you guys don't know anything about the bank heist. You had to see something? Hear something? What about the money? Surely he mentioned the money? Maybe even slipped a little out of the way before the fire? There was an entire ten hours between the robbery and the fire."

Plenty of time to hightail it out to Big Earl's, give the old man the money, and head back home to celebrate with too much liquor. Which was exactly what Silas had done.

Or so Jesse believed.

But they'd yet to recover the money. Instead, they'd been digging hole after hole, and Billy was starting to think that maybe, just maybe Big Earl and his great-granddaughter were trying to pull a fast one. A ploy to get money out of Jesse and his brothers.

That, or maybe they were after a story of their own.

A way to make a fast buck.

That's what logic told him, but Jesse seemed so damned sure. And while Billy had a hard time putting his faith in Big Earl and Casey, he trusted his oldest brother.

"I'll catch up to him eventually," Curt promised. "You know that. And then I'll ask him all the questions I'm asking you."

"I know, but it won't be tonight. He's got a rodeo to win."

Damn straight he did.

Billy pulled on his shirt and concentrated on snapping the buttons. But with every button, he thought of Sabrina and the way she'd popped off his shirt and slid it down his shoulders and—

Concentrate.

Tonight was all about the ride, not the woman he'd left at home.

Unfortunately, he couldn't help but wonder if she was still there, or if she'd gone back to her motel, or if she was actually sitting in the stands waiting for the bull riding to start.

"Sabrina's here with me," Eli told him when the old man called his cell to wish him good luck.

"And where exactly are you?"

"Picking up Melba. We've got a date for the Sweetheart Dance."

"I thought you were going to be here at the arena?"

"I've taught you everything I know. You're on your own, son. Now if you don't mind, I've got a plate of potato salad calling my name."

"But—"

Click.

So much for Sabrina waiting in the stands, eager for a glimpse of him. She wasn't here, and she wasn't coming, and Billy needed to cowboy up and get on with it.

He *knew* that.

But damned if he could stifle the disappointment that rushed through him as he opened the door and joined Jesse for the short walk to the main arena.

19

LATER THAT NIGHT, after an evening spent spying on
Queen Melba and Eli as they twirled around the dance
floor at the Sweetheart Dance, Sabrina pulled up in
front of the motel to find Billy's pickup parked in her
usual spot.

Her gaze swiveled to the man who leaned against her
door, arms folded as he waited for her. Her heart jumped
into her throat as she drank in the sight of him. He wore
a sleeveless white T-shirt with Eight Seconds and Then
Some emblazoned in liquid blue. Faded jeans hugged
his thighs and calves. Worn brown cowboy boots com-
pleted the outfit. His muscular arms were folded, his
expression serious as he waited for her. He looked hot
and incredible sexy and...worried?

Her pulse quickened and heat uncurled low in her
belly as she slid from the driver's seat. Billy pushed
away from the door as she started up the walk toward
him.

"What are you—"

"You missed the finals," he cut in. His brows knit together and his mouth pulled into a tight line. "You weren't there."

"I didn't see the point. Our business is—" She meant to say *finished,* but he didn't give her the chance.

He pulled her into his arms and hauled her up against his chest. His mouth covered hers. Strong hands pressed the small of her back, holding her close as he kissed her long and slow and deep. He smelled of soap and fresh air and a touch of wildness that teased her nostrils and made her breathe heavier, desperate to draw more of his essence into her lungs.

Excuse me? a voice prodded. *This is a bad idea. A really bad idea. The purpose of missing the finals was to avoid him. Kissing him is hardly an effective avoidance technique.*

She *knew* that, but he was so close and he smelled so good and she'd missed him so much.

"I can't stop thinking about you," he murmured when he finally tore his lips from hers. "I thought about you all afternoon and tonight. And I still won." He seemed surprised by the fact. "I *won.*"

"That's really great." She couldn't help the rush of warmth or the smile that tugged at her lips.

"It is," he said, the words more for himself than her. "But it doesn't *feel* great." His gaze collided with hers. "Not half as great as this." He kissed her again, fast and urgent, the way he'd done at the waterfall. "As you," he murmured when he finally pulled away. "I want you so bad."

Want.

That's what his sudden appearance was all about.

He was here for one thing and one thing only. Because his body drove him. It didn't go beyond sex as far as he was concerned. It never would. Even if he did seem different from the smooth-talking charmer who'd approached her that first night.

Honest. Sincere.

There's no such thing for his kind.

That's what she told herself, but she just couldn't make herself believe it. Not with her lips tingling from his kiss and her body buzzing with desire and her heart aching from the fact that she really *had* missed him. Sure, it had only been a few hours, but it felt like more.

Like a lifetime.

Anxiety rushed through her, heightened by the truth that echoed in her head.

This was it.

Her last night in town. Their last night.

And while an encore wasn't part of the agreement, ending things now before she'd had a chance to really say goodbye seemed like the worst idea ever.

She slid her arms around his neck, leaned up on her tiptoes and touched her mouth to his.

The kiss that followed was hot and wild and consuming. Her head started to spin and her heart pounded faster. He tasted of impulse and danger and a touch of desperation that made her chest tighten and her heart ache. As if he needed this as much as she did.

Her hands snaked around his neck and she leaned

into him, relishing the feel of his body pressed flush against hers.

He pulled free long enough to sweep her up into his arms and carry her inside. A few minutes later, they were inside her motel room. He let her feel every inch of his hot, aroused body as he eased her to her feet.

They faced each other then, and she knew he was waiting for her to make the next move, to show him that she wanted this, too.

She unbuttoned her blouse and let it slide from her shoulders. Trembling fingers worked at the catch of her bra and freed her straining breasts. She unbuttoned her skirt and worked it down her legs. Her panties followed, until she was completely naked.

He didn't reach out. He simply looked at her, yet it felt as if his hot hand traveled the length of her body along with his gaze. His violet eyes were dark and deep and smoldering as they touched on every hot spot—her neck, her nipples, the vee between her legs, the tender flesh of her thighs. Desire rushed through her, sharp and demanding, and she reached for him.

She gripped his T-shirt and urged it up and over his head. Her fingers went to the waistband of his jeans. She slid the button free and her knuckles grazed his bare stomach. He drew in a sharp breath, and then another, when she slid the zipper down and her thumb trailed over his hard length.

She hooked her fingers in the waistband of his briefs and tugged his jeans and underwear down with one motion. His massive erection sprang hot and greedy toward her.

She touched him, tracing the bulge of his veins and cupping his testicles. He throbbed at her touch and a surge of feminine power went through her—so opposite the crazy weakness she'd feared for so long.

She relished the feel of him for a few fast, furious heartbeats before he seemed to reach his limit. He drew her near and captured her mouth with his own. He drew the breath from her body with a hungry kiss that made her knees tremble and her hands shake and her head spin. A mix of desperation and desire fueled her response as she met him thrust for thrust, lick for lick, losing herself in the feel of him so close. A moment later, he pressed her back against the bed.

"Don't close your eyes," he murmured. "I want to know how much you like it when I touch you. How much you want me to touch you." He settled beside her and trailed his hand down the side of her neck, the dip at her collarbone, the slope of one breast. "Do you like it when I touch you here?" With his fingertip, he traced the outline of her nipple and watched it tighten in response.

"Yes," she breathed, the word catching on a gasp.

Her nerves came alive as he moved his hand down her abdomen to the strip of hair that bisected her sex. One rasping touch of his callused fingertip against her swollen flesh and she arched up off the bed. She caught her bottom lip and stifled a cry.

With a growl, he spread her wide with his thumb and forefinger and touched and rubbed as he dipped his head to draw on her nipple. Sensation speared her, and she had to fight to keep her eyes open. But she managed. She fixed her gaze on the blond head at her breast and trailed her hands over his shoulders, committing every ripple, every bulge to memory.

Desperate to keep him with her long after she left town.

When he slid a finger deep, deep inside, she moaned. Her fingertips tightened on his shoulders, digging into the hard, muscular flesh.

"You're so wet," he said, leaning back to stare down at her, into her. "So freakin' *wet*."

"So are you." She reached between them and touched the pearl of liquid that beaded on the head of his erection nestled against her thigh. She spread the liquid around the rock-hard shaft and watched his gaze darken.

"If you don't stop touching me, this is going to go a hell of a lot faster than I anticipated."

"I like it fast, and out of control." The words tumbled out of her mouth before she could stop them. "I like *you* out of control."

He shifted and reached for his jeans. His fingers dove into one of the pockets and he pulled out a condom.

Driven by her need for him, she took the latex and tore open the package. She eased the contents over the head of his smooth, pulsing shaft. He pulsed in her hands and hunger gripped her.

She spread her legs and waited as he settled between them. The head of his penis pushed a delicious fraction into her. Pleasure pierced her brain and hummed along every nerve ending. She lifted her legs and hooked them around his waist, opening her body even more. He answered her unspoken invitation with a deep, probing thrust.

Her muscles convulsed around him, clutching him as he gripped her bare bottom and tilted her so that he could slide a fraction deeper, until he filled her completely. He thrummed inside her for a long moment as he seemed to fight for his precious control.

But Sabrina had already lost her own and she wasn't going to go over the edge without him. She lifted her hips, moved her pelvis, and rode him until he growled and gave in to the fierce heat that raged between them. He pumped into her, the pressure and the friction so sweet that it took her breath away.

She met his thrusts in a wild rhythm that urged him faster and deeper and… Yes. *Yes!*

Her lips parted and she screamed at the blinding force of the climax that crashed over her. Billy grasped her buttocks and held her tight as he plunged one last and final time. A groan ripped from his throat as he followed her over the edge.

BILLY COLLAPSED ON top of Sabrina, his face buried in the crook of her neck, her muscles still clenched tightly around him. He felt every quiver of her body, every delicious shudder, every erratic breath. Her heart pounded against the palm of his hand and a wave of possessiveness swept through him. He had the sudden, desperate urge to tighten his hold on her and never let go. Because she was his.

She'd always been his.

Always.

He gathered her close and focused on the steady beat of her heart for several long moments, letting it lull him and ease the exhaustion in his muscles. He was tired. So damned tired. But he'd needed this in the worst way. He'd needed her. He still did.

The seconds ticked by, sleep pulling them both under. But he wasn't ready to give in. Not yet. Not until…

"I love you," he whispered the words that burned inside of him.

Her heart didn't skip a beat as he held her close and he knew she was already asleep. It didn't matter. He had tomorrow to get his point across. Then she would realize they had something special and change her mind about leaving. And all would be right with his world.

If only things were really that simple.

But Billy had been dealt a shitty hand too many times to think that the woman of his dreams would simply throw herself into his arms and life would be set. Instead, he knew good and well that he was in for the fight of his life.

He didn't care.

Sabrina was worth it, and he intended to prove as much. He just hoped she didn't run for the hills before he had the chance.

20

I LOVE YOU.

The words echoed through Sabrina's head throughout Sunday morning, taunting her as she tried to concentrate on entering her last ten profiles. She had to get back on track and forget all about Billy and the fact that he loved her.

Just where did he get off loving her? He wasn't supposed to love her and she wasn't supposed to love him.

No matter how desperate and out of control he'd been at the river, or how he'd taught her to make pancakes, or how he'd held her and listened to her talk about her mother and her father and her past.

Her heart pounded double time and tears burned the backs of her eyes as she tried to concentrate on her computer keyboard and the stats of cowboy one hundred and sixty-one.

James Early Harwell. James liked the occasional glass of whiskey, old Westerns and dancing until dawn down at the local honky-tonk. He was a ranch foreman at a large spread about twenty miles outside of town. The salt-of-the-earth type and every bit as good-looking as Billy Chisholm.

The exact type that her mother had always had a weakness for.

Weak. That's why she'd landed in bed with Billy. Not because he was different or because she sensed there was more beneath the surface. A man who was honest and loyal and all of the things her own father had never been.

Sure, he'd kept his word and handed her a neatly typed profile last night as promised once their deal was done. But that merely proved what she knew deep in her gut—he was a player like all the others, eager to move on to the next conquest.

That, or it means he's a man who does what he says, who keeps his promises.

One of the few she'd ever known. One of a kind. Special—

Stop. Forget him. Forget that he loves you and forget that you love him.

She couldn't. She wouldn't.

She stared at Billy's profile. Her very last one and the ticket to satisfying her investor and launching the website in a major way.

Her fingers went to the keyboard and she mentally commanded them to type. To enter the stats and get it over with. Then it would be really and truly done and Billy would be just another of the masses. Another sweet-talking, sexy-as-all-get-out cowboy with a sweet-as-molasses drawl and enough charm to make even a saint blush. He was perfect for the website. All the more reason to get him entered and get it over with.

Type.

But she couldn't force her fingers to make contact. They wouldn't move and, truthfully, she didn't want them to move.

Because she cared about him. Because she loved him.

Denial rushed through her. No, she didn't love him. She was close…dangerously so. That's why she couldn't make herself enter his stats and throw him to the masses who would be cruising their website in a matter of days, searching for the cowboy of their dreams.

But she wasn't falling all the way, not head over heels, body, heart and soul, in love with Billy Chisholm. Love required trust, and as much as she wanted to, she just couldn't trust a man like him. She wouldn't.

She wouldn't do something so self-destructive as fall in love with a cowboy like Billy Chisholm. She'd come too far, struggled too hard to escape her past to wind up living it once again. Only this time, she would be the one barefoot and pregnant in the kitchen, whipping up the pancakes and waiting for her man to come home.

If only that last image stirred the same distaste that it once had.

"WHAT DO YOU MEAN you can't see me?" Billy demanded when he stomped into the diner at lunchtime, after a very heated phone conversation. He'd called to ask for a date, no doubt to discuss the bomb he'd dropped the night before. Of course, she'd turned him down.

And turned him down again when he'd called back the second time.

And the third time.

Now here was Billy himself, standing in front of her table, wearing a black T-shirt that read It's All About the Ride and faded jeans and an intense look that made her pulse leap.

"Let me rephrase that—I don't want to see you." There. She'd said it, despite inhaling his all-too-familiar and terribly sexy scent of warm male and leather and him. Her nostrils flared and her lungs filled, and Sabrina damned herself for being so weak.

She wasn't weak. She was holding her own, keeping up her defenses and getting the hell out of Dodge. Fast. Before any more of Melba Rose's friends approached her to find them dates and she found herself agreeing to yet another day in Lost Gun and, more important, before she gave in to the hunger inside her and kissed Billy until her toes curled.

"We need to talk—"

"About last night," she cut in, "I understand completely. You were worked up and so was I and you didn't mean to say what you said."

"Oh, I meant it, all right—"

"Oh, wow, would you look at that? I've got a meeting over at the senior center and I'm late," she screeched, sliding out of the booth and scooting past him as if she'd been zapped by lightning. "Look, you just run along and don't worry that I'm making more out of it than you meant. We all get a little crazed in the heat of the moment. Chemistry is a powerful thing. People mistake lust for love all the time. Just look at the divorce rate. Lust," she rushed on before he could say anything to shake her determination. "Last night was just a bad case of lust, but now it's sated and—"

"Is it?" he cut in, his gaze deep and searching, as if he struggled to see everything she was trying so hard to deny.

"Yes," she declared with as much bravado as she could muster, considering he smelled so good and she had this insane urge to press her head to his chest just to hear if his heart was beating as fast as hers. "It's definitely sated."

He eyed her for a long, breathless moment, and she knew he was going to argue with her. That, or throw her over his shoulder and tote her back to his cabin and make love to her over and over until she developed such a craving for him that she couldn't keep from loving him. And damned if a small part of her didn't want him to do just that. To take the decision out of her hands so that she didn't have to think, to worry, to be afraid of what she felt for him.

What she *almost* felt, she reminded herself. She wasn't there yet. She wasn't in love. Not with him. She *wasn't*.

As if he sensed the turmoil inside her, his fierce expression eased into his usual charming grin that made her that much more wary.

"Listen, I didn't want to tell you this, but I've been writing a story about you and your brothers and your dad. An exposé to launch my journalism career." Okay, so she'd *thought* about writing an exposé, but she hadn't been able to make herself actually do it. Not after hearing the pain in his voice when he'd spoken about his past. Even more, she'd realized she wasn't cut out to be a journalist if it meant stirring up a world of hurt for someone else. She'd always thought that being a big-time journalist would make her happy, but she'd come to realize that just being good at what she did— namely hooking up Melba—had brought her a sense of accomplishment unlike anything she'd ever felt. But Billy didn't know that, and she didn't intend to tell him. "That was the reason I agreed to your proposition. So that I could get close to you and get the real scoop."

He eyed her for a long moment. "So did you?"

"Did I what?"

"Get the scoop?"

"Not exactly, but that's beside the point. The point is I had an ulterior motive. It wasn't just lust. I was using you."

"Where's the story?"

On its way to CNN. That's what she wanted to say, to prove to him that she didn't really care about him. But there was something about the way he looked at her, as if she was *this close* to disappointing him, that blew a hole in her entire facade. She shrugged. "I decided not to write it." So much for pushing him away.

"Because?"

"Because it's over and done with. Silas is dead. The money is gone. Might as well let sleeping dogs lie."

"What if I told you it wasn't? What if I said the money was still out there and there's proof that Silas had a partner?"

She waited for the rush of excitement at the prospect, but the only thing she felt was the desperate urge to kiss him. "Someone else can write about it then."

Something softened in his expression and she damned herself for bringing up the past in the first place. She'd meant to push him away with the news.

If only it didn't feel as if she'd pulled him that much closer.

"Maybe I will write about it," she blurted, gathering up her purse. "Right after I head over to the senior center."

"If you're no longer in lust with me, then I don't have to worry about you jumping my bones while I walk you over."

"I don't need an escort."

"But I do. It's been forever since I've been there, so I thought you could lead the way. I promised Eli I would stop by and let Melba know that he'll pick her up at eight tonight." At her blank look, he added, "Her cell's not working right now and he's tied up at the training facility." He shrugged. "You're going and I'm going. We might as well walk together."

"No." She shook her head. "I can't." She put her purse back down beside her.

"So you're not going?"

"Of course I am. Later. After lunch." She eyed the half-eaten hamburger in front of her. "You just run along and do your business and I'll stop by later. I think that would work much better. I mean, our time together *is* over. Business concluded. You really should get on with your life, and I'm already zooming right ahead with mine."

"You're still here," he pointed out.

She thought of lying. Of telling him she was doing research to blow the roof off him and his family. But she knew he wouldn't buy it any more than she could sell it. She shrugged instead. "I'm only sticking around for one more week, just until I find a decent prospect for Melba's friend. The VFW has bingo on Friday nights. It's also senior-discount night, which means every available man over sixty-five will be there. I should hit pay dirt there if all else fails this week."

"So you're here strictly for Melba Rose?"

"I made a promise."

He eyed her for a long moment. "You're stubborn, you know that?"

"I'm confident, not stubborn. I just know what I want out of life, that's all."

"Let's hope." He winked before turning toward the door. "I'll see you around, sugar."

"Not if I see you first," she murmured to herself as he edged his way around a table and walked out of the diner.

It was all a matter of keeping her distance until she left town. Rationally, she knew that.

It was the irrational urge to run after him and throw herself into his arms that scared the crap out of her, and made her all the more determined *not* to love Billy Chisholm.

SHE LOVED HIM.

With any other woman, Billy might have had his doubts. After all, she'd ditched him last night and given him the brush-off just now. Talk about rejection.

But this was Sabrina.

Bold, sassy, sexy as hell and scared.

Business concluded, she'd said.

He might have believed her, except that he'd seen the wariness in her eyes, heard the desperation in her voice. There'd been none of the cool confidence of a woman completely uninvolved, none of the nonchalance of someone ready to turn her back and walk away because she didn't feel anything for him.

Even more, she was still here.

While he had no doubt that she meant to keep her promise to Melba's friend, he knew that was just an excuse to stick around. Because she wasn't half as sure about leaving as she'd been the night they'd met.

Yep, she loved him, all right, and so Billy had backed off when he'd wanted nothing more than to pull her close and never let go. He didn't want her to feel pressured or anxious or afraid.

He wanted her willing, sure, certain beyond a doubt.

That meant she had to come to terms with her feelings in her own time, and so he decided then and there that he wasn't going to press or push.

Not too much, that is.

He certainly wasn't going to hide away and bide his time and simply hope that she came to her senses. Billy had never been a patient man when it came to something he wanted, and he really wanted Sabrina Collins.

And she wanted him back.

Now and forever.

She just needed a little help admitting it.

_**21**_

"There's a word for this, you know," Sabrina said nearly a week after Billy's declaration, when she opened her motel room door to find him standing on her doorstep. Again.

The devil danced in his eyes as he grinned. "Dating?"

She ignored the thumping of her heart and glared. "Harassment. You've shown up every night this week." Every night at exactly the same time. So punctual she could have set her clock by him.

As if his presence, so tall and sexy and reliable, wasn't bad enough, he'd come bearing gifts. Monday he'd shown up with a dozen pink roses. Tuesday, he'd brought a box of chocolate-covered strawberries. Wednesday had been cupcakes from Sarah's bakery. Today?

She eyed the starched Wranglers and pressed Western shirt. He'd traded the frayed straw cowboy hat for a sleek black one, his boots shiny and polished. He handed her a clear florist's box with a wrist corsage nestled inside.

"What's this for?"

"The Elks are having their monthly dinner and dance. While most of the guys are married, there are a dozen or so who are widowers. They gather in the back once the band kicks up to play dominoes and shoot the shit." He shrugged. "I thought you might find a few prospects for Ethel."

"That's a great tip. I'll head over later on—"

"You can't get in without a ticket."

"I'll buy one."

"It's members only. Eli's taking Melba to a movie tonight, so he slipped me his." He waved the slips of paper. "If you want to go, you have to go with me."

"You could be a nice guy and give me one of your tickets."

"And sit home all by my lonesome while you have all the fun?" He shook his head. "Not happening."

She thought of her plans for that night—sitting in her usual booth at the diner, hoping and praying for a new face to come in for the dinner special. She'd met all of two single senior men over the past few days, and both had been spoken for. They'd been picking up dinner for their intended, which meant she needed a new plan.

"Okay, but this isn't a date. That means no funny business."

He arched an eyebrow, his sensual mouth hinting at a grin. "Define what you mean by funny?"

"I mean it, Billy. No funny business. No thinking about any funny business." He didn't look convinced, so she added, "You stay on your side of the truck and I stay on mine. Tonight we're just two friends accompanying one another to a dinner dance."

His grin widened. "Whatever you say."

"Promise me." Her heart pounded for several long seconds as she held his gaze. "Please," she finally added.

As if he sensed her desperation, his expression faded and he nodded. "Just friends."

"This is my friend, Sabrina Collins." Billy introduced Sabrina for the umpteenth time to one of the elderly couples standing near the punch table and she did her best not to frown.

They *were* just friends, she reminded herself.

Which meant it shouldn't bother her when he said the word. Or left her sitting alone to dance with Mrs. Meyers, the chairperson for the event. Or Mrs. Davenport, wife of the head Elk. Or Mrs. Carlisle, newly widowed and president of the senior ladies' crochet circle.

She watched Billy lead the small, round woman around the dance floor. Her silver hair piled high on top of her head in a monstrous beehive. Bright orange lipstick matched the blinding shades of her flower print dress and her white patent leather shoes gleamed in the dim lighting. With every turn, Sabrina glimpsed the top edge of her knee-high panty hose just below her hemline. On top of that, the woman was three times his age.

It's not like Sabrina had anything to be jealous of if they had been more than friends.

Which they weren't.

"Where's the domino group?" she asked the minute

he walked back to their table. "The band's playing so they should be out back by now, right?" She pushed to her feet. "Lead the way."

"I promised Miss Earline I'd dance with her first."

"Then point me in the right direction and then go dance with Miss Earline."

He eyed her for a long moment and a light twinkled in the depths of his eyes. "If I didn't know better, I'd say you're jealous. But then that would mean that you actually do care and you've made it clear that you don't."

"I'm not jealous, I'm anxious. I've got a lot of work waiting for me back in L.A. I need to get this done and get out of here."

He eyed her for a long moment before he seemed to come to some conclusion. "Follow me."

A few minutes later, she found herself smack-dab in the middle of man heaven. Senior man heaven, that is. There were two dozen widowers in Lost Gun. All eager to find the next Mrs. Right. Provided she could cook as good as Shirley, or clean as well as Bernice, or rub a pair of feet as well as Corrine—God rest her soul. Every single man gathered in the domino room wanted to find a woman, and while a few of them weren't too jazzed about that woman being Ethel, more than half were willing to give her a try.

Two hours later, Sabrina stood on the doorstep of her motel room, profiles in hand, and stared at the man who'd walked her to her room.

"Thanks for tonight." She stuck out her hand to shake his, desperate to keep the distance between them and end the evening before she surrendered to the waves of emotion inside her and plant one on his lips. "I wouldn't have even known about the dinner dance if it wasn't for you and I want you to know that I really appreciate everything."

He stared at her, into her. "I don't want your thanks."

Her hand fell away. "Please, Billy. Don't—"

"I want you."

"It could never work. You live here and I don't. I could never be happy in a place like this." Even if she had grown sort of fond of all the senior ladies that she'd met, and the strong black coffee they served up at the diner and even the chicken fried steak. "I don't belong here."

And then she turned and walked away from him, because after years of clinging to her newfound city ways and keeping her distance from the small-town girl she'd once been, she didn't know if she had the strength or the courage to let go.

Not that she wanted to. She was happy just the way she was.

Wasn't she?

SHE WAS HAPPY.

That's what she told herself the next day as she narrowed down her newfound prospects to the three most perfect matches for Ethel and tried to forget Billy and the way he'd made love to her so furiously at the river. The way he'd tried his best to woo her the past few days. The way he'd stayed close to her at the dinner, his hand at the small of her back, possessive yet comforting at the same time. The way he'd said "I want you" last night.

Distance, she told herself. Out of sight, out of mind.

Which was why she did her best to look the other way when he showed up at the Bingo Hall on Friday night.

With a date.

She eyed the plain young woman wearing a pair of jeans and a Western shirt. She wasn't at all what Sabrina would have pictured, but then she never would have expected him to show up with another woman in the first place.

Proof that she was just as poor a judge of character as her mother. As weak. As gullible.

Really? You told him there was no chance and now you want to throw a pity party because he finally got the message and is now getting on with his life?

She watched him steer the young woman to a nearby table and pure longing shot through her.

Because she wanted to be that woman.

She wanted Billy beside her, smiling at her, loving her.

And he wanted someone else.

Walk away. That's what she should have done. What she'd wanted her own mother to do. But the woman had never had the strength. The balls.

But it wasn't about that, she realized as she stood there, her heart pounding in her chest. Billy had been right. Her mother hadn't stayed because she'd been weak. She'd stayed because she'd been too strong to walk away, to give up her chance at happiness. She'd wanted to fight for it.

Just as Sabrina wanted to fight right now.

And while it hadn't worked out for her mother any

more than it might work out for her, she knew that she would never forgive herself if she didn't at least try.

Panic bolted through her and she was on her feet before she could stop herself. She crossed the room in a few heartbeats and grabbed his arm.

"You can't do this," she blurted as her gaze collided with his. "Please. You can't. Not yet." She paused to drink in a frantic breath. "Not until you hear what I have to say. I love you," she rushed on before she lost her courage. "I always have, I just didn't want to tell you because I was afraid that it would put me at a disadvantage because I've always seen love as a weak emotion. But it's not. It takes courage to love. To admit love. To be in love. My mother had that courage, but my father was the one who didn't. He was the weak one. That's why he left. I know that now. I also know you're not him. You could never be him. That's why you can't do this."

"I have to."

The words tightened a vise around her heart and tears burned her eyes. "You can't. You can't date someone else, because I want to date you. I want to marry you."

He arched an eyebrow at her. "Is that a proposal?"

"Yes. So don't do this. Don't give up on me and start dating someone else."

"He's not on a date." The woman sitting nearby gave her a horrified look. "Hells bells, I wouldn't date the likes of Billy Chisholm. He's just dropping me off on account of my granddaddy's here and he can't see well enough to read his own bingo cards."

"I was doing some work out at her granddaddy's place and she needed a ride. Since you mentioned that you were coming tonight, I figured I would show up, too."

Her gaze swiveled back to Billy as realization hit. "You mean I rushed over here and made a fool of myself for nothing?"

"You rushed over here and made a fool of yourself because you love me and I love you. I do, you know. I have since the first moment I saw you standing at that bar." His grin faded and a serious light gleamed in his eyes. She saw the sincerity in his gaze, and felt it in her heart, and she knew. She gave in to the longing inside and threw herself into his embrace. Strong arms wrapped around her and held her tight.

"I love you so much," he murmured into her hair. "I love everything about you. I love the clothes you wear and the way you look curled up in my bed and the way your eyes glitter when you're mad. Everything. And that's never going to change. No matter how much you try to piss me off or push me away."

She pulled back and stared up at him, tears streaming down her face, happiness overflowing her heart. "You're stubborn, you know that?"

He grinned. "I learned from the best."

Warmth coursed through her and she smiled. "You really think I'm the best?"

"Most of the time. The rest of the time, I think I want to kill you, but I still love you regardless." A serious light touched his gaze. "I meant what I said. I want you. I want marriage and babies and a future, and I want it all with you. Only you. I don't care where we live. If you hate it here, we can move."

"I can't do that."

He stiffened. "Are you saying that you don't want to marry me?"

"I'm saying that I can't move away from here. I actually like it here."

"What about the website?"

"FindMeACowboy.com is Livi's brainchild, and now she's got the funding to make it a reality. I wrote the business proposal and worded all of the profile requirements, but now my work is done. Kat's doing the website and we're well past the idea phase. They don't need me anymore. Besides, I've got an idea of my own I'd like to work on."

"A job at the newspaper?"

"I was thinking more along the lines of a matchmaking service for seniors right here in Lost Gun. I could start with a storefront and then branch out on the web."

"So you're staying?"

"Only if you make an honest woman of me."

He grinned and drew her close. "You've got yourself a deal."

Epilogue

"THIS IS A WASTE of time," Billy Chisholm announced to his two brothers as he tossed a shovel full of dirt to the side and stared at the pastureland rutted with holes in all directions. "We've been digging for over four weeks now and we haven't found anything."

"It's here," Jesse said, but he didn't sound nearly as confident as he once had. "It has to be."

"Unless Big Earl is wrong," Cole pointed out. "The man's ancient. Maybe he hallucinated the connection to Silas."

Jesse shook his head. "Casey confirmed his confession."

"Yeah, but she's got nothing to go on except his word. That brings me back to my first theory—Big Earl could be wrong."

He _was_ wrong.

That was the conclusion that Billy had come to weeks ago. Big Earl was wrong and this was just a waste and it was high time the Chisholm brothers admitted defeat and went back to their lives.

A pretty great life, at least in Billy's opinion.

He had one now thanks to the woman waiting back at his cabin. Sabrina had moved in just over a week ago after giving up her apartment in L.A. and moving to Lost Gun for good. They'd announced their engagement just a few days ago and were now planning a wedding to follow on the heels of the PBR finals in November.

Billy hadn't wanted to wait, but Sabrina had been determined to keep him focused on his first championship. Thanks to the Lost Gun win, and the Houston Live Stock Show and Rodeo win right on its heels, Billy was a leading contender. He still had a long way to go, but if he kept performing the way he'd been, he was a shoo-in for the buckle.

"You're going to win," Sabrina had told him. "And then we'll get married. I don't want you worried about anything."

But he wasn't worried. For the first time in his life, Billy felt relaxed and confident and anxious. He wanted to say "I do" even more than he wanted a PBR championship.

But he also wanted to make Sabrina happy and so he'd agreed to wait. But only if she promised to let him help her with the wedding details. Because when it came to Sabrina, he had no problem making up his mind. She was his world. His future.

Which was why he was more than ready to give up this wild goose chase and get home. He'd come clean to Sabrina about the possibility that the money still existed and she'd been nothing but encouraging. There'd been no probing questions, no pushing for information, nothing to indicate that she was a journalist at heart. Because she wasn't. She'd found happiness in her matchmaking business, just as he'd found happiness in his bull-riding.

Still, she'd urged him to look, to help his brothers and lay the past to rest.

At the same time, Billy had already done that. He'd made peace and it was time to let sleeping dogs lie.

"The money's not here," Billy said again. Still, he rammed his shovel into the ground anyway, hard, eager to scoop up as much loose dirt as possible and prove a point.

And that's when he felt it.

The budge of resistance as the hard metal edge met something a few inches below the surface. He signaled Jesse and Cole and the three of them went to work on the spot.

A few breathless moments later, Billy retrieved a nearby lantern and held it up to reveal a large metal box.

His heart pounded in his chest as he broke the lock and pushed open the lid, and then the truth crystallized.

They'd done it. They'd really and truly done it.

After all these years and a world of heartache, they'd finally found the missing money.

* * * * *

Don't miss your

Blaze.

March books

From 1st March 2014, Blaze stories will be available as eBooks only.

Blaze fans SAVE 20%

Don't miss our special eBook offer—enter promotion code **Blaze20** to save 20% on all Blaze titles.

Find out more at www.millsandboon.co.uk/Blaze

PLUS, don't miss our special Blaze website hub for your favourite authors, new reads and the latest news at

www.millsandboon.co.uk/Blaze

Special Offers

Every month we put together collections and longer reads written by your favourite authors.

Here are some of next month's highlights— and don't miss our fabulous discount online!

On sale 21st February

On sale 28th February

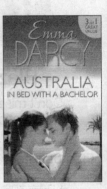

On sale 21st February

Save 20%
on all Special Releases

14/MB451

#1 NEW YORK TIMES BESTSELLING AUTHOR

SYLVIA DAY

*after*burn

COSMO RED-HOT READS
FROM MILLS & BOON

No.1 *Sunday Times* bestselling author Sylvia Day,
America's premier provocative fiction writer,
delivers the debut Cosmo Red-Hot Reads
novel for Mills & Boon.

**Download the eBook at:
www.millsandboon.co.uk/cosmo**

Discover more romance at

www.millsandboon.co.uk

- ❤ WIN great prizes in our exclusive competitions
- ❤ BUY new titles before they hit the shops
- ❤ BROWSE new books and REVIEW your favourites
- ❤ SAVE on new books with the Mills & Boon® Bookclub™
- ❤ DISCOVER new authors

PLUS, to chat about your favourite reads, get the latest news and find special offers:

- 📘 Find us on facebook.com/millsandboon
- 🐦 Follow us on twitter.com/millsandboonuk
- ❤ Sign up to our newsletter at millsandboon.co.uk

What will you treat yourself to next?

INTRIGUE... *A seductive combination of danger and desire...*
6 new stories every month

Awaken the romance of the past...
6 new stories every month

The ultimate in romantic medical drama
6 new stories every month

MODERN™ *Power, passion and irresistible temptation*
8 new stories every month

True love and temptation!
4 new stories every month